Tales From a Broad

by

Jeannine Henvey

Published by
Melange Books, LLC
White Bear Lake, MN 55110
www.melange-books.com

Tales From a Broad ~ Copyright © 2014 by Jeannine Henvey

ISBN: 978-1-61235-910-6

Cover Art by Caroline Andrus

To Sadie, Chloe and Carter—
For turning the wait to get published into a real live game of
Chutes and Ladders.
You learned math by tracking submissions and rejections, crossed
fingers at bedtime, chanted publishers' names around the house and
always made me smile. I love you with all my heart.

* * *

Acknowledgements

Thank you to the special people who took the time to read this when it existed in its earliest form. And especially to those who read it more times than I can ever thank them for. To my first unofficial editor, Tess Forte, who gave me the confidence to start a writing career, Samantha Skule who taught me the power of visualization, Karin Newell Piscitelli whose guidance extends from the characters in my book to the characters in my life, Allison Dickens and her creative suggestions, Nicole Pultz who has a magnifying glass for an eye, and to my husband Tommy who not only is a little bit Simon, but is a lot of bit wonderful.

Endless love and gratitude to my parents who taught me that anything can be accomplished, my sister who can read my mood better than any book, my amazing friends who give me daily focus, and my in-laws who have given me the actual time to focus. To my friends at Fiorello Dolce, whose cappuccinos on the sidewalk transported me back to Florence, to Caroline Andrus for the cover, and to Nancy Schumacher for turning my dream into a reality.

Prologue

```
Friends & Family
Date: 3/19/14 at 11:00 PM
Subject: Wedding

Dear friends and family,
    The wedding has been called off by
mutual consent.
    I apologize for the impersonal nature of
this email. We have been blessed with too
many loved ones to call individually.
Please accept our apology for any
inconvenience this may have caused.
With love,
Lucy and Cooper
```

I paused and held a trembling finger over my mouse. Was it okay to say "mutual consent"? That might be a bit of a stretch, considering I'd been dumped in a taxi and had tossed my three-karat ring out the window somewhere on the George Washington Bridge, but ... whatever. According to Google, this was the most eloquent way to announce the cancellation of a wedding.

I scanned the email for the 10th time and held my breath, hoping the message would send itself. "Here goes," I whispered and tapped the mouse. By the time the message was sent, I was practically gasping for air.

I took a gulp of wine and leaned on the kitchen island, waiting for the Chardonnay to calm my nerves.

Like it could.

Something stuck to my elbows, and when I lifted them, I saw a filmy substance across the granite countertop. Was it the orange juice I had spilled this morning? Or was that yesterday?

"Who knows, who cares," I muttered. My voice sounded hollow in the quiet apartment. I hadn't even brushed my teeth today, so the fact that I'd neglected another daily ritual—circling the island with a bottle of Windex in hand, didn't exactly come as a shock. What was a little dirt when my entire life had crashed and burned?

I pressed my fingers to my very swollen eyelids as if to counteract the damage that twenty-four hours of crying had done to my face. Even my contact lenses had suffered. They now felt like shards of glass on my eyeballs. I took my thumb and forefinger to carefully extract each one, rolled them into tiny little balls, then tore the lenses into minuscule pieces with my nails. Somehow, performing that ritual gave me a sense of satisfaction.

Ping. I snapped my head up and squinted at my laptop. An email from Aunt Louise. My stomach churned as I stared at my inbox. *Ping.* Cooper's cousin. *Ping. Ping. Ping.* F'ing ping!

Email vultures. It was as if they all had been hovering around their computers for the bad news and couldn't wait to respond within ten seconds. Each new email made a pinging sound on my computer, scraping at my nerves, and sending my iPhone vibrating on the kitchen counter. The reverberations might as well have been machine gun fire, straight to my heart.

Up until February fourteenth, I'd had a very lucky life. Since then, my whole world managed to unravel over the course of five short weeks.

First, I'd gotten the call that the parenting magazine I'd worked at for the past three years would be going under.

That was a setback, but with a wedding to plan, I didn't have time to dwell. Anyone who has ever planned a New York City wedding knows that doing so can be a full time job in and of itself. My newfound free time went to perfect use and even allowed me to plan ahead for the future.

I was already thinking about our first anniversary and knew I desperately wanted to give Cooper the baby we both wanted so badly. To hell with the clock, the modern, traditional, first anniversary gift. My own clock was ticking, and losing my job seemed to be one more signal that the time was right.

So when I wasn't busy with wedding plans, I caught up on all of the medical check-ups I was supposed to do when I turned forty, which had been two years ago. I wanted to get in as many appointments as I could before my kick-ass medical coverage expired. That's when I discovered that my eggs also had an expiration date, which had already passed. The fertility specialist told me that my body was in early menopause and I could no longer get pregnant. My heart was broken.

And then, I got clobbered with the last straw. I would never, ever have guessed in a million years that the man I'd loved for the past five years couldn't bear the thought of not having his own biological kids. The news about my fertility issues sent him running. He'd called off the wedding. I suppose it was probably a good thing I got my eggs in a scramble before we made the toast.

Still, it was hard to see the good in anything. As my grandmother always used to say, when it rains it pours. I was in the midst of a full-blown shit storm.

Ping.

"Oh shut the hell up." I slammed my laptop shut and tapped my shaking fingers on the aluminum case. There were 150 guests on our email distribution list. That probably meant I'd get about that many responses back.

I shook my head in disgust. Why was I the one who had to deal with this? Mutual consent, my ass. I didn't recall having a say in any of this.

I downed the last drop of wine, stood up to stretch, and blindly felt my way over to the Keurig, which had been an engagement gift from my marketing department. Maybe there was a bright side. Had I not been laid off last month, I would have had to face the office on Monday. That would've been a total nightmare.

Besides, at least now I get to keep the Keurig. After all, it was European, sophisticated, and could brew a warm beverage with the flick of a button. I placed an espresso pod into the machine and pressed the lever down. I may have tossed my engagement ring onto a bridge, but give back my coffee maker? No way in hell.

Chapter One

I refuse to empty the dishwasher today. My goal is to use every last utensil in there.
Facebook Status May 19 at 11:20am

I stretched my arm from beneath the down comforter and reached for my cell phone on the nightstand. I had a string of missed calls from my sister Morgan, and it was already a quarter past eleven. How did it get so late? I couldn't believe the racket on Lexington Avenue hadn't woken me sooner.

I closed my eyes and listened to the sound of life passing me by. Street drilling, the siren of a car alarm, and the beeping sounds of a garbage truck were comforting reminders that I wasn't completely alone. I put on my slippers, padded into the living room, and turned on the TV.

"Boy is it *beautiful* out there," Kelly Ripa chirped from her seat on "Live with Kelly & Michael," as her cheerful face came up on the screen. "There's something about this weather that makes you feel so, so … *alive*," she sang.

"Not feelin' it, Kel," I sang back. All I felt was guilt, and I certainly didn't need to get it from her. It had been two months since Cooper called off the wedding and still, I hadn't managed to reenter life. I didn't need to be reminded I was missing another quintessential spring day in the city.

I flipped the TV off, tossed the remote in disgust, and put my feet on the coffee table. Using my toe, I nudged the pile of accumulated crap on the table. It was a mish mash of magazines, unread mail, wedding responses from those who didn't get the memo, and my beloved journal, which had been oh so neglected.

I reached over and picked it up. A feeling of nostalgia washed over me.

"Bless me journal for I have sinned," I murmured. "It's been about a couple of months since my last confession. It's just that..." I paused to read one of the inspirational messages printed across an empty page, "I don't really write when I'm down. I eat. And it's just too darn messy to hammer cheese doodles and write at the same time."

Maybe I should go hands-free. Siri for slobs? A digital Dictaphone? I pondered whether they made waterproof ones that protected against flying crumbs and sticky fingers when I heard a knock at the door.

I froze for a moment. God strike down the person who invented the drive by visit! Luckily for them, my prayers were rarely answered these days. I tiptoed quietly over to the door and peered out the peephole.

I groaned inwardly. There stood Morgan, and I saw anxiety written all over her face, magnified through the tiny peephole. She bit her fingernail and knocked again, this time a little harder.

"Lu, open up! It's us!" Morgan sang in a chipper tone.

She may have sounded upbeat, but that didn't fool me. I knew my sister well enough to know she was nervous. She was probably worried about how her unstable sister would react to her unannounced visit.

She had called the night before with an invitation to take me out for a drink. When I told her that I wasn't in the mood for a cordial, her reaction was anything but. Over the past two months, the majority of our phone calls had gone in the very same direction. Bother, rinse, and repeat.

But last night, the routine was over. What had started with a friendly hello, ended with a not-so-friendly goodbye—on my part.

I looked out the peephole again and saw Tess, my twenty-four-year-old niece, staring back at me with apologetic eyes. Telepathically I told her, "Don't worry, Tessie. I know you're not responsible for this."

"Lu, we can see you," Morgan shouted through the door. I quickly ducked my head down. Busted.

I put my hand on the doorknob and froze in contemplation. They had driven an hour, so technically, that couldn't even qualify as a drive-by visit. Oh, how I wished it were a drive-by shooting instead. And I was the victim.

Then again, I wouldn't want to be found looking like this. I had been sporting one of Cooper's very old t-shirts with my pajama bottoms. It had been worn so thin that the grey material had become practically see-through. To make matters worse, I had cried myself to sleep the night before and used the shirt as an eye-makeup remover. Mascara as a pick-me-up is highly overrated.

What wasn't covered in mascara was covered in ice cream stains from a late night feeding frenzy. Classy. I wasn't sure what was more humiliating, the way I looked or the fact that I still slept in my ex-fiancé's shirt. And actually, my pajama bottoms were his boxers.

I swept my eyes around the messy apartment and caught a glimpse of a framed photo that hung in my foyer. Morgan had taken it years ago, but I remembered the moment as if it were yesterday. She and I had been shopping in Soho when we were caught in the storm of the century. In the photo, we were huddled under a plastic bag, soaking wet and giggling like silly schoolgirls.

My heart softened a bit, and I experienced a pang of longing for the simpler days. I knew I should just open the damn door. Morgan wasn't exactly the type to make a quiet exit. If I didn't acknowledge her efforts, she'd only try harder.

"Just a minute!" I shouted.

I looked down and knew I had to change my clothes, stat. I started to pull the shirt over my head and heard the doorknob click. I immediately froze as the door swung inward. I stood in the vestibule, topless, with the shirt over my face. I could actually see them staring at me, through the worn out material. Morgan's hand flew to her mouth, and Tess omitted a quiet giggle. Sheepishly, I pulled it back down.

"Hi," I said shame-faced. "I was just..." I trailed off. Morgan was speechless.

"We used the key," Tess said, shooting me a look.

I knew she was mortified for me. Boy, did I regret giving her a key to my crash pad for her twenty-first birthday. I was trying to send the message to drink responsibly. Little did I know that three years later, she would be using it to have an intervention with me.

"C … can you just give me a s … second?" I felt like a cross-dresser who had been busted. "Then we can have a proper hello," I said, walking down the hall towards my bedroom. "Make yourselves at home and I will be right…"

"Lucy," Morgan commanded. "Wait."

I stopped in my tracks, did a reverse, and slowly approached my sister. She rushed toward me, her eyes glistening with tears. She gripped both of my elbows and looked into my eyes.

"Lu, I'm really sorry about last night. I didn't mean to badger you. It's just that…. I wanted to see my sister. I've missed you so much."

As I stood face-to-face with Morgan, I suddenly felt foolish. I sheepishly ran my hand through my unwashed hair and waved it in the air. "Let's just forget it. I probably overreacted."

"No, you didn't. I was the one who overreacted. Lu," she paused and placed a hand on her chest, looking me up and down, "I didn't realize you were still in this much pain. You never even talk about it, anymore."

"Well,"—I widened my eyes—"I guess you had to see it to believe it, huh? Surprise!"

I held my arms up, and after Morgan's eyes darted to a hole in my armpit, I folded them protectively across my chest. Morgan's lips formed a sympathetic pout. I drew in a breath and released a long sigh.

"Look, I'm sorry too. I didn't mean to shut you out. From now on, you have an open invitation to my pity party. Come here." I tilted my head and stretched my arms out.

Morgan heaved a sigh as she came in for a hug. "I'm always here for you, Lu."

"I know you are," I whispered in her ear. "I love you."

"I love you too." She gave me a tight squeeze.

I drew in a breath of relief myself, and in doing so, I got a whiff of her signature scent. She'd been wearing Chloe for as long as I could remember. I, on the other hand, was aware that I smelled like a dirty sock.

"Now, do you mind if I shower quickly? You guys look so nice, and I just can't stand the thought of looking like a vagabond in front of you."

Morgan pulled away and gripped my elbows at arm's length. "But you look so handsome in men's loungewear."

"Shut up." I gave her a playful punch in the arm. "I can't even bring myself to hug *that* one." I pointed my thumb in the direction of Tess, who looked like her usual gorgeous self. Wearing jeans, a simple tee, and a long scarf, she looked perfectly put together.

"Oh, whatever!" Tess laughed and glanced up from her phone.

She was effortlessly beautiful. In fact, one of the things I loved most about her was that she was completely unaware of her good looks. I've come to realize that's probably why she's so awesome.

What I haven't quite figured out, though, is where her looks came from. Yes, my brother-in-law happens to be attractive, and Morgan has always been a pretty woman. She may be eight years older than I am, but for someone nearing fifty, she looks pretty damn good. Now, if she could bring herself to part with the minivan and her love of L.L Bean, she'd probably knock a few years off her look. But even if she were a Corvette driver, she still wouldn't look like an older version of her daughter.

Nor would I for that matter. Our side of the family just doesn't produce honey-colored hair and blue eyes. We're all dark-haired, dark-eyed clones of one another.

"Sweetie," Morgan called out to Tess. "Should we make Aunt Lu open our gifts first?"

"Gifts?" I echoed. "Is it my birthday?" I was only half-joking.

For a minute, I had to stop and actually think about the date. With no job, and no life for that matter, I was having trouble keeping track. My days had no beginning and no end.

"Mom and I brought you a little something," Tess said. "A peace offering." She stepped down from the barstool and gave me a wink. She walked over to the door, extracted a box from her oversized bag, and handed it to me.

"Ooh!" I smiled at Morgan while giving the box a small shake. "Let's sit." My shower could wait.

We took our places in the living room as they watched me lift the lid. Two books lay inside and suddenly my excitement began to dissipate. "*Eat, Pray, Love* and *Under the Tuscan Sun*," I read off the book covers. "Hmm. Old stories about lost women trying to find themselves," I said in a falsely upbeat tone. "Is this a hint?" I watched Morgan and Tess exchange a look.

"I'm sorry," I winced. "I don't mean to be unappreciative. I know I'm a mess." I crossed my legs to close the opening on Cooper's boxers.

Jeannine Henvey

"Actually," Morgan said with a smile, "it is a hint. We think it's time you give yourself a break for once in your life. Go find yourself."

I looked at Tess who was gazing at her mother, rapt with admiration. It was as if she had just witnessed her mom pass on the family stone. Yes, it was a nice gesture, but two books didn't quite warrant such a reaction. I drew in a slow breath.

I gave my sister a puzzled look and tucked my ratty hair behind my ears. "I'm not so sure I follow."

I extracted a peanut M&M from the candy dish that sat on the table, popped it into my mouth, and leaned back on the couch. I carefully bit the candy and released the nut with my tongue.

"Open the next one," Morgan said with a smile. Tess reached into her bag and handed me another gift.

Based on how it felt, I could already guess it was another book. "Did you ever think of starting a book club?" I said. I ripped open the paper. It was actually a journal.

"Okay," I smiled and nodded. "I'll give you an A for effort. I see you have a whole theme going on here. The books, the pep talk, the journal..." I waved the book in the air. A piece of paper slipped out and landed on my lap.

"What's this?" I picked it up and held it under my nose. "It looks like an airline ticket."

"It is!" Tess exclaimed. "We're going to Europe, baby!" With that, she leaped onto the couch and jumped up and down. She kind of reminded me of a judge on "The Voice." Or Tom Cruise, when he professed his love for Katie Holms on "Oprah."

Tess plopped back down beside me, barely taking a second to catch her breath. She grabbed my arm. "Aunt Lu," she panted, "this is going to be so much fun!"

I looked over at Morgan, who was happily nodding her head. "Go have the adventure of a lifetime." She leaned closer to me and tapped her hand firmly on the journal. "And remember it."

"But ... I thought.... Wait, what?" I shook my head in confusion.

"Okay, here's the deal." Tess clasped her hands together. "Since college, I've wanted to travel Europe, but never had the time—or guts, to do it. That's when my mom suggested that we go together!"

10

"How kind of her." I shot Morgan a silent look of death. "What about Jack?" He was the guy she had been dating for years.

Tess shrugged her shoulders. "We're on a break."

"I had no idea." I frowned. "What happened? Was it mutual?"

My stomach lurched, and I immediately regretted my choice of words. After calling the wedding off, I had received dozens of responses from friends who were happy to hear the breakup was mutual. I had come to loathe that word.

"Aunt Lu, I've been dating the same guy since high school. We've become more like brother and sister."

I glanced at Morgan. She tugged on her bottom lip to fight the corners of her mouth from twitching their way into a smile. I bit my own lip and turned my attention back to Tess.

"I don't know any man other than him, and I think it's time to experience new people, new things," she said with an eyebrow raised. "My life is so dull. Believe me, you're not the only one who could use a change. I took that job at the daycare center as a short-term plan while I waited to get a real teaching job. That was *two* years ago! I'm sick of wallowing about not having a 'real' job," she said, making air quotes. "I haven't done one productive thing since college."

She formed the letter "L" with her thumb and index finger and rested it on her forehead.

"That's not true, honey," Morgan said.

Tess cocked her head to the side and raised her eyebrows, waiting for her mother to elaborate.

"You made those beautiful window treatments for our living room," she offered.

"And let's not forget my gorgeous pillows, thank you very much." I picked up one of the throw pillows she'd made me for Christmas and hugged it protectively.

"Sewing is just a hobby," Tess admonished. "It doesn't pay the bills, and it's really depressing not being able to find a job. However, I can wipe a butt like it's no one's business." She held a triumphant fist in the air.

"Tell me about it," I scoffed. "Not the butt thing, although I wouldn't mind that either," I quickly added. My superstitious self never wanted the universe to hear any negativity when it came to babies. "But Tess," I furrowed my eyebrows, "do you really want to take this trip with *me*?" I scrunched my nose and tapped my chest. "Take your old aunt on a road show? An antique road show, no less?"

"Oh, please. There's no one else I'd rather go with. You're like a mother to me. Or big sister," she quickly corrected herself. "I have it all mapped out." Tess's eyes shone with excitement as she spoke. "We'll fly to London—"

I held a hand in the air. "I'm telling you right now. I am not a very calm travel companion. You do know how much I hate to fly, right?"

"I'll get you drunk and hold your hand," she encouraged.

"Ok, I'm just saying. On my last flight, the turbulence was so bad that—"

"So." Tess silenced me with her enthusiasm. "We'll start in London, take the train to—"

I groaned. "I get the chills when I even have to travel below 14th Street."

"Oh Lucy," Morgan chided. She gave me a sideways look. "Live a little. Go fill up that beautiful journal."

"Yeah." Tess gave my arm a supportive squeeze. "We can't allow our fears to hold us back. All you need is that journal and a backpack—"

"Come again?" My stomach dropped. "Backpack?"

"It's the easiest way to go from hostel to hostel."

"You're kidding me, right?" I laughed out loud.

"Would you rather roll one of your Louis Vuitton suitcases on and off trains and in and out of hostels?"

I held a finger in the air. "No, no, that's not what I meant. I already forgot about the backpack. That pales in comparison to the other thing you said. Hostels?" I made a face. "I'm sorry, do I look like I'm on summer break from college?"

Tess looked at Morgan with the same I-told-you-so look she'd been casting her mother for years.

"Oh, Lu," Morgan said, shaking her head. "I saw pictures on the internet. There are some really nice, clean youth hostels out there and they're so affordable."

"*Youth* hostels?" I sat back on the couch in defeat and looked at Tess. "Sweetie, you know I love you but if I were to do Europe, words like backpack and youth hostel would not be rolling off this tongue."

"Um, hello?" Morgan waved her hand in front of my face. "I hate to burst your bubble, but you're not exactly bringing in the big bucks, Lu. You may have done well in your heyday, but you should probably tighten your belt now. When was your last paycheck?"

"This is such an ego-boosting intervention," I said dryly.

Tess's phone rang and she held out a finger to pause our conversation. "It's Landon," she explained, looking at her phone. "Work it, Mom."

"Tell your brother to call me," Morgan shouted as Tess walked towards the kitchen. Morgan gripped the edge of her seat and leaned towards me. "Lucy, listen," she said in a hushed tone. "To be perfectly honest with you, this isn't just for you. I'm worried about Tess."

I sat up with a start and clasped my hands together. "What happened? What's going on?"

"Nothing," Morgan said with a hand in the air, "but that's just it. You heard what she said. All of her friends have found jobs they love, and there she is, feeling stuck in that dead end daycare. Then there's Jack," Morgan rolled her eyes and sighed. "I don't know, Lu. I just worry about her. I feel like she's falling into a rut, and she's too young to be stagnant. I knew if I encouraged her to take the trip to help *you*, she'd go. Look at how excited she is! I'm not trying to put pressure on you, but—"

"Oh no. No pressure," I scoffed and gave her a sideways glance.

I sunk into the couch and searched the ceiling, as if the answer to my life was written somewhere up there. I closed my eyes in despair and heard her rummaging through the mail piled high on the table.

"It's just that..." I cracked open one eye and watched her slip the unopened wedding response cards into her bag, completely unaware that she'd been busted. "I don't know if I'd be good company. I don't want to go all the way to Europe only to drag your daughter down with me. I saw that by the way. Sneaky envelope-taker."

Morgan chuckled. "Look, I came here to make peace with you, not stress you out even more. I'm sorry. I just think you should at least consider it. Please. It might be fun."

Tess had already emerged from the kitchen and stood behind the couch. "Oh, there's no might involved." Tess squeezed her fists in excitement. "Get this: Landon's company is sending him to Florence the same time we'd be there! If we were to go, of course."

"Wow. That's wonderful!" Morgan exclaimed. "Sounds like fate."

"No kidding. No pressure, Aunt Lu," Tess said, suddenly holding a hand up. "But, how cool would it be to see *Italia*," she said in a mock Italian accent, "with your only niece and nephew?"

I smiled fondly at Tess, whom I still saw as the little girl who had called me with anything newsworthy since the very first day she learned to use the phone. I've been her personal shopper, psychologist, and guidance counselor and have loved her like a daughter since the day she was born.

God only knows that Tess could be the closest I may ever get to a daughter of my own. I knew that while my life was in shambles, if I didn't go on this trip, then Tess probably wouldn't go either.

"Anyway," Tess continued. "We'll stop harassing you. Why don't you go shower and get dressed? Mom and I were hoping to take you for nails and lunch."

I was overcome with emotion. How lucky was I to have people in my life who cared so much about me? And to think I almost didn't answer the door. I paused for a moment in contemplation as tears pricked my eyes. Their faces began to blur in front of me.

"Shower," I scoffed, blinking rapidly. "Cleanliness is overrated. Besides, I should probably get used to skipping a shower here and there," I smiled mischievously. "They say backpacking isn't always so glamorous, you know."

Chapter Two

Two weeks later, Tess and I were on the redeye from JFK to London and arrived at eight the next morning. Heathrow International Airport bustled, and being in a foreign country was like getting an IV drip of caffeine straight into my bloodstream. Excitement coursed through my veins and gave me the jolt that I desperately needed.

After drinking two vodka tonics before the plane took off, I managed to fall asleep by the time we reached our cruising altitude. But my forty-minute nap actually ruined the rest of my flight. My subconscious mind had taken me off on a honeymoon with Cooper, so when I woke up to find Tess drooling on my shoulder, I wished to God I was still asleep. I desperately wanted to return to my dream and escape the real world, to go back to a place where I was a billion times happier.

Instead, while listening to Tess snore, I obsessed over the fact that my wedding day would have been two days away. I'd planned not to dwell on it, but the dream felt so real, and with the date looming in the air, my mind raced the entire flight.

Tess, on the other hand, slept like a baby and was perfectly rested by the time we landed. After months of succumbing to complete and utter lethargy, I struggled to keep up with her as she raced through the terminal, awestruck by the shops that surrounded us. I followed two paces behind, listening to the airport announcements that were being made in various languages while drawing in deep inhales of the eucalyptus citrus scent that wafted from Molton Brown.

Once we retrieved our backpacks and cleared customs, Tess and I clinked passports to celebrate our first stamps and our arrival. We hopped into the back of a Mercedes taxicab and gave the driver the address to our hostel.

Even though the car smelled like stale cigar smoke, I still felt a bit like royalty. Between the driver's three-piece suit, his crisp accent, and the fact that I was being whisked away in a luxury vehicle, something felt quite right as we drove on the wrong side of the road.

But when we got to the hostel, my grandiose delusions became more blandiose, and I suddenly felt like a poor college kid. There were about a dozen twentysomethings crowding the entryway to a dilapidated building. Its once-white cement, blackened from age, had dirty windows that opened up to rusty fire escapes. The building reminded me of the neglected low-income housing back home. Then again, that's basically what it was.

What did I expect for 20 euros a night? You get what you pay for, and that's exactly what we got. Two beds. Two of six beds in one very cramped room. But buttered toast was included. Thank goodness.

* * * *

An hour later in the cafeteria, I felt like a fish out of water among the hostel's much younger clientele. There was a definite style here—lots of tattered denim, sneakers, and greasy hair. Was that a current trend in London or just a dirty look accepted among the backpacking community?

A young guy sat in the middle of the room and strummed away on his guitar. Some of the diners sang along to his rendition of "Like a Rolling Stone" as they contributed to the already overpowering odor of marijuana that filled the air.

But since it was still the middle of the night back home, I imagined I was in a bread bar listening to an acoustic band. Plates were piled high with burnt toast while crumbs lay scattered all over the tables and floor. For some reason, as I sat on a chipped bench that was sticky from grape jelly and munched away on stale bread, I was suddenly feeling pretty psyched.

A voice in my head spoke as if it were an announcer at a Broadway show. *The role of Type A, anal-retentive Lucy Banks, will be played by her free-spirited twin sister. The two girls had been separated at birth.*

I always did the right thing in the right order. I finished college, went on to graduate school, and had a job lined up before I even had my diploma in hand. Not only did I lack the confidence to just take time off and go, it hadn't even crossed my mind. It wasn't an option. That wasn't on the road map of what was supposed to happen in life. People like me didn't do things like this.

I looked around and a slow smile spread across my face. I may not have looked the part, but I *was* a part of that freewheeling scene around me. Just like Mick Jagger's rolling stone, I was a complete unknown. I looked around at the young adults poring through travel books and maps. We all had the same thing in common. We were here to see the world.

"So, what do you want to do today?" Tess said. She popped a piece of crust into her mouth and opened her guidebook.

"Other than carbo-load? I think we've consumed enough bread to run a marathon." I laughed and brushed off the pile of crumbs accumulated on my lap. "Do you want to hit a museum? Or take one of those architecture walks?"

"Hmm," Tess drummed her fingers on the table and looked down at her book.

The thought of a walk sounded fun to me and I was pleasantly surprised I even wanted to take one. Fitness had always been a top priority of mine, but since the break-up, I had become overcome with a constant state of fatigue. My limbs had been feeling just as heavy as my heart, and I had never gone this long without actually wanting to move my body.

Tess snapped her head up. "I'd love to take a walk." She paused, thinking. "But how about we stroll through Regent Park instead? It says here we might see Madonna on one of her runs. Or have a David and Victoria Beckham sighting!"

"I'd say we'd probably have more of a chance seeing those guys at Madame Tussauds," I said with a chuckle. "Have you been to the one in New York?"

Tess wrinkled her nose and shook her head. "Nah. Wax museums are boring."

"Not this one. The statues looked so real. Especially with all the Botox the celebs are doing these days."

Tess didn't look too convinced. She giggled and turned her attention back to her book.

I rested my chin on my elbow and looked around the room. As my gaze fell on the Union Flag that hung on the wall, a red flag of my own went up in my mind. We had only been in Europe for two hours and already we couldn't seem to agree on our first outing. Not a good sign. It hadn't occurred to me that our ideas for the perfect trip might not be the same.

"So, is it wax museums you find boring or all museums?" I said with an eyebrow raised. My voice sounded casual, but I braced myself for her response.

"I have nothing against museums," Tess replied.

Oh, thank God.

"In fact," she added, "I'm dying to go to this one." Tess thumbed through her book and stopped when she found what she had been looking for. She turned the book around to face me.

I leaned across the table for a closer look. "The Dungeon Museum?"

"Yep. 'Gruesome events that span two thousand years of London's history'," she read aloud. "A museum of simulated horror from history."

I felt despair as I sunk back onto the bench. Tess looked at me with a glimmer in her eyes. "What do you think?"

I quickly shook my head. "I'm sorry. I'll never be able to sleep again. Especially here," I whispered. I pointed my chin towards an overweight guy who was cleaning his fingernails with a knife. Something that resembled a dog collar was wrapped around his neck and had a chain that connected to piercings in his ear and nose.

"Yikes," Tess said with grimace.

"Yeah ... terror's not my thing."

"Okay, fair enough." Tess handed me the book. "You pick."

I took the book and turned the page. "How about the Tower of London, famous for the execution of Anne Boleyn? I've become obsessed since I read *The Other Boleyn Girl*."

I filled Tess in on the tragic lives of the Boleyn sisters. She had been nodding her head politely, but I noticed that her eyes had glazed over.

"Or ... we can do a little shopping?"

Tess clapped her hands with delight. "Now you're talking. I'm dying to see the secondhand shops on Portobello Road."

Although, I had more of a firsthand experience in mind, I was happy to find something we would both enjoy.

She told me about a store called The Cloth Shop, where she had hoped to pick up some unique fabrics for her sewing. We headed in that direction and stopped in a few of the thrift shops along the way. While Tess found Nirvana perusing racks of worn clothing, I, on the other hand, felt like I needed to shower upon leaving each store.

"Tell me again what it is that you like about used clothing?" I hung a frayed skirt back up on a rack and reached into my bag for a bottle of sanitizer.

"They're vintage," Tess corrected, "and they're clean!" She held up a sleeveless shirt missing a button. "You can't find these kinds of things in department stores."

"Ain't that the truth," I muttered.

She shot me an amused look. "I heard that."

I smiled and squirted Purell into my cupped palm. "Tess." I paused to swallow. "Would you mind if we went our separate ways for a few hours?"

"You mean hang out alone?" Tess peered at me from behind a pile of hats and pushed out her lower lip in a pout.

"Well ... even though we'll be flying out of London at the end of the trip, we're only here for two days this time around. I kind of think we both should see what we want to see. Don't you?" I said apprehensively.

"I guess... Where are you going to go?"

"I don't know," I shrugged. "I'd like to pop into a museum or an old church. Get a little culture."

Tess suddenly looked like she had just dodged a bullet. She pulled a pair of jeans from the rack and nodded enthusiastically. "You're right. It's probably best we go our separate ways. Maybe I'll hit that Dungeon Museum after all," she mused.

She turned to face the pile of clothes that spilled out of her cart.

"When you do find that church, please say a prayer for me that I don't lose my shirt in this store."

"That might not be such a bad thing." I pointed to one of the faded shirts she had selected and wrinkled my nose.

"Keep an open mind, Aunt Lu," Tess sang, hitting me with the hanger.

"I know, I know. You're right. I'm probably just jealous." I eyed Tess in the mirror, watching her button the shirt over her own. "Actually, there's no probably involved. I *am* jealous. That,"—I waved a finger in the air up and down her body—"was never a look I could pull off. If I tried, that's exactly what I would look like: a woman trying to look like you, or even her, for that matter." I pointed to a mannequin sporting a basketball shirtdress and a fedora.

Tess laughed. "Halloween in June? She can't even pull it off."

"I'll just continue to play it safe and hide my lack of individuality behind designer logos," I sniffed, fishing through my Louis Vuitton wallet on a chain for a lip gloss. "Don't be fooled by these LV logos. You might think they stand for Louis Vuitton, but they're really screaming "lacking variety" like an obnoxious sounding parrot." I swung my bag with its colored logos like a lasso and threw it around the mannequin's neck.

Laughingly, we said our goodbyes and feeling rather vintage myself, I left Tess deliberating between a ten-year old skirt and a ripped up pair of jeans. I, on the other hand, opted for a little pop culture and went to check out the infamous blue door from the Julia Roberts movie, *Notting Hill*. Which, I discovered, happened to be black. Feeling rather let down, I hopped onto a tour bus for a quick spin around the city.

* * * *

"Our next stop is Piccadilly Circus, world famous junction of five major streets," Henry the tour guide spoke into his microphone.

I gathered my belongings, eager to get off the bus and stretch my legs. Henry had handed me a rain poncho when I climbed on top of the open-air double-decker bus two hours ago, and the plastic now clung to my neck. It had been drizzling for most of the tour, but I could see the sun peeking through the clouds. Of course it was. The tour was almost over.

I pulled the poncho over my head and felt my earlobe pull as the plastic tangled up in my gold hoop earring. If only I could've kept the damn poncho over my head. My shoulder length hair was a frizzy mess, and I kicked myself for not packing a hat.

"It would be quite the challenge to find a glitzier, busier place in London," Henry's voice boomed across the bus. Even with the microphone, it was still a struggle to hear his voice over a band of political protesters in the street. I strained to concentrate as he continued to speak.

"Walk a block or two and you will hit some of our poshest stores," he said and paused, with a finger in the air. "In fact, the name Piccadilly actually originates from a seventeenth century frilled collar named *piccadil*." The protesters' chants began to fade as the bus moved along.

"Interesting," I mumbled. I gave a sideways glance to the woman who had been sitting beside me since I had gotten on at the Notting Hill stop. My voice sounded raspy to my own ears, probably because it had been hours since I had spoken to anyone. I cleared my throat.

"Here I thought it had been named after a pickle." I scribbled notes on a pamphlet I had received when I purchased my ticket.

"And *Circus* comes from the Latin word circle," Henry continued. "A round open space at a street junction." The bus began to slow down.

"Here I thought it was 'cause of the freak show that comes here," my neighbor said. She nudged me with a dry, wrinkled elbow. She had coral painted nails, tan leathered skin and from the sound of her southern accent, I guessed she was from Georgia or maybe Alabama. A Disney World sweatshirt stretched across her large breasts. She pointed her chin towards the crowd that had gathered in front of the Piccadilly fountain. "Will ya look yonder?" Her eyes widened in horror. "Didja evah?"

I followed her gaze. I saw two men holding hands, one man with an earring in his nose and the other with pink hair. Slightly offbeat, but a circus act? Hardly.

"Here we are," Henry announced, rescuing me from a response. "Piccadilly Circus—home of the longest billboard in the world!"

He waved his arm with flourish into the air as the bus came to a screeching halt underneath a massive billboard. Henry stumbled backwards into one of railings but didn't seem to be rattled in the slightest. "Piccadilly Circus has been compared to New York's Times Square. A virtual twin sister," he smiled with pride. His face may have actually radiated more light than the sign that hovered over his head.

"Well, there ya go," my neighbor said. She gazed around with a critical eye. "That city's loaded with crazies. I went there once and was nervous as a whore in church."

I made a face, but just couldn't even bring myself to acknowledge her ignorance. She was probably also the type who thought all New Yorkers carried a gun. I stood up and walked toward the exit, taking in the sights around me. There were many fluorescent signs, a video display, lots of pigeons... Yes, I could see many similarities between the two tourist attractions, but Piccadilly didn't have the same feeling as Times Square. Piccadilly had a cool fountain, but there was no Naked Cowboy strumming on a guitar like the one I saw daily in New York.

I thrust a five euro bill into Henry's hand and climbed off the bus. The sun was completely shining now, and I reached into my bag for my sunglasses. Now, if only my mood would turn a bit brighter, I thought wistfully as my feet hit the sidewalk. I threw on my sunglasses and began to walk.

Throughout the tour, I had started to feel a little anxiety about the hostel. I had become rather exhausted and was really feeling the effects of no sleep. I reminded myself that this was all part of the experience and my chance to re-do my structured past. It didn't matter that we were staying in a dormitory setting. If this was the most affordable way to travel Europe, then so be it. The last time I checked, my name wasn't Paris Hilton.

Yet, I couldn't help but worry about how we were going to sleep that night. I pictured my valuables stuffed into my pajama pockets, nearly suffocating in my hooded cocoon sack with every toss and turn. Just thinking about the dirty bodies that have slept in the bunk I'd been assigned gave me a head to toe itch.

And as much as I wanted to scrub my body clean after we'd gotten off the plane, I came to the conclusion I was probably cleaner *not* taking a shower. Our loo looked like it had never been introduced to bleach. How on earth was I going to beautify?

We hadn't been gone for twenty-four hours, and already, I felt like the American Werewolf in London. I had a handful of stray eyebrow hairs, a sprinkle of clogged pores, and after sightseeing in the rain, my hair that was formerly just greasy, had turned into a greasy poof.

I took out my phone and dialed Tess's number. I tapped my foot impatiently while listening to the ringing in my ear. I hadn't heard from her since we parted ways, and I hoped that she was okay.

"Aunt Lu? Hi!" Tess's voice boomed through my phone. She sounded more than okay, and I wondered where she was and what she was doing.

"Hi!" I exclaimed, forcing myself to meet her level of enthusiasm. "Where are you?"

"At a pub," Tess replied matter-of-factly.

"Did the Tower of Terror drive you to drink?" I smiled.

"No." Tess laughed into the phone. "I actually met a couple of guys from Chicago of all places. They seem really cool."

"One is actually pretty cute," she added, her voice dropping to a whisper. "Come join us." Her voice sounded so hopeful I knew I couldn't say no.

"I think a drink is exactly what Dr. Jekyll ordered," I replied.

"Yay! We're at the Queen's Head on Knightsbridge. Kind of where we caught the bus this morning. By Harrods. And don't get any ideas. I promise we'll go to there tomorrow, *together*."

"Sounds like a plan." I smiled. "See you soon."

One hour later, I walked towards the pub, feeling slightly uplifted. I had passed Burberry on my walk over and picked up a new hat and sandals, which I had somehow managed to convince myself were authentic to London. I never shop at Burberry New York, but how could I pass up Burberry London? My new purchases made me feel like a real Brit.

I probably could've saved money and just bought a blow dryer, but there was nothing in the world like retail therapy. I couldn't wait to wash my hair and rid my locks from icky airplane germs. Only then would my head be worthy of the hat's fine silk lining.

I strolled down the street and paused in front of a general store that sat beside the pub. I peered in the window and caught myself in the reflection. My hands flew to my head and tried to smooth my wild hair down.

The window display held a mannequin family. They sported some pretty funky sunglasses as they picnicked on a teak table. The store seemed to have everything under the sun, so I wondered if they happened to sell a computer charger because I'd left mine back in New York.

Since I was living in a commune, I was hauling my dead laptop in my bag all day rather than risk it being borrowed by one of my fellow communers. It had literally become a huge pain in the neck. Figuring a laptop that actually worked would make the pain somewhat worthwhile, I walked through the automatic door.

"Hello," I said, smiling at the clerk behind the register. He was an elderly man who looked like he should have already retired. Years ago. "I'm looking for a charger for my Mac. Do you by any chance carry those?"

The guy scratched his bald head and gave me a sideways look. I self-consciously tucked my hair behind my ears. "For your *Mac?*" He looked rather perplexed.

"Yes."

"Mac n tosh?"

I nodded politely, inhaling slowly through my nose. Why was it so odd to charge a Mac? Were laptops solar-powered in London?

The man tapped a wrinkled finger to his lips for a moment. "I will be right back." He slowly disappeared through the double doors behind him.

When he returned several minutes later, he had a small plastic boot mat in hand. "Err, I'm sorry, ma'am. This is all we have, but if you fold your coat, you can probably use this as a charger."

I shook my head in confusion. "What? I need a charger for my Mac. My *computer*—I don't get it." I wondered if Brits were all stuffy PC users.

He stared at me for a moment as I brandished my dead laptop. Then rolling his eyes he pointed over my shoulder. "Of all the waste of time conversations I've ever had with daft Americans, this one takes the biscuit. Try aisle five." He walked off to help another female customer.

"I just don't speak American," he shrugged to the woman. She raised an eyebrow at me and bit her lip.

I stood there completely dumbfounded, probably looking rather fit for his accusation. My face burned half from anger and the other half from humiliation.

"AISLE forget it," I shouted, mocking his nasty tone with a pretend British accent. My ears prickled, and I swallowed hard. I couldn't believe I had allowed a perfect stranger not only to summon, but to actually release the inner bitch in me.

My embarrassment grew as I heard someone clearing his throat behind me. Anger filled me. Who was going to make fun of me next? Shame on me for letting myself go there, but I certainly wasn't going to take any more public mortification. I turned around to face a handsome guy who was grinning from ear to ear. I was momentarily taken aback. He may have had the nicest smile I'd ever seen in my life. I had yet to encounter a Brit with such fabulous teeth. I remembered the way I looked and suddenly a wave of insecurity washed over me.

"Ah." He wagged his finger. "It's people like you, young lady, who give us Americans a bad name."

Ah, he was American. That explained the teeth. I wondered whether he was an ex-pat or a vacationer like myself. But what was with the young lady bit? The guy seemed to be in his early thirties.

"Excuse me?" I purposely tried to use my best are-you-talking-to-me tone, but I wasn't sure whether he was flirting or picking on me.

"I, and probably the rest of the city, knew what you meant. The old timers here in London call raincoats, macs," he said with a chuckle. "And plates are chargers. I think he thought you were looking for a plate for your raincoat." He laughed.

My mouth started to drop. It probably was somewhat funny, but I was too embarrassed to be amused. I couldn't even bring myself to politely fake it. I shut my mouth firmly and spoke through gritted teeth. "So that's why I give Americans a bad name? Because I didn't know what a damn raincoat was called?"

"Nooo. *That* was funny. But your attitude?" He paused to give me a sideways look. "Not so much."

I opened my mouth to speak when he cut me off at the pass. "Smile." He shrugged his shoulders. "The sun is actually shining here today. What could be so terrible?" He held his hands up and looked at me expectantly.

"Quite a bit," I snapped. I crossed my arms across my chest and glared at the handsome guy. I wanted desperately to smile, toss my frizzy hair over my shoulder, and laugh, but I just couldn't. Laugh or toss. Frizzy hair doesn't exactly go there.

"Just because your day is hunky dory..." I trailed off, unsure of what to say next.

I felt kind of foolish for my bitter behavior. He actually looked like a really nice guy. I groaned inwardly and was about to apologize, but before I could gather my thoughts, he sighed and turned away.

"Um, excuse me," I said loudly.

Unfortunately, for me, at that very same moment "Penny" was desperately needed in the stock room. The intercom blared through the store and completely drowned my words. I watched him throw on a Yankee baseball hat and disappear through the double doors, looking as if he hadn't a care in the world.

Feeling silly, I waited for him to disappear before my dead Mac and I walked out with my tail between my legs. On a different day, I probably would've laughed at this classic example of cultural differences. But unfortunately for me, embarrassment is the same worldwide. And today, I just wasn't in the mood to laugh at myself with a better-looking member of the opposite sex.

That drink with Tess was sounding better and better. I stepped onto the sidewalk and drew in a breath of not so fresh air. The repugnant smell of body odor and Petrulli oil filled my lungs and its culprit, a young hippie, blocked my path. He shook a cup of loose change in my face, and too nauseated to take another sip of air, I held my breath and walked around him.

An ambulance whizzed by with a siren so unexpectedly loud, I was startled and jumped backwards into a puddle. I shook each foot, hoping to drain the water from my new sandals and listened to the stinky hippie guffaw in the process. Deciding I needed to make that drink a double, I bee-lined to the pub.

The heavy, dark wooden door to the pub made me strain from its weight as I pulled it open. Once inside, the smell of fried food enveloped me. My mouth immediately filled with water. I hadn't eaten a thing since that morning's all-you-could-eat bread buffet.

The establishment was everything I had always pictured an English pub to be. Worn oak flooring, wood paneling, gas lamps, and etched glass windows. I looked over at the bar and saw a dozen beers on tap, greasy potato chips, and jars of hard-boiled eggs. Since egg breath isn't exactly a turn-on across the Atlantic, I wondered whether people actually ate the eggs. That's when I heard Tess calling my name.

I followed the sound of her voice and saw her waving at me from a table in the corner. She was sitting with three guys, and yes, I had to admit, they were pretty cute. I pulled my hair into a pony and walked towards the group. Of course our never-ending travel day hadn't taken a toll on her. Tess's glossy hair was still shining, and she looked like she should be on the cover of a travel magazine. The guys were hanging on her every word as she sat there like Princess Kate holding court.

When I got closer, I realized with dismay that I was old enough to be the young men's mother. They were around Tess's age, and I suddenly felt ancient. There I was, in my Burberry shoes, leggings, and cardigan, which were perfect for afternoon tea at the Savoy. Then there was Tess and the rest of the pub, dressed in skinny jeans and graphic print tees.

One of the guys looked over at me and made a guttural sound that truly frightened me. I wasn't sure if he was choking or if there was a dog with a Midwest accent being strangled inside of his body.

"Are you okay?" I said. For reasons unbeknownst to me, his friends burst out laughing. Tess had to bite her lip to keep from laughing herself.

"I would imagine that was supposed to be a purr," Tess translated. "Aunt Lucy, this is Chaz."

Ah. That explained a lot. I've never met a Chaz, but he was exactly what I would have expected to go along with the name. He seemed to be fueled by their laughter, too pompous to even realize they were laughing *at* him.

"Aunt Lucy," Chaz said, giving me the once-over. "You are much hotter than I would have expected an aunt to be. A Brit would probably call you shagtastic, but I prefer the term cougar," he said, with a wink.

I raised an eyebrow. "I may look like one, sweetie, but I don't date younger men."

"Who said anything about dating?" he challenged.

I gave him my best fake smile and turned to Tess. "Um," I mumbled under my breath, "what do you say we lose the aunt title for this trip?"

"Good idea," Tess said. She smiled and handed me a Carl's Lager. "Let me introduce you to the *nice* guys. I had no idea," she said under her breath. "He hadn't really said much before you got here."

I waved my hand dismissively and took a big gulp of the beer. I hadn't expected it to be so bitter, and I forced myself to swallow.

One guy jumped to his feet and held out his hand. "Hi, I'm Mark, this is Sam, and that's an acquired taste." He made a face and gestured to my beer.

I shook their hands and smiled. "I'd heard English beer tasted a bit different, but ...wait, are you talking about the beer or your friend?" I pointed my thumb in Chaz's direction.

"Hey!" Chaz cried. "I take offense to that."

Sam snickered, and Mark held up his bottle to mine. "Good one."

"I'll clink to that," I returned.

"They have American beers on tap." Mark laughed and motioned to the bartender. "No offense, Chaz, but you do leave a bit of an aftertaste. He may be one of our friends," Mark said, with a hand on his chest, "but please don't hold it against us."

"I'm actually a fraternity brother," Chaz corrected with pride.

"And you think that helps your case?" I said.

My kind audience laughed again, and though I was serious, the reaction lifted my spirits. I might be old, but I could still hang.

"So you guys are from Chicago," I said. "For how long are you travelling?"

"These guys," Mark said, motioning to the others, "have been backpacking for a few weeks already. Can't you smell?" He winked at me and took a sip of his beer. "This is only my first stop. I'm traveling with my older brother, who you actually just missed. He went off in search of a converter. Anyway, he and I are planning to spend a week in Paris and a couple of weeks in Italy."

Tess rested her hand on his shoulder. "Aunt ... I mean, Lucy, you and Mark are cut from the same mold. He's doing the hotel thing."

"Ah," I said. "I'm jealous."

"Err ... excuse me," said a deep voice with a British accent, from behind us.

I turned around and came face-to-face with a young man. He had the whole rocker thing going on—long bangs, skinny jeans, and the tightest t-shirt I'd ever seen in my life. I was starting to doubt I'd be bumping into the Colin Firth type on this trip.

"I'm with a local British network, and we're currently recruiting for a new reality series. It's kind of like "The Real World," only cooler," he boasted.

Tess squeezed my arm so hard she actually left nail marks.

"Your mother would kill you," I whispered in her ear.

"Sweet," said Chaz. "Where's it gonna be?"

"I'm afraid it's still up in the air, but Amsterdam looks like a front runner."

"Dude, three months in Amsterdam. Sign me up," Chaz exclaimed.

"That actually sounds pretty cool," I admitted.

"Well, not you," the guy said. He gave me a strange look and scratched his chin. "Unless... Well, maybe we can use you, after all." He paused to look at me thoughtfully.

"No." I chuckled and held my hand up in protest. It never occurred to me I would be included in this. I hoped this trip would bring me more excitement than I had expected. However, I had been thinking more along the lines of a class act. Not a shit show.

"Yeah … wait … the more I think about this..." He slowly nodded his head.

"Are you kidding me?" I narrowed my eyes and wondered if I was getting Punk'd. I half expected Ashton Kutcher to pop up from behind the jars of pickled eggs, but the guy didn't seem to be joking in the slightest.

"Absobloodylutely not!" he exclaimed. "In fact, you may add a good twist to the season." He appeared to be getting rather excited, and although there was no way in hell I would ever allow myself to appear in a reality show, there was a tiny piece of me that enjoyed the attention. I may not have been a frontrunner, but it was nice to even be considered for a show with a young demographic.

"Well, I *am* a twisted sister," I joked, laughing awkwardly. Tess subtly held out her hand to me and wore an alarmed expression on her face.

The guy glanced down at his clipboard as I leaned towards Tess. "What's with the look?" I whispered.

"Twisted sister?" She cocked her head to the side and gave me a pointed look.

"It's a hip show," I hissed. "I was trying to sound..."

"Eighties?"

I feigned a hurt expression and was caught off guard when the guy looked up at me expectantly.

"Are you around tomorrow to pop in for an interview?" he said.

"Yes she is!" Tess shrieked. "We'll *make* her available."

I smiled modestly and shook my head good-naturedly. "Guys, I really don't think this is my thing." I placed a hand on my chest. Boy, did it feel good to be flattered.

"Nonsense," he scoffed. "I'm really liking this dynamic." He waved his hand around the group.

"What dynamic?" I said, fishing for compliments.

"Ya know … you hangin' with the younger blokes. It's brilliant! Most of the older women I come across are all fur coat and no knickers. You seem to have a little more depth. You got the whole fresh face thing working…"

I looked at Tess who grimaced. "I see," I said quietly, feeling suddenly foolish.

"Dude, I get it. Like a hot den mother type o' thing?" Chaz said, foaming at the mouth.

"Something like that, man," he replied enthusiastically. "We never had a season where the ages were totally mixed, and I think having a *mature* woman in the house could be interesting. A shag here and there…"

The network visionary continued on with his grand ole plan to make a spectacle out of me and I felt increasingly like a little girl who had been busted for playing dress up, but in reverse. I was an older woman who had been busted for dressing down. It wasn't my clothes, but rather my surroundings. What had I been thinking, trying to pass myself off as a carefree traveler? It wasn't as if I had deliberately tried to fit in with the younger, happy-go-lucky crowd, but still. I certainly wished I could.

"Helloooo, Mrs. Robinson!" Chaz exclaimed, snapping me out of my reverie.

"That's not my style," I said curtly. "I don't do younger."

"Oh, rubbish," the guy dismissed. "This is a once-in-a-lifetime opportunity."

"Not for me." I turned my back on him.

"It's a TV show, for shit's sake!" he cried. "Don't be an arse."

"I don't think so," I smiled through gritted teeth and muttered, "arsehole" under my breath. A raucous crowd of young men and women came through the door, and nobody protested when he walked off to make an introduction.

The group felt just as sorry for me as I felt for myself. What was I thinking, even engaging him in such a ridiculous conversation? There has never been anyone over thirty on a show like "The Real World" and I certainly didn't intend to be the first.

* * * *

The following evening, Tess and I waited in Covent Garden Plaza for a taxi to take us to the train station. The next Eurostar was scheduled to leave for Brussels in an hour, and we were still a forty-five minute cab ride away. It was starting to rain, so when one pulled over, naturally I ran to it and jumped in. I slid my bag across the seat to make room for Tess and was startled by the sound of frantic knocking on my window.

I saw an attractive young woman, and I cautiously unrolled the window. "Can I help you?"

"Oh sure, *now* you want to help," she spat, her face scrunched into a look of disdain. "Now that your *ass* is sitting on the seat I was supposed to have," she growled, poking herself in the chest. A big raindrop plopped onto her cheek, and I watched mascara run down her painted face.

"What are you talking about? My niece and I have been waiting for..."

"I was here before you!" she shouted.

"Noooo," I said slowly.

"Ladies, where are you going?" the driver called over his shoulder.

"Victoria Station," Tess replied. "Aunt Lu, roll up the window," she pleaded.

Tess didn't have to twist my arm. I rolled the window up as the car began to move.

The woman began to pound on the window fast and furiously. "Chav," she yelled. "You low-life, American chav."

The driver made a groaning sound. Tess and I looked at each other quizzically.

"*Chav?* Is that the best she could do? Is that even a word?" I demanded.

The driver looked at us in his rear view mirror. "She looked a bit dodgy. Pay her no mind. She's talking bollocks."

31

Tess had been fiddling around on her phone. "Give me a break... It says here that a chav is a term for an uneducated hoodlum in the United Kingdom. What an idiot." She shook her head.

I clicked my tongue. "Ew. Ignoramus. What else does it say?"

"A chav can be a juvenile delinquent who is amoral, vandalizes, paints graffiti, and speaks in slang. Or..." Tess gasped, "She can come in an older version and be a trashy, classless cheeseball." Tess winced and looked at me apologetically. "Aunt Lu, I really think we've read enough."

"No," I said through gritted teeth. "Go on."

Tess groaned and reluctantly looked down at her phone. "In London, the chav trademark is none other than Burberry." She pressed a button on her phone and tossed it into her bag.

My mouth fell agape. "Wow." I paused and swallowed. "*Wow*. The hat and shoes I've been proudly sporting all over London basically has marked me, a forty-two year old woman, as a certified chavberry."

"So much for playing it safe with labels, huh?" Tess poked me in the ribs with her elbow. "You hell raiser," she teased.

I pulled the hat over my eyes and slumped down in my seat.

Chapter Three

Goodbye London, Hello Amsterdam!
Facebook Status June 6 at 10:00pm

Tess and I ran to the platform just as the train to Brussels pulled into Victoria Station. I was pleasantly surprised when we stepped into the car, which was in pristine condition, both immaculate and rather luxurious.

The plush seats were also inviting with their soft, navy blue velvet covers. After we'd settled, I immediately reclined my chair.

"Ah," I sighed with a smile. "I hope our connecting train to Amsterdam is just as nice. Clean, comfortable seats, a menu... Now *these* are the unexpected joys of travel." I picked up the menu and read the dinner options.

Tess gave me a sideways look. "Well, what did you expect? You purchased first-class tickets."

I nodded. "True. Well, I've had enough of feeling like a second class citizen. All I have to say is, *Cheerio!*"

"Oh come on," Tess admonished. "We had some fun, no?"

"Absobloodylutely," I said in a British accent, mocking the guy we'd met the night before. "No seriously, London was amazing. I loved everything we did. St. Paul's Cathedral, Buckingham Palace, Westminster Abby.... " I frowned and paused. "It's just that some of the extraneous variables threw me off."

Tess nodded her head knowingly.

"I vote we stay somewhere a bit nicer when we stop back here on our way home. I need a re-do. Those living conditions were awful."

The train began to pull out of the station. When I looked at Tess for a response, I noticed she was staring out the window, looking forlorn.

"I'm sorry," I said. The last thing I wanted was for my niece to regret taking the trip with me. Because my wedding day was supposed to have been the next day, I think I was a little more down than usual. I bit my thumbnail and waited for her to look at me.

She seemed to be lost in a world of her own as she played with the hem of her skirt.

"Tess?"

She turned to look at me. "Hmm?" she said with a tight-lipped smile.

"I'm sorry I complained so much."

"Oh, please," she said with a wave of her hand. "We stayed in a dump. I just feel..." She paused and shifted uncomfortably in her seat. "Kind of bummed we're leaving. My experience was a little different than the one you had."

"Mark?" I wiggled my eyebrows and smiled.

Tess's cheeks turned pinkish as she nodded. "We had so much fun last night, Aunt Lu." Her eyes sparkled, and a slow smile spread across her face.

"I figured. I didn't even hear you come in." I hoped that I sounded nonchalant, but all day, I'd been dying for the details. Tess had always been honest with me, but still, I hadn't wanted to pry and make her uncomfortable. On this trip, I may have been more of a friend than an aunt, but one fact still remained. I was her mother's sister.

"I got back late. Very. We spent the entire night talking," she added quickly. "We stayed in the pub for about three hours after you left, and then we took a ride on the London Eye."

I sucked in my breath and placed a hand on my chest. "Doesn't that go like two hundred feet in the air?"

"Actually, to be exact, it went four hundred and forty three *amazing* feet high. The view of London was spectacular. Especially at night."

The look on Tess's face was really something. She seemed to have come alive as she talked. I opened my mouth to speak, but she cut me off at the pass.

"Hey, did you know Big Ben is really the name of the bell in the tower? Locals just call it the clock tower. That's what Mark told me. By the way, he's so smart, Aunt Lu. He just finished his M.B.A from Boston University."

I nodded in approval. "He sounds..."

"We have so much in common too!"

I bit the inside of my cheek to keep a straight face. I couldn't recall ever seeing her this excited about any guy.

"Books, movies, TV... You name it. Anyway, he and his brother are going to be in Paris at the same time we are. So, maybe I'll meet up with him. If that's ok with you," she quickly added. "I don't have to see him. We're just friends ... though it might be nice."

I looked at her and rolled my eyes. "Gee, you think?" I said pointedly. "Of course you're going to see him!"

I rummaged through my snack bag for peanuts and noticed a string had come loose on the hem of her skirt.

"You've been fiddling with this so much that you're coming undone." I reached over and twirled the string around my finger before I gave it a gentle tug. "It's really beautiful though."

And that it was. The skirt fell above her knee and was made from a thick lime green cotton fabric with pale pink swirls cascading throughout. The hem was about two inches wide and a darker pink textured ribbon.

"Did you get it on Portobello Road?"

"No." Tess smiled shyly. "You're kind. I made it the night before we left."

I swallowed the peanut whole. "You *made* this? *You* made this? Oh my God, Tess."

"What? It's not a big deal, Aunt Lu. It took me an hour. Finding the fabric was the hardest part."

"Oh, just shut up and say thank you. It's amazing. Here I thought home décor was your thing. This trip is getting better and better. I'm travelling with a designer."

Tess gave me a funny look as she paused to reach into my bag for a handful of peanuts. "And *I* am travelling with a total nut bag."

* * * *

We arrived in Amsterdam at nine that night. Since we had to change trains in Brussels, the trip had taken a little more than six hours. We went straight to the hostel, which was thankfully much nicer than the one where we'd previously stayed.

The brick hostel was a quintessential seventeenth century Amsterdam-style house: tall and skinny, but thick on charm. It sat across the street from a canal and overlooked the Jordan River through its massive windows. Wooden flower boxes adorned the windows and overflowed with sleeping tulips. The sweet smell from the flowers mixed with the salty scent of the canal, resulting in a soothing aroma that wafted through the air.

A bicycle built for two was parked in a rack outside the hostel. The whole scene reminded me of a postcard. It was somewhere I really wanted to be.

Tess and I were both tired and decided to go right to bed. The lack of sleep I'd accumulated had started to take a toll. I listened to the rhythmic sound of water lapping against the canal as I drifted off to sleep.

We woke up the next morning feeling refreshed and ravenous. Since we both agreed one of the first things on the day's agenda was to eat a hearty breakfast, we wandered next door to a diner.

"So how are you?" Tess asked me, her eyebrows knitted together in a concerned expression as we waited for our waitress to bring the breakfast we'd ordered. Her head was tilted to the side, and she looked at me expectantly.

"Good," I shrugged. "We have our own room for now, so let's just hope the other two beds stay vacant." I crossed my fingers in the air and cleared my throat. I had a hard time meeting her gaze.

"And hopefully we'll get used to the timed showers," I continued, forcing a chuckle. "I probably could have bucked up for the extra shower token. As you know, it is my wedding day." I pressed my lips together and gave Tess a half-smile, mid-babble. "We would've been blowing a load at the salon anyway, right?"

"Oh, Aunt Lu." She looked at me with sympathetic eyes as she reached across the table and squeezed my hand.

"Sorry." I cringed.

"Sorry? Are you kidding me?" Tess held my gaze as she slipped an elastic hair band from her wrist and twisted her honey-colored hair into a knot on top of her head. "I didn't want to bring it up, but I didn't want to not bring it up either." With creases of worry deepening on her forehead, she sunk back into the booth and cradled her coffee cup, resembling a therapist waiting for her patient to speak.

I nodded and poured some sugar in my coffee, stirring it. A lump rose in my throat and made me avoid looking her in the eye. When I drew in a breath, I could actually taste the sweet smell of syrup that wafted throughout the diner. I continued to stir.

"Do you want to talk?" she asked.

I whisked the coffee fast and furiously, making it splatter on the table. "Oh, shoot." A few of the hot drops soaked through my shirt to my skin. "This was my good tank." I blotted at my shirt with a wet napkin.

Tess grabbed a napkin and wiped up my mess while I sat staring into my coffee cup. She reached across the table and placed a gentle hand on my arm. Tears instantly clouded my vision, and even though I tried not to blink, they spilled over on their own.

"I'm sorry, I just feel so ... so ... empty," I admitted, surprised by how hard it was to get the words out.

"That's normal, Aunt Lu. Today was supposed to be a big day for you."

"I just want it to be over," I sighed, pressing my fingers under my eyes. "This day has been hovering over my head like a black cloud."

"Actually, that's pretty ironic. I talked to my mom this morning and, if it makes you feel any better, New York's having the storm of the century. There are power outages all over the city."

"So, I've heard," I replied dryly. Morgan had already left me several voicemails and text messages. "But isn't rain on your wedding day supposed to bring you luck?"

"Oh come on. That's total bull. Someone must have fed that line of crap to a lunatic bride when it rained on her wedding day. What else were they supposed to say?"

"Good point."

"No, really. How can a torrential downpour bring you luck? Your hair would've been a disaster and the reception would've sucked."

"I'd have taken that bet." I leaned my elbows on the table and rested my head in my hands.

The waitress appeared with a massive platter of Dutch pancakes, causing me to sit up and collect myself.

"Eet smakelijk," the waitress said with a smile before she disappeared.

Tess looked at me quizzically.

I shrugged my shoulders and shook my head. "I have no idea. She could've just said 'eat shit' for all I care." I unfolded the napkin and placed it in my lap.

"Oh. My. God. These pancakes look amazing." Tess drooled. "Cheese, bacon, brown sugar…"

"Pretty lethal. Well, it's not like I have a Vera Wang tank dress to squeeze into." I forced a smile as I helped myself to a pancake.

"Now that's a plus," Tess said, her mouth already full. "Because, let me tell you, these are to die for."

I took a big bite and closed my eyes as the flavors melted in my mouth. "Yum. You know what?" I paused to swallow. "Let's talk about something else. We need to enjoy this breakfast."

"Yeah, but…" Tess paused and rocked her head from side to side, "I feel like it might be good for you to…"

"Indulge me. Please." I leaned on the table and gave Tess a closed-mouth smile. "Plus, I'm dying to know. Have you talked to Mark?"

"Yeah, he called this morning when you were getting ready," Tess said with a wave of her hand. "It's no big—"

"Hey, I'm offended." I clicked my tongue and frowned. "Why didn't you tell me sooner?"

Tess looked down and shrugged. "I don't know. It's not a big deal," she said nonchalantly. "I didn't want to make you feel any worse than the way I figured you were already feeling."

"Tess, do not, I repeat, do *not* withhold information from me. Number one, I want to live through you, and two, I'm a big girl. I still have it in me to be happy for others. Especially you."

"Okay, okay, I'm sorry." She winced. "There's not much to say though. Other than he's a really great guy." Tess looked down and poked her fork into a pancake on her plate.

A smile spread across my face as I watched her swish it around the syrup.

She cleared her throat. "It's just that…" She paused and placed her fork down.

I raised an eyebrow.

"He kind of has a girlfriend." She wrinkled her nose and made a face.

"What do you mean, kind of?" I demanded. "He either has a girlfriend or he doesn't. Is it serious?"

"I don't know. He didn't say, and I didn't ask. He just mentioned he'd been dating someone for a long time, but it wasn't really working out."

"You'd make an awful detective, my dear. Well…" I tapped my fingers on the table. "If it was serious, wouldn't he be travelling with her?"

Tess shrugged. "I guess. Maybe. Oh, I don't know. He just finished business school and has pretty much given himself a year to do his thing, get a job, and find himself," she said.

"Hmph. Aren't we all?" I stared into my coffee cup for a moment. "Anyway, maybe the quest to find himself has a little something to do with his girlfriend."

"Maybe." Tess paused. "Whatever," she added with a wave of her hand. "I guess it doesn't really matter, anyway. I don't think he likes me like that." She shrugged and took another bite.

I just gave her a look.

"What?" she laughed. "I told you, we're just friends. We had a connection and to be honest with you, it was nice to be myself with someone other than Jack," she said rolling her eyes.

"Well, you guys have been together for a long time."

"We've practically grown up together, Aunt Lu. We've both changed so much we've kind of grown apart. I'd like to think I've become more insightful, and he's become, I don't know…" She frowned. "Kind of self-centered. He's been unsupportive throughout my whole job-hunting debacle. He seems to be more concerned with his own success and fixated on things that don't really matter in life."

"Like what?" I said.

"You know, superficial crap," she said, shaking her head. "He and his friends always seem to be one-upping each other, and to be honest, it's exhausting to listen to them."

"Not to mention boring," I exclaimed. I had to remind myself we were talking about Tess's boyfriend and not my own ex. Cooper had those same tendencies, and his materialistic ways often got under my skin.

"Sorry. I was engaged to an older version. In Jack's defense," I said, with my index finger in the air, "he is a classic case of a young kid making too much money, way too soon."

"So, what was Cooper's excuse?" Tess prompted, covering her mouth with a hand as she chewed.

I rested my chin on my hand and shook my head, affixing my gaze on a photo of a windmill that hung on the wall. "I don't know. I think who he is stems from his past."

I turned my attention back to Tess who had raised a quizzical eyebrow. "He grew up very poor, and I think it makes him feel good that he had done a complete 180 degree turn with his life." I shrugged my shoulders. "All on his own."

Tess didn't look convinced, but reluctantly nodded her head, obviously trying to cut him some slack.

"No, really." I rushed to defend him. "His dad ran off with another woman when he was twelve, his mom worked around the clock, trying to care for Coop and his younger sister, but she was left with very little money and a whole lot of resentment. According to him, she was a bitter woman for many years. He was a good kid, always taking on odd jobs to help out. Paper route, shoveling driveways in the winter, cutting lawns in the summer... You name it. But no matter what he did, there was never enough money and never enough smiles on his mother's face."

"Yikes," Tess said with a grimace.

"I know." I took a big forkful of my pancakes and shoveled it into my mouth, chewing thoughtfully.

It was hard to believe that Marjorie, the woman whom I had grown to love, was the same woman Cooper had described whenever he recounted his childhood. Whatever she had morphed into during Cooper's youth, she had morphed out of by the time I came along. She was loving and very proud of her children, and the feeling was mutual. Cooper truly believed that his mother did the best she could as a single parent with zero career skills and a broken heart.

"Anyway," I paused to sip my coffee, "I guess being abandoned by his dad, growing up poor, and not receiving any appreciation or love from his mom during his formative years, left quite the mark. Still, Cooper rose above it. He became Mr. Successful. Self-made." I sat up straighter, aware of the pride in my voice, but I couldn't help it. I *was* proud.

I leaned forward and stared into Tess's doe eyes. "I loved his vulnerable side. I saw the little boy in him, the one who just wanted to make his mommy proud." I paused to swallow, tears pricking my eyes. "I felt really lucky to land the wounded bird. He chose *me*." I pressed my hands into my chest for emphasis, simultaneously trying to suffocate the emotion threatening to pour out. "I was never anyone's plan A before."

"What?" Tess curled her upper lip, exposing her ultra white front teeth. "Are you kidding me?"

"Um, why are you looking at me like I have a penis coming out of my forehead? Or food all over my face?" I took my napkin off of my lap and wiped my lips, folding the napkin in half and resting it on the table.

"Why wouldn't you be someone's plan A?"

I drew in a deep breath and slowly exhaled. "Missy, you turn more heads than anyone I know." Tess rolled her eyes as her cheeks turned pink.

"I may look like I have it all to you," I continued. We locked eyes and began to laugh. "Okay, maybe not now," I said, wiping my eyes, "but in all seriousness, I was never exactly Ms. Popular with the boys. Glasses, braces, bad hair." I tugged on my air-dried hair and snickered. "Shocker, right?"

Tess leaned over and slapped my hand.

"No kiss until sixteen," I continued. "No date for prom..." I trailed off and made a sucking sound with my tongue, feeling sorry for myself.

"I'll never forget a party at my friend Tracey's when I was about fourteen. She was one of the cool girls, and we were family friends, so she always included me in everything. Long story short,"—I waved my hand—"we were playing spin the bottle, and Scott Kilogris, my crush of many years, spun the bottle, and it landed on me."

Tess scraped syrup onto her fork and licked it, her eyes rapt with interest.

"Oh, this is where it gets good." I made a sinister smile and nodded. "I was so nervous, my legs trembled when I stood up and I could actually hear my heart beating in my ears. Then I heard him say to one of the guys, 'I am NOT kissing Lucy Banks.' I stood there grinning like a fool, trying to be the girl with the sense of humor, but I wanted to disappear into the floor. My fake smile shook. Everyone was chanting 'Go, go, go...' and one of the cheerleaders actually dragged him to his feet." The painful memory made me cringe.

"No," Tess groaned, her hand flying to her mouth.

"Yep." I took a deep breath and continued. "So, we went into the dark closet, and despite all that drama, I was *still* excited and braced myself for my first kiss—my monumental moment. Oh, and it most certainly was."

Tess released her breath and smiled.

"Scott shut the door behind him, turned to me, and whispered, 'we really don't have to kiss. Let's just wait thirty seconds and come out.'"

Tess looked like a little kid who just discovered there was no such thing as Santa Claus.

I paused to sip water, hoping to hide my burning face temporarily behind the glass. I chewed on an ice cube and nodded.

"Yep. Heartbreak number one," I said, knowingly.

"Wow." Tess cleared her throat and shook her head.

"At the time it felt like the ultimate. Who knew that years later I would be faced with this gut-wrencher? Which leads me to the point of my humiliating story. The fact that someone who has it all actually chose plain ole Lucy Banks to be his wife, really made me feel like a million bucks."

"Okay ... totally get what you're saying, but Aunt Lu, that was like thirty years ago," Tess said. "Shouldn't you be a little more secure by now?" she said in a gentle voice.

"First of all, twenty-eight," I corrected. "But can you at least try to understand what I'm saying? Cooper had sky-high standards. So if he picked me, then wow, I must be something special."

"You *are* something special." Tess hit the table with her hand, making a saucer rattle on the table. She made a grimace and massaged her palm.

"Well, he ditched me, so clearly I'm not."

At the same time, we both let out exasperated sighs.

"Tessie, you can't relate to this. You've had an easy go at life."

Tess, who had been taking a sip of orange juice, snorted, causing a little juice to trickle down her chin. "Oh yeah, and that served me well. Now look," she said, wiping her lips with the back of her hand. "My mom took care of everything for me. 'Oh, you don't like your science teacher? I'll switch classes for you. Having a problem with one of your friends? I'll talk to her mother.'" Tess looked at me with exasperation. "She even made *you* take this trip with me."

I opened my mouth to protest, but she silenced me with her hand.

"I don't know how to figure it out on my own. I never had to. I can't get a job, so what do I do? Get depressed. It's like I can't handle the fact that I, or my mommy, can't fix this situation for me. The unknown with me in command has never been part of my life. I have followed all the steps I was supposed to, even as a child. I was a Brownie, then a Girl Scout, played sports in high school, went to the college Mom and Dad wanted me to attend, then to grad school. I did all the things I was supposed to do. All the things I was told to do. Now what? I'm trying, but..." She trailed off, looking miserable.

I reached over and covered her hand with my own. "There are no more mapped out turns on our GPS's of life," I finished. "It's like a car GPS. 'You have reached your final destination,'" I said in a computerized voice, "and are now on your own.'"

"The highway to nowhere," she muttered.

"Or the parkway to possibilities?" I offered.

Tess took a sip of her coffee, and I absently popped a blueberry into my mouth, sharing a moment of silence with my niece. I had never realized that despite our age difference, how similar we were. One generation apart and we were both kind of in the same place. Two structured women starting over.

"Well, Tess, you're paving a new route and giving it your all, honey. That's all you can do. All *we* can do."

I playfully slapped the top of her hand. "Hey, here's something that will make you feel better. Your situation could be worse. You can be forty-two and starting over." My stomach ached. "Forty-freakin-two and starting over..." I cleared my throat and waved my hands frantically, like I was shaking a heinous picture off of an Etch-a-sketch.

"What happened to 'parkway to possibilities'?" she demanded dryly.

"Touché. I guess it's easier to be the one giving the pep talk. Let's talk happy thoughts. Back to Mark." I swallowed hard and smiled. "Hopefully he's a little different than the men we're used to? Less attitude?"

"Oh yes," she beamed, eyes shining. "Mark seems to be the other way around. Growing up, his parents made him and his brother give away their birthday gifts to needy children in the area. I mean, c'mon, I know it's extreme, but it sounds like those values really stayed with him. He's so down to earth."

"Well, we're still going to see him again, right? Paris?"

"Actually, yes." Tess had an uneasy look on her face.

I raised my eyebrows in question. "Sweetie, that's a good thing."

Tess drew in a breath and twisted her fingers. "Aunt Lu, there's a slight issue. When I told Mark we were staying at that Lucky Youth hostel, he told me there was an age limit. Last summer, a few of his older friends were booted out for being overage."

I laughed. "Well, I knew the term *youth hostel* would eventually catch up to me somewhere. Don't worry, I'm sure there are hundreds more out there," I held my fists in the air, feigning enthusiasm. "I would just like to vote for a private bathroom this next time around. If possible."

"Actually, I had an idea." Tess's face turned pink. She sipped her coffee and placed it back down on the saucer, making it clatter loudly. "What do you think about staying at the hotel where Mark and his brother are staying?" She looked down and picked at one of her fingernails.

"Come again? Hotel? As in no 's'?"

"No 's'." She smiled. "They're staying at *Le Palais* in the Golden Triangle area. I was thinking it might be kind of nice to upgrade and see Paris in style. You've been such a great sport about the hostel thing, and I feel like now it's my turn to compromise."

"That's so nice of you." I pressed my lips together to keep from laughing.

"Don't you think we should treat ourselves? This hotel is in the middle of everything, and the view is supposed to be spectacular. I think we deserve it."

"And this has nothing to do with Mark?" I smiled.

Tess picked up a menu and hid her red face behind it.

I pulled the menu away. "Tess. You don't need to convince me. You had me at hotel."

"Really?"

"Um, really. No sleep cocoon? No shower shoes? Not squatting to pee? While my quads have gotten a bit tighter these past few days, it's really not good for my digestive issues," I said with a knowing look.

Tess looked giddy with relief.

"I can see it right now. A hot bath, blow-dried hair, champagne on the Champs-Élysées. I may even get this shirt laundered." I tugged on my newly stained tank top. "How do you like that?"

"I love it. Aunt Lu, you're the best." Tess walked over to my seat for a hug. "Before we go high class, don't forget you promised we would live like the Amsterdamians this evening." She pulled herself out of my embrace and did a little dance. "Red light district, baby."

"How could I forget?" I groaned. "We'll be observing, not partaking, young lady." I wagged my finger. "Your mother would kill me."

"I know, I know," Tess sang. She excused herself to use the ladies room, and I Googled the name of the hotel on my iPhone. That moment alone justified the international upgrades we'd made to our phone plans. I just couldn't imagine being out of reach for four weeks.

As I dialed the hotel's number, I noticed a girl who had walked into the diner. She instantly reminded me of a stereotypical Dutch girl in a movie. She looked as if she should be named Jolanda, with long, blonde, braided hair and red clogs.

"*Morgen,*" she sang to me, as she followed the hostess to the booth in front of us.

"Hello," I replied, kind of confusedly. The look on my face must have mirrored what was going on in my brain.

"Is something wrong?" she said in a kind voice. The waitress placed the menu on her table and walked away.

"Oh, no. I just think you might be getting me mixed up with my sister. It happens all the time. She looks exactly like me—in an older version," I said, chuckling.

Jolanda gave me a strange, sideways look. I tucked my hair behind my ears and started to fidget. I could actually feel my face flush. "It's been a rough week. I don't usually look this bad."

She shook her head quickly as if to erase me. "*Vaat?* I think I need my coffee. Vat do you mean ... your sister? I just said *Morgen*." She threw up her hands.

"Right. That's her name." I was starting to lose patience.

Jolanda drew in a breath. "I'm going to..." she trailed off pointing to her seat.

I simply nodded.

A man walked past us and smiled. "*Morgen*, ladies."

"*Goademorgen*," Jolanda answered.

I closed my eyes in shame.

"*Bonjour, Le Palais*," said the voice at the other end of my phone. I perked up, feeling much more hopeful for Paris. However, first, I just had to get through this day.

* * * *

A visit to the Van Gogh Museum, a tour of Anne Frank's house, and one boat cruise later, we stumbled out of a coffee shop in the red light district. "Pot and coffee—kind of counterproductive, no?" I grabbed Tess's arm for support.

"It works just fine for me, partner!" Tess sang gleefully. She linked my elbow with hers and swung me around as if we were doing a square dance. I planted my feet firmly on the ground and without missing a beat, Tess traded me for a lamppost.

"I don't know how I let you talk me into this," I said. "When you asked if I wanted to share a dessert, I was thinking more along the lines of oh, I don't know. Maybe a slice of Dutch apple pie? A piece of almond cake? Not a hash brownie. If your mother could see us now."

"Shh." Tess held a finger to her lips as she reverted back to her do-si-do with the lamppost. "I say, what happens in Amsterdam, stays in Amsterdam."

"You got that right," I agreed. "Isn't pot supposed to make everyone laugh and act silly? Figures I'm the one percent who has the adverse reaction."

"Maybe you need a little more help to beat the blues." Tess had a glimmer in her eye as she rubbed her hands together.

"Um, I don't think so. The pot did nothing but help me *greet* the blues, thank you very much. You know, you shouldn't have let me do this," I scolded.

"I don't recall tying your hands behind your back. Since when am *I* in charge of *you?*"

Her hand flew to her mouth in horror, and she gasped, stopping in her tracks. "Oh my God. What if I'm really Aunt Tess and you're really my niece, Lucy?"

I closed my eyes in despair. "We are going right back to the hostel, I can't even imagine what your mother would say if she knew ..."

"My mother would probably say we should stop and eat something. I've got the munchies and Dutch candy from the vending machine ain't gonna cut it!"

"Fine," I said sternly, steering her body in the direction of our hostel. "First food and then we're going back." I looked at my watch. It was eight p.m., which meant that it was two p.m., in New York, the exact time our ceremony was supposed to have started. I willed myself not to think about it. Eat and go to bed. The day would be over soon.

I sulked my way through the city, and we ended up at the same diner we ate at this morning. The waitress came to take our order.

"I would love some eggs, please." That's when the floodgates opened. I put my head down on the table, banged my fists, and started to sob. "I just want some friggin' eggs."

"She, um, can't have kids," Tess said in an obnoxiously loud whisper. "Then her fiancée cancelled their wedding. It would have been happening,"—she paused to look at her watch—"like now. O-M-G. Now!!!" she exclaimed. "Can you give us a minute please?"

The waitress seemed completely unfazed by my tantrum and Tess's dramatic narration. She must have been accustomed to stoned Americans. What she didn't realize was that if I had eggs, I wouldn't have been sitting in her booth. I'd be saying my vows right about now to the man I had thought was the love of my life. Instead, I was a grown woman half-baked into oblivion.

"I'm sorry." I sniffed when I looked up at Tess several moments later. "I'm not one for public meltdowns. I think the pot made me extra emotional. It's just..." I wrung my hands together in despair and felt stickiness from the tears and mascara. "You know, I think there was a part of me that was hoping Cooper had kept his hold on the Waldorf-Astoria and would whisk me away right to the wedding I'd always wanted."

Tess's eyes widened upon hearing her delusional Aunt's true confession. After a moment, she reached across the table and folded her hands over mine, looking stone-cold sober.

"I'm sorry, Aunt Lu. You do not deserve to be in this much pain. Cooper has no idea what he's lost."

"Thanks," I sighed and gave her hand a squeeze back. "Hey, would you mind if we went back to the room? I promise, I'll treat you to a feast in the morning. I have no appetite and can't sit here anymore."

"You're on, but if you think I'm waiting until morning, you're crazy. The vending machines will have to suffice. I have munchies that cannot be controlled!" Tess popped a piece of gum into her mouth.

We walked out of the diner, and suddenly I had an impulse I couldn't control. I took my phone out of my bag.

"Tess, please don't tell your mother what I'm about to do. I need closure," I declared.

"No," Tess said firmly. "You don't mean…"

I nodded. "Remember, what you said earlier, what happens in Amsterdam, stays in Amsterdam." Just the thought of making some sort of contact, any contact, with Cooper, was enough to make me smile. "Don't worry," I said, waving my hand. "I'm just going to say a quick hi. Keep it light."

"Aunt Lu, you're going to regret this. You do not want to go there. Remember our conversation earlier today? Materialistic? Damaged?"

"Aren't we all, Tessie. I just told you the negatives. We didn't get into his positives. As you know, a negative and a positive balance each other out. They equal a neutral. That, my dear, is exactly what I am about to make. A neutral hello."

"No, a negative and a positive equal a big, fat zero." She formed a circle with her fingers and waved it in front of my face.

I just smiled. I began to dial.

"Oh my God, it's ringing." I looked at Tess, who was gnawing away on her nails.

It rang four times and then his voicemail picked up. I could feel the color drain from my face as I listened to his recorded voice.

"He changed his message," I whispered. I felt as if I had been kicked in the gut. What else had he changed? Was he dating? Did he ever think about me?

Hearing his voice brought up so many emotions—bitterness, sadness, hurt, jealousy, betrayal, and major anxiety, followed by an enormous wave of nausea. My hands shook at the beep of his voicemail. I cleared my throat and watched Tess crack her knuckles.

"Hi Cooper…it's me. Lucy. It's been awhile. Three months actually," I laughed bitterly into the phone. "But who's counting, right?"

I cleared my throat again. "Happy wedding day," I sang in a too-high, slightly manic tone. "I'm in Amsterdam. Celebrating the single life. Celibacy…" I looked over at Tess and cringed. She had her face buried in her hands.

"I'm kidding. Not really." A lump rose in my throat and it actually hurt to swallow it. "Cooper," I choked, "why did you leave me? Why did you do this to us?"

Tess lunged for my phone, and I turned my back to her, walking towards a footbridge. "I figured you would come to your senses, but maybe you already had. Did you ever love me? You were my life!" At that point, I was sobbing into the phone.

Some nasty comments may have followed, but if they had, within seconds, my mind had blocked them. I heard Tess's heavy footsteps coming up behind me.

"We had plans," I wailed and tripped onto the bridge to get away from her. "We were supposed to grow old together. We were supposed to…"

"Hey!" I yelled angrily at Tess who had pretty much pushed the phone out of my hand while pressing buttons to end the call. The phone fell to the ground near my feet. "Why did you do that?"

"Why did *you* do that?" Tess sighed and shook her head sadly. She leaned against the bridge and stared at me with her arms folded defensively against her chest. "Can't you think a little more of yourself? Or if you don't, at least pretend you do. For once?"

I pushed out my lip and folded my hands across my chest. "You're too young to understand." The heart to heart we'd had earlier that afternoon felt like it had never happened. We were back on two different playing fields.

"No, Aunt Lu, that's where you're wrong. I was never, ever, too young to understand how special you are."

I wiped my eyes with the back of my hand and looked away, unable to meet her gaze. I was beginning to feel mortified about my actions in front of my niece. Once upon a time, she had looked up to me.

A tour boat passed beneath the bridge, and despite the happy sounds of music, laughter, and clinking glasses, an awkward silence hung between us. I took a few sips of air to steady my breathing.

Suddenly, my phone rang, and Tess and I sprung into action. We simultaneously bent down to grab it and bumped heads in the process. The phone lit up and Cooper's name and number flashed across the screen.

"Please." Tess placed a gentle hand on my arm. "Don't pick it up. He hurt you so bad."

My forehead smarted, but I remained frozen in a crouched position, listening to it ring for the third time. I grabbed onto the bridge to help support my wobbly legs as I stood up.

"I'll just let him leave a voicemail," I said weakly. He never did.

Chapter Four

"I feel like I've died and gone to Versailles," I whispered loudly as Tess and I stepped into the lobby of the hotel we'd booked in Paris. "Thank you for this brilliant idea. *Merci, merci, merci!*" I enthusiastically tugged on her arm as we both looked around the majestic hotel.

That morning, I'd woken up in Amsterdam, feeling surprisingly optimistic. It was a brand new day, and taking a break from roughing it definitely upped my happiness quotient. With the promise of a high thread count ahead, I was hardly bothered when the hostel shower refused my token again that morning. My irritation level was fairly low on the Richter scale, and I'd decided it was going to stay that way.

I'd survived the would-be wedding day, the sink baths were over, and to top it all off, on the train from Amsterdam to Paris, I'd gotten an email from Janice Preston, an old friend with whom I used to work. She was now an editor at a travel magazine, and after she'd heard I'd gone to Europe for an extended period of time, she'd written to ask if I'd be interested in pitching an idea or two for an article.

Au revoir to yesterday. Paris was definitely off to a great start, and today I planned to sip champagne in style.

"Aunt Lu, you're the one I should be thanking," Tess said. "I still feel really guilty. My plan wasn't to pick a fancy hotel and have you pay for it. Mark and his brother have great taste."

"Yes they do, and thank God for that. Don't even give it another thought. This is my gift to you." Excitement filled me as I looked around the lobby. My eyes wandered from the marble floor, to the dark antique furniture and works of eighteenth century art, and then up to the crown moldings and crystal chandeliers.

"After that last place..." I said with a shudder.

"Oh, come on. It wasn't that bad."

I gave Tess a sideways glance. "It may have been charming on the outside, but I'm too old for dormitory living. And will you look at that guy behind the front desk? Are all French men that handsome?" I whispered.

"Who, him?" Tess followed my gaze. "You think he's better looking than the guy we gave the key back to this morning?"

My mouth fell open, but turned into a smile when I realized she was kidding. The man who had checked us out of the hostel in Amsterdam had looked as if he had been on a three-month bender.

"Justin Bieber's greasy older brother? Just a tad. C'mon, let's check in so we can ditch these things." I adjusted my heavy backpack.

We approached the front desk, and I began to feel self-conscious about the way we were dressed. "I cannot wait to get out of these clothes," I murmured to Tess through gritted teeth.

She was wearing jean shorts and a t-shirt, and I had on my well-worn leggings and a stretched-out tank top. That would've been fine if we had Louis Vuitton luggage as arm candy, but the backpacks did little to enhance our look.

"*Bonjour, Mesdemoiselles,*" the handsome man said, making my arm hair stand on end. He could have said, "Hello, you dirty American sluts", but with his beautiful French tongue, anything would've sounded seductive. I glanced at his nametag: *Claude.*

"*Bonjour.*" I smiled and tapped Tess's foot with my own. I leaned on the counter and drew a hand to my face, tracing the not-so-hollows of my cheeks.

"*Parlez-vous francais?*" he said.

"No," I said apologetically, half-attempting to look sexy. I had been warned the French don't appreciate it when Americans won't even try to speak their language. Yet, I had nothing to say. *"Un poco español,"* I offered, with a friendly chuckle.

"I see. Name please?" He smiled tersely.

"It's under Tess McNally." I handed him my credit card.

Tess shifted uncomfortably and gave me a gracious smile. She had never been good at accepting generosity from others.

"Mesdemoiselles, where are you traveling from today?"

"We're from New York," I answered in my best Audrey Hepburn impression. "City." I straightened up and tossed my hair over my shoulder. I needed him to know that we were on his playing field. I also hoped to impress my niece while I was at it. Especially, after my pathetic display the other night in Amsterdam.

"Ah, very nice." He inserted keys into a folder. "You will certainly approve of our hotel and find it quite delightful. The view of the Seine is simply divine."

"Oh, I'm sure," Tess gushed. "We're easy to please. We've been doing the hostel thing for the past week, so anything's an improvement!"

As Tess twirled her unwashed hair, Claude gave her a not-so-subtle once over and paused for a moment with the folder mid-air. He turned to his colleague and began speaking in French.

I leaned on the counter next to a wheeling rack holding several Chanel, Fendi, and Jimmy Choo shopping bags. It looked like someone had had a field day on the Champs-Élysées.

"Oh my gawd," cried the woman who'd been standing next to us. "I couldn't help but ova-hear. We're from New Yawk, too. Yous are gonna doy when you see the riva view. I feel like we're staying on the Hudson."

Considering that the Hudson is notorious for its brown filth, I wasn't so sure she drew a kind comparison.

I watched the men behind the counter exchange a look of disapproval.

"How nice," I politely murmured. After our faux pas of not speaking the language, I certainly didn't want to be associated with anyone who spoke our own language incorrectly.

Claude turned back to us, removed the keys from the folder, reinserted them into his machine, and punched in a code. "Enjoy your stay at *Le Palais.*" He handed the key to us with a flourish.

"Will you be needing help with your..." He pointed down at our clunky backpacks, which had shed a fine layer of dust on the hotel's immaculate floor. "Luggage?"

He quickly withdrew his finger. It was as if he feared a bedbug would pop out and bite it off.

"We're fine, thank you," I answered.

A few minutes and three flights of stairs later, we walked into the room.

"Wow, wow, wow," Tess said. She fell face first onto one of the big queen poster beds.

"Ack! Didn't your mother ever teach you not to lay on one of these dirty bedspreads?" I scratched my head. "The first thing I do when I get to any hotel is flip the bedspread and sanitize the toilet seat. If these rooms could speak," I shivered at the thought. "Just think of what goes on in here."

"Okay, okay." Tess gave me the hand and jumped off the bed. "Thank you for that visual."

"Just protecting my little niecie." I smiled sweetly, heading to the large windows. "And now for the most spectacular view in all of Paris. Drum roll please."

I dramatically ripped open the curtains and heard Tess gasp behind me. "What the—"

"Fuck," I finished. "This is a good view?"

I pointed my finger towards our magnificent view of an alley behind a restaurant. "Unless the river view is that stream coming from those pots of water the kitchen staff are pouring onto the street, we are in the wrong room," I declared.

"It's okay." Tess sighed. "It's not like we're going to be spending all of our time in here, anyway. This room is still fabulous, and I can't say thank—"

"That's not the point. I think he downgraded us because he thought we were dumb American backpackers. Well, no one is going to make a fool out of me." I picked up the phone.

Tess pressed her cheek on the glass. "Aunt Lu, if you look all the way left, you can kind of see a glimmer of water." I knew she was probably hoping to appease me, and I waved my hand in response.

"*Bonjour*," said the operator who answered my call. "*Puis-je vous aider?"*

"May I please speak to Claude? We were promised a spectacular river view, and I think there may have been a slight mistake," I said as I smiled into the phone.

"I'm sorry, *Mademoiselle,* but Claude is with another guest. May I help you?"

"Actually, I'll come down and wait."

Five minutes later, Claude wore a strained smile on his face as he watched me approach the front desk. Clearly, he had been warned I was on my way.

"*Bonjour, Mademoiselle.* Colette said you were not pleased with your room?"

"The view," I corrected.

"Ah, I see," he nodded. "Even though you can see the river?"

"Not without sticking my head out the window," I answered with artificial gaiety as I skewered him with my eyes.

"I'm sorry to hear that. You have one of our finest rooms in our hotel, but if you are that unhappy…." He held up a new key.

"Thank you." I exhaled and reached for the key.

"This key will grant you access to our rooftop where you can enjoy a 365-degree view of Paris. Complementary coffee and tea are served from seven o' clock—"

"Wait," I insisted. "This will also lead to a new room, right?"

"I'm afraid not, *Mademoiselle.* There are no rooms with a better view." A flicker of fear crossed Claude's face. His face, once irritatingly handsome, was now just irritating.

"But you said,"—I paused to draw in a breath—"that our view was spectacular *before* you changed our keys at check-in. Were my niece and I not worthy of your finest? Was it because she said we were backpackers?"

"No, as I said—"

"I know what you said and it is *not* acceptable. Our stay is a gift for my niece, and if I wanted to stare at the back of a filthy kitchen, I would have stayed at one of *her* youth hostels."

As angry as I was, I still wanted to make one thing clear: I had nothing to do with her previous choices of lodging. Claude's upper lip curled up ever so slightly as he listened to me speak.

"Don't you judge me, *Claude,* with your perfect"—I waved my hand in front of him—"everything."

"Just so you know," my hand remained in the air as if I were testifying, "I don't usually look like this. I know I need tweezers. They took it away on the airplane. Silly me thought plucking stray hairs in the natural sunlight would be a bonus. Like I'm really going to hijack the plane with a Tweezerman?"

Claude folded his arms across his chest and tapped his lips with a finger. A smile tugged at the corners of his mouth.

"In Amsterdam, I had to use a three-minute token to take a shower. And do you know what my window overlooked? A view of an apartment where an old man was not a fan of wearing pants."

All the pent up agony and exhaustion of the past week exploded from me. I knew I was ranting, but I was powerless to stop myself. I hadn't exactly been sleeping well in those hostels, and the emotional rollercoaster and stress of getting through the supposed wedding day had caught up to me.

Claude had covered his entire mouth with his fingers, but I could still see the crinkles around his eyes.

"I may sound like a drama queen to you, but my dear Claude," I said with my eye narrowing as I paused to take a breath, "If I don't get a room with a freaking view, I am going to *lose my shit.*"

The phone rang, and Claude held up a finger. "Excuse me for a moment, please." He lunged for the phone.

"Ahem," I heard a voice behind me.

I turned around and came face-to-face with the handsome man I had met in London, when I had come close to verbally assaulting a store employee. What were the odds? He even wore the same Yankee hat and shit-eating grin.

Oh my God, oh my God, oh my God. Feeling like a fool for the second time, I subtly wiped the trickle of sweat that had formed on my upper lip.

"I … I didn't realize anyone was waiting behind me. What are you doing here?" I stammered, mortified but also still on a rage, high from my adrenaline-fueled tirade. "How long have you been standing there?"

He looked amused as a smile teased his lips. "Long enough to see that the angry American strikes again." He nodded his head in Claude's direction. "I never saw anyone answer a phone so fast in my life." He winked at me. "Is there a problem with your room?"

"The room's fine, it's just that..." I closed my eyes and shook my head. "I'm really not an angry person."

He raised an eyebrow. "Forgive me. I don't know where I got that idea from. Not that it's any of my business, of course."

"Of course," I responded with a fake smile.

I turned my attention back to Claude who was still on the phone. Through the reflection of a mirror behind the desk, I could see Tess headed towards me. She was carrying two coffees and walked beside a man. As she got closer, I realized it was Mark and couldn't help but feel a bubble of happiness rising inside of me. I was excited for her to have a new love interest and relieved to be saved from the Yankee behind me.

"Hi Mark," I called out as I turned around. "How funny that you ran into each other already." I winked at Tess.

"Yeah, really," Yankee answered. "That was quick."

I shot him a look. Mind your business.

"Hey Lucy," Mark said, greeting me with a kiss on the cheek. "I see you've already met Simon?" He handed a cup of coffee to the Yankee.

"Sort of," I answered and felt my throat catch as I realized who the baseball cap guy was. "Is this your—"

"Brother," Simon said, flashing his perfect grin. "How do you do?" He extended his hand.

"Nice to meet you." I clenched my teeth and accepted his hand.

I flashed back to the night I met Mark when he had said that I just missed his brother who'd gone off to the store. I hadn't put two and two together and realized he'd walked into the same store I'd had.

"But why do you wear a Yankee hat if you're from Chicago?" I blurted out the first foolish thing that popped into my head.

"My dad was born and raised in the Bronx. Is that okay with you?"

"This is my niece, Tess."

I pulled my hand away and lunged for one of the coffees she held. Her eyes shone as she greeted Simon. There was no mistaking that Mark's presence made her glow.

Simon pointed towards Claude, who had just hung up the phone. "Do you mind if I ask him something real quick?"

"Go nuts," I said dryly.

"So," Tess began, flashing me a quizzical look. "Were you able to change rooms?"

"No, he claims there are no rooms left that have a view. Whatever." I rolled my eyes. "Mark, have you checked in yet?"

"Yes, we checked in this morning, threw our bags down, and went for a walk. We haven't even unzipped our bags and already managed to lock ourselves out." He pointed a thumb towards his brother's back.

I couldn't help but chuckle. "How's *your* view?"

"Pretty spectacular I have to admit." Mark cringed and gave us an apologetic look.

"*Was* pretty spectacular," Simon said, joining the conversation. He dangled a key in front of me.

"What's this?" I said. "Trying to pick me up?"

Both Mark and Tess laughed, but Simon just shrugged, his eyes twinkling again.

"I am offering you our room," he said with a tiny half bow that suddenly had me thinking of princes and courtly manners. For the first time, I looked Simon square in the face and was taken aback by the kindness in his big brown eyes.

"Simon, don't be ridiculous," I said.

"Yes, stay with us," Mark pleaded. "The more the merrier." He looked longingly at Tess.

"What I meant," Simon said, shooting his brother a look, "is that you can have our room, and we will have yours. A new room with a new view."

"Oh. Yes, be ridiculous," Tess said. "That's so nice of you!"

I stepped on her toe.

"Good idea," Mark agreed. "Not as clever as mine…" He laughed and said, "but still good, nonetheless. A view is wasted on two guys who would rather sleep with the curtains tied closed."

Simon nodded. "I barely even noticed the view," he confessed.

"We couldn't," I said, out of principal alone.

"I think you could manage," Simon said, narrowing his eyes. "Obviously, it means more to you than it does to us. I work at a camp and spend most of my summers sleeping on top of a cobweb-covered bunk bed. We can roll anywhere."

"A camp?" I said before I could stop myself. I recovered quickly. "I mean, um, we can roll anywhere, too. Right, Tess?"

This time it was her turn to shoot me a look.

Simon raised his eyebrows and gave me a sideways glance. "I somehow find that hard to believe."

I wondered where this thirtysomething grown man, a camp counselor sporting a baseball cap, came off judging me. Wasn't he too old to be working odd jobs, anyway?

Sensing she needed to run interference, Tess quickly spoke. "It's just that she, *we*, would feel bad taking your room away from you."

Simon groaned and downed the last of the coffee he had been chugging. "Mark, can you please talk some sense into these crazy women? I'm going to ditch this." He waved the empty cup.

We watched Simon walk towards a trashcan by the lobby exit. For a moment, I lost my train of thought when I couldn't help noticing, despite myself, he had a really nice ass.

"Honestly, guys," Mark said, "we really don't need it. That's all there is to it."

Mark's phone rang and as he stepped away to take the call, and Tess placed a hand on my arm. "Please, Aunt Lu," she whispered. "Just take it. Simon's being so sweet and I really like Mark. Can you please be a little nicer to his brother?" It wasn't like Tess to reprimand her elders, and I felt a little foolish.

"I'm sorry," I said, crinkling my nose. "I'll definitely be nicer, but..." I paused to sigh. "I'm not so sure we should take their room."

"Why not?"

"I don't know." I frowned and paused for a moment. "I don't want to feel ... oh, you know ... obligated."

"Obligated?" Tess stared at me in disbelief. "Obligated to what? Oh no," she gasped and placed her hands on her cheeks. "Are we going to have to have sex with them now? I mean, clearly if you take his room, you're going to have to marry him, right?"

I looked at Tess and chuckled. "I'm being silly, aren't I?"

"Just a tad." She pinched her thumb and pointer finger together.

"Aunt Lu, this isn't the 1900s. No one is going to label you a whore or expect you to put out. Unless, of course you want to." She winked. "Simon's pretty cute, huh?"

I rolled my eyes and looked away, only to see Simon heading towards us. He held the key out like a peace offering. "Last chance, ladies. I would like to head to my room. Whichever room that may be."

"Thank you." I smiled through gritted teeth as I took the key. "We appreciate it."

Twenty minutes later, Tess and I eagerly opened the door to our new room. I dropped my backpack on the floor and strode over to the window.

"Shall I?" I dramatically placed a hand on the curtain. This time, when I ripped it open, the view really did take my breath away.

Tess made a gasp. "Aunt Lu! Now *this* is a view." She jumped up and down with excitement.

The city seemed to go on for miles, and seeing my first glimpse of the Eiffel Tower over the Seine, I felt overcome with emotion. I think it was a combination of joy for going where I've always dreamed, pride for breaking out of my comfort zone, excitement to share it with Tess, and gratitude that Simon and Mark allowed us to enjoy such a wonderful view.

I opened the French doors and leaned on the railing, lost in thought.

Tess appeared next to me, snapping pictures on her phone, fast and furiously. "I can't wait to update my Facebook, Instagram, Twitter ... Oh my God, this is amazing!" she sang, jumping up and down. "Ok stand here." She pushed me up against the railing and stepped back to take my picture. After she examined it with a critical eye, she nodded with satisfaction.

"What's this?" she asked.

I followed Tess's gaze and watched her walk over to a wrought iron table and pick up a book.

"Looks like a guidebook of Paris. Someone is going to be very bummed." Tess thumbed through the book. "It's filled with notes."

"Is there a name on it? Maybe it belongs to Mark or Simon?"

"No," Tess said with conviction. "Mark said they barely set foot in the room. Besides, you heard Simon. It didn't sound like he logged in any time appreciating *this*." She swept her hand across the balcony. A used airline ticket flew to the ground.

60

I bent down to pick it up. "Simon Anderson," I read, standing back up.

"Wow, he's quite the details man," Tess murmured. She handed me the book and disappeared inside the room.

"No kidding," I murmured.

I opened to an earmarked page, which happened to feature our hotel. It had notes all over it about the beautiful view and historical buildings nearby. He obviously enjoyed the view way more than he cared to admit. The back jacket listed all the things he hoped to do while visiting Paris. Feeling as if I had violated his privacy, I quickly slammed the book shut and instinctively hugged it to my chest.

Chapter Five

Café au lait and a croissant. Twenty euros.
Eating the overpriced breakfast in a
chenille robe and fuzzy slippers.
Priceless.
Facebook Status June 9 at 7:00am

Fifteen hours and two long hot baths later, I ran downstairs to get an extra toothbrush from the front desk. I'd had to use my old one to clean my iPhone charger port. Remnants of the hash brownie were so embedded in the crevices that I'd started to get a little paranoid. All I needed was for a drug dog to come sniff me out at one of the major tourist attractions.

It was a pretty humbling experience to check into a four-star hotel looking and feeling like a sloth, and then have to ask for a hygiene kit. Thankfully, Claude was nowhere in sight.

On my way back to the room, I stopped by the concierge desk to pick up a map of the area. That's when I noticed a sign-up sheet for a day trip to work on a local farm in Bordeaux. Picking grapes sounded like the perfect French adventure. I figured we could try something different, broaden our horizons, and spend the day outdoors in the majestic French countryside. Yet when I called Tess from the lobby, she said she'd rather stay in Paris and had no interest in seeing Bordeaux.

Okay, I could do this alone. At the very least, I'd have a good idea to pitch to Janice. Sure, I would've loved to stay in my cozy robe, but who wanted to publish an article about a lazy woman in a robe? I signed up at the desk and ran upstairs to get dressed.

My plan was to perfect my pitch on the bus ride to Bordeaux, and I had to remind myself of that when my mind began to wander for the tenth time.

Focus, I told myself. Get something on paper.

I shifted in my seat to make room for a rather large man who was trying to squeeze himself through the tight aisle. After one of his thighs threatened to take my journal with him, I slid onto the empty seat next to me. I looked out the window for inspiration.

"How's the view?" A voice interrupted my thoughts.

I turned, and my eyes widened as I realized the owner of the voice was Simon, who was staring down at me. I immediately straightened up in my seat. I felt a surprising frizzle of excitement and tucked my hair behind my ears. Dressed in khaki shorts and a navy blue Polo shirt, he looked as if he were headed to the golf course.

"View's not bad." I paused and looked at Simon thoughtfully. "I mean, you do clean up pretty nice. I almost didn't recognize you without the Yankee hat."

Simon flashed a boyish grin.

"Oh wait … did you mean that view?" I pointed out the window. I couldn't believe how smooth I sounded.

You hand a girl an assortment of top-notch beauty products and a blow dryer in a luxury hotel room, and bam—a confident woman is born. It was either that or I was channeling a flirtatious French spirit.

"May I?" Simon said. He pointed toward the empty seat next to me. "Or would you rather be alone?"

"Please." I couldn't waste a blowout. Besides, I had promised Tess I'd be nicer to him. I slid my bag over to make some room and patted the seat.

When Simon had settled, he gave me a sideways look.

"What?" I heard the paranoia in my own voice.

That morning I had tweezed a lone piece of wiry hair sticking out of my chin. Thank God for magnifying mirrors. Please, please, don't tell me I missed another.

"Nothing," he smiled. "It's just that … you clean up pretty nice, too."

I sighed inwardly with relief and blushed. Good thing I put on my dressier tank top. A little ruffle goes a long way.

"In fact, I'm kind of surprised to see you here."

"I must've sounded like a real diva yesterday, huh?" I cringed and waited for Simon's response.

"Nooo. Why on earth would you say that?"

"Ugh. I'm so not like that," I said with a grimace.

"Actually, you sounded more like a woman who had hit her breaking point. No judgment here," he said, holding up his hands. "The fact you're choosing to roll up your sleeves and do a little manual labor ... well, that says a lot."

"You're here, too," I reminded him.

Simon waved his hand and smiled. "That's only because I saw your name on the signup sheet at the concierge desk."

"Oh, yeah right." I laughed, but I was blushing. "What guy would choose to spend the day with a woman he witnessed having a nervous breakdown?"

"And," he said, holding up a finger, "let's not forget the attitude you copped in London."

I rolled my eyes. "You've gotten such a bad impression of me. I really am a nice person."

"I'm sure you are. I asked my brother about you and he gave you a good report." Simon winked and I blushed again under his gaze.

"You did?" For a minute, I forgot I was trying to play it cool.

"Mm hmm," he nodded. "What can I say? You intrigued me. Although ... I'm not so sure about those mood swings of yours."

I chuckled. "I swear those were just backpacking side effects. Let me tell you something, a dirty youth hostel is no place for a forty-two-year old woman."

Simon's jaw dropped.

"Oh, yeah. Mark didn't tell you?" My heart sank, just a little. I felt ancient.

Simon shook his head.

"We've been staying in youth hostels. See? I'm not a diva." I sniffed. "As a matter of fact,"—I sat up a little straighter and continued—"you're talking to a member of Hostelling International."

"Wait. I need to get something straight. You're forty-two?"

64

I clenched my teeth. A woman should never divulge her real age. Did I just reveal mine unsolicited?

"Yep." The cougar's been let out of the bag.

"It's not a big deal or anything." Simon shrugged. "You just happen to look a lot younger. I thought you were around my age."

"And you're...?"

"Thirty-two."

I had to laugh out loud at that one. "Aren't you quite the charmer? I wish I was your age."

"I'm only ten years behind you. That's nothing."

"Maybe in dog years," I snickered.

"Well, I'm still intrigued by you."

My palms were sweaty. "Speaking of intrigue, I think this belongs to you." I reached into my bag and fished out his book. "I didn't look in it," I lied.

It wasn't like I had any idea this volunteer program was on his list of things to do. Nor did I know he wanted to climb to the top of Notre Dame. Or bring home healing waters from Lourdes. Or see a sunset from the top of the Eiffel Tower. I especially had no clue he planned to take an evening bike tour that night. I swear I hadn't read it.

Simon took the book. "Oh man, I was looking all over for this." The bus suddenly made a sharp turn, and my journal slid from my lap into his hands.

"Good catch," I exclaimed.

"That's what the ladies tell me." He winked. "I know you're vacationing with Tess, but are you also traveling for business?" He looked down at my book, and our fingers brushed as he handed it back to me.

I hesitated. "No. This is just a little writing book, and if I were here for business, I'd be up a creek." I flipped through the empty pages and laughed. "However, as of yesterday I may have become a freelance travel writer." I told Simon about the recent email from Janice and also filled him in on my previous job at the parenting magazine.

"A-ha," Simon said. "Sounds like a little inspiration is in order. Another reason why you needed a good view."

"What about you?" I smiled. "You mentioned you work at a camp? Are you a counselor?"

"Something like that."

"What do you do during the year?"

"Oh, you know … the summer takes up so much time and mental energy that I kind of need to take the rest of the year to recharge."

I couldn't tell if he was joking, but he looked pretty serious. Who knew that a camp counselor ranked high on the list of America's most stressful jobs? I didn't. And I sure as hell didn't know anyone over twenty-one in the field. I hated that I was judging him, but I couldn't help it. What thirty two-year-old man still worked as a camp counselor? I bit my lip.

"How long do you plan to travel?"

"Camp starts in three weeks, so we'll hit a few more places and then head back to reality."

Maybe you should step into reality, Mr. Hardly-A-Care-In-The-World. I politely smiled back. But as I listened to the world's oldest camp counselor talk about his life in Chicago, I actually began to enjoy myself. So much so, that I began to open up as well.

As we rolled onward, I found myself telling him about my own life in New York City. I told him about my apartment, my obsession for romantic comedy films, my addiction to Chinese take-out, and my love-hate relationship with the treadmill at the gym. I confessed that I ended up in physical therapy after running a half marathon with zero preparation, and Simon admitted to needing shoulder surgery after doing a triathlon without swim training.

"Ok, so basically we both rush into things." I laughed, as the bus finally pulled into Chateau Les Artistes. I heard the sound of gravel crunching underneath the bus tires.

"Good one." Simon poked me in the ribs and smiled, deepening a dimple in his cheek.

My face flushed, and I bent down to adjust my shoelaces, which didn't need any adjusting, whatsoever. "So, there you have it," I said, once my composure returned. "You now know my life story. The abridged version, anyway. Lucy-Lite."

"You know what?" Simon said as he stood up and stretched. "I like Lucy-Lite."

"Thanks." I smiled and looked at him in earnest. "Have I redeemed myself?"

"Oh, about two hours ago." Simon winked as he held out his hand to help me out of my seat.

I walked ahead of him, suddenly self-conscious that he had a view of my rear. I quickened my pace and hurried off the bus steps. Once my feet hit the ground I gasped at the idyllic scenery that lay before me.

"Wow," Simon exhaled as he approached me.

I nodded and looked around. The vineyard could've been used as a set for a movie. An eighteenth century castle stood off in the distance, and rows and rows of grapevines stretched on for as far as we could see. The trees were all the same height and were filled with green leaves and purple grapes that stood out against the clear blue sky.

I drew in a deep breath, and as the clean country air filled my lungs, I knew I'd made the perfect choice for the day. Simon's sleeve brushed against my arm as we stood together in a moment of blissful silence. I turned my head to look up at him, and he smiled back at me.

Suddenly, feeling a bit anxious, I grabbed the wooden bucket and immediately headed off to pick grapes. My legs were wobbling oddly beneath me.

"Lucy, wait up!" Simon called.

I turned around and watched him walk towards me.

"That's it? You're done with me?" he said.

"Of course I'm not done with you. I mean, well, you know what I mean," I mumbled.

The look on Simon's face told me he had no idea what I was trying to say. How could he? I hadn't a clue myself. I was so out of practice talking to men.

"I just wanted to get a head start. There are a lot of grapes out there that need to be picked. I also wanted to get a good spot. As a matter of fact, this looks like a good one." I took a break from my babbling to pluck a few grapes from the tree. Simon was staring at me, and I grew warm under his gaze. *Breathe*. In through the nose, out through the mouth...

"Well, is there room for one more over here? I'd hate to crowd you out." Simon said, tilting his head to the side.

I looked around to see that we were the only two people in that row. "Ha, ha," I said and tossed a grape at him.

Simon got to work, and we immediately fell into a good rhythm. I discovered more about Simon and also learned that working on a farm in Bordeaux is not all red wine and olives. It started off as therapeutic. However, as the hours passed, the sun grew hotter and the dust grew dustier. A layer of grime formed on my face, and I paused on top of the ladder.

"By any chance, do I look as dirty as I feel?" I asked Simon. "I feel like I see something dark on my nose." I closed one eye and used the other to look at the side of my nose.

"Dirty, no. Silly, yes." Simon smiled and leaned over his ladder to wipe my nose with a paisley handkerchief.

"Thank you," I laughed. "You know, I'm really impressed you carry a handkerchief."

"It comes in handy with the ladies." He winked.

"Yes, you never know when you might encounter a dusty gal in a vineyard." I rubbed my hands together to remove some of the dirt stuck to my palms.

Simon watched me with a half-smile.

"What?" I said, feeling paranoid.

"Nothing." He shrugged his shoulders. "I'm having a nice time with you."

"Me too." My heartbeat quickened as I reached for a cluster of grapes. "Who knew picking grapes could be so much fun? My ex would never have done this."

"Why not?" Simon popped a grape into his mouth.

"Oh, a number of reasons. Manual labor, dirt…finger cramps."

I paused to stretch out my hands. After a few hours of picking those slippery suckers, my hands were starting to feel rather tight.

"A little manual labor is good for the soul," Simon said.

The whistle blew for lunch. "As is a picnic. I'm famished." I started to step down the ladder, but whether it was because of Simon's presence or because I was so tired, I missed a step going down.

"Shit!" I cried. I fell to the ground and knocked over my bucket in the process.

"Lucy, are you okay?" Simon rushed over to help me.

"Talk about grapes of wrath," I grimaced. I slid the bucket out of the way.

"Don't worry about the damn grapes." He looked worried. "Let's get you up."

He bent down to help me, but as I stood, I realized I couldn't bear any weight on my ankle. "Oh my Lord," I groaned. "I feel like such an ass."

"Put your arm around my waist," Simon directed. As I grabbed on for support, I could feel the firm muscles under his shirt, and all I could think about was that his hand was wrapped around my muffin top. I sucked in my stomach with such a vengeance that I was pretty much gasping for air as we hobbled over to the picnic area.

"Hang in. We're almost there," Simon said, apparently mistaking my gasping for pain.

When we got to our destination, an attractive blonde woman with a bag of ice ran over to us, her long floral skirt bellowing behind her as she ran.

"I saw you coming and made you a pack. Please, sit down." She ushered me over to a white Adirondack chair.

"I'm Charlize. My husband and I own the vineyard. I'm so sorry about this. Our daughters ran up to the house for some pain reliever and wrapping. There they are now." Her face broke into a smile, and I followed her gaze to see three little Asian girls running towards us.

"They're adorable," I smiled.

"Are they triplets?" Simon asked.

"Thank you," Charlize smiled at me again. "And yes, they are," she answered Simon. "We fostered them back in San Francisco, and they officially became our daughters one year ago yesterday. We moved to Paris and bought the vineyard shortly after. I guess you can say it's been a wonderful year for us."

"It also happens to be their fourth birthday tomorrow," she said with a twinkle in her eye. Charlize held out two very toned arms and opened them to greet her daughters. "Group hug!" she cried.

The girls fell into her arms and gave their mother a tight hug. A knot formed in my throat, and I actually had to put on my shades.

Simon cleared his own throat. "Looks like you girls brought enough supplies to open a hospital. Thank you." He took the first aid materials from their hands. The three sisters smiled proudly.

"And here comes Daddy with the food, so we're all set," Charlize said.

A husky man on a tractor pulled up, and we watched him unload picnic baskets from the back. He called out to the girls in French, and they ran towards him to help out.

"Do you need anything else?" Charlize asked.

Simon held up his hand. "Thank you, but we're all set. I've been doing this for years."

As Charlize joined her family at the tractor, Simon turned to me with a wrap. "Ahem. It's a good thing you're with an Illinois certified emergency medical technician."

"Thank God for that," I said. "I fall so easily. And when I fall, I fall hard."

"Thanks for the warning. I used to be like that. I'm trying to take my time now. I mean, you can't rush into love, right?" Simon's eyes twinkled as he waited for me to respond.

I laughed, then turned my head and watched the three little girls. They were happily handing out lunch bags to the volunteers.

"Those three are adorable, eh?" Simon said as he followed my gaze.

"Beyond," I said with a sigh. "Charlize and her husband are very lucky."

"Seriously. Three sisters. It doesn't get any better than that. I would love to adopt when I…"

"Grow up?"

"Cute. Get settled was what I was going to say," Simon corrected. He pulled the wrap tightly around my ankle. "You better take it easy or Dr. Evil is going to come out."

"Do you really? You would adopt?"

"Sure. Why not?" Simon shrugged.

I stared at him in silence. That didn't sound to me like someone who had a Peter Pan complex. Maybe Simon had a few more layers of depth than I had given him credit for.

"Why do you seem so shocked?" he said.

"Why do I seem so shocked?" I sorted through the many thoughts whirring around in my head. "Well, for one, what I didn't tell you in the Facebook version of my life is that my ex-fiancée basically said if we

70

couldn't have kids, for whatever reason, there was no way he would adopt."

"What?" Simon grimaced. "So he's opposed to giving a child a better life?"

I actually felt goose bumps on my arms as Simon spoke. I wondered if there were other men out there who shared his thinking.

"I don't know. He wants to keep his name going, pass down his genes..." My voice trailed off.

"Sounds like he has some set of genes," Simon said dryly. "Not to mention, balls." He looked at me pointedly.

He must have seen the mixed emotions crossing my face because he backed down and reached out to touch my shoulder before saying, "I'm sorry, but the guy sounds like a real tool. Especially, if he let you go."

"Thanks." I gave him a closed-mouth smile and tried to ignore the heat from his fingers as they brushed my upper arm. "It got pretty complicated."

Simon paused to look me square in the eyes. "Well, I'm sure you'll find better."

My stomach did a flip as he turned his attention back to the wrap he was now winding around my ankle. He secured it tightly with a piece of tape.

"You're good to go." He looked proud as he assessed his handiwork. "Ready to get back out in the field?"

"I guess," I said doubtfully. I couldn't help but wonder which field he was talking about.

Each time Simon came to check on me, he told me about the antics of the other visitors out in the vineyard. Apparently, I wasn't the only one with the grace and balance of a hippopotamus. I wasn't sure Cooper would have been as amused as Simon was. Coop tended to equate clumsiness with carelessness, and he certainly wouldn't have laughed at smudges of dirt or sweat marks on my face. Not that he would have ever seen them there in the first place, since I was pretty sure Cooper's alleged allergy to anything resembling dirt would have kept him far from these fields.

I was having a great time, and Simon's obvious care for the other people here—I saw him taking water to an older woman, and he helped the triplets carry the remains of our lunch baskets back up to the house—

made me think about what kind of man I really wanted.

There were probably men out there who wouldn't make me feel like I was ancient, men who were older than this thirty-two-year-old camp counselor. Men who shared Simon's belief that a family didn't have to be biological and that caring for others was the first priority. I'd allowed myself to feel like damaged goods, a failure of a woman, that in the midst of my wallowing I had failed to see something important. Something really important: Not all men were like Cooper.

With that hope in my heart, I enjoyed the bus ride back, said goodbye to Simon, and collapsed happily into the bathtub at the hotel. As I relaxed in the bubbles, I hoped Tess would be on board with my plan to watch an in-room movie. Until I found that man, a good chick flick would have to fill my void for romance.

* * * *

"Aunt Lu?" Tess called from behind the bathroom door. I sat up with a start and looked down at my pruned fingers.

"Just a sec, Tessie. What time is it? I think I fell asleep."

"Six o'clock. Oh my God, I have so much to tell you!"

"Hang on, I'm coming out." I couldn't believe I had been in the tub for an hour. The water had turned cold, and the bubbles had all flattened.

I stepped out of the claw foot tub and winced when my injured foot hit the floor. "It's a good thing you came home," I shouted through the door. I dried my body with the towel. "I could've—"

"You would not believe the day I had," Tess interrupted. "I met the cutest guy. His name is Pierre. Pierre! How much more French can you get?"

I threw on a robe and opened the door. I came face-to-face with Tess, who was aglow with excitement. "Well, hello." I smiled.

"*Bonjour.*" Tess beamed back at me. "Then, I ran into Mark who—"

"Wait." I held up a finger. "I'm coming out. Start at the beginning." I ducked back into the bathroom to grab a hairbrush.

"Okay." She paused to take a breath. "First I took a bus to Montmartre. You know, that cool area where you and I had planned to go?" Her voice trailed off as she walked towards the beds.

"I'm sorry I went without you, but I was just dying to check it out.

When I left the hotel, there was a bus that happened to be heading..."

Tess babbled on so fast that in my post-bath haze, I was having trouble keeping up with her. I emerged from the bathroom and watched as she rifled through her backpack.

"Tess," I commanded. Her head popped up to look at me. "Slow down. I'm not going anywhere. You sound like you're about to pass out."

"I'm sorry." She turned her attention back to her bag. "I've learned that there's a big difference between American coffee and French. I'm so caffeinated it's like *whoa!*" she exclaimed. "A-ha! There you are."

I watched as she extracted a wrinkled dress from her bag. My hopes of watching a movie began to diminish.

"Oh my God! Aunt Lu, what happened to your foot? You're limping."

"Oh." I rolled my eyes and took a seat at the desk. "It was nothing. A vineyard casualty."

"Ugh." She furrowed her eyebrows and frowned. "I feel so self-centered. I ripped you out of the tub, didn't even ask about your day—"

"I'm fine. We'll get to that later. You first." I clapped my hands. I was dying to know who or what had gotten her this excited.

Tess drew in a breath and smiled. "Okay. Well, I have to say, I felt really independent today. I conquered climbing the steps of Rue Foyatier!" She threw her hands up in victory. "You know, that crazy staircase that takes you up to Sacre Coeur?"

"Oh yeah," I said nostalgically. "I actually had a poster of those steps in my college dorm room. Are there really as many steps as there appear to be?"

"More," she replied with a face. "Two hundred and thirty-four! When I got to the top, I just *had* to sit down. I was totally exhausted, but more so, blown away, by the surrounding sights. It was like I'd climbed a staircase to heaven. I've seen photographs of those steps for years. Wait till you go. You'll get goose bumps."

I was having a magical moment of my own. It was so nice to see my niece expanding her horizons. At that moment, I was so glad we'd taken the trip together.

"Now, here's where things took a turn. I had bought a crepe at this stand back by the hotel. You know, one of those yummy thin pancakes they stuff with Nutella and fruit spread. Mmm! I carried it around for hours and ripped into that bad boy like it was my j-o-b after I finished the steps. When I went to reach into my bag for a napkin, there was nothing there. Some creep must have swiped it, from right under my nose. My wallet was gone!"

"Wait. You mean to tell me someone took your money? Why didn't you call me? We have to call the bank." My mind immediately went into protective overdrive. Morgan would kill me if Tess lost money, or worse, had her identity stolen on this trip.

"It wasn't so bad. You have all of my credit cards," Tess reminded me in an accusatory tone.

"Oh. Right," I said with a grimace. On our way out the night before in Amsterdam, she had wanted to leave her credit cards in the hostel. I had insisted on holding them for her and forgotten to give them back.

"Well, I guess it worked out for the best, didn't it? Maybe you'll remember that next time you question your older and wiser aunt's decisions," I teased and sighed in relief that I wasn't going to have to tell my older-but-never-wiser sister I had put her daughter's financial future in jeopardy.

"Don't be. Talk about a happy accident … Anyway, I went from floating to freaking. How would I find my way back to the hotel, without speaking any French? My map was totally gone."

"So, what did you do?" My heart was in my throat. I had to remind myself she was fine. After all, she was sitting right in front of me telling the story.

"What did I do? I planned to take the Montmartre Funicular back down, but without any money, I had to drag my sorry ass back down the 234 steps. By the time I got to the bottom, I probably looked like a sweaty beggar as I walked past the cafés, searching for a friendly face. I felt someone staring at me and looked to my right where I locked eyes with a very attractive man. We're talking Chace Crawford handsome."

"Who?"

Tess paused for a moment and looked at me in disbelief. "We'll get to that later. Anyway, the guy was leaning against the wall of a café, and I knew right then and there I'd discovered the hottest piece of French bread in all of Paris. So, I walked right up to him." With that, Tess covered her mouth in mock horror.

I laughed out loud. "Only you." I shook my head. "Did he work there?"

"Yes. He had the whole black pants, black shirt thing going on, the red apron tied around his waist—in fact, he actually wiped his hands on it. I think I made his hands sweat," she said in amazement. Tess stood up and I couldn't help but notice how awesome her legs looked in the jean shorts she was wearing.

"Gee, you think?" I said.

A blush crept across her face. "I told him I was lost and asked if I could trouble him for a glass of water. That's when he led me into the café. He disappeared behind the counter and held up two bottles. 'You like sparkling or flat?' he said in a very sexy French accent. This is where I almost had a panic attack. Aunt Lu, I had no money!"

"What did you say?" I cringed.

Tess walked off towards the closet. "I told him that I had no money and was hoping for tap. He looked so confused. It may have seriously been the most humiliating moment of my life. He had no clue what I was talking about. I had to point to the sink."

I watched her take the ironing board from the closet and wondered if I would have to put on a dress tonight, too. She plugged the iron into the wall and plopped on her bed.

"Then he was actually relieved. He thought I wanted him to do a dance!" Tess laughed. She folded her legs into a cross-legged position and hugged a pillow on her lap.

"He practically threw the two bottles at me. Then, oh my God, you're *not* going to believe this one." Tess buried her head into the pillow and giggled.

I was really enjoying her little show and sat on the edge of the bed for more.

"He went over to his tip cup and pulled money from it. Aunt Lu, it was as if I were watching a train wreck. He set the money down and proceeded to fill a bag with baguettes. He truly thought I was a homeless woman."

Tess and I both started to laugh simultaneously.

"Nooooo!" I yelled.

"YES. At that point, I was *hanging* over the counter, basically contorting my body into a pretzel, just so I could have him see me through the bread displays. I pretty much had to shout, 'I'm not looking for money … or food!' I told him that I just needed directions to get back to our hotel. When I said '*Le Palais*,' he was all like, '*Tres* fancy. Clearly you don't need my little tips,'" Tess said in her best French impersonation.

"He was joking, but as he stuffed the money back into the jar, he kind of looked ashamed. I told him how the hotel was a gift from you and we were just taking a break from hostelling."

I looked at Tess and sighed. I affectionately caressed the hotel's plush robe. "I'd like to think we are taking more than just a break. Once you go hotel, you never go back."

"This is pretty nice," Tess nodded. "Anyway, he asked me to go out tonight. See the city as a local. He's picking me up in an hour." She began to twirl her hair, a nervous habit she'd had ever since she was a little girl. "Is that okay?"

What was I supposed to say? I knew Morgan would kill me if anything happened to her, but I also couldn't tell a twenty-four-year-old what to do. "Well, do you think he's normal? I hate the thought of you out with some random French guy. What do we know about him?"

"Nothing," Tess admitted.

I massaged my temples. "Oh, that's reassuring."

"But his dad owns the café, so you'll know where to find him if anything happens to me," she offered. She got off the bed and walked back towards the ironing board.

"Tess! Don't even say that. Promise me you will stay in public places." My voice sounded just like Morgan's.

"I promise."

"Remember, you don't owe him anything."

"I know," she sang. "My mom would say the same thing." She picked up the iron.

"Now, what happened with Mark? You mentioned his name before."

"Oh. This is where I question if I'm doing the right thing by going out on the date. I ran into him on my way back to the hotel. He had gone sightseeing with Chaz, but apparently Chaz wanted to stay behind at Pere Lachaise Cemetery. Seems he wanted to spend the day mourning the loss of Jim Morrison." She rolled his eyes. "You know, since they were so close and all."

I bit my lip to keep from laughing. That Chaz was something else.

"We ended up walking around, and Mark totally opened up about his relationship. Lately, things haven't been working out so well, and they're at a major crossroads, too. Jen, that's her name," she said with her nose crunched, "wants to meet up with him at some point on this trip, but he's not sure he even wants that."

"Interesting." I made a mental note to ask Simon about their situation the next time we bumped into each other.

"He actually asked me if I wanted to have dinner with him tonight too. I kind of wanted to cancel on Pierre, but I felt bad, especially after he had been so nice to me. I told him I had a date with a guy I had met earlier."

"Good girl." I nodded in approval.

"He seemed kind of surprised, but was pretty cool about it. Do you really think I did the right thing? I mean, Mark does have a girlfriend who might be meeting up with him, for God's sake. I don't need to date anyone who's confused, even if he's totally awesome, right? Ugh." All of a sudden Tess looked absolutely tortured.

"Right. Mark is a great guy, but I don't want you to fall for someone who has a girlfriend. Nor do I want you to fall for a Frenchman and move to Paris. Your mother would kill me."

I remembered the conversation we had the day before in the Amsterdam diner and clenched my fists. "Just have fun tonight," I said with authority. "Remember, we're here for new experiences."

"Aunt Lu, why am I suddenly attracted to multiple men? This is so unlike me."

"And it's like me to encourage you to date a stranger?" I laughed. "Enjoy it. You've been in a relationship for a long time. It's totally normal," I reassured. "I wish I had your problems."

Tess frowned. "Do you mind that I'm going? I feel bad leaving you alone."

"Don't be silly! I was only joking. Do I look like I'm in any rush to part with this robe?"

Tess looked me up and down and smiled. "No. You did change out of the robe today, right? It's pretty much all I've seen you wear since we've come to Paris."

"Yes, and it was hell getting out of it." I nestled my cheek against the soft fabric. "I didn't think it would go over so well at the vineyard."

"Speaking of that, tell me about your day. What was it like to be a grape picker?"

"Draining and staining." I wiggled my purple-stained fingers and then pointed towards the bathroom. "Go get ready. I'll fill you in on my day later."

Tess smiled in anticipation. "You're the best, Aunt Lu!" She skipped off to take a shower.

The water turned on as I sat back and kicked my feet onto the bed. A feeling of contentment washed over me, something I hadn't felt in a really long time. I didn't have my usual feeling of doom and gloom.

I looked forward to living vicariously through Tess that night, but since she wouldn't be home for hours, I needed to pick someone else's adventures to live through. I picked up the remote and scrolled through the in-room movie selections. I decided I was finally in the mood for a little romance.

Chapter Six

```
The   Eiffel   Tower   and   a   bottle   of   red.
Feeling oh-so-French!
Facebook Status June 9 at 8:00pm
```

I picked my phone off the nightstand and sent Tess a text.
How r things?

She responded immediately.
```
Just buckling up on a scooter. Imagine me,
cruising on the back of a Vespa!
```

My reply:
*Remember—safety first & hair second. Wear a
helmet!*

I felt bad for checking up on her, but I knew I wouldn't be able to live with myself if anything happened to her.

I placed my phone on the nightstand next to the bed and couldn't help but feel a stab of envy. I could just picture Tess, riding off into the sunset, her long hair flowing out from beneath the helmet that I prayed to God she'd worn. Blessed with perfect tresses, Tess wasn't one to obsess about her hair, so hopefully tonight would be no exception. Besides, she had looked beautiful enough for a little hair flattening to go unnoticed.

She'd been so excited for her date. When the clock struck seven, she had pretty much skipped to the door.

"I feel like Cinderella going to the ball. Are you sure I look okay?"

"Honey, you look more than okay." I smiled.

Together, we had pieced together the perfect date night outfit for a Saturday dinner in Paris. She wore an off-white strapless cotton eyelet dress, my new Burberry sandals, and a handful of gold bangles she'd bought this afternoon, before she'd lost her wallet.

Tess raised her shoulders and smiled. "Well, here goes. Don't wait up."

She walked past the dresser and did a double take when she spotted a long gold chain hanging from a knob on one of the drawers. She gently took it off, and I watched her unhook the clasp, and wrap the chain around her waist.

"Oh, I'm waiting up, alright." I cast aside the magazine sitting on my lap. "How could I sleep knowing you are out God knows where with God knows who?" Up until then I'd been playing it cool, but I could no longer hide the concern that had slowly crept up on me.

"Aunt Lu, I'll be fine. Don't worry."

I looked at her makeshift belt and nodded. "Nice."

"*Merci.*" Tess curtsied and put her hand on the doorknob.

"Wait, just a minute." I sat up in bed with a start and readjusted my robe. "Where are you going?" I sounded like the wicked stepmother.

"Um, to meet Pierre," she said in a condescending tone. I almost expected her to follow her words with a loud, "*Duh!*"

"He's not coming to the room? What kind of gentleman is that?" I hated him already.

"What kind of lady has a stranger pick her up in her hotel room?" Tess crossed her arms like a defiant teenager.

She had a point. I couldn't argue that one.

"Besides, he *is* coming to pick me up. We're meeting down in the lobby."

Okay, so maybe he was a gentleman, but I still wasn't completely satisfied. It looked as if I had no choice.

"Well, then I'm coming with you." I swung my legs off the bed. It was time to part with the damn robe.

"Aunt Lucy, I'm not two. *Please*." Tess clasped her hands together and held them in front of her. "What would I say? Uh, Pierre, this is my aunt. She needed to scope you out to make sure you didn't look like a serial killer?" She looked at me and rolled her eyes. "That's *so* embarrassing."

"Okay, fine. Then I'll follow you down to the lobby. Just in case I have to identify him to the police. Please, Tess. Humor me."

"Fine," she groaned. "Promise me you'll stay far behind."

"I promise. Just give me one sec."

Tess sighed as I hobbled over to the bathroom. I quickly threw on black leggings and a faded tank top hanging behind the door. Because I'd been washing my clothes somewhat half-assed at a Laundromat, the off-white tank had become more of a very off-white.

"Don't mind the way I look. You're rushing me." I smiled sweetly.

Tess looked at me with a critical eye. "Here," she said, unclipping two silk flower pins from her backpack. "Put these on. Pick a shoulder. Just in case you run into someone you know."

"Okay, Donatella. Especially, since I know so many people in Paris."

Tess gave me an amused look and led me out the door. I pinned the flowers on the strap of my left shoulder as I followed her to the elevator. Once inside, I caught a glimpse of myself in the mirror.

"Wow, you're right," I said with an approving tone. "That tank was shot. Not anymore. Maybe greige will be the new black." I adjusted my bra straps and rolled my shoulders back. "You know, Tess, you have a real eye for fashion."

"Well, you better have a real eye to spy," Tess hissed as the elevator stopped in the lobby. She gave me a quick peck on the cheek and jumped back to the other side of the elevator.

The doors opened to the lobby. Tess went on her merry way and I followed behind, keeping a safe distance between us. I watched her greet a tall guy who must have been Pierre with a demure French double cheek kiss.

He wore tan linen pants, a thin white sweater, and some sort of European looking sandal. I had never been a big fan of a guy who wore sandals, but on this guy, it worked. Tess had been accurate with her assessment. With a combination of sandy blond hair, high cheekbones, and full lips, he was absolutely gorgeous. On a scale of one to ten, he was a definite ten. And as a couple, they were well off the charts.

Pierre may have gotten a check in the box from me for good looks, but that hadn't been one of my concerns. I smiled to myself when he handed her a rose. Check. I was more than relieved to witness a sign of chivalry. Then, he helped her put on her sweater. Double check. After Pierre extended his arm to Tess, escort-style, I knew I'd seen enough.

Tess casually looked over her shoulder at me with one eyebrow raised. I gave her two thumbs up, and she blew me a kiss in return. As I watched them disappear through the revolving doors, I felt like a mom who had just sent her daughter off to college. I wrote the checks, was all alone, and didn't know what to do with myself.

I moseyed over to the centerpiece of the lobby, a circular table with a spectacular floral arrangement. There were about a dozen three-foot hurricane vases that housed submerged cherry blossom branches and white tulips. I took a deep inhale through my nose and detected a faint, but pleasant, aroma.

"Excuse me?" I heard a voice say.

I turned my head to see a woman standing beside me with a camera in her hand.

"Can you please take a picture of my family," she asked. Behind her stood a man and two teenage girls.

"Oh sure," I said. She handed me the camera, and I stepped back, waiting for the foursome to position themselves in front of the table. She sandwiched herself between her two daughters and they all stood close with arms wrapped around one another. Her husband was at one end and she was on the other, yet his hand still managed to reach across and cup her shoulder.

"Ready?" I looked into the camera and centered the photo against the floral backdrop. "Say *fromage!*"

"*Fromage!*" they cried in unison, laughing.

I handed back the woman's camera. The family bid me a good night and as they walked off arm-in-arm. I wished they would adopt me for the night, or at least take me wherever it was they were going.

I'd been content to hang in for the night, but now that I was in the hustle and bustle of the lobby, solitude was no longer looking so good. I meandered into the gift shop and picked up a newspaper. We'd been gone for almost a week, and I had no clue what was happening in the world. CNN hadn't been a part of our daily activities.

I flipped through the newspaper, but was distracted by the activity happening outside the window on the street. It was a lovely night, and the streets were packed. Happy faces filled the tables of a neighboring outdoor café. Families, couples, and friends strolled by, all looking as if they were on their way to do something spectacular.

The grass was really starting to look much greener on the other side of the window. I reminded myself how happy I had been to be in my robe ten minutes earlier and that leisure once again awaited me upstairs. Somewhat reluctantly, I put down the paper and walked to the elevators trying to recapture my indulgent relaxed mood.

But back in the room, my earlier feeling of contentment had dissipated. I picked up my phone and scrolled around to read the posts of my Facebook friends. Were their status updates as misleading as the one I had just written?

Eiffel Tower and a bottle of wine.

It sounded like I was living the life on the top of the tower. Little did they know the "Eiffel Tower" was really the name of the purse Carrie Bradshaw carried in the *Sex and the City* movie playing on the TV. As for the bottle of wine, Charlize had sent me away with the vineyard's finest, and I was debating whether I should open it or wait for Tess to return. There was something pathetic about drinking alone in a hotel room. Especially when the room happened to be in one of the most romantic cities in the world.

A knock on the door shook me out of my thoughts. "Hello?" I called out.

"Room service," said a voice on the other side.

"I didn't order anything," I shouted. My ankle was throbbing again after my trip to the lobby, and I didn't feel like hobbling over to answer the door, just to smell food I wish I'd ordered.

"Room service. Can you please open the door?" The voice had an Indian accent with an impatient tone.

I forced myself to get up and limped over to the door. I peered through the peephole and much to my surprise, I saw Simon standing there.

I flung the door open and laughed. "I should've known it was you."

"Why?" Simon looked so innocent, despite the mischievous gleam in his eyes.

"I think it's safe to say that not one employee of this hotel sounds like they're from Bollywood."

"Indian?" he cried. "You mean I didn't sound like Gerard Depardieu?"

"Hmph. Not so much." I smiled and gave Simon the once over. He wore dark jeans and a buttoned-down shirt, and he smelled like sandalwood and citrus as he stood before me.

"What are you up to?" With an eyebrow raised, I looked down and noticed he held a rather large shopping bag. A box of candy slipped from under his arm, and I reached out to catch it in midair.

"Nice save. May I?" Simon peered over my shoulder into the room.

"Oh, of course." I stepped aside to let him enter.

I watched him cross the room to set the bag down on the bed. I placed the candy box beside it. My mouth watered when I saw it was French nougat, my favorite after dinner treat from a bistro near my apartment. "What happened to your evening bike ride?"

He cocked his head and gave me an odd look. "How did you..." A flicker of recognition registered on his face. "Ah. I had a feeling you read my notes in the guidebook." A slow smile spread across his face.

I cleared my throat. "I, um, the book fell open to that one page, but that's all I saw."

Simon smiled and nodded slowly. "Well... I decided to pass. Today's manual labor totally wiped me out."

"Oh, I hear you." I tucked my hair behind my ears. The front and sides were still intact from this morning's blowout, but the back was pure frizz from the powernap I had taken in the tub.

As I touched the straight portion of my hair, I realized I was wearing ratty clothes and no makeup. I wished I had at least left Tess's flowers pinned on to my tank. "Will you please excuse me for a moment? I'm going to use the bathroom."

"Sure, take your time. I'll just be outside," Simon said, pointing to the balcony.

I disappeared into the bathroom and closed the door. I went over to the basin and gave myself a silent lecture while my brain screamed, "Lucy, get it together!" Why did I care so much? He was far too young for me.

I flushed the toilet and ran the water, using the sounds to disguise my freshening up process. I'd rather be dead than have him think I was primping for him. By the time I emerged, I found him leaning over the balcony railing.

I approached him from behind, noting once again, with a little embarrassment, just how nice the back view was. "Please don't tell me you came here to kill yourself."

"Well, that depends." Simon turned around to face me, and I quickly looked up with a start. "Mark told me Tess had a date, so I thought you might like some company. Was I right?"

I didn't answer right away, struck by the sight of him. Standing on the balcony with the sun setting behind him, he definitely looked like a Mr. Right. Well, a younger version, anyway.

"What did you have in mind?" I raised an eyebrow.

"Why don't you let me show you?" He took a step back into the room. My heart stopped as he walked towards the bed. He didn't mean...? Really?

My heart started to race again. Should I? How would that feel? How could I even be thinking this? Just as I was about to say something, Simon reached into the bag and pulled out a bottle of wine and two glasses.

The clinking of glasses brought me back to reality. Of course, that wasn't what he intended. *Get a grip, Lucy.* One day with Mother Nature, and I was losing it. The guy was just being nice. He probably has his pick of women back home. And they're probably twentysomethings. He doesn't like me. He's probably just bored. What else would he have done tonight without Mark? Some people just don't like to be alone.

"Well, if you *do* want company, I brought these. The wine happens to be the fruit of our beloved vineyard. And if you're not in the mood for company, at the very least you can use and abuse me." Simon winked as he pulled out a roll of medical tape. Ah, that kind of using and abusing. The medical kind.

"I can wrap your foot again and then you can throw the other glass at me. I even brought Moor mud for you to drown me in." Simon held up a jar, and I noticed he had nicely groomed and squared off fingernails. My own cuticles hadn't been pushed back since we left New York.

I clasped my hands behind my back. "What the heck is Moor mud?"

"It makes a good foot bath. So I've heard."

I let out a slow whistle. "How do you like that? A guy that knows more than me about foot spas." I nodded with approval and forced the corners of my lips to go up, even though they were fighting their way down. Was he gay? More high maintenance than I was? A Cooper dressed in casual clothing? I dug my nails into the palms of my hands. Why did I even care?

"Let's not get carried away," he said with a hand raised. "We use it for bee stings at the camp."

A giggle escaped me. He probably wasn't gay or high maintenance. However, while I felt momentarily lifted, the mention of his job as a camp counselor reminded me just how young he was.

He reached his hand back into the bag, oblivious to my reaction. "For snacks, I wasn't sure if you were salty or sour, having seen a little of both out of you. So, I chose vinegar chips and chocolate covered pretzels." Simon placed the snacks on the bed. "But, I have a feeling you're mostly sweet. Am I right?"

He waved the box of candy he had dropped. I cocked my head to the side and smiled demurely.

"And in the event you wanted to see some of Paris, I brought you..." Simon reached into the bag and dramatically unfolded a large stick, "Voila! A cane."

"Wow, I'm impressed. You've really thought of everything," I laughed uneasily.

"So, what do you think?" He tilted his head and smiled.

"I can't believe you did all of this for me." I held a hand to my chest. "You just might be the nicest guy I've ever met. Thank you for this ... all of this." I waved my hand over the items.

"My pleasure. Now, what do you think of my proposals?" He raised his eyebrows and cracked his knuckles. He certainly put in a lot of work for a little company.

"Well, funny thing ... I found a book yesterday, right here on this balcony in fact. In that book, I may have read a handwritten note, which said that seeing a sunset in Paris is a must-do."

"Really." Simon stood up a little straighter. "Whoever wrote that sounds like a very smart guy."

"That's what I'm thinking." I paused and tapped my finger to my lips. "Should we take his word for it? Maybe crack open the wine and enjoy it on that very same balcony where I found the book?"

"Works for me." Simon exhaled loudly.

We looked at one another and smiled. I gathered the bottle and glasses, grabbed a corkscrew from the table, and led Simon back out to the balcony.

"This really is some view," he said. He took the bottle from my hand. I felt the warmth of his skin as his hand brushed against mine.

I winced at the memory that the view could have been his every day. "I really am glad you're here to enjoy it. Thanks for coming." I handed Simon the corkscrew.

"I had a really nice day with you, Lucy. I was actually starting to miss you a little bit."

Simon busied himself with the wine bottle, and I tried to hide the silly grin that popped on my face. There was something about this guy that made me feel pretty damn special. He was very charming and no doubt, had his pick of women back home.

I chewed my bottom lip and watched him pour the wine with the grace of a professional. He swirled it around, stuck his nose inside the glass, and took a dramatic inhale. I suddenly felt giddy and burst into laughter.

"What?" Simon looked at me and chuckled.

"Nothing," I shrugged. "You're just funny."

"You don't think I'd make a good *sommelier*?"

I raised my eyebrows in response as he took a sip of the wine.

"That's dreadful." Simon spat.

"Oh, come on. Or are you still in character? I find it hard to believe you're a wine snob."

"First of all, I take offense to that. But I'm actually not. You've got to try this." Simon offered his glass to me.

"How could I resist with an intro like that?" I took a generous sip and nearly choked as it hit the back of my throat. "Oh my God. It tastes…" I forced myself to swallow. "Like—"

"Ass," Simon finished.

"Yes." I groaned, after managing to swallow. "You took the words right out of my mouth."

"Look at that. We're already finishing each other's sentences."

I placed my glass on the black wrought iron table and watched Simon lean against the railing.

"This figures," he said and tossed his hands in the air. "Just when I get you to have a drink with me, I bring over the crap wine." He stuffed his hands into his pockets and made a face.

"Please. I was about to open my own bottle of crap wine. So…" I paused. Now that I had company, I was in no rush to part ways. "What's our plan B?"

"How about we take our show on the road? Maybe … a dinner cruise on the Seine?"

"Talk about one extreme to another! *Nah.*" I wrinkled my nose. "Too touristy."

Simon took his hand and wiped it across his forehead. "Whew."

"Well, then why did you ask me?" I leaned against the railing next to him and folded my arms across my chest.

"I just thought that … well, maybe it would be up your alley."

"Yeah, maybe back in the day, like oh, you know … about a week ago when I played it safe. But now that I've lived in a commune, ridden the Euro Rail, and picked grapes with the locals, I think I'd like to try something a bit more … authentic."

"Like steak and *pommes frites*?"

"Mmm, yes." I licked my lips. "Can you just give me a minute?" I looked down at my wrinkled tank top and leggings. "I feel so…"

"Gorgeous?"

I figured he was kidding, but the look on his face was anything but.

"No." I stepped back into the room and turned around to face him on the balcony. "I was going to say that I look like a hot mess."

"Nope," Simon shook his head. He walked towards me and leaned his tall body on the balcony doorframe. "Just hot."

"You're good for the ego. I'll just be a minute."

He's definitely not gay. Neither was I. Oh, neither was I. My entire body tingled.

Simon followed me into the room and lightly touched my arm, sending an electric current down my body. "Lucy, don't change. You really look great."

"Okay, okay," I groaned outwardly, but was secretly flattered. We locked eyes and I wondered for a fleeting second if he was going to kiss me. I felt my heart beat faster and forced myself to swallow. What the hell was I doing? I quickly stepped back and turned to get my bag from the bed. I was hoping to disguise the effect his touch had on me, but could already feel my face burning.

"In fact…" Simon paused, waiting for me to turn around. "I'll bet that you'll be tonight's finest looking lady on a cane."

I held my hands to my chest as if I had just won the Oscar. "Ooh, what an accolade!" I cried a little too loudly, hoping to change the mood in the room. "Now I can bet you've never been out on the town with an older lady on a cane."

Simon narrowed an eye and nodded his head. "I like the sound of that."

"Being out with a cougar?" I raised a shoulder suggestively.

"Well, not just any cougar. This one, in particular."

"Ha ha." Was he trying to get into my pants? Did I even care? Was it really only one week ago that Chaz had called me a cougar? Now there I was, wanting to go in for the kill. I must've been temporarily insane.

"I was kidding, by the way. I just like the sound of being out with *you*." Simon handed me the cane with one hand and took a hold of my arm with the other. "Shall we?"

"We shall," I said. I took an awkward step with the cane. Simon flashed a boyish grin, and I suddenly felt like a senior citizen being led on my walker by a boy toy.

"You know what? I don't think I need this." I pulled away and looked down at the cane.

"Are you sure? It may minimize some of the tension."

"Positive." Only a cold shower could possibly minimize the kind of tension I was feeling. It had been a long time since I'd felt this alive, and boy, did it feel good. I took a breath and propped the cane against the wall behind the door.

"Worst case, you can always lean on me." Simon grinned and offered me his arm. As I wrapped my hand around his strong forearm, it sure felt like the best-case scenario to me.

* * * *

Despite my ankle, we managed to walk around for quite a bit. We had gotten to know each other all afternoon, but physically holding on to him for support, I felt a level of comfort that hadn't been there before. By the time we stumbled upon a local haunt with a line out the door, I felt like I was with someone I'd known a lot longer than one day.

"*Le Relais de L'Entrecote*," Simon read from the sign. "Oh! The concierge told me about this restaurant. He said it was the best kept secret in the neighborhood."

I looked at the line out the door. "I think someone spilled the beans."

"Excuse me, sir? How long is the wait?" Simon spoke to a man who stood at the end of the line.

"Ninety minutes," he replied with a French accent. "Totally worth it, though. Zee best rib steak ever." He kissed his fingers and tossed them in the air.

"Their sauce is a gastronomic delight," added the woman who accompanied him.

Simon looked at me with an eyebrow raised. "That sounds hard to beat. What do you think?"

We peered into the small glass windows and saw people crammed together drinking wine and laughing. It looked like a quintessential French restaurant. Black and white tiles covered the floor, and rattan chairs surrounded wrought iron tables. The waiters with their classic white shirts, black waistcoats, and aprons, raced around, carrying carafes of wine and baskets of bread.

"It does look rather inviting," I said wistfully. "And sounds delicious." I swallowed the saliva that had formed in my mouth. I was starving.

"But are you up for standing this long? We've done so much walking already." A crease slashed across his brow with the question.

Oh, had we? I had been floating on air and hadn't noticed that my feet had actually hit the ground. "I'm fine." I waved my hand, dismissing his concern. "This reminds me of one of the restaurants in *Julie and Julia*. Did you see that? I think I left the theater and ate an entire quiche."

"I didn't see it. Meryl Streep?"

"Yep. It was soooo good. If you hadn't shown up, I probably would've ordered that in my room tonight."

"The quiche?"

"No, but that sounds pretty good right about now. I meant the movie."

"I hope you don't mind that I changed your plan." I could see Simon's Adam's apple bob in his throat as he swallowed.

"Of watching a movie that I've already seen? Not at all," I smiled.

"Well, I know how you women are with chick flicks. Besides, you already told me about your addiction."

"*Julie and Julia* is not a chick flick," I shook my finger at him. "Not that it matters. I must've seen *Pretty Woman* at least a dozen times."

Simon shook his head in disbelief. "A movie about a prostitute? Really? I'm a big fan of Julia Roberts, but I really don't see the appeal of a hooker landing a rich guy."

"That's not the point. It's like..." I looked up in the sky for a moment. "A modern day Cinderella," I said with a finger snap. "Every woman dreams of being rescued by a handsome prince."

"So, what about you? Do you dream of being rescued by a knight in shining armor?" The corners of his mouth rose with his grin.

I blushed. "Yep. Still waiting for my *Pretty Woman* moment."

"You mentioned an ex-fiancée. I take it you're … single?" Simon shoved his hands into his pockets.

"Correct." The knot in my stomach now synonymous with thoughts of Cooper tightened. "What about you? Are you single?"

"Very," Simon said. I exhaled through my nose, not even realizing that I'd been holding my breath. "You see, the problem with women is that you're all so high maintenance."

I wondered whether he really felt that way or if it was just an excuse for commitment issues. "Well, sometimes it's you guys that make us that way."

The look on Simon's face made me think he hadn't a clue what I was talking about. "Let's take my ex. He never would have let me go out looking like this." I tugged on my tank top. "And God forbid I wore jeans!"

"What did he want? Formal attire? That's ridiculous. What's that expression? Clothes don't make the woman? It's the woman *in* the clothes. You could probably make a sweat suit look fancy."

I cocked my head to the side and smiled. "That's sweet of you to say."

Simon bent down and lifted up the ankle band on one of my leggings.

"What are you doing?" I looked around to see if anyone was watching.

"Oh, nothing." Simon caressed my shin. "I just wanted to see if you're rebelling now that you're free from his scrutiny. You know, braiding the hair on your legs to make a statement."

I laughed and placed my hands on either side of his head, pretending to squeeze it in a vise. "I always shave my legs, thank you very much."

I silently thanked God that I had. Two days ago at the hostel they had been anything but smooth.

Simon's wavy brown hair was so soft that I had to force myself to pull my hands away. I reached one hand down to help him up off the sidewalk. He took my hand, and even after he stood up, he continued to hold it. I could feel my heart beat so heavily that when the line began to move, I quickly dropped his hand to adjust the bag on my shoulder. Through the window, my gaze fell upon a family who were raising their glasses to make a toast.

"It must be so weird to grow up legally drinking alcohol." Nerves turned the words into a chuckle.

"Well, they don't know any other way. Do you remember your first legal drink? It's so monumental. Europeans don't have that rite of passage."

"Ugh. Memories," I groaned. I wasn't sure whether I was groaning from the memories or from the realization that my first legal drink was before Simon even hit puberty.

One hour later, I was the one feeling like a pubescent kid, with a crush, as I listened to Simon speaking to the waiter in a lovely French tongue.

I sat there completely rapt. I couldn't help but feel as if he was somewhat of a mystery man. The moment the waiter walked away I leaned across the table.

"Where did that come from?"

Simon looked at me from behind the wine list. "Where did what come from?"

"Um, your beautiful French?" He might be young and a camp counselor, but mastering a foreign language definitely boosted him on the maturity scale.

"Oh. I studied abroad during my last year at Boston University. It's been so long that I still need a guidebook and a map of Paris, yet I somehow managed to retain any words that involve wine and food," he said sheepishly.

"I'm very impressed, not to mention jealous. I regret that studying abroad never even crossed my mind. What was your major?"

"Business." Simon closed his eyes and made a snoring sound. "It's what my dad wanted me to do." Clearly his father's intentions hadn't worked out so well.

I nodded and thought about what to say next. "Now you're happy … at the camp?" I reached into the breadbasket to select a piece of bread.

Simon's face lit up with a smile. "Couldn't be happier. What about you? Do you love to write?" He leaned his elbows on the table.

"Well, I was really happy when I wrote for that parenting magazine, until it shut down a few months ago. But I'm excited to pitch some ideas to my friend at the travel magazine." I twisted my hands under the table. "It's just that lately I've been a bit creatively blocked. It's been a rough few months."

"I see," Simon nodded, gazing at me intently. "Well, don't give up." He reached across the table to squeeze my hand. "Something great is going to happen for you, Lucy. You probably won't even remember the way you've been feeling."

"Thanks." I was so touched that I felt a lump rise in my throat and smiled through gritted teeth. I took a swig of my water.

"Hey, maybe I could be your muse." Simon narrowed his eyes and gave me a come-hither look.

A chortle replaced the lump in my throat. "Well, you most definitely *a-muse* me, that's for sure."

I took a generous dollop of butter and began to spread it on my bread. I could feel Simon's eyes on me, and I paused with the knife in hand.

"I know," I said and nodded. "I'm disgusting. In the past forty-eight hours, I've become obsessed with French butter." I took a bite of bread and my teeth sank into the soft center. The butter tasted so rich and creamy.

"Well, then we're both disgusting." Simon reached his own knife into the bowl of butter. "I've had butter on pretty much everything since we got here. And it's refreshing to be with a woman who will actually eat it."

"Oh, not as refreshing as being with a man who actually lets me eat it."

Simon opened his mouth to speak and quickly shut it, pressing his lips together. "You know what? The beauty of an ex is that his issues are no longer yours." He reached across the table and tapped his buttery slice against mine.

I looked Simon in the eyes and took a revengeful bite. He laughed and playfully tapped my foot under the table as he glanced down at the paper menu.

"The French sure know how to do it," I murmured, swallowing the monster bite I had been chewing. "I pick and choose my battles, and I refuse to pass up their butter. I'll have something that is starred low vat to offset the damage."

Simon paused with the bread to his lips. "Did you say low vat?"

I sat up a little straighter in my seat. "Yes I did. See? You're not the only one who can find your way around a French restaurant." I picked up the menu and gave it a quick scan.

Simon glanced at his menu and began to read aloud. "Items that are starred indicate low vat. Is that what you're talking about? The lentils?"

"*Oui.*" I tossed my hair over my shoulder and took another bite. "They were starred at last night's restaurant, too."

The corners of Simon's mouth twitched as he placed the menu down. "Um, Lucy, VAT means Value Added Tax. It's like a sales tax."

I felt like the bread had suddenly lodged its way into my esophagus. I took a sip of water and wished it were the wine we had ordered. "Are you sure?"

Simon held up a hand in oath. "One hundred percent."

I sunk back into my chair. "Do you mean to tell me I've been eating lentils for nothing? I don't even like lentils. Fuck, is all I can say."

"I think you meant to say ... vuck?"

I closed my eyes in shame and rubbed my eye sockets.

Simon gently tapped my foot under the table with his. "You are so cute, Lucy."

I peered at Simon through open fingers. "Cute?"

"Yes. Especially that first time I spotted you in London on your mad quest for a charger." He sighed and omitted a slight chuckle.

"Let's not go there." I slid my fingers down my face. If Simon's foreign tongue added a few years to his age, then my lack of common sense knocked a few years off of mine. It looked like our age gap was narrowing.

The waiter appeared with a carafe of wine and two glasses.

"Oh, thank God. Saved by the wine," I said with relief.

After the waiter poured the wine, I gratefully accepted a glass from him.

Simon raised his glass. "To the best non-date ever."

And that it was. When the check was placed between us I couldn't believe that three hours had passed. When he reached for it, I wasn't sure what to do. I knew Simon's camp counselor salary must be low, so I felt I should offer, but at the same time, I didn't want to offend him either.

"Simon?" I watched him unroll a haphazard wad of euros that he had taken from his pocket. "Can we split this?"

Simon redirected his gaze from the crumpled ball of bills and gave me a firm look. It pretty much demanded I let him treat me like a lady. Which, he continued to do the entire walk back to the hotel. It felt so nice to be taken care of that by the time we got back to the hotel, I really didn't want the night to end. We stepped into the elevator, and Simon pressed the button for our floor.

"I had a really good time tonight. Thank you." I smiled as the doors closed.

"Thank *you*. That place was totally worth the wait. The food, the wine, the company..." Simon elbowed me gently.

"Don't forget the ab workout." I placed a hand on my stomach, sucking in my food and wine induced bloat. "I can't remember the last time I laughed that hard. My abs are actually sore."

"Better than a movie in bed, right?"

"Well, that depends with whom." I winked.

The wine must have gone to my head. I bit my cheek as the elevator ascended and wondered what I was supposed to do next. Was I supposed to kiss him on the cheek? Give him a hug? Shake his hand?

The elevator stopped, and the doors opened. We stepped out, staring at each other awkwardly, and Simon shoved his hands into his pockets. I guess shaking hands was no longer an option.

I felt a yawn coming on and clenched my jaw to suppress it. "I don't know about you, but I'm pretty beat from all that manual labor," I said after the urge had passed, smiling brightly to hide my confusion.

"I won't keep you." Simon smiled down at me.

I couldn't help but feel disappointed by his words. I'd enjoyed his company so much that I wasn't in a hurry to part ways, although my inner voice was screaming that I should be the mature older woman and step inside the room with a polite goodnight and thank you. I hadn't felt this carefree in months and didn't want to burst my lighthearted feeling and happiness bubble with a random hook up that would lead to nowhere. Not that he was rushing to take advantage of me either. But still.

He put his hands on my shoulders and gave me a soft kiss on my left cheek, followed by an even softer one on my right. Genius.

"Two kisses are better than one," Simon said as if he had read my mind. His hands remained on my shoulders as he locked his eyes with mine.

All of a sudden, I didn't want the date to end, nor did I care about protecting my heart. Instead, I wanted him to kiss me—on the lips. "Yes, but three is my lucky number," I said before I could stop myself.

Simon dropped his hands to my waist and pulled me close. I closed my eyes and enjoyed the sweetest kiss I had ever received. I felt like I was having an out of body experience. My knees went weak, my stomach did flip-flops, and I saw colorful swirls from behind closed eyes.

Did I wish it were Cooper? No. To my surprise, I was exactly where I wanted to be. I pulled back to look up at Simon. His smile caused my stomach to do another flip. This time, I wrapped my arms around his waist and leaned my head on his chest. We fit together so well. *Why, why, why* did he have to be so goddamn young? I was only going backwards in the looks department. He, on the other hand, would just get hotter and ...

Ding. The elevator doors opened and interrupted my mental anguish.

"Aunt Lucy?"

My eyes flew open in alarm, and I looked up at Simon. "Oh my God," I whispered.

I fixed my gaze on Simon as he looked over my head. He turned his attention back to me and gave me a subtle nod.

No, I mouthed. I took a deep breath and turned around. Simon's hands remained on my waist, and I pushed them away.

I stood face to face with Tess and Mark.

"Hi. Um, what are you doing?" I said in what I hoped was a casual tone. "Did you guys have a fun date?" I subtly used my knuckle to wipe my bottom lip.

"Well…" I could tell Tess was trying not to laugh. "It wasn't exactly a date, more like a bail out."

Wait a second. Her date wasn't with Mark. I shook my head in confusion. "I'm sorry ... how did..." I pointed at Mark. "What happened to the Frenchie on the Vespa?" I blurted.

"Long story," Tess said with a look.

I glanced at Mark, and he shifted uncomfortably. We all looked as if we were up to no good.

"And what about you guys?" Tess asked.

"We just grabbed a bite. It was no big deal." I looked at Simon, and he quickly looked away.

"In fact, I'm so tired." I felt another yawn coming and welcomed it with an open palm. "I'm going to..." I pointed my finger to our room.

"Right," Simon said.

"Um, thanks again for dinner." I bit my lip.

I reached up and gave him a kiss on his left cheek. One good old American-style cheek kiss. My lips brushed against the stubble on his cheek. It hadn't been there at the vineyard that morning.

"It was just a bite. No big deal," he said with a wink.

"Bye, Mark. Thank you so much." Tess smiled brightly.

"Maybe we'll catch up with you guys tomorrow," Mark replied.

I was surprised to see him give Tess a quick peck on the lips. I unlocked the door and went into the room. When I heard the door click shut I turned around to face Tess.

"Lucy, you got some 'splainin' to do!" Tess cried. "This time you're going first."

"It was so not what it looked like," I said with a hand on my chest. I walked to the bed, kicked my shoes off, and massaged my sore ankle.

"Oh, I hope it was exactly what it looked like." Tess kicked off her own shoes and plopped onto her bed.

"You do?" I said, amazed.

"He's so cute, Aunt Lu. And nice." Tess eyed the items Simon had brought over. "What's all this?"

"Oh, just a few things Simon brought over."

Tess looked up and gave me a knowing look. "See, what I mean? So nice."

"I know. He's wonderful. You don't have to convince *me* of that, but I'm practically old enough to be his mother!"

Tess gave me a look. "His mother? Really? I know people start young these days, but I don't know any ten-year-old mothers." She gave me a sideways look. "C'mon. He's not *that* young."

"Okay fine, but he's young enough for a thirty-year-old hottie with a tight butt and perky boobs to turn his head. He also happens to be unsettled, and that's a bad combination. It's one thing to date a younger man, but a camp counselor? No ma'am. That's just crazy. We really are worlds apart."

"He wouldn't understand the pressures of the business world and the deadlines I face. Or hope to face again," I said, making a face. "Life isn't one big party. I want a child in my life, but not in the form of a boyfriend I would have to support. This is definitely not the conventional route."

Tess lay on her side and propped herself up with an elbow. "First of all, take a breath. You sound manic. Who are you trying to convince here? You just met the guy, and second, I thought we were trying not to take the road we're 'supposed' to take," she said making air quotes.

I dismissed her with a wave, even though her words rang true.

"Why don't you just have fun? Don't analyze it. You might learn something about yourself."

"I already have. I've learned that I'm capable of having fun with another man. Yay!" I clapped my hands. "This might actually be the first day when Cooper didn't consume my brain. Instead of twice an hour, he may have only crossed my mind twice the entire day."

Tess narrowed her eyes and studied me. "Maybe Simon is the antidote to Cooper. You were looking pretty chummy when we saw you."

"Hey, speaking of *we*, what were you doing with Mark, anyway? What happened to Pierre?"

Tess flipped on her back and looked up at the ceiling. "He was a nightmare, Aunt Lu." She sat up to face me. "He might seriously be the Don Juan of Paris."

"The Jean John?" I joked. I ripped open the box of French nougat Simon had brought me and held it out to Tess.

She sampled one. "Mmm. This from Simon, too?"

I nodded and popped a chocolate in my mouth. She smiled and shook her head with disbelief.

"Shut up." I laughed and a chocolaty dribble slid out of my mouth. I used the back of my hand to wipe my chin. "Okay, go on."

"Very chewy." Tess used her tongue to work a piece of candy stuck to her tooth. "We went to a wine bar, and Pierre must've turned his head every time someone with boobs walked past. *I* felt like the biggest boob. I pretty much watched him ogle women."

"Eww," I groaned. "So how did Mark come into play?" I put the box of nougat onto my lap and debated my next selection.

"Basically, Pierre had too much drink, and instead of taking me back to the hotel, he took me to his cousin's apartment."

My mouth flew open in horror, and Tess nodded her head somberly.

"Problem was, by the time I realized it, we had made so many twists and turns I didn't even know where we were. The apartment was totally vacant. Suddenly he was miraculously sober and asking me to spend the night."

"Oh my God, Tess. I can't even listen to this." I pushed the box of candy off my lap. I had suddenly lost my appetite. "You could've been date raped. I told you to stay in public..."

"I know, and believe me, that was my intention. But how was I supposed to know where he was taking me? We've only been here for two days." Tess stared at me and chewed her lip. "Do you want to hear more? It gets worse."

"Go on," I sighed. I made a mental note not to let her out of my sight for the rest of our trip. Maybe the rest of her life.

"I went to use the bathroom, and when I came out he was lying in bed wearing nothing but underwear. Total tighty-whities." She wrinkled her nose in disgust.

"NO," I yelled.

"'You like?' he said with a ridiculous come hither look on his face. All I could think about was Mark. Not Jack, the boyfriend I am on a break from, but Mark. I passed up a date with a nice guy for that loser?"

"Oh, sweetie." I sighed.

"So, I told him I didn't feel so well and had to go home. Then suddenly, he was drunk."

"What do you mean? Did he start drinking again?"

"No. He said, 'Since you aren't feeling well and I am already undressed, can I just take you back to the hotel in the morning? I'm in no condition to drive.'"

"What a jerk."

"Yup. So I went outside to take a deep breath. Never mind, date rape. I wanted to commit date *murder*. I tried to call for a taxi, but couldn't seem to reach anyone who could speak English. I didn't even know how to pronounce the cross streets. All I knew was that I was somewhere in between scared shitless and freaked out," she said with a bitter laugh. "That's when I texted Mark."

"Why didn't you call me?"

"I figured you'd be sleeping. It hadn't occurred to me you'd be out getting your groove on." She wiggled her eyebrows. "Anyway, it wasn't a big deal. He was just hanging out and watching TV. He said he would have the concierge send a cab and twenty minutes later the taxi came, and he was in it. My knight in a shining taxi cab."

I took a breath and slowly exhaled. "I should never have allowed you to go out on that date. I wanted to be the cool aunt and not tell you what to do, but next time I'm going to speak up. No more foreign men for you, young lady."

"Don't worry. There won't be a next time."

I smiled with relief.

"American-made men here on in!"

"Tess," I warned.

Suddenly, a knock on the door interrupted our conversation. Tess and I looked at each other and froze. She clapped her hand over her mouth to suppress a giggle.

"Who do you think it is?" she whispered.

"I don't know. You go." I felt like a teenager waiting to see which one of our crushes had come to visit. I smoothed my hair down and tucked it behind my ears.

"Coming!" Tess got off the bed and ran to the door.

"Wow, these are beautiful," I heard her exclaim.

"They were just delivered. Enjoy," said a man with a French accent.

"*Merci*," Tess said and closed the door.

I heard her pull out a card and squeal. She walked towards me and held a big bouquet of orchids under my nose. I inhaled a sweet scent that reminded me of vanilla with a touch of cinnamon.

"Aren't these gorgeous?" she beamed. "Guess who?"

"*Tres magnifique*. Let's see. Could it be an apology from Pierre?" I said. "No. It sounded like he was too banged up. Scratch that. I bet they're ... missing you flowers from Jack!" I cried. "Yes, that's my final guess."

"Aunt Lu," Tess said with a glimmer in her eye. "They're for you."

She handed me the envelope marked with my name. I didn't have to open the card to know who they were from.

"Simon." I smiled. He may be young but he sure knows how to woo a woman. My hand shook with excitement as I tore open the card.

Fleurs de Berri| 12 Rue de Berri| 75008 Paris | France

Dear Lucy,

It was great to hear your voice the other night. I'm sorry I caused you so much pain. For what it's worth, I think I may have made the biggest mistake of my life. Can we talk?

Love always,

Cooper

Chapter Seven

Speechless.
Facebook Status June 10 at 12:10am

I stared at the floor as Tess finished a dramatic reading of the card. I had read it to myself, read it aloud and even after she read it, one question still remained, so I said it aloud.

"Is he *fucking* kidding me?"

Tess looked at me and shook her head in disbelief. She slipped the gold bangles off of her wrist and twirled them around her finger.

I jumped up and winced from the throbbing pain of my ankle. "Now he does this? *Now?*"

Fueled by anger, I began to pace back and forth. After I'd completed two laps between the bed and coffee table, I made a pit stop to stuff one of Simon's chocolates into my mouth.

"Orchids. He sends me goddamn orchids," I muttered, wiping another drip of chocolate drool that escaped from my mouth. I looked over at the flowers with disdain.

"Are orchids bad?" Tess asked. "Do they symbolize something inappropriate? Friendship? Deception? Death?" She had a horrified look on her face.

"Um, considering orchids were what I had planned to carry down the aisle? Yeah, I'd say they symbolize something *very* inappropriate. Not to mention the stupid fights we had over that goddamn flower. Mr. Control Freak wanted me to carry lilies. Who carries lilies?" I plucked another chocolate from the box.

"Nobody?" Tess offered. "Besides, what guy actually cares about the flowers at a wedding, anyway?"

"Seriously. Besides, a lily pollen stain is a bitch to get out. I finally won that argument. Or did I? It seems to me that Cooper got the last laugh." I hobbled over to the bed and plunked myself down with the chocolates on my lap.

"Well maybe now you'll really get the last laugh," Tess said with her finger pointed at me.

"How? By blowing up like a balloon?" I groaned and pushed the box off of my lap. "Seriously, what the hell am I supposed to do? Should I be doing cartwheels that he's finally come to his senses? Play hard to get?"

"Um, how about none of the above? He broke your heart, Aunt Lu." Tess walked over to my bed and helped herself to a chocolate.

"I know." Tears stung my eyes, and I reached across the nightstand to grab a tissue.

"Ugh," I exclaimed, ripping it out of the box with vengeance. "I'm so mad. Can't I just feel happiness for one stinking day? Is that too much to ask?"

"Ugh, is right." Tess stood up and shook her fists. "Not only did he break your heart, but he humiliated you on top of it. The more I think about it, the more I want to take those pollen-infested flowers and shove them up his ass."

"Those weren't the pollen ones." I smiled despite myself and wiped my nose.

"Whatever. They still suck and so does he. He abandoned you at a time when you needed him most. You shouldn't play hard to get. You *are* hard to get. I'm sorry, but that man does not deserve your forgiveness."

I felt a stress headache coming on. I gathered my hair in a tight ponytail and gave it a hard tug to massage my scalp. "I don't know about that, Tess. Doesn't everyone deserve a second chance? Maybe he's finally come to his senses."

"Nope." Tess crossed her arms in front of her. "He's come to his senses," she paused and looked at her watch, "oh, about three months too late."

"I know, but it takes a big person to admit he was wrong."

"And it takes a crummy person to break off an engagement. Why are you defending him, anyway? You're always selling yourself short."

"Tess," I sighed. "This is really complicated. I know everyone hates him right about now, but let's not forget that he was the love of my life. Maybe even still is. He did, I mean *does*, have some pretty amazing qualities."

"I'm not so sure my mother would agree with you on that one."

I closed my eyes and rubbed my temples. She was actually starting to sound like my overprotective sister, and I was no longer in the mood for a debate. I limped over to the dresser and opened the top drawer.

"How did he even know you were here? The only person who knows where we are is my mom, and there is no way in hell she'd ever tell him your whereabouts."

"Gee, I don't know." I turned around to give her a dirty look. "Did you by any chance tell five hundred of your closest Facebook friends where we are?"

Tess sucked in a breath. "I might have mentioned something to my friend Riley ... on my wall." She looked at me and cringed apologetically.

"Tess, I know I've said this before, but you really shouldn't use Facebook as your personal GPS. Turn your location services off and let's keep our whereabouts confidential. And while we're on the topic, I'd also like to keep the flowers confidential."

"Simon?" Tess said with a knowing look.

"I don't care about Simon." I knew that wasn't true, especially since the mere mention of his name had caused my stomach to do a flip.

I quickly turned around and pretended to be quite absorbed with my pajama drawer. "Your mother is the one I have to hide this from. I don't need her two cents. Especially when I already have you to keep me in line. I'm starting to see that the apple hasn't fallen far from the judgmental tree."

"It's all out of love, Aunt Lu," Tess reminded me gently. I knew it was out of love, but still, I was the only one allowed to bash my ex-fiancée.

"So. What are you going to do?" she said.

"I have no idea." The one thing I knew was that this topic of conversation was officially off limits.

Physically exhausted and mentally drained, I wished there was another room for me to escape to. I just wanted to be by myself. Seeing no other option, I pulled off the top sheet and hopped into bed, fully clothed.

"Actually, I do know. I'm going to go to bed." I rolled my pajamas into a ball and tossed them on the floor.

"Just like that? You've been telling me for years that a woman should never go to bed without washing her face."

"Not everything is black and white, sweetie." I paused and gave her my biggest and brightest fake smile. "I'm wiped." I shut off the light that sat on the nightstand. "Besides, things always looks clearer in the morning. Goodnight, Tess."

"I hope so. Goodnight, Aunt Lu. Sweet dreams."

Like that would be possible. I closed my eyes and gave myself permission to let my thoughts run wild. In the process, I must've hit every emotion on the spectrum. I started out with hate, went to sorrow, then love, and managed to end with a sliver of hope.

But I sadly reminded myself that no matter what happened, I still wouldn't be able to have children. Would Cooper ever be okay with that? Would another man be able to accept that about me?

All of a sudden, I had babies on the brain, and it wasn't just the type I prayed to God I could have. I thought about Cooper, who had acted like one and Simon, who, well, seemed young enough to be one. Oh, baby.

Hours later, I sunk into a state of semi-consciousness. The last thing that popped into my head was a flashback of the kiss I'd shared with Simon. Despite everything, I actually managed to fall asleep with a smile.

* * * *

The next morning, I woke up to the ringing sound of the phone in our room. I cracked open an eye and sat up in bed with a start. My contact lenses were stuck to my eyeballs.

"Hello?" I said, groggily.

"Hi."

I recognized the voice immediately and felt my stomach flip. I looked over at the lump in Tess's bed. It hadn't moved, despite the interruption.

"Hi, Simon," I said, dropping my voice to a whisper.

"Did I wake you?"

"No, not at all. How are you?" I put the phone on mute and quickly cleared my throat before I unmuted it.

"I'm good. I just wanted to say I had a really nice time with you last night."

"Me, too." I smiled shyly and bit my nail. I tasted the remnants of last night's chocolate binge and a sinking feeling washed over me as I remembered the way the night had ended.

"Did you sleep well?"

"Like a baby." A newborn baby, that is, who woke up every two hours. I pulled a bottle of saline solution from the nightstand and poured it into my eyes.

"I was just sitting here wondering what would've happened if we hadn't been interrupted by Tess and Mark."

"Hmm," I paused to swallow. Let's see ... we probably would've still been kissing in the hallway or worse, back in my room. Then the flowers would've been delivered and the interruption would've been far more awkward.

"Something tells me it worked out for the best," I said.

"Well, I beg to differ."

His morning voice sounded sexier than usual, and my heart skipped a beat, reminding me of the effect he had on me. I smiled and stretched my free hand overhead.

"What are you guys up to today?" I said in a hushed tone.

"Well, that all depends on you. How's your ankle?"

"Much better, thanks. It must've been the first aid."

I peered down to make sure that it looked as good as it felt. For all I knew, it had swollen up to gargantuan proportions. Thankfully, it hadn't. Then, when I stepped out of bed I was relieved to discover it actually did feel much better.

"That's good news. Mark and I were wondering if you and Tess would like to join us for a little sightseeing action. We're dying to see the Catacombs."

"No pun intended?"

On the phone, Simon chuckled as I walked over to the balcony and quietly opened the French doors. When I stepped outside, the cool morning air gave me a jolt I hadn't quite expected. The hair on my arms stood on end, reminding me of an angry cat.

"Sounds kind of creepy." I shivered and gave myself a hug to get warm.

"Maybe a bit, but where else can you find a labyrinth under the city that holds the bones of six million starting from the 1500s? C'mon, you have to admit it sounds pretty cool. It's supposed to have a maze of passageways and…"

As Simon talked, my mind began to race. I'd had such a fabulous day and night with him yesterday, but what was the point of getting together again? Sure, I could say screw it and have fun, but where would that leave me in the end? I'd be back home and back to where I started. Alone. Not to mention feeling worse because this temporary happiness band-aid would be ripped off.

Or, would I be with Cooper? If I hadn't drunk-dialed him in Amsterdam, would he have thought of me? I peered through the glass at the flowers and saw Tess walking out of the bathroom.

"So what do you think?" Simon said.

I made a face into the phone. "I don't know. Part of me feels like I should just stay here and flush out an idea for an article I want to pitch."

"Oh come on. You can do that anytime. Perhaps a visit to the underbelly of the City of Light might inspire you. I bet the bones of some very intelligent people are resting down there. Their souls might find you."

I needed to do my own soul search. What the hell was I going to do about Cooper? I looked down at the table where Simon's glass of wine still sat. Absently, I picked it up and traced my finger around the top.

"What time is it anyway?"

"9:10. Mark made me wait until a socially acceptable time to call."

I laughed and quickly calculated that it was the middle of the night in New York. It's not like I could call Cooper now, anyway. Besides, he made me wait three months. I should at least make him wait a day.

"Okay, I'm in. Let me go ask Tess." I hit the mute button one more time and walked back into the room.

Tess was climbing back into her bed and looked at me through hooded eyes. "Morning. Who was on the phone?"

"Oh, just Simon." I rolled my eyes in response to the slow smile that spread across her face. "He wants to know if you and I would like to sightsee with them today."

Tess's eyes grew wide. "Like a double date?"

"No, not like a double date. More like a double hang."

"Or a pick up where you left off?"

I drew in a breath and gave her a sideways look. "You know what? Maybe this isn't such a good idea."

"It's a great idea!" She jumped to her knees, suddenly wide-awake, and clasped her hands together. "Say yes."

"Okay, fine, but, just so you know, the only reason I'm going is because I know how much you like Mark."

"Oh, whatever," Tess said, rolling her eyes. "You didn't exactly look miserable yourself, last night."

"No more of that." I held up a finger. "Now shut up," I whispered as I unmuted the phone.

"Hey Simon. We're in."

"Cool. Dress warm. I've heard it gets pretty chilly down there."

I hung up the phone and looked over at Tess who was already rifling through dresser drawers.

"I have no clothes," she whined. "What does one wear to an underground cemetery, anyway?"

"Well, it's not like we have too much to choose from. Plus, Simon said we should dress warm. So, I'm going to go with leggings. I may even use the very same ones I wore to bed, as a scarf. And make no bones about it!" I laughed.

"Stylish. Why don't you wear this, instead?" Tess pulled a thin chocolate brown knit scarf from her backpack, rolled it up into a ball, and tossed it to me from across the room.

"I made it, so technically it's not a real scarf either, but it's probably a little better than wearing a crotch around your neck." She chuckled and turned her attention back to her own clothing crisis.

When I caught the scarf, it unraveled to reveal thin multi-colored swirls that blended into little circles. They were made of pale pastels and the pink, green, and yellow hues really stood out against the rich brown background. My mouth was agape as I marveled at my niece's handiwork.

"Aunt Lu, we really need to shop. It's so hard to live out of a backpack in the fashion capital of the world."

"No kidding," I mumbled. I wrapped the scarf around my neck and looked in the mirror. I'd definitely pay money for this.

"Well, we'll be back amongst our peeps again in two days," Tess sighed, focusing her attention on her backpack. "I'm sorry we already paid for the hostel in Germany."

"You and me both," I replied with a chortle. "Although I think we could probably swing the thirty dollar loss."

Tess didn't reply, and from the way she was just staring into her bag, it looked as if she had been instantaneously sucked into a vortex of dreamland.

"However, maybe in the meantime," I said, giving her butt a playful swat, "you can whip yourself up another one of your homemade skirts. Show those Parisians what a real designer can do." I wiggled my eyebrows as Tess turned to face me with a smile.

Never one to take a compliment, her cheeks had turned a deep pink. She glanced at the scarf around my neck.

"Ooh, that looks good on you. Do you like it?" She crunched her nose as she waited for me to respond.

"Are you kidding? I love it. You know, Tess," I paused thoughtfully and caressed the soft fabric on my cheek. "You could probably make a career out of this."

"Please." Tess said with a wave of her hand, "I'm a teacher. Well, I will be if I ever find a real teaching job." Her face grew solemn and she looked at me in alarm. "Aunt Lu, what if I never find a job?"

I frowned. "I know it's what you went to school for, but have you ever considered trying something else? Is that the only thing you want to do?"

Tess shook her head. "I don't know," she said with a sigh. "I've been saying that I wanted to be a teacher ever since I was old enough to play school."

"I remember. I spent many, many Saturdays in your school." I smiled fondly at the memory of the makeshift classroom that Landon and Tess had set up in the basement of their house. "You were a very impatient teacher."

Tess grinned. "Well, now I'm learning I'm a very impatient nose wiper. As a matter of fact, I'm beginning to wonder if teaching is what I really want or just something that I *think* I want?" Tess groaned as she picked up a towel that hung from her bed.

"Or was it another one of your mother's suggestions? Something that she might have reinforced over the years?" I said with an eyebrow raised.

"Hmph." Tess nodded thoughtfully.

I felt a stab of disloyalty towards my sister and immediately regretted opening up that can of worms. "Well, who knows," I said quickly. "But what I do know is that it's normal to be confused at your age. If it makes you feel any better, I'm still confused."

"It does. Thanks for the support, Aunt Lu. Jack's eyes would glaze over whenever I talked about this." She rolled her eyes and stretched her arms overhead. "That's why I sew. It takes my mind off the job stuff and mellows me out after those exhausting days at the daycare. And speaking of jobs, how much do you *love* being on vacation? It's been so nice taking a break from reality."

"It really has," I replied with a smile. Especially from the reality I'd been living in.

"I'm going to take a quick shower."

I sat on the bed and leaned back on my hands, smiling to myself. I could still feel Simon's presence in the room from the night before. There was a definite aura of happiness hanging around, and I sure was going to miss it there. That room had nothing but good memories—with the exception of the not-so-special delivery.

I looked at the flowers and felt a knot form in my stomach again. Just when I was finally on an upswing, Cooper had to come and torture me. I walked over to the flowers and pulled them from the vase, wrapping my hands around the stems.

"Dum dum dee dum, Dum dum dee dum." I hummed the wedding march and stopped in front of the garbage can. It seemed to have beckoned to me. I paused for a moment and then stuffed the flowers, with all thoughts of Cooper, straight into the receptacle with vengeance.

Chapter Eight

Feeling the love at the Louvre!
Facebook Status June 10 at 1:00pm

"I feel like we're still at the Musee d'Orsay. How is a subway station just as nice as a museum?" I said to Simon as we entered the Cite station stop.

We had been walking around Paris for hours and had seen everything from the Louvre to the Arc de Triomphe. Moments ago, we had stumbled upon the ornate Art Nouveau metro entrance, and it had lured us like an exquisite menu on a restaurant wall.

Orange globe lamps surrounded the entrance and loomed over the *Metropolitain* sign, like two flowers in bloom. A cast iron balcony enveloped the staircase that led underground to a sea of shiny white beveled tiles. Mass transit never looked so good, and it wasn't just because we were tired of walking. My eyes surveyed the station.

"Well, I've read the subway stations in Paris are often works of art," Simon commented. "Apparently the Abbesses Station is a spectacular sight. Like graffiti-covered walls—done on purpose. I think Hector Guimard also designed this one."

"I think you might be right." I nodded but had no clue what the hell I was talking about.

I'm sure Simon couldn't spot the difference between a real Fendi and a fake one, but he probably could sniff out a phony person. So what if he'd been rattling off all sorts of cultural trivia today? And that I barely understood any of it. How the hell did he know so much, anyway?

I followed Simon as he walked towards the tracks. Old-fashioned glass bulbs lit up the tracks as far as we could see. The ceiling and walls looked as if they were covered with thousands of tiny prisms as light particles radiated from the tiles.

"Hey, I thought this was supposed to be a subway station," I heard Mark's voice behind us. "Where's all the litter? The homeless?"

I turned around and saw him approach with Tess.

"Yeah, it doesn't quite remind you of Chicago, does it?" Simon said to his brother. "Marko, I have a feeling we're not in Kansas anymore."

At that moment, I spotted a homeless looking man who happened to be rummaging through the garbage. Simon followed my gaze, and we shared a smile. He and I locked eyes, and a moment of intimacy passed between us.

Mark held up a hand. "Hey, take it easy, bro. Don't disparage our great city. They'll never come visit."

I glanced at Tess and once our eyes met, she quickly looked away. The corners of her mouth turned up, and she pressed her lips together, probably in attempt to wipe off the silly grin that threatened to take over her entire face.

"Oh, please. You can't scare us. I've actually seen a homeless man doing *numero deux.*" I laughed and held up two fingers. "These walls would never make it in New York. In no time, they'd be covered with urine and God only knows whatever else."

"Gross," Tess replied, wrinkling her nose.

"Very gross, but very true," I said as I walked down the track to a bench. I plopped down and stretched my arms overhead. "Speaking of which, I don't know about you guys, but I'm pooped," I called out.

Simon laughed and took a seat beside me. "Oh?"

"You Anderson brothers take sightseeing to a whole new level. Who makes a pit stop at the Louvre?"

"Well, when we were at the Eiffel Tower, you declared you desperately wanted to see Mona. What's a guy to do?" Simon tossed his hands in the air.

"I didn't mean right then and there."

"Well," he shrugged, "I wanted to be the one to see her with you." He opened up a bottle of water and held it out to me.

"You're the best." I gratefully accepted the bottle and sipped. I paused and held the bottle mid-air. "Note to self: I must watch what I say. I also happened to mention I wanted to *see* the top of the Eiffel Tower. That didn't mean I needed to walk to the first and second levels. I feel like death." I handed Simon the bottle and watched his Adam's apple bob as he took a big gulp.

"Perfect timing. We'll be at the Catacombs in no time." Simon's cheeks formed perfect dimples as he smiled.

He patted my knee and let his hand linger there for a moment. A tingle swept over my body and I felt anything *but* dead. My racing pulse reminded me how very much alive this guy made me feel.

I looked over at Tess and Mark who stood close together at the track. Tess turned her head in our direction, and I jumped up with a start, causing Simon's hand to fall from my leg.

It had been like this all morning. Simon would reach for my hand and I'd shift sideways to stay out of his way. When he met us in the lobby at the hotel, I thought he was about to lean in for a hug or kiss, but thinking of Cooper's flowers and Tess and Mark watching, I just couldn't add anymore fuel to my mental fire. I simply gave his arm a pat and said, "Let's go. Can't wait to see the sights!" Tess had given me a strange look, but I just couldn't go there with Simon this morning.

"I think I hear the train," I sang.

"You must have bionic ears," Tess cried. "We see lights in the tunnel but can't even hear a sound."

"Interesting," Simon said with a wry grin.

Not knowing how to respond, I smiled awkwardly at him and walked towards the track.

The train pulled into the station, and as it slowed down, the only sounds that could be heard were the whispering from its rubber tires and the whine of its brakes. We hopped on and a short ride later, we reached our destination. After we walked up the stairs and stepped onto the street, I stopped to catch my breath and survey the neighborhood.

The area definitely was different from the one where we were staying. Markets and cafés replaced the upscale stores. Instead of Hermes or Christian Dior—boutiques, cheese shops, bookstores and antique shops filled the streets. Bohemians replaced the stylish. Despite the people that loitered, there was a sense of calm in the air.

"Is it just me or is everything abnormally peaceful here?" I said. "It even smells relaxing." I took in another breath and a strong scent of lavender filled my nose and lungs.

"Well, we are on top of a cemetery." Mark laughed.

"Creepy." Tess shivered and buttoned up her sweater. A sudden gust of wind blew her hair over her face.

"Where did that come from?" she demanded.

"Must be the ghosts," Mark said. "They don't like to be called creepy."

He gave Tess's ribs a gentle jab with his elbow. She swatted at his arm and in turn, he grabbed her hand. Simon shot me a quick glance and took a guidebook from his back pocket.

I pulled myself into my jacket like a turtle and kicked around a coin that lay on the ground. Using my toe, I flipped it over and wondered if I'd hurt his feelings when I knocked his hand off my knee earlier.

"It says here to enter through a green ticket office," Simon murmured from behind the book. He lifted his head and squinted across the street. "*Voila.*" He pointed his finger to a green hut.

The streetlight changed and Tess and Mark began to walk ahead of us. Still hand in hand, they laughed together as they walked in step.

"Hey, how come you don't let me hold your hand?" Simon asked, giving me a slight nudge.

I swallowed and shoved my hands into my pockets. "You didn't ask," I said with a forced chuckle.

Once we had safely crossed the street Simon took hold of my elbow and turned me to face him. "Are you okay today?" His eyebrows were furrowed together.

"Yeah, why? Do I seem weird?" I opened my eyes wide and waited for him to respond.

"Well ... last night we seemed one way and today, well, you seem a bit distant. I thought I pulled out my best moves, but you don't seem to bite."

I looked into Simon's eyes and took a deep breath.

He reached out and cupped my shoulders with his hands. "Lucy, I wanted to kiss you so bad before." He began to massage my shoulders with a soft pressure.

"When?" I swallowed. I had wanted him to kiss me so bad too.

"All morning," Simon said softly. My lips parted as he took the words right out of my mouth. I pressed them together.

"I wanted to kiss you hello when we met in the lobby, as we crossed the Pont des Arts bridge, when we were in the Eiffel Tower... Let's see when else?" Simon paused and tapped a finger to his lips. A blush swept across my face as a smile teased his lips. "Now?"

I paused for a moment and chewed my bottom lip. I stole a quick peek over his shoulder at Mark and Tess. "I'm sorry. It's just that..."

Simon took his hands off of my shoulders and cracked his knuckles.

"I feel a little weird with PDA in front of my niece," I concluded.

Simon crinkled his nose and shook his head. "Why?"

I gazed at the newly coupled couple now locked in a tight embrace. Simon followed my glance and gave me a sideways look.

"Tess doesn't seem to mind. Shouldn't *she* be the one who feels weird?"

"You would think," I said with a nervous giggle. "You see," I paused to take a breath, "part of the reason for this trip was to get my mind off of the fact that I was supposed to have gotten married." I looked up at Simon and cringed.

Simon took a step back. "Oh."

"Yeah." I nodded and closed my eyes before they flew open as I realized what he must be thinking. "Wait, Cooper, my ex has nothing to do with my weirdness."

A look of relief crossed Simon's face. "That's all you?"

"That's all me." I smiled and waved a hand over my body.

"Well, that's good to know. I mean, you mentioned an ex-fiancée, but I didn't realize he had earned the title so recently."

My jaw tightened as I clenched my teeth. "Oh, he didn't earn the title. He chose the title. I guess you can say things got a little messy, which is why Tess and her mother, my meddling sister, banded together to get me on this trip. They've been treating me like a wounded bird." I scoffed and picked at one of my fingernails.

"Are you? A wounded bird?" He sipped water as he waited for my answer.

I inhaled, hoping the lavender-scented air would calm my nerves. This time it was laced with an aroma of coffee wafting from a nearby cart. "I was and then I wasn't and then now..." I gazed into Simon's warm eyes and faltered. Why did I need to tell him this?

Screw Cooper and his stupid flowers. "I'm doing great." I smiled and much to my surprise, it actually felt genuine. I still may have had a way to go, but Simon was definitely chicken soup for my f'd up soul.

"Well, I'm glad to hear that. I'll just have to steal you away from your niece for a bit," Simon said with a wink.

"I know it sounds silly." I rolled my eyes and shook my head. "I just think that it's best to keep my private life to myself on this trip. Tess is a hopeless romantic and will conjure up her own ridiculousness. The next thing I know, my sister will be calling for the scoop. That's all I need, for them to start yapping that we're having a thing."

Simon cocked his head to the side and raised his eyebrows. "God forbid they think that."

I looked up at Simon's tone. Was he offended? How could he be? Had no one ever turned him down before? Did I step on his playboy party toes by rejecting him? Suddenly I was annoyed. This girl wasn't going to just fall at his feet because he had a killer smile and mesmerizing eyes. I was wiser than that.

"That's not what I meant. It's just that..."

"No need to explain," Simon interrupted. "Do you want to...?"

I felt a knot in my throat and swallowed. "Simon, I love your company. It's just I'm so much older and I ... I..." I was so goddamn attracted to him and was absolutely terrified to get close to another man. Especially, a younger one. Would he reject me one day too? Cooper left me because of my rotten eggs. What would do Simon in? A fresher set of hot cross buns? I narrowed my eyes at him.

Simon took his hands and placed them on my shoulders. That wasn't helping; it just made me want him to kiss me.

"Relax, you ageist. I can almost hear the wheels spinning in your head. You think too much. What I was about to say before you cut me off, was, do you want to head over to the line?"

My face burned, and I closed my eyes for a moment willing my embarrassment away. I opened my eyes and began to walk ahead. In doing so, I tripped over a mound of God knows what on the sidewalk and stumbled into Simon's path.

He reached his arms out and managed to catch me right before I hit the ground. After he helped me up, one hand remained wrapped around my waist. The heat from his hand warmed my entire body and I jumped back with a start. I readjusted my clothing and tucked my hair behind my ears.

"You know, I'm starting to think you might be doing this on purpose." The creases by his eyes folded as he smiled. "Is this your way of making a move?"

"You wish." I snorted. "What the hell was that?" I took another step back from Simon while trying to peer behind him and see what had tripped me.

That's when a man jumped up from a crouched position on the sidewalk and blurted something out to us in French, an inquisitive look on his face. He held a shiny gold wedding band under my nose. He was on the short side and standing before him, after tripping over him, I felt like a big oaf.

I looked up at Simon for a translation. He shook his head impatiently.

"Um ... *Non merci?*" I offered.

"Is yours?" the man asked.

"Oh. No," I replied. I looked around to see if anyone was searching for a ring.

"Want to buy ring for mademoiselle?" the man said to Simon. "I need food. You make money when you sell. Twenty euros."

Simon put his hand on my back. "Come on. Let's go," he said abruptly.

"Please," the man begged. "You can sell for *beaucoup* money. Is pure gold."

I gave Simon a look. "I'd like to help this man. I'll buy it myself," I whispered. I gave the man a warm smile and reached into my bag. His eyes were grateful as he murmured something in French.

"It's a scam, Lucy," Simon sighed, pulling on my arm.

"You're such an American. You don't have to be so defensive." I fished through my bag and realized that all I had on me was plastic.

"Simon, I don't have cash. Can I borrow a twenty?"

"I don't have change. Let's go."

Simon muttered a few words to the man in French. Then he pulled on my arm again and steered me away.

My heart went out to the stranger. There he was trying to sell me an expensive ring just to get a meal and this cheap guy couldn't reach into his pockets. I gave the man a tight smile, and he gave me a dark stare in return. Then he spit in our direction and walked away.

"Lucy, did you see what he just did? It was definitely a scam. A nice guy doesn't hock a loogie at a lady."

I shook my head and looked away. A massive line had formed, and judging from the crowd of people camped out on the floor, I assumed the wait would be longer than we thought.

"I'm going to grab a few coffees. Hopefully they'll take credit since you can't seem to spare a few bucks." I shot Simon a look over my shoulder and walked towards a coffee cart at the top of the line.

Cooper would never have done that. He probably would've given the man an extra twenty, given me the ring, and then bee-lined to Harry Winston for a matching bracelet. Cooper always did the right thing. Well, most of the time anyway.

I drew in a breath and counted to three as I inhaled. *Let-Cooper-Go*, I reminded myself on the exhale.

While I waited, an old lady with a shopping cart sidled up beside me. It looked as if she had just raided a dollar store with her cartful of trinkets. I looked at her goods and saw a bag of gold rings that were marked two euros. I inched closer and realized the rings were identical to the one I had almost bought. The guy *was* a scammer.

Argh. I stamped my foot on the sidewalk. Did Simon really have to be right? More importantly, did I have to be wrong?

I ordered the coffees and looked over at the group. It looked like Simon was telling a story, and the dimple in his cheek moved as he spoke and deepened when he smiled. I folded my arms across my chest and tapped my fingers. Damn that stupid smile... not only did it cause my stomach to do a flip, but it also kicked my conscience into overdrive.

Maybe I should just suck it up and say I was sorry. I sighed and returned to the group with the coffees in hand. As I handed them out, I spotted the guy with the ring. He was eyeing an elderly couple like a hawk. The couple had just climbed onto a pair of rented bicycles, and I watched him approach them with the ring in hand.

"No!" I cried. I hit Simon on the chest with the back of my hand. He was in the middle of taking a sip.

"What?" he sputtered. I pointed to the man and Simon followed my gaze. "You were right. We can't let him try to pull one over on that elderly couple. I'll be right back."

"*We'll* be right back," Simon said as he followed me over to the couple.

"Give me twenty euros," the beggar was saying.

"Leave them alone, man," Simon said.

I turned to the older couple. "The guy's a scammer. Did he ask if it belonged to you?" The woman nodded and held her hand to her chest, as if she were about to have a heart attack.

"Don't feel bad. He did it to us too. The ring is worthless," I said.

The beggar shoved the ring into his pocket. "*Baise toi*. Fuck you!" he exclaimed before he spat at my feet.

I don't know what shocked me more—the fact that he insulted me, or that his insult actually sounded glamorous in French.

Simon grabbed the guy by his collar and growled something in French. I didn't know what he said, but I could tell it wasn't very nice. The tips of Simon's ears had turned red, and a vein bulged from his neck.

My heart began to race, and I could actually taste the rise of vomit in my throat. The last thing I wanted was for Simon to get into a fight over a ring that had probably been mass-produced in China. I took him by the arm and dragged him away. The Frenchman brushed off his clothes and skulked away.

I turned to Simon with my mouth wide open. "Are you crazy? Thank you for defending me, but you could've gotten killed. What if he had a knife?"

He gave me a sideways look as he removed his hat. "C'mon. I could've fit that little twit in my back pocket. It's really not a big deal." The front of Simon's hair was matted down and I resisted the urge to rumple it.

"Well, it is to me. What did you say, anyway?"

"Spit at her one more time and so help me God, I'll kick your ass," Simon replied nonchalantly.

I formed fists with my hands and tapped my knuckles together. "I once got spit on by a Met fan at a Yankee game. Cooper simply grabbed my arm and said, 'Keep walking…don't look back.'"

Simon threw his hat back on and opened his mouth to say something, but then stopped himself.

"Go ahead. You can say it. I totally deserve it. You were right, and I'm sorry." I looked up at Simon and cringed.

"Sorry for what? Seeing the good in a person? I don't need to be right Lucy, and that wasn't what I was about to say. There are a lot of things you deserve. An I-told-you-so is definitely not one of them." Simon put his hat back on and looked at me.

I pursed my lips together and twirled the bottom of my hair. "Chivalrous and kind. Who knew?"

"Oh, there's quite a bit you don't know about me." Simon reached over and gave my arm a squeeze. He was definitely inching his way up the appeal-o-meter.

"Aunt Lu!" Tess called. "C'mon." The line had begun to move, and it was finally our turn to enter.

As we walked through the entrance to the cemetery under the city, I began to feel a little unsteady. Especially when I saw an oxygen tank encased in glass and labeled with all sorts of warning signs.

I took a deep breath, peered around the entrance, and noticed a digital number on the wall. "Look," I said, attempting to sound casual. "That must be the amount of people down there." The others were silent as they followed my gaze.

"One hundred and eighty three. Wow, that's a lot of people in a small space," Tess said.

"Actually, I think it's the amount of oxygen that's left," Mark replied with a straight face. "The number just went down as that guy entered." He pointed to a grossly overweight man.

I looked at Simon in horror and he gave me a reassuring pat.

"Not for persons with a nervous disposition," Tess read off the wall. "Oh, Aunt Lu. Maybe you should sit this one out."

"Are you an anxious person?" Mark asked. "You seem so chill."

"Ha!" Tess cried. "She's a nervous thinker."

Mark laughed.

"I'm so glad you're amusing yourselves at my expense," I muttered as we approached the ticketing window.

We descended the dark and narrow staircase and as we wound around and around, I became dizzier and dizzier. By the time we got to the bottom, a dark opening, I paused and placed a hand on Simon's shoulder to steady myself.

The air smelled like mold and dampness. Even in the dark, I saw tiny drops of water that glistened on the ceiling. Mark and Tess walked ahead.

Simon turned to me and placed his hands on my shoulders. "Are you okay? Thousands of people pass through here every day. There's nothing to worry about, I promise."

I looked up at him and nodded.

"Ready?" he said.

"Ready."

Out of the corner of my eye, I saw rows of stacked skulls and squeezed my eyes shut. I peered at Simon from under hooded lids and saw him approaching for a kiss. I closed my eyes again and felt his soft lips on mine.

He managed to take away the little breath I had left. My knees buckled, and I pressed up against him for support. The kiss we'd shared the night before had been soft and sweet. This one was completely different. Cooper definitely never had this much of an effect on me.

"Sorry," Simon whispered, several seconds later, when I pulled away. I felt as if there were thousands of eyes watching us. I reminded myself they were only skeletal sockets.

"You looked a bit woozy," he continued. "I thought a kiss would revive you, but then I realized that a slap or a shake is what usually does the trick."

"Oh, that did the trick all right. As did your attempt to get me alone in the dark." I smiled weakly and looked away at the limestone wall I wanted to bang my head against. Did the spirit of an old French lover cast a spell on me? My brain said one thing, but my body screamed another.

The mixed messages made my mind whirl, and I floated through the maze, viewing the skulls and neatly arranged piles upon piles of bones. I also peeked from the corner of my eye to get a sense of what Simon was thinking.

Several times, he and I paused to look at the signs, and I could feel his arm brush up against mine as I pretended to focus on what we read. I wasn't taking in a word. The only thing I was conscious of was Simon standing so close to me.

"Oh look; here's a quote in English," Simon said.

"Henry David Thoreau," I read aloud. "It doesn't matter how rich you are, how poor—"

"How much older you are than the man who is trying to woo you," Simon interrupted and nudged me.

A chuckle escaped me, and my mouth fell agape. "I don't think that's what it says," I replied, amused. The kid may have been relentless, but his confidence was rather intriguing.

"Maybe not, but I'm sure that's what it meant."

I rolled my eyes as he moved ahead to read another sign next to the exit. Was he really trying to woo me? I knew he'd been flirting with me, but to come out with such a bold statement made me a touch uptight and slightly euphoric at the same time.

Okay, more than slightly. But, hey, was there any harm in having a little fun? I deserved it. Life was short, as I had just witnessed in the underground cemetery. Maybe the universe was trying to send me a message. Live for today and stop worrying about tomorrow. The Catacombs may have been better than a shrink. Who knew? At that moment I was happy, and I was going to do whatever, or *whoever*, to stay that way.

My phone vibrated, indicating a new email. I reached for it immediately, needing an escape from the visions in my brain. When I realized the email was from Cooper, my blood chilled.

I looked at Simon. He appeared absorbed in the display, so I leaned against the doorway to read what Cooper had to say for himself. As I waited for the message to open, a tap on my arm caused me to jump.

"*Pardon.*" A young French man stood before me.

"I'm so sorry." I realized I had been blocking the entrance. I slid over to the left and felt something probing my back.

"Ouch," I muttered, rubbing the small of my back. I turned around to see what it was and was greeted by what must've been a pile of legs many centuries ago.

I inhaled a sharp breath and somehow jumped my way back into Simon's arms. His eyebrows flew up as he clutched my arms to keep me from falling. He tenderly kissed my cheek and pulled me in for a protective hug.

"Sorry," I mumbled.

When we pulled away, Simon offered me his hand, which I accepted gratefully. I clutched my phone tightly with my other hand. As much as I was dying to see what Cooper had written, I was really enjoying Simon's comfort. I stuffed the phone into my bag and allowed him to lead me through the exit and up the stairs to the street. When we got outside, I drew in a deep breath and leaned against the wall, after checking to be sure I wasn't blocking the door or any body parts.

"You made it," Simon said, holding out a fist.

"There's a first time for everything." I tapped his fist with one of my own. I wasn't even talking about the Catacombs. When had high fives become a thing of the past?

I felt my phone vibrating inside my bag and immediately a pit opened in my stomach. "Let's wait here for Mark and Tess."

"*Pardon, Mademoiselle?*" a man said.

I looked up at a man who was wearing gloves and had a trash bag in hand. "Yes?"

The maintenance man frowned.

"Er, *oui?*" I offered.

His expression softened. "You can't stand here. You are blocking the exit."

"What is it with me and exits today? I'm sorry, I was just waiting for my niece." I reached into my bag to retrieve my phone.

"You and your nephew can wait over there," he said, pointing to a bench.

I nodded politely and gave Simon a terse smile.

"Ouch," Simon whispered as we walked away.

Nephew. That sealed the deal. If there were any doubts, they were all buried in the Catacombs. I busied myself with my phone and saw I now had not one, but two missed calls, and they were both from Cooper. I could no longer wait to see what he had to say. I bee-lined over to the bench.

"Hey, slow down, Luce. What, do you have a ghost following you?" Simon called out as I ran ahead.

"Pretty much." I plunked myself down on the bench like a pile of bones.

I wasn't sure if it was Simon, Cooper, or the thousands of body parts we had just seen, but suddenly an overwhelming feeling of dizziness struck. I slumped down, rested my head against the back of the bench, and closed my eyes.

Simon stood behind me and placed his hands on my shoulders. I sat up straighter as he massaged a muscle that was quickly becoming a knot. "Are you okay, Luce?"

"Yeah, I just feel a little weird."

"I know. I do, too. It's not that big of a deal. The hat makes me look younger. I hear that all the time."

I tossed him a look over my shoulder. "Maybe I should try wearing a hat."

Simon laughed and leaned closer to me. "You're beautiful," he whispered.

His breath was warm on my neck and a shiver ran down my spine. I clasped my moist hands together and gave them a supportive squeeze as he continued to massage me.

"Thank you, but for once, it wasn't your age that made me feel weird. I just got an email from my ex, followed by two missed calls." I glanced at my phone and felt Simon's hands stiffen on my shoulders.

"Oh?" Simon walked around the bench to face me. "Cooper?"

I squinted my eyes to see Simon through the brightness of the hazy sky. "Yep, the one and only. First, he sent me flowers last night and now..."

"He did?" Simon said, with an edge to his voice.

I saw a glimpse of some emotion cross his face, but it became carefully blank again as he sat on the bench. "I thought you said he was history."

"I thought so too, but apparently ghosts never really go away, do they? It's kind of a long story." I waved my hand dismissively and reached for the guidebook Simon held in his hands.

He lifted it higher in the air. "Nope. I want to hear your story first."

"Oh, come on," I whined. "Actually, it's really not much of a story and is exactly what I just told you."

"Well, flowers, an email, phone calls ... It kind of sounds like a story about a man who is in hot pursuit of you. Is this out of nowhere?"

"Nowhere." I rolled my eyes as I turned my body to face him. "We haven't spoken since we broke up a few months ago."

"And you broke up because...?"

I leaned my arm on the back of the bench and rested my head in my hand. My chest tightened as I debated how much to tell him. Hell, I may as well practice my spiel. It wasn't like he was going to be a long-term contender in the dating game. No matter how much I happened to enjoy his company.

"Well, the long and short of it is that I waited too long to have kids."

I shifted my body and sat on my hands to keep them from shaking. I sneaked a peak at Simon, but he didn't seem to have much of a reaction. He just sat there and looked at me through narrowed eyes.

"What?" I felt paranoid and braced myself for his answer.

"I don't get this. You're a little over forty. How is that possible?"

I shrugged my shoulders. "Who knows? For whatever reason, my eggs have expired. My fiancée was pretty shocked too."

Tears welled in my eyes, and I pressed my lips together. I looked down at the ground, nervous to see if his reaction was going to change. I wasn't even sure why I cared, but suddenly I did.

"Hey." Simon touched my chin and gently tipped it up to meet his gaze. "Let me get this straight. This is why he broke up with you?"

I chewed my bottom lip and nodded.

"Unbelievable." Simon shook his head. "He doesn't realize what he had, Lucy. Maybe now he does but I really hope it's too late ... for you. I'm sorry, but that's unforgivable."

"Is it though? I changed what he thought he was getting out of life. Out of a wife."

"Lucy." Simon took a firm hold of my arms. "That doesn't change who he was marrying, who he would grow old with, who he would weather the storms with. The going gets tough, and he gets going? This is

126

the twenty-first century. There are other ways to have a family. Please," he muttered.

My heart melted, but I fought it tooth and nail. "Says the man who wants to adopt. Not everyone feels the way you do. You already know that's something you want to do."

"I also know whomever I fall in love with, I will stay in love with, through good times and bad. *Especially*, bad. I'm sorry, Lucy, but if you ask me, the guy did you a favor." Simon may have spoken in a gentle tone, but his words cut through me like a knife.

"I know it sounds that way." I sighed and absently twisted the non-existent ring on my finger. "But we have history, Simon. I loved him."

Simon nodded solemnly. "Are you going to call him back?"

"I don't know." I took a hair band from my wrist and pulled my hair into a ponytail. "Believe it or not, he really is a nice guy, despite the little details I've shared."

"Little details," Simon muttered and rolled his eyes. "I'm sorry, but what you just told me is not a little detail, so I need to hear more. What did he do for you?"

"What did he do for me..." I paused and considered. "Well, for starters, he treats me like a queen."

"As long as you look like one, right?"

I furrowed my eyebrows and stared at Simon.

"Didn't you say he prefers it when you're all dressed up?" I could detect a hint of impatience in Simon's voice.

"Well yeah, he's more on the formal side, but the plus to that is he always looks really put together."

"Go on." Simon compressed his lips into a line.

"Okay, he's funny. Not funny like you." I smiled. "But he does make me laugh."

"Is he ... successful?"

"Oh yes. Very. He's always been career driven, and he's settled and in a good place. In fact, he motivates me to work harder and stick to my goals. He was really good for me."

Simon's face wore no expression, whatsoever. I bet he made one hell of a Poker player.

"Is he fun? Not many people can pull off success and spontaneity."

I stumbled for a minute. "Well, we've definitely had some good times. He's not wild and crazy." I laughed. "I mean, he would never take weeks off to travel the way we all are. And if he ever did, it would have to be perfectly planned with reservations at the finest restaurants and hotels. He's a bit anal like that and his career always came first, but that's what makes him so successful."

"So, where did you fit in?" Simon prompted.

I closed my eyes and wished that I hadn't opened up to him. I should've just walked away and read the damn email from Cooper in peace. "That's not fair, Simon. This," I said, opening my eyes and waving my hand between the two of us, "is not reality."

"Ouch," Simon said with a wince. "It feels pretty real to me."

I shook my head quickly. "That didn't come out right. What I meant was, my life isn't spent waiting for summer camp to start."

I didn't need to see the hurt look that appeared on Simon's face before I immediately regretted my choice of words. My hand flew to the sides of my face and I let out an exasperated sigh. What was I doing? What was I trying to prove? And to whom?

"Look, I'm sorry. It's just … this situation is stressing me out. I know you mean well, but I don't need to defend him to you. You and I are in different phases of life, Simon. I was ready to settle down with a settled man. You couldn't possibly understand how I'm feeling."

"You're right. I apologize," Simon said quietly.

I closed my eyes again for a brief second. "I have to figure out what to do." I rose to my feet. "I'd like to read this email. I'm dying to know what he had to say that was suddenly so important."

Uneasy, I loosened the scarf around my neck. "I'm going to go back to the hotel and deal with this," I waved my phone in the air, "and freshen up for dinner. Can you just tell Tess I went on ahead?"

"Sure." Simon gave me a blank stare.

"What time did you guys want to meet later? Mark mentioned a sunset boat ride on the Seine?" I gathered my things and tossed my bag over my shoulder.

"Lucy," Simon said, looking up at me. "I think I'm going to pass on tonight. You need to deal with things that are far more important than a night out with me."

"Simon." I twisted my ponytail around my finger. "I want to go out with you tonight. Please," I said softly.

"Lucy, you just said…"

I held up my hand. "I know what I said. I've been sending mixed messages, and I'm sorry, but that's exactly how I feel. Mixed up," I cried.

"Well, let me make it easier for you," Simon said wearily. "Go sort out your head. I hate to say it, but I think you might be right." He looked down and made circles in the dirt with his sneaker. "You're out of my league," he mumbled.

My mouth fell open. "I never said that."

Simon looked at me with sad eyes. "You didn't have to."

Chapter Nine

```
The living freak me out more than the dead.
Facebook Status June 10 at 4:00pm

Lucy
Date: 6/10/14 at 3:01 PM
Subject: Hi

Dear Lucy,
    I hope you're having a good trip. Ever
since you called, you've been on my mind
non-stop. Did you get the flowers I sent? I
thought you would've called by now, so I
wanted to double check.
    Hope to hear from you.
    Love,
    Cooper
```

I suffered a state of confusion after Simon kicked me to the curb, but once I read Cooper's email, my brain reeled with something entirely different. How dare Cooper harass me on my vacation? Who did he think he was? And shame on me for allowing him to ruin my date. Probably even the whole rest of my day. Sorry wasn't good enough, and did he really think he could just say it with flowers?

With anger coursing through my veins, I backtracked my way to familiar territory, and by the time I returned to the Louvre grounds, I was able to take my first slow breath in an hour. I didn't know whether it was the memories of my visit with Simon or the calming nature of the gardens outside the Louvre, but something turned the X-rated language in my brain to plain old PG-13.

I found a seat at the Tuileries and opened the lunch I had bought from one of the cafeterias on the street. I scooped a forkful from the beet and mache salad that rested on my lap and dipped it into the cup of champagne dressing perched on my knee. I discovered the dressing tasted like truffle oil and poured the contents of the container all over the salad. The balancing act had not been an easy feat, considering that my knees had been knocking since I'd left Simon.

A group of American tourists congregated around me, nose deep in identifying the different flowers in the magnificent park. I tried to pay attention to the botany lesson, but was too distracted by their attempts to look French. There were a whole lot of berets and striped shirts going on.

Once I'd finished my lunch, I tossed the remnants in the trash and leaned against a tree to reread the email from Cooper. I slid down to the ground as I read the words that were almost committed to memory by then.

The bark stuck to my leggings, and when I separated myself from the tree, I discovered a tiny hole in the seat of my pants.

"Just what I needed, another a-hole," I muttered aloud as I began to type a response.

Dear Cooper, thank you for the flowers.

No. Too nice.

Cooper, the same flowers I planned to carry down the aisle? Really? Too late.

Was it though? The jury was still out on that one.

Dear Cooper...

Oh, f… this. Before I could change my mind, I pressed the numbers I had dialed thousands of times before on the phone.

Ring.

I swallowed and took a breath. Please don't pick up. *Ring.* Please let it go to voicemail. *Ring.* Oh, thank God.

Three rings down meant that I was probably safe. I cleared my throat and swallowed in anticipation of leaving a message.

"Hello?" Cooper said breathlessly.

I closed my eyes and clenched my fist. "Hi," I said coolly.

"I was hoping to hear from you."

The sound of his familiar voice brought tears to my eyes. I inhaled to steady my shallow breaths.

"Did you…?"

"Yes, I got your flowers. Thank you." Don't be a wuss. Make him work.

I cleared my throat and sat up straighter, feeling the bark scrape along my shoulder. "You were right, by the way." I winced and cast a sideways look at the long scratch. "Orchids do not withstand the humidity too well. Good thing we didn't make *that* mistake."

My forced chuckle, which sounded more like a horse being strangled, was met by an awkward silence.

"Um, Luce, I was really happy to hear from you. When you called the other night…"

The all familiar twisting in my stomach started, and I pulled my knees to my chest to make it stop. "Cooper, um, I was stoned. Calling you was not part of my plan that day."

I swallowed the hard lump that formed in my throat and wondered if he could hear the razzing sound as it dissipated. "It was a really emotional day for me. Had my wits been intact, I never would have called."

"Oh. Well, I'm glad that you did. How've you been? Where are you?"

"I'm doing great. I'm at the Louvre." I smirked to myself, knowing he and I had talked about going there together.

"Good for you. You've always wanted to go there. How is it? Did you see Mona?"

"Yeah. She was about the size of a postage stamp, but for a little lady, she attracted quite the crowd." I clenched my teeth. Why was I being so nice?

I cleared my throat and tried a different tactic—to say what was on my mind. "Cooper, do you really think I can just make small talk when the last thing you said to me was that you didn't want to marry me? What do you want from me?"

"Luce, I'm sorry. I know you probably hate me right about now. I just want to talk to you."

"About what? What can you possibly have to say? Where have you been for the past three months? I'm trying to move on with my life. If I wanted to pine away for you, I would've stayed in New York. Do you have some sort of a radar on me?"

"What do you mean?"

"Did you sense I was having a good time? Did you *feel* I was getting over you? Don't worry. I'm not there yet."

"I don't need any reminders of you. It'll be a long time until I stop thinking about you. Are you happy now? Yes Cooper, I still think about you. So please…" My voice broke and I rested my head against my knees. "No more flowers. No more emails."

"How about a visit?" he said in a quiet voice.

"What?" I snapped.

"Can I come see you?"

"See me? Where?"

"Paris. Or wherever you'll be this weekend."

Was he kidding? He would come all the way over here? Just to talk? I rapidly tugged on the grass to the rhythm of my heartbeat.

"Please, Luce. I can be there by Friday."

I chewed the bottom of my lip and tore off a piece of skin.

He began to talk faster. "We can meet for dinner, and if it goes well, I'll stay. If not, I'll never bother you again. Please, just give me one chance to talk to you."

Holy mother of God. He wasn't kidding. I rubbed my eyebrows back and forth, a weird nervous habit of mine. "Cooper, I don't think that's such a great idea. I'm vacationing with Tess, and I don't need her to see you skulking around."

"Luce, it's just one dinner. Please?"

One dinner. Tsk. One dinner could do a lot of damage. Look at what one dinner did last night. It led to a knee-buckling kiss and intense feelings for a younger man. Cooper's flowers pretty much ruined the high I had been riding. Who did he think he was, anyway?

"No, Cooper. I've come here to start my life over."

"I'm really, really sorry," he said in a low voice.

I tapped my toe against a root. "Oh wow. Finally. Wait; I'm assuming you're apologizing for breaking up with me on the day I discovered I couldn't have kids, right? Or are you just sorry for hunting me down on my trip? I'm supposed to be on my honeymoon, you know," I spat.

"I just thought that after you called, maybe you still cared."

"*Maybe* I still cared? Do you seriously think I can just shut my feelings off? Cooper, I have to go. I should never have called you the other night. Or today, for that matter."

"Lucy, wait. Please don't hang up. Please give me the chance to explain."

"Goodbye."

I hung up the phone and tossed it into my bag. An instant later, it began to ring.

"Yeeees?" I sang wearily.

"Aunt Lu? Are you ok? Simon told us you weren't feeling well, and you don't sound too hot either."

I was relieved to hear it was Tess and not Cooper, but dizziness washed over me, the aftermath of my emotional roller coaster ride. "Oh no, I'm fine," I answered with artificial gaiety. "Just tired. I felt a little claustrophobic in the Catacombs, but once I got more air, I felt better."

"You and Simon both."

"Oh?"

"Yeah. When we got out of the Catacombs, he seemed a little off. He said he was going to walk back and pick up a few souvenirs for his buddies. Can you believe it? A guy who shops for souvenirs? I think he's a keeper."

I leaned my head against the tree and looked up at the sky in despair. "I don't think he wants to be kept," I muttered under my breath.

"What's that?"

"Nothing."

"Aunt Lu, I have to ask you something and please be honest." Tess continued talking, oblivious to my emotional turmoil. "Would you mind if I went out alone with Mark tonight? He wants to have an official date and I kind of want to go."

"No, go ahead. I have work to do anyway."

"Are you sure?"

"Positive."

"Thank you!" she squealed. "What do you think of him, anyway?"

"Well, just last night I had said that I wasn't going to let you out of my sight. So, the fact that I am sending you off with my blessing should be an indication of just how much I like him. He seems great, Tess. Really." I smiled.

"He is. We just stopped for a glass of wine at this adorable little bistro. We sat outside at a table for two, chairs facing the street. Just like they do in the movies! We could even see the Eiffel Tower. It was so romantic." She sighed. "He even bought me a rose from a vendor on the street. The rose man didn't even ask him. Mark called him over."

"That's serious business, Tessie. You watch 'The Bachelor.'"

"That's what I thought, too! *And* the best part is that he and his girlfriend broke up. I noticed he was being overtly flirtatious all of a sudden, and now I know why. I guess last night after he and I parted ways, they had a heart-to-heart on the phone."

Tess paused and seemed to take a deep breath. I was about to say goodbye and wish her luck on her date when she suddenly continued. "Um, Aunt Lu, can I confess one more thing?"

"Sure, hon." What now? I loved my niece, but I was suddenly so exhausted I just wanted to get off the phone and get back to the hotel.

"I wasn't sure how to handle this with Jack. That was, before—"

"Yikes. I almost forgot about him," I interrupted with a cringe.

"You and me both. When we decided to take a break, without saying it in so many words, we both knew it was the softer version of breaking up. Kind of like a pre-break up, an easier way to end things without feeling the finality of our six and a half year relationship. Regardless, we promised to be honest with each other before anything happened with anyone else. I just logged onto Facebook to see what he was doing ... okay, truth be told, I was going to shoot him a message and take the easy way out."

"Tess!" I cried.

"I know, I know, I'm a wimp. But let me tell you, he's worse. Not only had Jack changed his relationship status to single, he also had been tagged in about a dozen photos, looking anything *but* single. You have to check out Facebook and Instagram. You'll see he's moved on pretty fast."

"What is with men these days? They're all cowards. Did that bother you?"

Tess hesitated before she answered. "No. I felt more relieved than anything. I guess in my mind it has been over for a while, but it's kind of sad to think this is like the end of an era, you know?"

"It *is* the end of an era. But now you're free to explore whatever this thing with Mark is."

"I know," Tess said happily. "I really like him."

"Good for you honey. I hope it works out the way you want it to."

I was happy for Tess, yet I couldn't help but envy her newly discovered carefree ways. Had I been a little more carefree, I wouldn't be sitting here all by myself.

"Well, wish me luck on my first official night as an unattached woman."

"Good luck, and you know the drill. Be careful." I wasn't too worried since I knew she was in good hands.

We ended the call, and I straightened my legs on the ground and exhaled. I was alone, once again, in the city of love. What a difference a day made.

I took out my notebook and inhaled the sweet scent of the yellow daffodils that surrounded me. My eyes swept around the Tuileries, first at the flowers and then the pairs of people scattered throughout. I wondered how many people got engaged here each year. It looked like a Mecca for people who were in love.

One, two, three, four ... I counted at least two dozen couples locked together, one way or another. Hands, arms, lips.... Paris really did bring out the romance in everyone.

I let out another wistful sigh and tapped my pen to my knee as I thought about some of the places I'd visited earlier that day. Then I began to write out one of the ideas for Janice that had been brewing in my mind.

The Best Places to Kiss in Paris
By Lucy Banks

It has been said that Paris is a kissing city and the romance of the City of Love is contagious. Pretty much anywhere is a good place to lock lips, but whether a sidewalk café, street corner, or park, don't forget that a kiss is not just a kiss. It is where everything begins or ends. The following hot spots will make that special moment even more unforgettable.

- Take it to the top. The Eiffel Tower will get your head in the clouds and provide a panoramic view of the city.
- The Pont des Arts was the backdrop for an epic scene in *Sex and the City*. Carrie and Big shared their fairytale moment on this pedestrian bridge that crosses the Seine River.
- Set on a hill, Montmarte offers breathtaking views of the city. This quaint village has starred in many movies, including *Amelie*, *An American in Paris*, and *Sabrina*.
- On top of the Arc de Triomphe is an open terrace, which overlooks the famous Champs-Élysées. For those who find shopping to be an aphrodisiac, this is a must-see.
- The Pont Marie is known to be the Bridge of Lovers. Legend has it that a kiss under the bridge will make any wish come true. Sail into the sunset on a riverboat cruise.
- Once the backyard of royalty, the Jardins des Tuileries is one of Paris's most visited gardens. Stroll arm in arm on your way to the Louvre or cozy up on the grass with a romantic picnic for two.
- My personal favorite is the Catacombs of Paris. An underground ossuary is not traditionally known for romance, but will send the message to live for the moment. There's nothing like your own mortality to make you take a chance on love.

Chapter Ten

Last mango in Paris.
Facebook Status June 10 at 7:00pm

On my way back to the hotel, I stumbled on a store that made its own soaps and bubble bath. It wasn't until Tess mentioned Simon and his souvenir shopping that I realized I had forgotten all about Morgan in my travels. She had sent me to Europe, so the least I could do was send a little Europe to her.

I chose an assortment of bath products and threw in an extra bottle of mango bubble bath for myself. I couldn't wait to get back to the room and run a bath. This was our last night in Paris and in a real hotel, so I wanted to soak up the luxury while I still had the chance.

Plus, I really needed to relax. It had taken a couple of hours to organize and write out my ideas, and my head pounded from too much thinking. It wasn't the writing that had gotten my brain in a twist; it was the two men tangled up in my thoughts.

The first thing I did when I got back to the room was run a bath. I took off my clothes, climbed into the deep tub and submerged my body in the warm water.

The bubbles rose to my shoulders. "Ahhh." I sighed. "Never underestimate the healing powers of a bath."

I closed my eyes and rested my head on an inflatable pillow that hung from the back of the tub. I knew I should apologize to Simon, but I wasn't sure what to say exactly. I stuck my head under the water and gripped the bottom of the tub to keep myself from floating. Maybe I should stop at his room with a bag of treats. I could bring salt for his wounds and a muzzle for my big fat mouth. I should also throw in a filter while I am at it since I never seem to say the right thing.

I came up for air and heard loud knocking at the door. I sat up with a start and reached for my glasses that I had thrown on the floor.

"I'm coming," I called out. It had to be Simon. Suddenly, I was a big fan of the pop-in visit.

After using the robe for a towel, I threw it on and tied the belt around my waist. My wet hair clung to my head as I ran to get the door, but shockingly I didn't even care what I looked like. Now was not the time to be vain. We were leaving in two days and this would probably be my last chance to make things right with Simon. *Carpe Diem.*

I took in a breath and smiled as I opened the door.

My heart sunk when I saw that it was Tess.

"Surprise," she said in a sarcastic tone.

I hate surprises.

"I am *so* upset," Tess whined, charging past me.

"You and me both," I muttered under my breath. "What happened?"

"You're not going to believe this. Mark is such a jerk!" Tess shook her fists and started to cry.

My hand flew to my chest and a sinking feeling washed over me. "What did he do to you?"

I ran over to Tess and looked her up and down. My mouth had gone dry, and I nervously licked my lips. "Did he force himself on you? I swear to God, I will kill him. I should've learned my lesson with Pierre." I clenched my fists and my nails pierced into my palms. "I should never have...."

"No, no! He didn't *do* anything to me. That would've meant that he actually showed up. He blew me off," Tess sniffed. She brushed her cheeks with the backs of her hands, leaving mascara streaks behind. "I sat at the bar for oh, forty-five freaking minutes."

"What?" I giggled with relief. "Tess, there has to be an explanation."

"Oh, there was." Tess's eyebrows were knit so close together they had practically become one.

"Okay." I walked over to the mini-bar and pulled out a bottle of water for Tess and a can of Diet Coke for myself. "Sit down," I ordered while I handed the bottle to Tess. "Now tell me what happened."

She reluctantly took a seat on her bed. "Well, I had been waiting so long I finally decided to text him. Get this one. All of a sudden, out of nowhere, he didn't feel well. Uh, was he planning to tell me?" Tess looked at me with wild eyes.

"Okay, calm down. It sounds like he caught some sort of bug. Maybe he was too sick to call or text right away? Then again…" I frowned and stroked my chin. "He could've still texted, even if he were hanging over the bowl. But you know men. They're such babies when they're sick."

Tess clasped her hands behind her back and simply stared at me.

I raised my shoulders. "It's true. Your father's the same way. Let's just hope we don't catch it. I once came down with something so bad that—"

"Aunt Lu, there was no bug," she said pointedly. "I left my key here and figured you were probably out, so I went to the front desk to get a new one. That's when I saw *her*." Tess's bottom lip trembled, and she pressed them together.

I froze with the can of soda mid-air. "Her? Who her?"

"His ex," she spat.

"Shut up!" I slammed the can down and some fizz spilled over the side onto the top of my laptop. "How do you know? Are you sure?" I pulled out the desk chair and sat down.

Tess framed her face with her hands and took a deep breath. "Positive. When I got to the front desk, there was a girl about my age already being helped. I heard her. She was all like 'I just flew in from Chicaaago, and I believe my boyfriend left a key for me. Mark Anderson?' Ugh." Tess groaned as she stuck out her tongue.

"This can't be," I said, shaking my head from side to side. "There has to be two Mark Andersons."

"Well, it seems there are. One is a charming phony, and the other happens to be a total dick. C'mon Aunt Lu. What are the odds that two women from Chicago know a Mark Anderson? I'm such a fool."

"No. *He's* the fool. Did you call him out on it?"

"No, but I texted him right back. I was like 'how about I bring you some soup or maybe we can watch a movie together?'"

"Good for you. Make him squirm." I nodded my approval.

"Well, I don't know how much squirming he did. He wrote back before I could even get to the elevator. He said he was going to lay low tonight. Oh! And tomorrow, too."

"Okay." I took a deep breath, thinking fast how to reassure my niece and get back at that slime ball for hurting her. "You need to let him know that you know what he's up to."

I may have sounded calm, yet I felt anything but as I jumped up from the desk and began to pace. "This is all my fault. Again. Had we stuck together you would never have gotten your heart broken."

"Oh, come on. I'm a big girl, Aunt Lu. He seemed great. So did his brother. They could be serial players for all we know."

"You're right. Maybe they are. How would we have known?" I stood still and pinched the bridge of my nose. A thought occurred to me. "Is he even aware tomorrow's our last full day in Paris?" I wondered if Simon was.

Tess nodded her head sadly.

"So you mean to tell me that after all the time you spent together, this is it? This is how he chooses to end it?"

"Oh," she said with a face. "He thinks we're meeting up in Rome this weekend. *Whatever*."

"He does?" I took a sip of soda to hide the smile that teased my lips. I let the soda bubble on my tongue before I swallowed the fizz.

"Yeah. It came up this morning. They planned on going to Italy so they figured they'd meet us in Rome before we leave to see Landon in Florence. I figured you wouldn't mind since you and Simon were looking pretty chummy."

I blushed and hid my face behind the can.

"So, that's how he left it. 'I will see you in Rome,'" she concluded. A lone tear rolled down Tess's cheek, and I got up to hand her a tissue.

"I really liked him, Aunt Lu." Tess paused to blow her nose. "He was different from most guys. I know we only spent a few days together, but I never felt that way before. I hope for your sake that Simon is different," she said with a sigh.

I rolled my eyes and made a frown. "That, whatever it was, is done too." I told Tess about the real reason I left the Catacombs. I happened to leave out the part where I called Cooper back. Minor omission.

"Aunt Lu, it sounds to me like Simon completely overreacted. We all have a past, and it's not your fault that yours is still a tiny piece of your present. Your break up just happened."

"I know," I agreed reluctantly. "I did send mixed messages though. Regardless, it never would have worked out. It's not as if I liked him the way you liked Mark."

I got a funny feeling in my stomach and wasn't sure why. I held it in tight and then slowly released the muscles. That move was supposed to be a tension buster, but today it did little to alleviate the strange sensation inside me. I reached my hand into the bag of chips that Simon had brought last night.

"I don't want to see him in Rome, Aunt Lu," Tess whined.

"No, no, no. I agree, totally."

"Thank you. You're okay with rerouting?"

I was momentarily taken aback. I had meant Tess should avoid Mark. I wasn't talking about a reroute, but it was my duty to protect my niece. I certainly didn't need for her to get mixed up with a boy like that.

"Of course," I said.

"Okay, so we'll stop in Munich like we planned, but then how about we go right to Landon in Florence? The only guy I want to hang out with right now is my brother," she sniffled. "Can we please get out of here in the morning? I would die if I saw them together, and since you don't seem to care about Simon..." Tess trailed off and looked at me with pleading eyes. The look on her face reminded me of the one she had worn the day she begged me to take the trip.

"Right," I said through gritted teeth, my stomach churning even more. Simon and I would never have worked out, so of course we should go straight to Florence. I put my hand on my middle and shifted on the bed in an attempt to get more comfortable. What was up with my stomach? Suddenly it was bubblier than the bath I'd left behind.

"Thank you, Aunt Lu." Tess crossed the room and gave me a kiss on the cheek. "We make a good team. To hell with cowardly men. First I discover Jack is dating through a Facebook status and then Mark disses me on text. Is there anyone out there who has enough balls to end something face-to-face?"

I thought about Cooper as I smiled back at my niece. He, at least, had the decency to look me in the eye when he broke my heart. Was I a coward for avoiding a face-to-face meeting with him? Or was I just protecting myself?

"I'm going to call my mom," Tess said as she opened the door to the balcony.

"Okay," I said absently.

Tess and I made a good team, but I knew we wouldn't be together until death did us part. What I needed was a real partner, the kind that would stay with me for life.

I picked up my phone and fell back onto my bed. After I'd reread the email from Cooper, I rolled onto my stomach and rested my chin in my hands. For a moment, I allowed my mind to drift down memory lane. Cooper and I really did have some pretty fabulous times together. Yes, he acted like a total jackass, but what if he really was the one for me? What if this break-up was just a speed bump in what was to become a very long road ahead of us? Would we laugh about this one day, like on our twenty-fifth wedding anniversary? Or our fiftieth?

How would I know? I probably wouldn't. Unless...

I jumped up and sat on my knees. Should I just let him come see me? If he wanted to spend eight hours on an airplane for a two hour dinner, then who was I to stop him?

I picked up my phone and began to type a reply back.

```
Cooper,
    I thought about your invitation. We will
be in Florence on Friday night, so if you
want to grab a bite, I'm game. Let's meet
at your hotel and keep it simple.
    -Lucy
```

Then I pressed my fingers into my aching stomach and positioned myself into a child's pose. My gut was trying to tell me something, and I wished it would just pipe down already. I sure was getting tired of the way my stomach, head, and heart worked in tandem. They were the three amigos from hell and always had each other's backs.

"What do you want?" I groaned. "Are you hungry? Mad that I may see Cooper? What are you trying to say? I've had it with mixed messages..." Before I could change my mind, I hit send.

Five minutes later, I received a reply back. I jumped to my knees and read Cooper's message.

```
Lucy,
     Thank you for putting the biggest smile
on my face. I've booked a room at the Four
Seasons Hotel Firenze and will meet you in
the lobby at 6pm on Friday. I promise you
won't regret this. Can't wait to see you.
Love,
Cooper
```

Filled with nothing but regret, I looked over at the balcony at Tess. She was pacing around with the phone to her ear, making sharp turns every ten feet, alternating between wild hand gestures and rapid twists of her hair.

I shook my head. I had forgotten all about her in my temporary insanity. How was I going to explain Cooper? It felt like an ulcer was forming in my stomach, and I fell into the fetal position, hugging my knees to my chest.

C'est la vie, bebe. C'est la vie.

Chapter Eleven

Hi ho, Hi ho, back to the dorms we go.
Facebook Status June 11 at 4:00pm

When we checked into the Munich hostel the next day, I actually had to take a long hard look at my watch. The time may have read two o'clock, yet the ambiance screamed midnight. Between the insanely loud Katy Perry music and the beer bottles scattered around, it looked like a cross between a fraternity party and a rave.

After our peaceful stay at the Parisian hotel, the raucous scene was a shock to my system. Where the last hotel had votive candleholders and hurricane vases scattered throughout, the Munich hostel seemed to favor ashtrays and the random left-behind pint glass. All the posh people had been replaced with sloshed people.

I was, however, quite pleased to discover that for once, I wasn't the oldest person in the crowd. The owners themselves were older Americans, and although they looked as if they belonged on the set of *Animal House*, the place itself wasn't actually that bad.

An antique looking glass chandelier hung from a stucco ceiling and shone light on dark wood moldings and exposed beams. The wood was so dark it almost looked black and formed a nice contrast against the cream color of a veined marble floor. There was a whole lot of old age charm, even though the ambiance gave it a new age feel.

Tess and I weren't really in a party mood, so after walking around the city for a bit, we called it an early night. The highlight of our evening was

145

when we received a box of marzipan in our room at turndown. It sweetened the fact that we had roommates, who happened to be out on the town.

So what if no one offered to turn down my sleep sack? I got to go to bed sacked out with a fistful of everyone else's candy.

* * * *

The next morning, my internal alarm clock screamed for me to get out of bed way too early. By the time evening came and we were en route to the notorious Hofbrauhaus, a beer hall in the Munich City Center, I was already on my fourth cup of coffee.

"I'm exhausted," I said to Tess, stifling a yawn. "I'm not so sure the Glockenspiel show was worth getting up for at the butt crack of dawn."

"Waste of time?" Tess said vaguely, slumping down in the backseat of the white Mercedes taxicab. She hadn't been herself since Mark stood her up at the bar, but I couldn't help wonder if perhaps she had come down with something. She'd still been incoherent when I left that morning, even though we'd already put in a full night's sleep. She'd ended up sleeping most of the day away.

"Was it a waste of time?" I repeated Tess's question as I tapped the empty coffee cup on my lips. "Well, I wouldn't go that far. It was definitely cool, for about the first five minutes, anyway. These little men marched out of the clock and danced in memory of the black plague and then jousting knights came out to kick a little ass."

I paused and slashed the air with an imaginary sword.

"I read it was some sort of reenactment from back in the day. It was cute, but after about ten minutes of annoying yodeling music, by the time the bird tweeted three times to signal the finale, I just wanted to stuff him back into his little house myself."

Tess had been looking out the window and turned to give me a distracted smile.

"I think the show is just another excuse to gather around and party. At half past noon, a band was in full swing, and the beers were flowing. By the way, I really think that beer is a basic part of nutrition in Munich."

Tess didn't respond, and I reached over and tugged the back of her smooth ponytail. "Hey, shouldn't you be smiling? This is supposed to be happy hour, right?" I gave her a playful nudge with my elbow.

She looked at me and put on a strained closed-mouth smile.

I cocked my head to the side and raised my eyebrows. "Are you kidding me? I can spot a real versus fake anything in an instant. Smiles included."

Tess looked down and fiddled with a string hanging from her purse.

I reached into my bag for my nail clippers. "It's not like you to be so doom and gloom. I thought that was my job."

I slid over and cut the loose string, which made Tess look up at me in surprise. "Yeah, that's right. I've become quite the savvy traveler," I said with pride.

The taxi came to a sudden stop. I looked out the window at the traditional Bavarian fixture that sat in front of us.

"Hofbrauhaus," the driver said over his shoulder.

"It looks like Germany in Epcot. Too bad we can't just walk next door to Italy," I said with a chuckle. I knew Tess was really looking forward to seeing Landon in Florence the next day.

I laughed at my own joke and handed the driver ten euros. When I stepped onto the street, I pulled my damp hair out of the ponytail I'd been wearing and shook it free.

"Did my air-dried pony do the trick? Do I look like one of those women in the hair commercials?" I batted my eyelashes as Tess came around the back of the car to join me.

"What did you say?" Tess glanced up from her phone with a distracted look on her face.

The door to the beer hall opened and I heard the sounds of Bavarian music and laughter until it closed shut again.

"Okay, that's it. We need to talk. You spent the entire day in our room. You haven't laughed at any of my jokes, and I'm sorry, but you always laugh at me." I sniffed. "Are you okay? Is it Mark?"

"Yeah," Tess said wistfully. "He called me like ten times today." She held up her phone and showed me the missed calls.

I stepped back in surprise. "Wow." That lucky girl. I wouldn't have minded a call from Simon.

I sucked in a breath and widened my eyes. *Simon?* Where did that come from? I thought I had moved on to Cooper, but then again, my own thoughts never ceased to amaze me. I wouldn't have wanted ten missed calls from Simon. Well, one might've been nice though. I wonder if he had thought about me at all. Would he have called if he had my number?

"I just don't know what to do. I shouldn't call him back, right?" Tess said.

"No," I said in a firm tone. "No way, no how, no, no." I pursed my lips together and winced as my teeth bit down on my lip.

"I knew you would say that," Tess said, as she pushed out her bottom lip. "See, what comes around, goes around. I practically yelled at you about Cooper, and you listened to my words of wisdom. I just wish I could follow my own advice."

Just thinking about the secret I'd kept from Tess made my stomach drop. I planned to see Cooper the next night and still didn't have an exit strategy for Tess. Suddenly, my stomach was swimming again.

Another string from Tess's purse had come unraveled and was clinging to her tank top. This time I just wrapped it around my finger and yanked it off.

"Stay strong. You know it's best to cut all strings," I scolded.

Tess gave me a funny look and I too, was surprised by the firm tone of my own voice. It was as if my own subconscious was giving *me* the lecture.

"C'mon." I took a hold of Tess's arm and gave it a pat. "Let's go drown our sorrows. I think we could both use a drink."

Tess's eyes widened and she nodded. "You can say that again. Let's do it, and while we're at it, let's get shitty."

I snickered as we headed to the entrance. "Your mother would be so proud of me. How about we just start with a drink?"

From the street to the door, I managed to not only berate myself about Cooper, but also question my chaperoning judgments. First, I got stoned with my niece in Amsterdam, and now I was her accomplice in Operation Get Shitty? I should never have allowed Tess to spend so much time alone with Mark.

I opened the door to the beer hall and was immediately slapped across the face with life. The smell of roasted meat and beer wafted through the air and gave me a jolt of energy.

The sounds of music, singing, laughter, and conversation filled the room and drowned out the noise in my head. Hundreds of people sat at long wooden tables. They held massive mugs of beers and swayed along to the beat of the Oompah band.

The wait staff was dressed in traditional Bavarian clothing. The women wore white blouses with a black dirndl and red aprons, while the men wore Lederhosen and white shirts. They raced around the room, balancing a dozen heavy steins at a time.

People were laughing, yelling, and singing in German. My senses came alive and my worries began to slip away.

"This is so cool!" Tess shouted over the music. Apparently, the vibe was contagious. "You want to sit?"

"Sure," I said, eyeing the big baskets of salty hot pretzels scattered around the tables.

"I can practically taste those." I pointed to a waitress who walked by with a tray full and swallowed the saliva forming in my mouth. "There's nothing like a little carbohydrate therapy."

"Aunt Lu," Tess's eyebrows were knit together, "I'm really sorry. I've been in my own world today. You don't seem quite like yourself either."

"Ha. Who the heck is that? Honey, I don't even know who my real self is anymore."

Tess cringed and made a clicking sound with her tongue. "Do you miss—"

"No one," I finished her sentence, dismissing her words with a wave.

I was sorry I had opened my big mouth. All I knew was that I needed to stuff in a pretzel, asap. I looked around for an empty table and froze when I saw a table of senior citizens gaping at us.

"Hey, is it me or are those old men checking us out?"

Tess followed my gaze to the table of men. There were about seven of them, and they were all motioning for us to join them. "I think the beer went to their heads," she said.

"No kidding. They look like smitten little dwarves who just found Snow White and her sister."

"Well, in that case, you can be Snow White. It looks like Happy is on his way." Tess nodded towards one of the old men heading towards us. Like the rest of his senior posse, he was short, chubby, and grinning from ear to ear.

"Hello ladies." He tipped his hat and smiled.

I was pleasantly surprised to hear an American accent. "Hi there," I replied.

"This is totally innocent, and I can promise you we are not dirty old men. Well, most of us, anyway," he said with a wink.

Tess and I looked at each other and shared a smile.

"You girls remind us of our granddaughters. Where are you from?"

"New York?" Tess answered.

"It sounds familiar," he answered while bobbing his head. He looked over at me and winked.

"We're your neighbors over in New Jersey. The German-American Club has taken the show on the road. Please, let us buy you a beer."

He pointed to the table where the rest of the group sat. They were all smiles as they sat on the edge of their seats, waiting for their fearless leader to return.

"You'll make us all look good, and at the very least, please don't make me look bad." He placed a hand on his chest. "Whadaya say? Just know that if you say no, I will never live this down back at the clubhouse."

Tess and I looked at one another. The expression on his face was so endearing that neither of us had the heart to turn him down. Tess gave me a subtle nod.

"Let's do it," I said. I linked arms with Happy dwarf who had already given his group the thumbs up sign. "I'm Lucy. This is Tess." I had to shout as he led us past the band to his table.

"And I'm drunk," he yelled back.

And that he was. I don't think he stopped talking from the moment we sat down. He and his friends showered us with so many compliments that I was actually starting to feel like I could be a contender in the Miss Germany contest. They were interested in everything I said, laughed at all my jokes, and complimented me into oblivion. I was like a queen holding court, and I ruled the kingdom with a beer stein.

After we had been there for about an hour, Tess announced she needed to use the ladies room. As she pushed her chair away from the table, I watched her remove her cell phone from inside her bag.

My eyes narrowed, and I pointed an unsteady finger to her phone. "Who are you calling?"

Tess wobbled as she stood up. "No one," she protested.

I nodded and turned my attention back to a man named Dan, for whom I was starting to have a real affinity. He was a dead ringer for Cooper's deceased German grandfather, and, while initially I had found it to be endearing, at that particular moment, it began to bother me.

I felt a lump in my throat, and a melancholy feeling washed over me. Over the past few months, I had been so Cooper-centric that I hadn't even thought about the baggage that came along with him. Now that we had crossed the border where there were oodles of German stuff to remind me of Cooper's family, I was suddenly aware that our breakup probably hadn't affected only me.

Not that I thought Cooper's family was weeping and mourning, but I realized we had all lost more than just a glamorous wedding day. And shame on me for not realizing that sooner.

Cooper's mother had left two messages after the breakup. Why hadn't I had the courage to return her calls? Chances were pretty high that Marjorie wasn't calling for the crock-pot she had given us. She was probably just trying to help, and I suddenly felt terrible that it had taken me so long to pull my head out of my ass. I made a mental note to reach out when I got back to the States.

All of a sudden, I longed for my past. Since the day before, I had been prompted by the embroidered pillows and cuckoo clocks that were the cornerstones of Cooper's grandmother's interior decorating. The blueberry pancakes I'd had for breakfast took me back to many lazy Sunday mornings at Cooper's apartment, and the weinerschnitzel I'd eaten for lunch tasted exactly like his mother's. I became completely nostalgic for the life I had shared with him.

Sitting there, even the little old men affected me. Dwarf Dan was the icing on the apple strudel. Add to that all the beer I had consumed, and I wasn't sure what was happening. It was as if I had gone from doing a hundred-twenty on the Autobahn to about ten miles per hour, and I struggled to pull the breaks on the waterworks.

"Did you?" Dan said, suddenly interrupting my train of thought.

I blinked at him. "Did I what?" I responded, completely bewildered, subtly dabbing my eyes while pretending to wipe beer foam from my upper lip.

"Did you hear the latest joke about Jane Smith who lives over on the next block?"

"No, what about her?" I forced a polite smile.

"She had triplets. Then two weeks later, she had twins."

"That's impossible." I dismissed it with a wave of my hand.

"One of the triplets got lost." Dan laughed so hard his shoulders shook. His red cheeks looked like shiny little apples.

The harder he laughed, the more I wanted to cry. Feeling like I was on the brink of a breakdown, I pretended I was laughing too.

I let my tears fall and wiped them away as if they were tears of laughter. Fake laughing while crying is pretty draining and borderline creepy. I think I even managed to freak Dan out. He anxiously excused himself to use the bathroom, and I closed my eyes, rubbed them hard, and reopened them to see the profile of a man in a Yankee hat.

Was that...? *No way.* My heart pounded in my chest and I swooned from dizziness. I closed my eyes again and reopened them. Oh my God. Oh. My. God. It was Simon.

I took a deep breath and looked down at the table. My body didn't know which end was up and anxiety kept me riveted to my seat. When in doubt, bottoms up. I chugged the entire liter of beer that sat in front of me. That was the third one in an hour.

One of the men who sat beside me leaned closer. I winced as he yelled in my ear. "Surely, I must be looking somewhat attractive to you by now?"

My ear buzzed from the loudness of his voice. I made a mental note to tell Tess the man we coined Dopey was actually rather slick.

"We're gettin' there," I winked while I rubbed my ear. "Can you excuse me for a sec?"

"Of course. You can't ignore the call of nature."

"You got that right." Nature was calling, and I was a dog in heat. I stood up and smoothed my tank top.

I made my way over to Simon. There were about a dozen guys standing with him, and they were in the midst of a toast. As I waited for them to clink glasses, I took several deep breaths to relax and wondered if they were friends of Simon's from back home. After the mug chug, I tapped him on the back and braced myself.

Simon turned around, and without even allowing him a nanosecond to see me, I kissed him square on the lips. After a small pause, he hungrily returned the gesture with wet, sloppy kisses that were nothing like I remembered. It felt like a stranger was kissing me. I pulled back and smiled at him.

All the blood drained from my face. Sweet Jesus, a stranger *was* kissing me.

An alarm went off in my head, and I quickly pulled away to face the pimply mess I'd just kissed. I inhaled sharply and sucked in some of his bad breath in the process. My hand flew to my mouth in horror. His friends roared with laughter. As the sounds around me became deafening, I could actually feel vomit rising in my throat.

"I … I…" I swallowed. "You're not Simon.

"And you're not a *girl*," not-so-Simon said with his lip curled. "You're like, old!"

"Excuse me?" I tasted bitter saliva in my mouth and swallowed hard. I looked down at his University of Wisconsin t-shirt.

"It's my twenty-first birthday," the guy slurred, glaring at me. "My buddies dared me to kiss a random girl tonight. I didn't expect her to be someone my mother's age."

Twenty-freaking-one. I shook my head in disbelief and rubbed my burning lips. "Well, I didn't expect you to be a child," I snorted. Or a he-she. I had noticed flabby breasts underneath his shirt.

"Dude, you landed a MILF," his friend said, slapping him on the back.

"I don't know about that," he sneered.

I felt my hands shaking with rage. "You're right. I'm not a mother and—"

Suddenly, the loudest belch known to man came roaring out of the dark depths of my soul. It was if an alien had escaped me in his entirety.

Then suddenly I felt something else escaping, and before I could move, vomit erupted and landed all over the feet of the birthday boy.

"What the fuck?" He stood frozen in a puddle of regurgitated food.

My tongue seemed to be attached to the roof of my mouth. With shaking fingers, I wiped the corners of my mouth and pried my mouth open. It definitely was not my finest moment. I did my best to recover.

"I'm sorry. Your breath was just so, *ugh*," I said with a shiver.

His face turned various shades of red as his friends roared with laughter around him.

"Happy birthday," I grumbled.

I spun on my heels and surveyed the room rapid-fire. I needed either an exit sign or a suicide bomber to come rolling in. I couldn't get out of there fast enough. I saw the exit and bee-lined towards the door. Keep walking, don't look back, keep walking, don't look back. I repeated the chant over and over until I busted my way outside.

I glanced over my shoulder, and once I knew that I was alone, I bent down to rest my hands on my knees. I felt like a marathon runner who had just crossed the finish line. My chest was tight, and I struggled to release the breath I'd been holding. I spit at the ground several times, hoping to rid myself from the taste of that nasty kid. I took a tissue out of my bag and licked it fast and furiously.

"Ack," I groaned while moving little pieces of tissue around my mouth with my tongue.

I saw a taxi idling across the street. The little red walking man was on the sign, but since there were no cars coming, I began to run. I was about one foot into a sprint when someone yanked me back onto the sidewalk.

Oh, sweet Jesus, I was being mugged. I'd read that crime was rising in Germany, but right outside a major tourist attraction? Please don't kill me. How will Tess ever find me? What if she thought I ditched her in a foreign country?

I snapped my head around to look at my assailant. I was momentarily taken aback when I stared into the beady eyes of a policeman. He was a big, burly guy with puffy cheeks and blond hair that curled around a very scary looking hat. He looked like an evil doll come to life. Still, the alternative was worse.

"Oh, thank God! You scared me," I cried.

He shouted something in German, and I cringed as I clasped my hands together. I looked around and all I saw was a teenager who was leaning against a nearby building, his ears stuffed with headphones.

"*Ich verstehe nicht?*" I ventured. I clenched my teeth and prayed I retained the three words I read earlier in my guidebook. They meant "I don't understand" and it was one of the few phrases I really did understand.

He narrowed his beady eyes and pulled a pad from his pocket. "Jaywalking is illegal. Do you understand that?" he announced in a heavy accent.

"Yes, sir." Something pounded inside my head as I nodded.

"You cross like this in America?"

"No. I don't feel well, and I am having…" I paused to swallow a sour taste that had reappeared in my throat. "A bad night." My eyes watered, and I blinked several times to stop the tears from falling.

"Well, do not do it again." He wagged one of his pudgy fingers and tucked the pad back into his pocket.

I knew if I opened my mouth to speak, the tears would flow faster than a beer on tap. I nodded again and made the hand signal for ok. I connected my thumb and forefinger into a circle and held the other fingers straight up.

"Really?" he said. His beady eyes bulged and his face reddened as he spoke. "I need to see your identification." He whipped out his pad again and clicked the pen open with rage.

I couldn't even imagine what I did to make him so upset. I hastily took out my passport and handed it to him. He snatched it from my hands and began to scribble wildly.

"Don't insult the *polizei*," he spat. He tore a ticket from his pad and waved it in front of my nose.

"I didn't." I accepted it reluctantly, and he strutted away, looking like a ten-pound bratwurst stuffed into a five-pound bag. I looked down at the ticket.

"What the … one hundred euros!" I cried aloud.

"You gave him the driver's salutation," said the teenager in a nonchalant tone, as he pulled his ear buds out of his ears and held his fingers up in the same sign I had made moments earlier.

"The ok sign?" I held my hands up in the air. "Why did that make him mad? I was agreeing with him and promising never to do it again."

"It means arsehole," the teen said smugly.

"Excuse me?"

"That's what you called him." The guy shrugged and put his headphones back on.

My mouth fell open, and I stood on the sidewalk completely dumbfounded. "Are you serious?"

He closed his eyes and began to play the air guitar. Dipshit.

Feeling like the biggest arsehole that ever lived, I crossed the street and got into the taxi.

The driver made a u-turn and pulled up next to the one-man band. He had apparently moved on to drums and shook his wrists in the air.

We locked eyes and when the light turned green I gave him a sweet smile and flashed the ok sign as we pulled away.

* * * *

"Stop," Tess hissed in a loud whisper from the top bunk. We were back at the hostel and one of our roommates, a Japanese student, had fallen asleep with a book on her chest. "You actually threw up?"

"Yep." I dried my hair and hung the towel off of the railing on her bed. I tossed my toiletries bag onto the bottom bunk. "So, that's why I left you. I hope you understand. I was totally—"

Tess held up a hand. "Say no more, Aunt Lu. I hope you ruined that loser's birthday."

"Let's just hope someone bought the guy a bra. He's the one who should have been ticketed for walking around with his big ol' man boobs."

"Zits and moobies? Wow. And you thought he was Simon? How exactly?" Tess picked up her pillow and covered her face.

I could see her shoulders shaking with laughter. I stepped onto my bed and reached up to take the ticket that sat on hers. I tapped Tess on the head with it and jumped down to the floor.

"I'm sorry," she giggled. "And I'm even sorrier about that." She made a face and pointed to the ticket. "I say rip it up. You've already paid the price."

"Wait, there's more. After I called you, I went straight to the showers. I needed to wash my sins down the drain. You know how I feel about communal showers—get wet and jet. Well, no one was there so I decided to take the time to catch up on all of my grooming."

"Okay..." Tess reached into her backpack hanging from a hook on the bed and pulled out a bag of M&M's. She tore it open and offered it to me.

I shook my head. "Well, I was enjoying my solitude so much, I guess I just got a little lost in thought. By the time I shut the water off, I saw I had over-shaved during my musings and I was no longer alone. There were three other women present, and all eyes were on me."

"I had gone into the shower already feeling like a dirty old woman. I seriously feel like I have been violated on so many levels."

"Ew," Tess cried. She folded over the bag of candy and stuffed it back into her bag. "How did you not notice them? What the heck were you thinking about?"

"Oh, I don't know," I said with a shrug. "I was just reflecting on who I was becoming on this short trip."

Tess raised an eyebrow and waited for me to elaborate.

"Well, I left New York feeling like a total loser, and now here I am, trying new things, chasing the illusion of Simon, of all people, in places I never dreamed I would ever be," I said. "Maybe I was wrong about myself and who I really was when I was with Cooper. I really don't think I should have—"

"Should have what?" Tess sat up straighter, and the top of her head grazed the ceiling.

Oh, I don't know. I really don't think I should have just walked away from Simon. I really don't think I should have invited Cooper to come. I really don't think I should have opened my big fat mouth to Tess ... something stopped me from confiding in my niece completely.

"I don't think I should have ... bared my accidental Brazilian bikini line tonight." I forced a chuckle and climbed into the bottom bed.

Tess's head appeared next to me as she hung upside down like a bat. "You know, you should write an article on that—trends for pubic hair all around the globe."

I wrinkled my nose. "No thanks. I'd rather not research that one. My evening may have inspired another article though. Gestures in different cultures."

"You know, I've been thinking, would you ever consider writing a book?"

"Me? Write a book?"

"Why not? You love to write and are so good at it."

"Tess, I appreciate the vote of confidence, but I'm a magazine writer. I don't have what it takes to write a book."

"You always sell yourself short," Tess said, shaking her head. "Just like you did when you were with Cooper." Her honey blonde hair looked like a curtain as it fell across her face.

"I think I'll just stick to magazine articles for now," I replied, ignoring her comment about Cooper. "Like the one I just mentioned. This way, at least I'll have someone to invoice for this ticket, to cover the cost of my alleged road rage," I scoffed. "I seriously should've told that fatty to go eat another schnitzel."

I placed my hands on the side of my head and massaged my temples. "Well, here's to new experiences. Strange kisses, peepshows... Who knows what Italy will bring."

Tess's eyes shone with excitement, and I heard her giggle as she tucked herself back into the bed above me.

I lay back and tapped the bottom of Tess's bed with my foot. "Hey, what's so funny up there?"

"Oh, nothing. You just make me laugh. Good night, Aunt Lu."

"Good night," I sang in a suspicious tone.

I was happy to see her in a better mood and wished I could say the same for myself. I didn't know what Italy would bring, but I sure knew who it would bring, and I was starting to feel anxious about seeing Cooper again.

Deciding that I would channel my anxiety into my next article for Janice, I rolled over to reach into my bag for my laptop.

~~Sex~~ Six Tips for the Single Girl in Europe
By Lucy Banks

One letter can make all the difference in the world or around the world. If someone in France warns you something is high vat, it may trim your travel budget, but it certainly won't make you thin. Six more things you need to know:

1.   Burberry isn't always the best choice in London. No matter how badly you want to break out your beloved plaid, don't do it.

2.   Berets aren't cool in France unless you want to look like an American.

3.   In France, high heel ankle boots with short shorts aren't just for hookers. If your boots were made for walking, pack 'em. Just don't try this at home. Style non-transferrable.

4.   If it's a simple cup of coffee that you want, café Americano is what you need to order. Europeans take coffee to a very dark place.

5.   Not all gestures are created equal. Steer clear of signing unless you do your homework first. Gesturing "okay" isn't always. In Germany, it's an insult, and in Greece it means homosexual. And in certain parts of Europe, "thumbs up" gets a serious "thumbs down".

6.   The same goes for words. Don't try to get fancy. *Kussen* means kiss in Dutch and vagina in Danish. If a guy tells you he wants your *kussen*, tell him to kiss your ass.

Chapter Twelve

Tess and I arrived in Florence at about one o'clock the next afternoon. From the moment we pulled into the Santa Maria Novella Station, a wave of excitement washed over me. Both sets of my grandparents had been born in Sicily, four hundred miles from where I stood. I was actually in the country of my family's origin! I belonged here.

We walked off the train, and I had goose bumps as I heard the beautiful sounds of Italian filling the air. The station was alive, as people greeted loved ones with cheerful salutations, tight embraces, and double kisses. The body language that surrounded us was almost louder than the kind that could be heard.

I wanted to shout, "I'm one of you!" but I couldn't. I didn't speak the language. It had always been on my list of things to do one day, and never before had I wanted to learn as badly as I did at that moment.

Tess and I walked past a pack of fellow Americans we easily identified as such because of their familiar accents. They were dressed in baggy shorts, faded t-shirts, and, like us, were laden down with heavy backpacks. As we maneuvered our way around them, I gave them a polite smile and wondered if we looked as out of place as they did amongst the well-dressed Italians.

I was just looking down at my sleeveless yellow and white gingham button-down when I heard a loud voice bellow in my ear.

"Ciao, signora. What are you doing, checking yourself out?"

I spun around and took a step back, stunned to see my handsome nephew standing in front of me.

"Landon," I exclaimed. I grabbed his cheeks and gave him a kiss on the side of his lips.

Tess, who had been walking one step ahead of me, stopped dead in her tracks and whipped her head around. "Landon!" she yelled. "What are you doing here? I thought you had a conference this morning."

Landon pulled Tess and I into in a tight embrace. "I do, but how often do I get the chance to welcome my only sister and favorite aunt to a foreign city? *Benvenuti.*"

Landon took my backpack and slung it effortlessly over his shoulder. He was just under six feet, and with his muscular build, my bag suddenly didn't look so big.

"Bless you," I smiled, rolling my tired shoulder. "When did my little nephew grow into such a gallant gentleman?" I reached up and pinched one of his cheeks that had turned pink.

"He may be chivalrous, but he is far from grown up. Trust me." Tess laughed.

"Aren't you sweet? I see your preschool buddies have rubbed off on you, sis."

"Ha-ha-ha," Tess replied.

Landon reached down and put a playful headlock on his sister, gently grinding his knuckles into her forehead.

After Tess wriggled free, she removed her backpack and thrust it under Landon's chin. "Just for that, you can carry mine too, wise ass."

I clasped my hands together and stretched my arms overhead. My load felt light without the heavy pack, but I also felt light in my heart. Landon was right. Being together in a foreign city was pretty extraordinary indeed.

I smiled to myself as Tess and Landon continued their sibling banter. It had been awhile since I'd seen them side by side, and I'd forgotten just how much they looked alike. Both were tall, thin, and had honey blond hair and green eyes. There was no denying they were siblings, and quite often, they'd even been mistaken for twins. The only difference was that

Landon had inherited his mother's darker complexion.

"So, how's the trip going? Aunt Lu, do you have flyer's remorse, travelling with this one?" Landon pointed his thumb at Tess.

"Are you kidding? I don't regret a mile. Do you?" I creased my eyebrows and waited for Tess to answer.

She slung an arm over my shoulder. "Not a one," she reassured. "This whole trip has been amazing. And quite ... interesting." She gave me a knowing look.

"Oh yeah," I said with wide eyes. Tess and I looked at each other and giggled.

"Sounds like you have a few stories to tell over drinks." Landon paused to look at his watch. "And speaking of drinks, I better get back to work."

"How is that, speaking of drinks?" Tess said with a face. "Are you at an AA meeting or an architect's conference?"

"The latter, unfortunately. Or should I say fortunately?" Landon wore a bemused expression and shook his head. "Regardless, the longer I sit in a windowless conference room, the more I want to drink. Learning about low energy architecture is seriously making *me* feel lethargic. Hopefully they'll still be serving lunch when I get back."

My stomach growled at the mere mention of lunch. I looked around the station.

"Tess, would you actually mind if we grabbed something to eat here?" I said.

"What?" Landon looked at me incredulously. "You did not come to *Firenze,"* he said with an affected accent, "to eat in a train station. It's too early for you to check in, so I'm going to take your bags to the pensione, but first, I will drop you off at the Central Market. I may have only been here a few days, but I've picked up a few tips from the locals."

"Lead the way," I ordered. Tess and I linked arms and followed Landon out of the station.

Ten minutes later, a taxi dropped us off in front of a rather plain looking building. Feeling skeptical, we said our goodbyes to Landon and went inside to search for a taste of Florence.

"Um, Aunt Lu?" Tess said when we stepped inside.

I paused for a moment to swallow. "Sorry. I have an excessively watering mouth."

I knew we wouldn't have to search hard to find something to eat. The room was covered from wall to wall with booth after booth of all sorts of Italian delicacies.

I drew in an exaggerated breath and inhaled the fresh aroma that came from a large cheese stall. The pungent smell of Parmesan wafted into my nose and had me suddenly craving a plate of homemade pasta.

"Um, my mouth is also watering, but I think it's a warning that I am about to throw up." Tess pulled on my arm and pointed her chin to the other side of the room.

I sucked in my breath and stood up straighter. "Ohhh." Without moving my head, I glanced at the neighboring stalls and saw all sorts of unrecognizable intestines hanging from the ceiling. "Don't think about it," I commanded.

I turned my attention back to the vistas of cheeses and steered her past the stalls of slaughtered animals. When we got to the end of the first floor, I made my way over to the various vinegars, olive oils, and produce. Chilled eggplant, porcini mushrooms, and buckets of dried fruits created a sweet scent in the air. The colors of the dried peaches, apples, bananas, and plums were visual eye candy.

After walking through the two-floor supermarket, Tess and I bought paninis with mozzarella cheese, which didn't even make it to the door. The cheese was fresh and warm and practically slid down our throats. A drizzle of olive oil on top had soaked into the thin bread and the combination left behind a pleasant artichoke aftertaste.

Florence was off to a delicious start.

We wandered around and caught glimpses of the city's most famous cathedral, Il Duomo, off in the not so far distance. We followed the distinctive Renaissance dome until we came face to face with the colorful marble façade of the Gothic cathedral. Stained glass windows depicted the saints, while bronzed doors lined with scenes from the life of the Madonna led to the vast interior.

Once inside, we paused to light a candle. As I bent my head in prayer, I couldn't help but sneak a peek at my watch.

Time flies when you're having fun, and my date with Cooper was getting closer. My throat tightened, and I inhaled slowly to steady my breathing.

While falling in love with the city, I had almost managed to forget about Cooper. Yet all of a sudden, I felt as if I were about to be executed in the piazza. I reminded myself it was just dinner with my ex. I didn't have to count down the hours to a beheading, and I certainly didn't need to waste valuable prayer time.

I clasped my hands together and squeezed my eyes shut, hoping to focus a little more on my spirituality, and a little less on my insanity. This was a new one for me, the first monumental decision I had made without initially bouncing it off my sister. How could I be sure I was doing the right thing? I stuffed another euro into the donation box and prayed someone would send me a sign—or at least help me blow off my family for dinner. I looked up at the stunning ceiling fresco and pleaded with the Lord.

I still wasn't sure how I was going to sneak away from Tess. I didn't want to tell her about dinner with Cooper, because I knew she would tell Morgan. I needed my secret guest to remain just that, for now.

I fretted all the way to the Ponte Vecchio and felt like I was just going through the motions as we snapped pictures of the medieval bridge across the Arno River. The bridge sat on top of three stone arches, and we took our time walking through the raised pedestrian passageway, which happened to be lined with little jewelry and goldsmith shops.

Tess browsed through the shops while I leaned over an opening that was midway across the bridge. From where I stood, I could see the colorful wooden shutters hanging from the bridge on either side of me. Each shop had their shutters open, probably to enjoy the glorious view of the river.

I watched a young couple fasten a lock on the bridge. Ah. I recalled reading about the legend of the Ponte Vecchio padlocks in one of the guidebooks. Apparently, so had many others before them. Several thousand locks had been fastened all over the bridge. The couple looked around and giggled. The man kissed the key and tossed it into the water.

Once they'd locked in their love and thrown away the key for eternity, the couple walked off arm in arm. I couldn't help but wonder if they really would be together forever. I slumped down and wrapped my arms around the railing.

I used to be such a romantic. What had happened to me? I clung to the bridge and almost wished that *I* were locked to it forever. If only. What had I been thinking when I accepted Cooper's invitation to talk? What could he possibly have to say?

A headache was coming on, and I massaged my temples when Tess joined me to snap pictures of the sun glistening on the Arno. She agreed we had seen enough when I suggested taking a break, so we walked back over the bridge and headed to the pensione.

It was a short walk, and I shielded my eyes from the setting sun to give the pensione a once over as we approached it.

"Only in Europe would affordable lodging be housed in a place fit for a king," I observed. Cornice molding lined the top of the building and looked like eyebrows over large semi-circular arched windows. "In New York, the only places that look like this are the multi-million-dollar apartments that line Central Park."

"Well, Landon did say that this place is quite popular with American travelers." Tess pulled open the front door and grimaced from its weight.

"Gee, I wonder why." I chuckled and pointed my chin to the left toward the common room where a flat screen TV hung front and center. An X-box console was positioned directly underneath and shared a shelf with dozens of game choices. There was a vintage looking Coca-Cola sign resting on a mini-fridge, and I was so thirsty from the walk back that I could actually taste the sodas that were lined up behind the glass door.

"It looks like the owners really do know the American way," I murmured as I headed toward the fridge to grab a soda.

"Either that or they got the memo that Landon was coming to town. He may have played the professional part this morning, but according to his email yesterday, he's already logged in an awful lot of hours playing X-box. I think he wishes he was at a video gaming convention instead of the boring architect's round-up."

"Well, I'm glad we're here. You did good, kid." I looked over at Tess, who beamed back at me.

"*Ciao*, may I help you?" called a woman from behind the front desk.

"*Ciao*. We would like to check in. My nephew already dropped off our bags." I looked at my watch and felt a sinking feeling in my stomach. I had only two hours until it was time to meet Cooper.

"Ah, *si*." She traced her finger down a list of paper. "McNally and Banks?" she said.

I nodded and smiled.

"*Un momento, por favore*," the woman said holding a finger in the air. She disappeared into a room behind the desk, and I leaned against it.

The scent of cappuccino wafted through the room, and I wondered if having a cup after finishing my soda would be caffeine overload.

My eyes darted around the room and went from the soft, fluffy couches to the colored photographs of Florence hanging on the walls. All sorts of books, travel guides, candles, and ceramic dishes filled the shelves.

"This place has an interestingly cluttered vibe," I murmured. "Pottery Barn meets Grandma Maria's living room."

Tess stifled a laugh as the woman reappeared. She wrung her hands and leaned on the other side of the desk.

"All of our doubles seem to be *occupate. Mi dispiace.* Is a double bed okay? Or we could give you two rooms, one for each of you?" The creases on her forehead deepened as she waited for our reply.

"I guess a double bed is fine," I replied. However, after the words left my mouth, I wondered how true they really were. I needed to pull out all my best beauty tricks. Quickly. How was I going to get ready for my date in front of Tess? Would I be able to pull this off?

"Well, what do you think?" I raised an eyebrow and looked at Tess. She seemed to be lost in thought and shifted uneasily.

"I don't know, what do you think?"

I exhaled impatiently. I held my palms up and shrugged. "Your call. Do you want to go solo or not?"

"Sure."

"Oh." I was momentarily taken aback.

Tell me what you really think. That answer rolled off her tongue a little too quickly. Was she getting sick of me? Hell, I was getting sick of me. I got what I wanted. Let it go. This must be the sign I had prayed for at the church.

"Okay," I said to the woman. "We'll take two rooms."

She gave us the keys to our rooms, and we headed up the creaky stairs and stepped onto a carpeted landing.

"Three oh one, three oh two, three oh three... Looks like this is my stop." I put the key in the door and turned the knob. Tess followed me into the room.

"This is..." I paused and gave the room a quick once over. "Kind of plain, no? The owners must've put so much effort into making the common area an inviting place that they gave up on the bedrooms."

The room was Spartan in style with just a simple bed and wooden wardrobe. A tiny table by the bed held a lamp and under the window was a ladder-back chair, like one used at a desk. There were no extras. Not even a cushion on the chair. Outside I heard bells from one of the churches, and I wondered briefly if the monastic look was all the rage in Florence.

I placed my backpack on the bed and looked down at my watch for the hundredth time. Tess was prowling around the room looking at the non-decorations, her backpack waiting in the open door. She looked over at me and suddenly I couldn't take it anymore. I hated secrets.

"Tess?" I took a breath to steady my nerves.

"Yeah?" Tess walked over to the window. She opened up the shutters and threw her hands in the air towards the street. "Ahhhhhh!" she sang loudly in a soprano voice. She immediately turned around and sat on the window ledge, facing me. "I'm sorry." Her cheeks had turned slightly pink, and she looked down at her feet.

"Sorry for what? Being happy? That's hardly a crime. I noticed how euphoric you seemed today. It must be nice for you and Landon to be together." I smiled and looked at my niece. "Your mom may be a wackadoo, but she did some job raising a tight knit family." I nodded in approval.

Tess raised an eyebrow. "Oh … yeah, it was so nice to see him, but I'm just happy in general." Tess smiled and lowered her head.

I couldn't help but wonder why. It had only been a few days since Mark had crushed her hard. "What are you up to?" I narrowed my eyes.

"Nothing." Tess giggled and quickly shifted her gaze back to the street. "This room just makes me happy. It reminds me of one of those Italian movies with the shutters, where the guy calls up to the girl from the street," she said wistfully.

I walked over to the window and looked down at the cobblestone street. There was a man selling chestnuts out of a pushcart and a woman sitting on a bucket, peeling fruit. The air smelled like lemons.

"It kind of does." I drew in another breath, hoping to bring the conversation to this evening's plans. "I wonder what it's like at night."

"It's so nice to have a good view," Tess said, completely ignoring me. I momentarily closed my eyes in despair. "God, the last view we enjoyed was when you officially met Simon. Doesn't that feel like a lifetime ago?" She looked at me searchingly.

I felt like I had been kicked in the stomach. "Tess," I said, clasping my hands together. "I really don't want to think about Simon. Not today."

"Sorry." Tess cringed. "The other night you chased his twin, so naturally, I assumed he was on your mind."

"Okay, that pimply post-teen was far from Simon's twin. Let's be honest. Simon was hot. His olive skin, his hair..." I sighed. "That's water under the Ponte Vecchio."

"It doesn't have to be. Aunt Lu, you could've told me how into him you were. We didn't have to flee Paris on my account."

"I wasn't into him," I suddenly snapped. "Can you please stop talking about Simon? I'm not that desperate that I need to date a kid from the middle of nowhere."

Tess gave me a sideways look. "Thirty-two isn't a kid, and Chicago is hardly in the middle—"

"Tess," I said sternly. "Enough. I barely know the guy." From the corner of my eye, I saw her look away.

"I'm going to see if Landon's back," she said, jumping down from her seat at the window. "I'd like to go out with him for a quiet bite and catch up. Do you mind?"

"No, of course not." I felt taken aback for a moment that her plans didn't include me. But my insecurities were immediately replaced with a gust of relief. Now I didn't have to explain myself.

"Enjoy," I said with a smile.

She left, and I perched myself in the same seat where she had looked so happy, only minutes before. I looked up at the sky and clasped my hands together in prayer. Please God, don't let meeting Cooper be a mistake. Please do not let this sick feeling in my gut be another sign.

I made my own sign, one of the cross, and slid from the window to the floor. When my feet hit the ground, I walked over to my backpack and pulled out the one date night option I had packed, a short black dress.

After I tried it on, I decided it was too sexy, and since I really didn't want to send that message, I opted for my uniform as of late: black leggings and a long, loose-fitting tank. It was far from sexy, but it was a dressier version of what I wore on my night out with Simon, and he'd seemed to find that look perfect. Anyway, I didn't really have many other clean options from which to choose.

I hopped in the shower, blew out my hair, and after an hour of the up-do, down-do game, I settled on leaving it loose. When I was finished, I looked in the mirror and gazed into my eyes.

"Hi Cooper!" I exclaimed, while flipping my hair. My eyes bulged and my phony grin made me look somewhat manic. No way. That wouldn't be a good hello.

But I did notice a stray hair on my chin during the hair flipping process. There's a reason for dress rehearsals, I thought as I yanked it out with tweezers. I applied a light pink gloss to my lips and cleared my throat.

"Hi," I said quietly and flashed myself a tight-lipped demure grin.

I shook my head in disgust. We weren't meeting at a funeral. Take three.

"Hello there, *dick*," I said coolly. The tone of my voice seemed to evoke a tiny feeling of confidence. My eyes lit up as I giggled in the mirror. "What's that, jackass? Oh, I'm doing great, thank you."

I smiled at myself like a proud mother. "Yeah, baby. *You're* in the driver's seat. You're a strong, beautiful woman." I puckered my lips and blew myself a kiss.

I started to walk out of the bathroom before I popped my head back in to take one last look at myself.

I narrowed an eye and pointed a finger at the mirror. "Listen bitch, do *not* cave," I commanded.

I retreated the finger that shook back at me and formed a tight fist. With fingernails digging into my very sweaty palm, I grabbed my purse and headed out the door.

Chapter Thirteen

Never judge a person on the first date.
Facebook Status June 12 at 9:30pm

Cooper's hotel was only a few blocks away, so I chose to walk, hoping my nerves would calm down in the process. Unfortunately, they only ended up making me walk faster. I got to the Four Seasons in record time and wasn't surprised to see that it was, of course, top notch. If there's a luxury hotel in any city, leave it to Cooper to find it.

I arrived ten minutes early, so I set myself up in a comfy chair to deep breathe and hopefully calm down. I found it hard to meditate since the people-watching was so spectacular, but at least the view gave me something other than Cooper to think about. I focused on a small group of businessmen who must've been in a meeting. They were yelling at a laptop in Italian, hands flying passionately in the air.

A pack of beautiful women clipped past them in their stiletto heels and even in the midst of the men's debate, all of them turned their heads to check out the women. The men actually had a moment of silence, smiled knowingly at one another, and then resumed their wild gesturing.

I smoothed my hair, feeling suddenly frumpy and self-conscious as I thought about the Italians and their candid appreciation for beauty. Why hadn't I interrupted their meeting when I walked by moments earlier?

The ding of the elevator doors opening interrupted my soliloquy of insecurity. My heartbeat quickened, and a feeling of relief washed over me when I realized Cooper wasn't in it. A couple walked off, hand in hand, lost in a world of their own. Even their shiny gold wedding bands screamed happiness. I watched them disappear through the hotel doors and I wanted to run out after them.

What was I doing? My anxiety was in overdrive, and I suddenly wished I could just shit-can the whole thing. What if he saw me and decided I wasn't worth the trek? Would he regret coming? What would we talk about? Where would we even begin? I sat on the edge of an antique chair and firmly planted my hands on my knees to keep them from knocking.

Ding.

The elevator doors opened again and this time it was the one and only Cooper. I clenched my body as I watched him step out of the elevator. Good God, was he handsome.

I had almost forgotten just how good-looking he was and immediately found myself comparing him to Simon. Both men were attractive in completely different ways. Simon had rugged good looks with tousled brown hair, a strong, muscular build, and a casual style of dress. Cooper had more of an elegant look—short, dark hair with a classic side part, a long and lean build, and a penchant for tailored clothing. Cooper was always impeccably groomed and tonight was no exception. He wore white pants, a navy sports coat, brown loafers, and looked as if he had lived in Florence his entire life.

Our eyes met, and as his pace quickened toward me, my heart skipped a beat. I realized with relief, I had made the right decision to meet him here. Boy, had I missed him. As he smiled at me, I had to swallow the lump in my throat. Be strong, I scolded myself. Show a little self-respect.

"Hi, Luce," Cooper said when he stopped in front of me. His smile looked a little shaky as he looked at me expectantly. I was relieved to see I wasn't the only nervous one.

"Hi, Cooper." I smiled.

I went to kiss him on the cheek, but at the same time he went in for a hug. While I switched to give him a hug, he switched to give me a kiss. It wasn't the smoothest start, and after the volley of awkward movements, he basically ended up with a handful of my hair in his mouth.

I laughed as we pulled away awkwardly. "Sorry."

Beads of sweat shone on Cooper's forehead. He quickly pulled a tissue from his jacket pocket and wiped his forehead. "Is it warm in here, or is it just me?"

I looked around at the other guests who wore sweaters over their summer dresses. "I think it's just you. I feel pretty good." A trickle of sweat slid down my stomach and I prayed fast and furiously that I wasn't spotting through my tank top.

"Luce," Cooper said, taking in a shallow breath, "you look great. You're even more beautiful than I remembered. Single life suits you." He gave me a tight grin.

I wanted to say, 'Oh yes… I love being a lost soul roaming Europe with my young niece with no job, man, or prospects at home. It's so great to be free.' Instead, I smiled modestly.

"Oh, I don't know about that." I waved my hand dismissively. "Besides, I've gained so much weight since I've seen you. I kind of fell out of my gym routine."

Oh, shut the hell up, Lucy. I immediately wished I could pull the self-deprecating words back into my mouth. Why did I feel the need to make excuses for the way I looked? I'd been making such strides on learning to take a compliment before I was ripped away from therapy to take this stupid trip. It had been so great until now.

"Well, if you had," Cooper said looking me up and down, "I would never know." He also didn't seem to know that *he* was the reason I fell out of my gym routine in the first place.

"I do have a question." Cooper looked at me with an eyebrow raised. "I had said we would meet here because I assumed you would want to avoid your hotel."

"I do. That's why we're here," I said pointedly.

"But … are you planning to change?" Cooper sounded bewildered. "I thought we would go somewhere a little more…"

I looked down at my outfit as he gestured at my clothes, clearly disapproving. Unbidden, the memory of the night Simon made me feel like the most beautiful girl in Paris while I wore a similar outfit popped into my mind. My face flushed, and I drew a breath.

"Cooper, the plan was to talk. Not go to a five-star restaurant."

"Oh, right. I know. I just thought… Never mind. You look great. Would you excuse me for a moment?"

I nodded and Cooper turned around and walked over to the concierge.

I saw them speaking for a few minutes as the man behind the desk jotted some things down. He looked over at me, smiled, and then picked up the phone.

"What was that all about?" I said when Cooper returned.

"Nothing. I just wanted to cancel the reservation I'd made. Let's do Florence your way."

A flash of anger bolted through my gut. At home, Cooper had always chosen where we ate and with whom. I realized the number of times I had chosen our destination were few. I wasn't sure if it was his general nature to want to control the situation, if he just assumed I liked the same kind of places he did, or if he thought he was being kind by showing me the right places to go.

Usually I didn't mind. After all, what girl didn't love shopping in designer stores on Fifth Avenue, dining at top spots, or getting her nails done behind the red doors of Elizabeth Arden instead of at the corner sweatshop.

Suddenly, though, I wasn't quite so amused by his need to be the one in charge. Maybe I liked eating with my hands in a tiny Ethiopian hole in the wall in the East Village—a place Cooper refused to go even after I read a flattering review in *The Village Voice*—or casually dine in a Florentine *trattoria* on a side street. I had always played along, stifling my wants just to please him. Well, not anymore. He lost that right.

"Do Florence my way? And what way is that?" I said dryly, while Cooper laughed aloud.

"Casual, no pressure. Whatever way you want it to be."

I gave him a sideways look. "Are you talking about Florence or us?"

Cooper narrowed an eye. "That's subjective, my pretty lady," he said with a smile. "Shall we?" He offered me a bent arm.

I went to take his arm and stopped myself, folding my own arms awkwardly across my chest. "Sure."

"You're not going to make this easy for me, are you?"

"Not a chance." I smiled sweetly and started to walk. "I passed a quaint little restaurant right outside the hotel. Want to try it? I looked it up in Fodor's," I said, waving my phone, "and it seems to be a favorite amongst the locals."

"Sure." Cooper walked alongside me. "I'm all yours. Just lead the way."

"So, how are things at work?" I said, as the doorman opened the door and we stepped onto the sidewalk.

Cooper rolled his eyes. "Stressful, as usual." He groaned reaching for his phone. "I think you just put a hex on me. As soon as you said the magic word, it began to vibrate."

"What word? Work?"

"See?" Cooper cried, holding the buzzing phone in his hand. "You did it again."

"Oh, for God's sake, just turn it off."

"Ah, yes, have you heard the news, ladies and gentleman?" Cooper pretended to speak into the phone. "The market will now cease all financial affairs while Cooper Thomas is on vacation."

"Very funny," I said, shooting him a look. "Now tell me something, how did our dinner turn into a vacation?"

"I had the days," he said with a shrug. "Don't worry. I'm not expecting anything from you." He stuffed the phone back into his pocket.

"Good, and thank you for putting your phone away. That damn thing buzzing on the dresser all night long is one thing I do not miss at all," I said holding up a finger.

"Are you saying there are some things you do miss?" Cooper wore a hopeful look as he awaited my response. I didn't give him the courtesy of one.

"Here we are," I announced with a flourish instead, stopping in front of the restaurant, relieved I didn't have to answer Cooper's question.

"Luce," Cooper said gently, placing his hands on my shoulders. "Can you please answer the question? Do you miss me at all?"

My eyes welled with tears. "That's not fair, Cooper." I looked away and my gaze fell on a gaggle of teenage students who stood in school uniforms, armed with books and Grande cups of Starbucks. For a brief moment, I wondered how Starbucks could be so popular in the motherland of espresso.

"Hey," Cooper said, tipping my chin to look up at him. "I'm sorry. I would do *anything* to take back all the hurt I caused you." He had become teary-eyed as well.

"What are you doing here, Coop?" I looked into his watery eyes searchingly. "I was trying to forget about you. I was trying to find myself," I cried, with my hand on my chest. "Why are you doing this? Why *now*?"

"I messed up, Luce," Cooper replied, throwing his hands in the air. "I took the best thing that ever happened to me and threw it all away."

He ran his hands through his hair, clasped them behind his head, and looked up at the sky in despair. "And you want to know the worst part of it all?" he said, snapping his head back down. "I failed you. I let you down. I abandoned you at a time when you needed me by your side."

Cooper looked down at the street and hung his head. He looked like a pathetic little kid, and part of me wanted to hug him tight and tell him that all was forgiven. The other part, the angry part with the broken heart, just wanted to slap the shit out of him.

I groaned inwardly, feeling like a fish being reeled in slowly. This was the side of Cooper that always got me. I had always melted when I saw glimpses of that vulnerable child, the one who always tried so hard to get his mother's approval. The one who blamed himself for his father's abandonment so many years ago. The one who was so afraid of being hurt again, that he had built a wall around him.

"But why now?" I said again. "Why all of a sudden?"

He looked up at me and stared into my eyes. "This isn't all of a sudden, Luce. I came to my senses about a month after we broke up, but I was afraid."

He saw my incredulous look. He was admitting to being afraid? Macho-in-charge Cooper?

He nodded. "Yes. I was afraid to admit I was wrong. I swallowed my pride and thought I would get over you. Of course I didn't," he said. "Then that night when you called…"

The reminder of my juvenile behavior in Amsterdam caused me to cringe. "I was really banged up."

"I figured you were. You made some pretty bold statements." Cooper frowned and looked at me gravely.

I squeezed my eyes shut and massaged my temples. "Was it that bad?" I peered at him with only one eye open. "Please don't tell me I was mean," I whispered.

"No, not at all. It made me feel great that you gave all my jewelry away. To the homeless woman on the corner of Fifth Avenue and Fifty-Seventh Street, no less."

I bit my lip. "I told you that?"

"Oh yes. That was one of the nicer things to which you confessed."

I waved both hands in front of him. "No more, please. I am so sorry." I placed a hand over my chest and looked him in the eyes.

"*You're* sorry?" Cooper sounded shocked. "I deserved every word of it. Just so you know, you could've said a hell of a lot worse and I would still be standing here."

We stood awkwardly in front of the restaurant. "Do you want to…?" I motioned to the window.

"Sure. 'Mama Lucia'," he read from the sign. "Based on the name alone, I like it already." Cooper opened the door with a flourish. "After you, *bella*."

I walked past him, and if there were such a thing as a gastronomical orgasm, then I had one upon entry. The smell was amazing. We walked by a circular table with platters of fresh antipasto. A massive bowl of basil was the centerpiece, and I had to curl my fingers to resist the urge to grab a sprig. I drew in a deep breath of what was probably responsible for the overpowering scent that filled the air.

I looked around at the locals and listened to their lively language bounce around the room. The tables were covered with red and white checked table clothes, vases made of old bottles, and more breadcrumbs than I could imagine.

I expected Mama Lucia herself to come waddling out of the kitchen. Again, it seemed I had stepped onto a movie set, and like the day I spent with Simon in the French countryside, I couldn't keep my heart from beating a little faster. I felt higher than I had gotten in Amsterdam and took in a slow breath, enjoying the scent of fresh basil and truffles that wafted through the room.

"This is…" I began.

"Not ideal, right?" Cooper said, pulling a face.

I blinked at him. "I was going to say, perfect." I felt somewhat deflated and frowned. "What don't you like about it?"

"I don't know." Cooper's lip curled as he looked around. "I know it's your namesake," he laughed, "but it's kind of loud, no? And wouldn't you rather go somewhere a little … nicer? I can call the concierge and try to get our reservation back. Or maybe he can suggest something a bit fancier, with casual dress?"

"A-ha. I was wondering when the old Cooper would be making an appearance," I said, rolling my eyes. While I had warmed up to Cooper's vulnerable side, his snobby side was far harder to overlook.

"What does that mean?"

"Well, I know how you like things to be just so."

"*Buona sera*," the maitre d' came over.

I looked at Cooper uneasily.

"*Buona sera*," Cooper's voice boomed. "Table for two, please."

I looked at Copper and raised my eyebrows in question. He gave me a subtle nod and smile.

"Right this way," the maitre d' said. On our walk through the restaurant, we passed the biggest wheel of Parmesan cheese I'd ever seen in my life. I turned around to point it out to Cooper, but he was already tapping away on his phone.

"Here we are," the maitre d' said, holding out the chair for me.

"*Grazie*." I grinned at him.

"Can I see the wine list?" Cooper requested.

"*No signore*. No list," he replied, wagging his finger. "Just a nice house red. *Delizioso*," he said, kissing his fingers. "All you can drink."

A waitress appeared behind him with two glasses and a jug of wine. She put a loaf of bread on the table and poured a bowl of olive oil. "*Buon appetito.*"

"*Scuzi?*" Cooper said. "Can we have menus?"

The woman laughed. "There are no menus, *Signore*. We bring lots of food, and you eat lots of food," she replied. I gave her a warm smile, which she returned, before walking away.

"I hate places like this," Cooper muttered. "You get stuck drinking shitty wine and food you didn't even want."

I took a sip of the wine and smacked my lips. "It's actually pretty good. Try it."

Cooper made a face and raised his glass to his lips.

"Wait," I cried. "Thank you for coming to see me," I said, holding my glass in the air.

"What do they say in Italian? Salude?" Cooper clinked my glass.

"*Salute*." I took another sip. The maitre d' walked hurriedly past our table.

"Sal-*ick*," Cooper groaned loudly, making a face as he wiped his lips. The maitre d' stopped dead in his tracks and whipped his head around.

"You no like?" he said defensively.

"No. Not at all, man. Sorry," Cooper grimaced. "You must have something else?"

"We have a house white, but it's no good. This is the best," he said with pride, hands flying in the air.

"It's perfect," I said. "We love it."

"But the *signore*," he said, with a look of pain. "He—"

"My friend isn't a wine drinker," I interrupted. I leaned closer towards him and gave him a knowing look. "He doesn't know shit from Shinola."

The maitre d' broke out in peals of laughter. "*Bella*, I don't know what that means, but I like," he said, cupping my shoulder. "*Grazie, bella, grazie*." He smiled and walked away.

"Very kind of you to have a laugh at my expense, *friend*," Cooper said as he played around on his BlackBerry.

"You," I pointed my finger at him, "were very rude. As is this," I reached across the table to tap his phone. "Maybe you can save the blackberry for dessert?"

"Sorry." Cooper slipped the phone into his breast pocket. "So... How's the trip been?"

"Fabulous." I looked at Cooper earnestly. I was eager to welcome a more neutral topic of conversation. "I can't believe how much I've enjoyed seeing this part of the world. Oh, and in case you're wondering, I didn't even need Valium for the flight." I sat up taller and shimmied in my seat.

Cooper gave me a half-smile and a puzzled look.

"Remember?" I looked at him pointedly. "I hate flying?"

"Oh. Right, right." He nodded quickly and took a sip of wine, wincing as he swallowed. "How could I have forgotten?"

I threw my palms up and wondered that very same thing.

"Come to think of it..." He unbuttoned the cuff on his sleeve to look at his arm. "I think I still have nail marks from that first flight we took together."

I rested my chin on my hand and grinned from behind my knuckles. There was a pregnant pause as we stared at each other in an awkward silence. I tucked my hair behind an ear and looked down at the table.

Cooper cleared his throat and swallowed. "So, how's Tess been? Are you enjoying your travel companion?"

"Actually, I really am."

"You sound surprised by that."

"Well, when we started out, I wasn't sure what my role was. We both had different agendas, and I tried to expose her to the things that ..." I paused, placing a hand on my chest, "I deemed important." I lifted the linen napkin that covered the bread and extracted a warm chunk of freshly baked bread.

"And now?" Cooper said, eyeing my bread.

"Well, I think we have a nice pace. I've loosened the reins as 'chaperone extraordinaire' and gave her the space she deserves. She even went on a date." Cooper reached for a piece of bread. "She got lost one day in Paris and met a nice guy who waited tables at a café and ..."

He froze with his hand mid-air. "You're kidding me, right?

"No," I said furrowing my eyebrows. "Why would I be kidding?"

"I just can't believe you would let your niece, for whom you happen to be responsible, go out on a date with a ... a waiter." Cooper wrinkled his nose and made a face.

Just when I thought I had broken out of the chaperone box, he put me one foot back in it. "She's twenty-four," I said sternly. A sudden tightness formed in my chest, and I picked up my glass of water. "And what's wrong with being a waiter?"

Cooper raised an eyebrow. "I'm going to use the bathroom." He pushed his chair back and stood up.

Good idea. I nodded politely.

"Do you think there's even soap in there?" he said in a condescending tone.

"Of course there's soap. What's your problem with this place?"

"Nothing." Cooper sat back down and leaned across the table. "It's just so ... low brow," he whispered.

"No, Cooper, it's not low brow. It's local. Big difference. And isn't it great to experience a real Florentine restaurant?"

I looked over and realized he wasn't buying any of my enthusiasm. I shook my head, disappointed.

"We should've just stayed at your hotel. Done dinner the Four Seasons way: elegant, upscale, and totally predictable." I dipped a piece of bread in the oil and popped it into my mouth.

"I would've loved that. However, one of us was a little underdressed." A sarcastic grin crossed his face.

The man was very lucky I had food in my mouth. It gave me enough time to think before I lashed out at him. I held my fist to my mouth, swallowed, and drew in a deep breath.

"Cooper," I said calmly, "would you like to leave?" As I waited for his answer, I played with the side of the olive oil bowl.

The tiny hand-painted black olives on the bowl morphed into question marks as all sorts of things ran through my head. How could I have loved this man? Had he always been this way? And why hadn't it bothered me in the past? Was I that blinded by his success and so flattered to have been 'the chosen one' that nothing else mattered? Or had he just gotten worse since we split? Did a little attention from a down-to-earth man open my eyes? Perhaps I was the one who changed and now saw him through fresh eyes. Whatever the reason, one thing was certain: he could be so goddamned obnoxious.

"So? Are we leaving or not?" I said again.

"Actually," he said tightly, "that would be too late." I followed his gaze to the platters of food heading towards us.

"Well," I sighed. "I guess it's settled. Can you please make the best of this?"

"Sorry," Cooper smiled sheepishly. "I think I'm just nervous. Of course I can make the best of this."

Shockingly, for the next two hours, he actually did. Not that it was all that difficult. The food was outrageously outrageous. We had an unbelievable Gorgonzola gnocchi and probably the best steak I've ever eaten in my entire life.

We kept the conversation light by sticking to neutral topics like friends and family. By the time we walked out of the restaurant, I knew we needed to talk. Really talk.

Cooper and I turned to face each other at the same time and practically stepped on one another's toes in the process. We were so close I actually felt the tip of my nose brush up against his shirt. He placed his hands on my shoulders, and I was aware of his gaze, but couldn't bring myself to look up and meet his eyes. The familiar scent of his clean skin and woodsy cologne gave me pangs of nostalgia and sadness.

We stood silent, enveloped by the sounds of traffic on the street. Cars honked and scooters whizzed by while I watched Cooper's shirt move to the rhythm of his breath. I closed my eyes and inhaled deeply. Despite all the food we'd just consumed, his breath managed to smell like mint. I, on the other hand, could still taste the remnants of garlic in my own mouth. I pursed my lips and took a step back.

Cooper released his grasp on my shoulders and reached a hand down to take a hold of one of mine. The intimacy of his touch caused my lip to tremble. I pressed my fingers on my lips and looked away.

"I know," he whispered, giving my hand a squeeze. "I feel it too."

I looked into his eyes and felt my nose sting with emotion. "Cooper, it's been fun chatting with you, but I can't just pretend like nothing ever happened."

"Luce, don't you think I know that? I've been dreading this moment all day." Cooper closed his eyes and rubbed his forehead. "I even rehearsed what I was going to say to you in the mirror."

I fought an overwhelming desire to laugh out loud.

"It's true," he said with a shrug. "But in all seriousness, Luce, no rehearsal in the world could have prepared me for the way I feel right now. Seeing you makes me feel like shit. Absolute shit." He grimaced and clenched his fists. "How could I have hurt you so badly?"

I gritted my teeth and shrugged my shoulders. "Only you can answer that one, Cooper. Why didn't you call me sooner? If I hadn't called you..."

"I'm so glad you did," he exclaimed. "Honestly, I didn't think you'd ever want to hear from me again," he said with a groan. "Everyone in your world must hate me." Cooper shook his head sadly.

I wasn't sure how to respond to that one. They did.

"Would you even consider taking me back, knowing people may think you're crazy for giving me a second chance?"

"Cooper, have you met me? People's reactions are the least of my concerns." I shook my head with exasperation. "I don't give a crap what people have to say, and yet that's all you seem to care about. You've mentioned people's opinions of you, people's opinions of me taking you back ... to hell with people."

Cooper forced his hands into his pockets and let his shoulders slouch as he stared back at me.

"Wasn't that the reason you broke up with me in the first place?" I continued. "Because God forbid, *people* thought we were flawed by our, no I'm sorry, *my* inability to produce a child? Who are these people that have so much power over you? You're like a one-man government, ruled by the goddamned people."

I sighed loudly and rolled my eyes. My head was pounding, but I just had to know one thing immediately. "Tell me something, Cooper. Has anything changed?" I said pointedly. "Do you still feel the way you did about the baby thing?" My eyes filled with tears.

"No," he exclaimed. "Not at all. I was stupid. I think I just freaked out and that was my pathetic way of dealing with the news. Now that I know what life without you is like, it really doesn't matter to me as much. I don't need to have a baby."

"No, you aren't getting it." My heart hammered in my chest as I placed a firm grip on his arm. "I *do* need to have a baby."

He had a bewildered look in his eyes. "But you can't. We can't."

"Oh, I will," I said with conviction. "And if you're lucky enough to be a part of it, will you be able to face your 'people'," I said making air-quotes, "with the shocking news that we aren't perfect? That your wife is flawed?"

Cooper drew in a sharp breath and pressed his lips together. I clasped my shaking hands while I waited for his response.

He tilted my chin up and locked my eyes with his. "Listen to me Luce. You're far from flawed. And I am so sorry I made you feel otherwise."

I nodded and chewed the bottom of my trembling lip.

"Really. You're absolutely right. There are plenty of other ways to have a family. I'm sorry it took me so long to understand and accept that."

My body trembled with excitement. Maybe he had changed.

"Right," I said. "I know it's not ideal, but think of all the kids out there who need a mom and dad."

A flicker of surprise crossed Cooper's face. "True. But like I said, there are other ways to have a family. A guy at the office just had twins through a surrogate mother and egg donor. It was all his sperm, though, his flesh and blood." He paused, and looked at me with an eyebrow raised. "You'd really want to adopt?"

My eyes practically bulged out of my head. "Why not?" I demanded.

"I don't know. Do you really think you can ever love someone else's baby?"

"Someone else's baby? It would be *our* baby. I'd be the mother. You'd be the father."

"Right. That's what I meant," he said, rather unconvincingly.

"So now you're asking if I could ever love our baby? Okay..." I trailed off and curled my lip. "Cooper, I will love whatever God gives me."

Cooper ran his hands through his hair and exhaled. "Did you ever consider becoming a lawyer? You're really making me nervous." He used the back of his hand to wipe the beads of sweat that had formed on his upper lip. "I hear what you're saying, and I'm sorry."

I folded my arms across my chest and tapped my fingers.

He reached over and gave my shoulder a squeeze. "Relax. We're just talking. It's not like we're anywhere close to that point."

"You can say that again, but to even get close to that point, I really need to know how you feel about this." Hysteria began rising within me.

"When we get back together..." Cooper began.

"*If* we get back together," I corrected.

Cooper placed a finger on my lips to silence me. "If you forgive me, and if we get back together, then yes, we will adopt as many kids as you like," he said in a gentle voice. "You have my word."

I know I'd told myself to play it cool, but that didn't seem to stop the corners of my mouth from turning up. What happened to the bitch in the mirror?

Cooper pulled me close and I stiffened as we came together. He planted a kiss on the top of my head, and I let my body relax as I leaned against him.

Jeannine Henvey

The vehicles on the street slowed down next to us when they stopped for the red light. The hum of the idling cars seemed to match the pace of my brain waves. It was almost as if my running thoughts had also ceased with the traffic. At least for now, for the first time in months, my racing mind was finally at a standstill.

Chapter Fourteen

```
Woo is me!
Facebook Status June 13 at 10:00am
```

The next morning, I woke up way too early, feeling excessively thirsty from dinner the night before. I reached for the bottle of Pellegrino that sat on my nightstand and thought about Cooper as I chugged the lukewarm water.

The last thing he had said when we parted ways was that he promised to leave his BlackBerry back in the room if we met up first thing in the morning. I wasn't sure what amazed me more, his pledge to leave work behind or that I really looked forward to seeing him again so soon.

My mind flashed back to the quick peck he'd given my cheek when we said good night in his hotel's lobby after our after-dinner walk. Despite the embrace we'd shared on the street, the kiss wasn't any different than the way he kissed his grandmother, and I was also surprised that I didn't want it any other way. Was I scared? Taking it slow? Playing hard to get?

Whatever the reason, now that the initial date was out of the way, I could honestly say I was thrilled he had come to apologize. I was also especially glad we'd gone somewhere authentic to Florence, even if he had spoiled the beginning with his attitude. That restaurant had reminded me of the little French place where I'd gone with Simon. The only difference was that Simon was in his element, whereas Cooper was like a fancy fish out of sparkling water.

I couldn't help but wonder if perhaps that was what threw him off his initial game. Cooper had always been a wooer and I hadn't really allowed him to woo me. I was sure the buzzing sounds coming from his jacket pocket didn't help either. Maybe there was something to be said for a non-career man. Simon had certainly never interrupted any of our time together to take a call.

I fell back asleep mid-ponder and woke to the buzzing sound of my own phone. When I saw it was a text message from Tess, I sat up with a start. In the past twelve or so hours of my own self-absorption, I had managed to forget all about her. Thankfully, before I could even decide how to disappear for the day, she beat me to it by saying she had gone to the convention center with Landon. There was a fashion show scheduled to take place in that same building, and she wanted to check it out.

Once again, I was relieved she'd done my dirty work for me, but I promised myself I would come clean after that day's sightseeing date with Cooper. With Tess already gone, I invited Cooper to pick me up at the penisone.

He texted me upon his arrival, and when I came down the stairs, he had an arm resting on a bookcase and was looking around the pensione with a critical eye. I saw a frown cross his face, although his expression was carefully blank when he turned and saw me. He straightened, glanced at his sleeve, and brushed his hand along his arm.

"What? Are you afraid you'll get bitten by the pensione bugs?" I wiggled my fingers as I walked towards him.

"Something like that." Cooper grinned and grabbed my hand, trying to joke about his obvious displeasure with my choice of lodging. I decided to ignore his superiority complex and squeezed his hand slightly.

"One would think you grew up with a silver spoon in your mouth," I teased. I could already tell we were both feeling way more comfortable than we had felt at the start of the previous night's date.

"What do you mean?" The creases around his eyes deepened as he smiled.

"Well, you're eyeing the place as if you're a Rockefeller in the slums. This is a warm and wonderful pensione, and I don't want to hear one word out of you, mister." I pulled my hand away and wagged a finger at him. "You can check your materialism at the door."

"That sucks. If I have to check my materialism at the door, then I guess that means I can't give you the gifts I brought," he said with a frown.

"Gifts?" A smile teased the corners of my mouth.

Cooper laughed and motioned to the couch where a dozen shopping bags sat. From where I stood, I could make out the logos from all my favorite designers.

"Ooh," I said with anticipation.

"Go ahead. They're all yours."

I walked over to the couch and ripped open the Jimmy Choo bag first. In it, the most exquisite pair of strappy sandals stood tall. When I caressed the muted gold, the leather felt like butter in my hand. I looked at the bottom of the shoe. "Size nine. You remembered?"

"I may have had a little help from some friends," Cooper admitted.

"What friends? Tess?" My mouth went dry, and I anxiously licked my lips. Had Cooper told Tess he was here? Had I been busted?

"No, not Tess," he assured me.

I sighed with relief, but for a moment I wished Cooper had done my dirty work for me. Of course, it couldn't have been Tess. Cooper didn't have her email or cell phone number.

"The secret shopper was actually the concierge at my hotel. When I cancelled our reservation last night, I asked him to send out for a few things. He worked with Barneys in New York to pull some sizes from their database. I know you like to shop there at home."

"Why did you do all this," I asked in disbelief.

"I figured you might be sick of your backpacking attire. You're not exactly the type to rough it, Luce."

I feigned a hurt expression. "I think I've done just fine, thank you very much."

"You have, but I know the girl I love is hiding somewhere under those plain Jane clothes of yours."

He pointed a finger at me, and I looked down at the little black dress I'd decided it was finally time to wear. It was more of a sexy Susie than a plain Jane. I was momentarily taken aback. Did he not like the no-frills version of myself?

I opened my mouth to speak, but then quickly closed it as he continued. "Besides, I wanted to take the time to do something to make you feel special."

While it was very kind of him to think of me, placing an order with the concierge was hardly taking the time to do something special for me. But he was just trying to treat me like a lady. Be thankful and shut up. I didn't want to sound like a spoiled brat.

"Thank you for thinking of me, Cooper." I smiled and placed a hand on my chest. "Shall I open another?" I couldn't help but feel excited as I eyed the rest of the bags.

"Why don't you go upstairs? Take your time going through it all and pick something out for today."

"Now? Don't you want to go out?"

Cooper's phone rang. He looked at me with a conflicted expression.

"Ah … I get it." My jaw clenched as I nodded. "I thought you said..."

"I know," he said, cringing. "I did. Honey…" He looked at his phone and groaned. "It's a call from Asia. After I left you last night, I dealt with such a mess back in New York," he said waving his phone. "I can't be out of reach all day. I just have to take this quickly."

"Please?" He sandwiched his phone within folded hands and gave me a pleading look. "Then I promise I'll be all yours. I just need thirty minutes … tops."

Twenty-seven minutes later, I stood naked in my room. Cooper had bought me so many cute things that I actually had too many choices. Finally, I settled on a pair of fitted white pants, a strapless Pucci bandeau top, and of course, the Jimmy Choos. Whatever issues I had about Cooper's gesture had been hung up in the closet with my new rags. I had to admit, it was nice to be in dry-clean-only clothing again. And if I said so myself, damn I looked good.

I blew myself a kiss in the mirror and left the room to unveil the sophisticated version of myself to the Florentine world. My legs felt a bit wobbly as I went down the stairs. I clutched the banister for support, but the heels weren't really the issue.

Cooper sat on the couch thumbing through pamphlets for local attractions, and I suddenly felt nervous to be under his scrutiny. I was in dire need of moral support.

I cleared my throat and bit the inside of my cheek. He looked up at me and let out a slow whistle.

"What do you think," I asked, but the look on his face said it all. I exhaled the breath I had been holding and unclenched my fists.

"What I think," Cooper said, walking towards me, "is you may have to come back to my hotel later."

My face flushed, and I opened my mouth, but couldn't come up with a snappy retort.

"Don't worry," Cooper said, "not for that. Although … don't get me wrong," he said, putting his arm around me, "that would be nice too. It wasn't easy being a perfect gentleman last night. What I meant to say was that I don't think you fit in here anymore."

"Yeah, yeah, yeah. Nice save." I pressed my lips together and smiled. I had to admit I was enjoying his flattery. "If you think this is bad, which it's not, then you would've needed a tetanus shot just to step foot in our London abode."

Cooper shuddered and made a face. "Well, it's a good thing I'm here now. You know, to take your trip up a notch. I did a little research," he said, waving the pamphlets, "and happen to have a chauffeur waiting outside to whisk us away." Cooper paused and a slow smile spread across his face as my mouth opened wide with surprise.

I giggled and clasped my hands together. "Really?"

"Of course." He nonchalantly shrugged his shoulders. "So, I'm thinking a day trip to Chianti. We can see the vineyards. What do you think?"

"Hmmm...." I flashed back to the experience I had in the French vineyard and laughed. "Well, my last experience in a vineyard was in France where I volunteered for the day. I…"

"Wait, what? Volunteered to do what?" The look on his face reminded me that while he was big on donating money, Cooper had never been one to donate his time.

"Pick grapes," I shrugged. "Nothing too tough."

"Was it fun?"

"Yes, it was fun, you lazy ass." I felt a pang of nostalgia mixed with regret and immediately pushed it away.

"I don't know why I can't seem to picture you up on a high ladder." Cooper looked at me and chuckled.

"Well, maybe you can picture this one then. Me, falling off the high

189

ladder," I said.

"C'mon." Cooper guffawed.

"Yep. I twisted my ankle so badly I could barely walk."

"So, what did you do?"

"I'd met a guy," I said dismissively, "who was very sweet. He happened to be staying at our hotel and actually took pretty good care of me." I smiled at the memory of Simon and quickly shook my head to erase the barrage of thoughts that accompanied it.

"Okay, I'm officially jealous," Cooper announced. "Am I allowed to say that?"

"Yes, you can say that." I laughed. "And, I'm officially happy to hear that." I looked in his eyes and saw that his expression had grown rather solemn.

"Luce..." he began, "I don't think I will ever be able to let a day go by without another apology."

I held my hand up in protest. "Not now. This is fun day."

"Okay, okay." He sighed.

"I mean, I can't get all crazy emotional in this beautiful get up." I waved my hand over my body.

"Ooh, I think you can." Cooper winked.

I bit my lip, but a shiver of excitement hit as Cooper walked me to the Mercedes parked outside. I relaxed in the backseat as I waited for him to finish his last phone call for the day.

* * * *

The driver took us on a winding road through the magnificent Tuscan landscape, and I felt as if we had driven straight into a postcard. Rows of pencil thin cypresses alternated with patches of vines and olive trees and stood like a proud committee welcoming us to the Chianti region.

The windows were open, and I had to hold my hair back as fresh gusts of air whipped through the car. We cascaded though the rolling hills and fields and followed the road towards a moss-covered castle.

When we drove through the wooden vineyard gates, I sucked in the fragrant air. The sweet scent of the grapevines and fresh dirt filled my lungs and energized my body. We stepped out of the car and a middle-aged man who introduced himself as Sal immediately greeted us.

Cooper and I followed Sal down a cobblestone walkway as he told us a little bit about the vineyard's history. Apparently, the eleventh century castle was a former Florentine fortress used today as a vineyard that churned out wine and olive oil.

We walked underneath a stone archway that led us into a stunning, trellised garden. I was so taken by the creeping vines and delicate flowers overhead that even though Sal had a fairly good grasp on the English language, I had a hard time concentrating on his words. I sniffed the herb and lavender air and half-listened to him as a chorus of birds tweeted around us.

The other side of the trellis opened to a vast field, and my mouth fell open when I saw dab smack in the center of its edge, there was a table set for two. It was covered with a white linen tablecloth and adorned with candles and fresh flowers.

I turned to Cooper. He had his hands in his pockets and pointed his chin in the air.

I closed my mouth and gave him a questioning look. "Is this ... for us?"

"Perhaps," he said with a slight shrug. He may have been trying to act modest, but the smile on his face was anything but.

I folded my hands across my chest. Times like this had always made me feel special. "This is…" I looked around at the vista of green trees that stood against the plowed, brown fields. "Unbelievable. Really something else."

"Well, you're something else." Cooper took my hand and walked me to the table, where a bottle of champagne rested in a bucket of ice.

"I'll open that for you, and then after your champagne toast, we'll be on our way," Sal called out from behind us.

Cooper pulled out a chair with flourish. "*Per favore, signora.*"

"*Grazie*," I said with a curtsy.

I sat down and smiled as Sal approached the table. He pushed up the sleeves of his white shirt and pulled out the bottle of Prosecco. I noticed his arms were rather tanned, and I guessed it was from spending so much time outside at the vineyard.

I gripped the sides of the chair and locked my arms. It couldn't get any better than this. "Where might I ask, are we going?"

I sat on the edge of my seat and looked back and forth at the two men. Cooper wore a mysterious smile, and Sal simply winked as he opened the bottle.

"Let's just say we are going to take this tour to a whole new level," Cooper answered.

"What do you mean," I asked.

The cork made a distinctively loud sound as it popped. A small cloud escaped the bottle and disappeared into the air. Sal poured the champagne, and I watched the bubbles dance to the top of the glasses.

"*Salute*," Sal said as he handed us the glasses of champagne.

Cooper tapped his against mine. "Cheers, Luce."

I smiled from behind my glass and sipped the champagne. It tasted fruity and smooth in my mouth.

"Shall we?" Sal said to Cooper.

I sat up a little straighter in the silver chiavari ballroom chair and felt a flutter of excitement and nerves.

"We shall." Cooper took my hand and helped me rise from the table.

I really felt like a princess. First the clothes and the chauffer, and now I was being wined, dined, and only God knew whatever else was in store. What a day it was turning out to be.

"Will you please tell me where we're going?" I pleaded with Cooper as a smile stretched wide across my face.

Sal led us around the corner of the castle, where a rainbow-colored hot air balloon awaited.

I felt like someone had punched me in the stomach. "No." I shook my head and looked at its large, chocolate brown passenger basket. My knuckles turned white around the champagne glass. "Please tell me, we are *not* going in there."

"Of course we are." Cooper gave me a strange look.

"Cooper, we've been over this a million times."

I looked away, took a deep breath, and slowly exhaled. Just the thought alone of going airborne in a basket made my chest feel tight.

"I'm really sorry to burst your balloon," I said, "but I've told you, time and time again, I would never set foot in one of those."

Cooper looked at me momentarily with a blank stare and then a flicker of recognition crossed his face. "I know that," he said in a patronizing tone. "But c'mon Luce, look at where we are." He swept an arm majestically across the field. "You can't be afraid here."

"Oh I can't? A hot air balloon in Italy is still a hot air balloon." I loosened my grip on the glass for fear it would break in my hand. Hoping to swallow the anger that burned my throat, I took a big sip of champagne.

Cooper looked crestfallen and cast his eyes in Sal's direction.

"That's like me saying you can't be addicted to work here. C'mon, Coop, we're in Italy," I mocked.

Sal cleared his throat and stepped forward. "*Signora*, it's *magnifico*. You will love it. I promise."

"Come on, Luce. I was trying to be romantic," Cooper said. "You know, make one of those grand gestures." He looked at me with a pout.

I shifted my stance and took another swig of champagne. Was a grand gesture supposed to make a woman feel sick? I knew he'd meant well, and I certainly didn't want to spoil the mood, but part of me was upset. Either he had forgotten about, or was just minimizing a great fear of mine. Regardless, I had to stop myself from showing *him* a grand gesture.

Cooper stood there and tapped his foot. "I'm going to use the bathroom," he announced. "Try to keep an open mind while I'm gone."

"Right that way," Sal said and pointed to a wooden door on the castle.

"Thanks." Cooper walked off and turned around to face us. He walked backwards towards the castle, with his hands in his pockets. "Hey Sal," he called out, "I'll throw you a few extra euros if you can convince that stubborn woman." He turned back around, and I saw him pull his phone from his pocket.

I sighed and looked at Sal. "I'm sorry. It's not you. It's just that this has been an incredible fear of mine. He should know that by now."

"*Signora*, men are *stupidi*. We don't always think." He tapped his salt and peppered colored head. "He's trying to impress. When he called, he kept saying everything had to be *perfetto*." Sal pressed his fingers together. I thought you were a *nuova coppia?*"

I didn't understand. "New..." I furrowed my eyebrows and stared at Sal.

"Couple?" he finished.

"Oh. Well, that's debatable. We're an old couple that's well, maybe about to be new again? Who knows..." I muttered.

"There's a saying. *Tutto il vecchio e nuovo anchora.*" He pulled on his lips as he paused to think. "Everything old is new again."

I nodded and ran my hands through my hair. In the distance, I could see a few men picking grapes. My mind wandered back to the day I'd spent with Simon.

Sal reached over and tapped my head. "Don't listen here. Listen here." He thumped on his chest.

I wondered if he had read my mind, but then realized we were still talking about Cooper.

"And if that don't work, then here." He pressed his fingers into his stomach. "*Il stomaco* never lies. So what do you think?" He pointed at the balloon.

I placed a hand on my churning stomach. "My stomach says...."

"Eh, fuggedabout the stomaco," Sal said with a wave. "Trust me. Make a memory."

I took a deep breath and saw Cooper walking towards us. He paused at our table and grabbed the bottle of champagne. I readjusted my bandeau and reminded myself that Cooper was just trying to give me a perfect day. This was his way of trying to win me over. Besides, wasn't this trip about breaking out of my comfort zone? I was in the midst of downing the last of my champagne when Cooper rejoined us.

"Just in case," he said, waving the half-empty bottle in the air. He looked at Sal and then at me, as if trying to get a sense of the situation.

"I hope you have another one for yourself," I said with a tight smile and grabbed the bottle from his hand. "Let's do it."

"To new beginnings," Sal exclaimed as he helped refill my glass.

Twenty minutes later, I clung to Cooper as we ascended into the sky. With a hand over my eyes, I peered between my fingers for a one-eyed peep show as we drifted over old churches, farmhouses, and fields of green and dirt. Even scared out of my mind, it was pretty exhilarating to see Tuscany from that vantage point. I let my viewing window get bigger and bigger, and by the time we touched ground an hour later, my eyes were fully uncovered. I'd survived.

Sal escorted us back to our table for a champagne brunch, and I was insatiable as we devoured the fresh cheeses, jams, and pastries. Anxiety had always caused me to overindulge, and I wasn't sure whether I was trying to fill a hole of post-traumatic stress syndrome or simply celebrating the fact that I had faced a fear. My feet were back on the ground, and I felt a sense of triumph.

After a wine tour, where we learned about the fermentation process and how wine is made from vine to bottle, Cooper and I lingered in the tasting room. Between all the champagne we had and then the wine, I was feeling more than comfortably numb. We sat on bar stools and faced each other, our knees lightly touching.

A plate of green grapes sat beside us on the table. Cooper plucked one from the bunch and held it out to me. "Grape?" Without waiting for me to answer, he popped it in my mouth.

"You know what," I said once I finished chewing, "I think you're kind of like a grape." I nodded at my own revelation.

"A grape?" Cooper looked bewildered. "Are you talking about a mature one that's finely wrinkled and plump? Or one that's immature? Hard, but small?"

I opened my mouth to answer, but he held a hand up. "Stop right there. I don't think I want to hear the answer to this. I may be buzzed, but I have feelings." He laughed and took a sip of his red wine.

"Oh, shut up," I chuckled. I took a few grapes and stuffed them into his mouth. Cooper may have shown a little insensitivity with the balloon ride, but when all was said and done, I felt as if I were still flying high on top of the world.

"What I meant was, like a grape, there are times when you're a bit sour and hard to swallow, but on the inside, well, you're pretty sweet."

"Thanks." Cooper cocked his head to the side and gave me a look. "I think?" He slid my wine glass aside and picked up my hand that had been resting on the table. "No more wine for you, missy. I'm cutting you off."

I gave his hand a reassuring squeeze. "What I said wasn't a bad thing. I think the same could be said for our day here in Chianti. At first it had a tough skin and a bitter bite, but it ended with a real sugary finish."

"I knew you would enjoy yourself once you let go," he said. "I'm glad you had fun, and I'm proud of you." He tapped his glass against mine. "And, while we are drawing grape comparisons, I have to say, you my dear are like a fine wine. You only get better, not to mention bolder with age."

"Ew." I tucked my hair behind my ears and looked into his eyes. "You are so cheesy." I raised my eyebrows, "The balloon ride was pretty much thrust upon me. I didn't want to hurt your feelings."

He placed a finger on my lips and leaned towards me. "I see that you've sweetened with age, too."

I couldn't help but smile as he lightly brushed his lips against mine.

"Now, what do you think?" he murmured.

"Still cheesy," I teased. "However, if you were a wine, I would say ... somewhat aggressive, very smooth, and..."—I tapped my finger on my lips and leaned towards him again—"I think I'd like another taste."

* * * *

"Well, I guess this is goodbye," Cooper said, squeezing my knee.

The car stopped in front of my pensione. We were right back where we started, yet mentally a lot had changed over the past four hours. The awkwardness between us was gone, and things were heading in a good direction. We held hands the entire ride back, and I rested my head on Cooper's shoulder in a buzzed state of bliss.

"It doesn't have to be goodbye, you know." I turned my head to look up at him.

"Ah, I thought you would never ask," he said with a wink. "I would love to come upstairs with you." He traced my knee with his finger.

"That's not what I meant." I swatted his hand away.

Cooper grabbed my hand, kissed it, and then gazed into my eyes. "Well, what did you mean? Luce, there is nothing I would love more than to spend the rest of the day and night with you."

Nerves fluttered in my stomach, and a titter escaped me. All day I had been feeling like I was back together with my best friend, and while it was fun kissing Cooper at the vineyard, I didn't quite have a burning desire to rip his clothes off. I chalked it up to jitters and figured that the lust would kick in eventually.

"How about you come in, I'll change into something a little more comfortable..." I paused as Cooper nodded his head enthusiastically. "Then maybe we can grab a bite and come back here to hang?"

I noticed a slight frown cross his face.

"Maybe do a little snuggling?" I quickly added. "Get reacquainted?"

More than anything, I had really missed sharing my bed with someone.

"How about we just go back to my hotel? Twelve hundred count bedding, pillow top mattress, a towel warmer…a towel warmer, Luce. Need I say more?"

I paused and looked at him thoughtfully. I had somehow managed to forget that the Cooper I had pined away for had a tendency to whine.

"Oh, just come in." I stepped out of the car gracefully, offered Cooper my hand, and pulled him out to the street. "Let's pretend we just met and you don't have a high horse to come down from."

"Ooh, role play. I like that."

"You're hopeless." I shook my head.

"And you're sexy," he murmured, leaning towards me to give me a kiss. I turned my head and his lips landed on my cheek.

"Not here." I looked around the street, half expecting Tess and Landon to be there. I had texted Tess from the vineyard, but I conveniently neglected to say that Cooper was with me.

"If not here, then where? We're in *Italia, bella*." With that, he put his arm around my waist and dipped me low to the ground.

"What are you doing?" I cried.

"Pretending I don't know you. Isn't that what you wanted?"

I looked into his eyes and saw a playful glimmer.

"Alcohol suits you," I said, after he had tipped me back up to standing.

I felt woozy from the blood that had rushed to my head and held onto his arm to steady myself. I looked around and saw a few faces staring at us from the front window of the pensione.

"I can't remember the last time you were this relaxed," I mused.

"Life is good." Cooper smiled, grabbed my hand, and we walked into the pensione.

As soon as we got through the door, the first thing I saw was Tess. I could've sworn my heart stopped. I squeezed Cooper's hand so tight he yanked his hand away immediately.

"Jesus Christ, Lucy. What the hell?" Cooper whispered, shaking his hand.

I pointed my chin towards Tess. She had been pouring sugar into her coffee, and the frozen smile on her face was far from sweet. She looked at us like she had just seen the walking dead. At that moment, I wished I had told her about the ghost of my love life's past. I cracked my knuckles.

Tess put down the coffee and walked towards me.

"Hi," I said softly.

"Hi, Aunt Lu," she said cautiously. "Hi, Cooper." Tess gave him a closed-lipped smile.

"Hi, Tess."

If Cooper noticed Tess's lack of warmth, he certainly didn't indicate it. He leaned in to give her a hug, and I could actually see her body tense. He cast me a look over her shoulder. The three of us stood there and awkwardly stared at each other.

"Ahem," I heard from the other side of the room. I looked over at the window and saw Mark, of all people, standing there.

I squinted in confusion. "Mark?"

I looked at Tess. "What's he doing here?"

"I'm sorry," Tess said quietly. She twisted her fingers and chewed her bottom lip.

"Why should you be sorry? You're not the only one who owes an explanation. Cooper, I'll be right back."

Cooper nodded as I took a hold of Tess's hand. She held up a finger to Mark. The guys stood on opposite ends of the room as I led Tess back toward the entryway.

Tess looked at me with pleading eyes. "Aunt Lu, I really should've minded my own business."

"Please," I said dismissively. "I was going to tell you about Cooper but…" I paused. "Wait, what do you mean you should've minded your own business?"

Tess looked towards the couch and I followed her gaze, until my eyes landed on the infamous Yankee hat. I was suddenly sober and stood breathless with a hand over my mouth.

"Oh my God," I mumbled from under my hand. I shook my head in disbelief and walked closer to get a better look.

Cooper rejoined me and placed a gentle hand on my arm. "Is everything alright?" His were eyebrows furrowed, and he took a step closer towards me.

I bit my knuckle and took a step back as I nodded.

"Hey, Tess," Landon shouted from the couch. "Can you get me a Coke?"

He turned around abruptly and popped his head over the couch. "Tess, hurry. It's my turn and...*Cooper?*" Landon removed his headset and stared at me with curious eyes.

The Yankee hat turned around, and I locked eyes with Simon. A current ran through my entire body.

"What's up man?" Cooper said to Landon. His voice sounded as if it were coming from a faraway place. It was as if my body was unattached and I watched the events unfold as I floated toward the ceiling.

"I didn't expect to see *you* here. How's it going?" Landon said politely. He got up off the couch and went to shake Cooper's hand.

"Are you freaking kidding me?" I hissed to Tess. "A little warning would've been nice."

"Um, I like your outfit?" Tess said loudly, in a questioning tone.

I looked down and suddenly felt like a little girl who had been busted for playing dress up in her mommy's designer clothes.

"Yeah, you clean up nice," Simon said. He looked at me with sincerity as he stood and approached our dysfunctional little group. He held his hand out to Cooper. "I'm Simon."

Cooper accepted his hand. "I'm Cooper. Lucy's..."

"Ex. I know. Heard a lot about you." Simon gave Cooper a once over.

Cooper groaned. "I was going to say stylist, but I see my reputation precedes me," he said sheepishly. "I've come to redeem myself."

"Well, they say the key to a woman's heart is through her wardrobe, right?" Simon said in a flat tone. I closed my eyes in despair.

"So they say," Cooper smiled oblivious to the sarcasm.

"Um..." Landon began uneasily. "Are you just passing through?"

"That's to be determined." Cooper winked, putting a protective arm around me.

I gave my audience a weak smile and wished that I were the one who was just passing through. I drew in a shaky breath.

"I'm going to use the bathroom," I said. "Care to join me?" I said to Tess, shooting her a look of death.

"No, I'm good," she responded, an octave too high. Then she inched away towards Mark.

"Oh, I think you do," I smiled sweetly and grabbed her wrist.

I led her down the hall and opened the door to the ladies room. Once inside, we both began to talk at once.

"I don't think so," I said, holding up a finger. "Me first. Why didn't you tell me you invited the boys here?" I folded my arms across my chest and leaned against the sink.

"I'm sorry," she cringed. "I thought you would think I was stupid for trusting Mark ... and..."

I raised an eyebrow. "How stupid do you think I am?"

"Okay," she sighed. "We, that is, Mark and I, thought you and Simon would like to see each other. He's been asking about you and—"

"He has?" My mouth twisted into a smile, which I quickly wiped away. This was no time to smile.

"Yes!" Tess practically shouted with excitement.

A flutter in my stomach made me press a finger to my lips. "Shh," I whispered. "Go on," I encouraged in a stern voice.

"Okay." Tess took a breath and begin to talk in a fast pace. "Mark said that Simon really missed you and totally regrets that he bailed our last night in Paris. We all know your hang-up about the age difference," Tess said, rolling her eyes, "so, he figured it wouldn't have made a difference anyway. Was he right?"

I ran my hands through my hair and held it up in a tight ponytail, not giving Tess the satisfaction of appearing to care.

"Anyway, that was until Mark decided to come see me. I guess Simon wanted to see you one last time before he lets the old ship set sail."

"Ha ha," I sneered, releasing my hair. "The old ship, eh?"

"I didn't mean it like that." Tess grimaced. "Anyway, Cooper's here," she said dismissively. "So, I guess it really doesn't matter whether Simon's hot for you or not, right?"

"Right," I said, although I didn't quite believe it myself. My stomach suddenly ached and I placed a hand under my rib cage. "And I'm sorry I didn't tell you about Cooper. I feel kind of silly myself. Not to mention I feared your mother's wrath."

"Oh I hear that." Tess smiled, and then her face grew serious. "Aunt Lu, we just want you to be happy, with whoever that is." She paused to give me a questioning look. "If Cooper makes you totally happy, and you love the way he makes you feel, then you have my blessing."

"Thanks, Tess," I said, suddenly unable to look her in the eye. I reached over and gave her a hug.

"Wait a minute." I pulled away from her and firmly cupped her shoulders. "You still haven't told me how Mark got here."

"Long story, but to sum it up, his ex decided to surprise him back in Paris. He wanted to tell me, but was afraid I wouldn't believe they really had broken up."

I narrowed an eye. "How do you know he's telling the truth now?"

"I trust him," Tess shrugged. "Besides, it was all laid out on Facebook anyway." The look in her eyes matched the light-heartedness of her voice.

"What is it with your generation and relationship announcements on Facebook? Anyway, speaking of happiness, the most important thing is that you're happy."

"I couldn't be happier," she said, beaming. "Now, let's go back to the group." Tess took a hold of my elbow.

"Ugh," I groaned, feeling a massive pit in my stomach. I looked in the mirror and rubbed my temples.

"Aunt Lu, if you don't feel anything for Simon, then you have nothing to worry about, right?"

"Right." I nodded weakly, following her out of the bathroom and down the hall.

We went back into the common room. Landon, Mark, and Simon were still playing the game and shouting at the TV. Cooper sat perched on a chair, tapping away at his phone.

"Aww, man," Simon cried. "I'm out." He tossed the control on the table and walked towards the refrigerator. "Anyone want one?" He waved a Coke in the air.

"Um, I'll take a Diet." I dug my fingernails into my palms as I walked towards Simon. "So, how have your past few days been?" I wished the light tone of my voice matched the feeling in my heart.

"Pretty good," Simon answered. "One vat-free soda coming right up."

Simon winked as he handed me the can. Our hands brushed, and a spark passed between us.

"Thanks." I swallowed and toyed with the pull tab on the can.

"How's your ankle?" Simon asked.

"Good." I said with a nod. "Well, it was until I put these shoes on anyway." From the corner of my eye, I saw Cooper's head snap up.

"I was going to say, I almost didn't recognize you," Simon said.

"The places I like have dress codes," Cooper interrupted.

Simon and I both turned to look at him. I had always hated his jealous side.

"Is this the guy who helped you when you fell?" Cooper said to me.

"Yep." My cheeks grew warm, and I sipped the soda.

From behind the can, I saw Cooper eyeing Simon with interest. My gaze shifted back and forth between the two men who were polar opposites. Cooper wore leather loafers, linen pants, and a seersucker shirt, while Simon was sporting khaki shorts, a Polo t-shirt, flip-flops, and of course, his signature hat.

"So, what have you guys done over the past few days?" I said to Simon, hoping to start a more neutral conversation.

"I had some work issues to take care of back home. It actually took up a lot of my time."

I nodded, but had to wonder what kinds of things a camp counselor could possibly have that required his attention. Ordering sunscreen? Bug spray? I suspected he was trying to impress Cooper, who had been firing off emails from the moment we entered.

"See, Luce?" Cooper said. "Every guy takes work on vacation with him."

I gave him a sideways look in response.

"What do you do, man?" Cooper said to Simon.

Simon opened his mouth to speak, but I cut him off at the pass. "He works at a camp."

I ran a fingernail around the rim of the can and looked at Cooper, silently willing him to change the subject. The last thing I wanted was for Simon to be subjected to Cooper's career scrutiny.

"Lucky you," Cooper said, clearly misreading my mental telepathy. "I wish I worked at a camp. Now that, I could probably leave behind."

Simon gave Cooper a half smile. "It entails more than you might think," he said dryly. "But regardless of the job, at some point you just have to let it go, right?"

"It's not that easy for me," Cooper said. "I have millions on the line every day. Each ignored email is like dollars trickling away."

"Well, you also have your life trickling away, one day at a time. I know it's hard, but you have to keep it in perspective," Simon said. He removed his hat to run his hands through his rumpled hair.

Cooper was getting irritated. He folded his arms across his chest and shifted uneasily. "Want to go to your room?" he said abruptly.

Just the mention of the word 'room' caused my upper lip to moisten. Suddenly, it was as if I was about to cheat on Simon with Cooper and that I had already cheated on Cooper with Simon. Both notions were preposterous, but suddenly I just wanted to be alone.

"You know what, Cooper? If you don't mind, I think I'm going to take a quick shower. I'm feeling a little hung over ... or something."

"Do you want company?" Cooper said suggestively.

I glanced at Simon who looked away. I wondered if my cheeks were as red as they felt. "No, thanks," I replied.

"Ok," he said coolly. A flicker of annoyance crossed his face, but was immediately replaced by a neutral expression.

"Cooper, you're more than welcome to play with us while you wait," Landon offered.

"Video games?" Cooper said with disdain. "No thanks. I haven't done that since I was a freshman in college." He snickered.

"It's fun," Landon responded. "What else is there to do? I've done my sightseeing for the day, meetings are done ... The Italians don't start partying until late."

"You're such a loser, Landon," Tess teased her brother.

"The guy makes a good point. It sounds kind of nice to relax before we go out," Mark admitted, putting an arm around Tess. "Do you guys want to watch a movie? They have a pretty good collection in the library."

Cooper walked over to a shelf that contained the movies. "Please don't tell me this is the library? What is this, 1980?" he said, picking up a VHS. "No DVD's?"

"Who cares?" I joined him at the shelf and peered closely at the row of movies to get a better look. "These are classics. *Roman Holiday, Before Sunrise...*"

"Obviously they're used to dreamy Americans blowing through here," Cooper said.

"What do you mean?" Simon demanded.

"I hate these movies. They're so cliché. Guy and girl meet in a foreign country, gaze at the Eiffel tower, and find love. *Blah, blah, blah.* Ridiculous," Cooper scoffed. "Or what about the ones where two people from opposite walks in life come together?"

"It's been known to happen," Tess said, looking over at Mark.

"You sound like your aunt," Cooper said, pointing his thumb at me. "You gotta love her idea of hopeless romance, but c'mon, love doesn't work that way in real life."

I looked at my ex-fiancée as if he were a stranger. Was this the same guy who had just taken me on a hot air balloon ride? The flirtatious one who kissed me in the tasting room?

"What?" He stared back at me. "Remember that J-Lo flick you made me watch? The one where she gets hit by a car or some crap, the guy comes to her rescue, and they fall madly in love? Like that would ever happen," he said with a sneer.

Landon laughed. "Ooh you better watch out, Coop. Simon rescued Lucy when she fell off of a ladder."

I looked over at Tess, who gave me a helpless shrug. Clearly, she hadn't told him there had been something between us.

"Well, I'm sure they didn't fall in love after she fell off," Cooper said with a fake smile on his face.

Simon was picking away at a cuticle on his finger, and from where I sat, I could see the tips of his ears redden. An awkward silence filled the room.

"Cooper," I warned.

"Luce, I was kidding," he muttered, but he looked back and forth between Simon and me, obviously wondering what he had started.

"I'm going upstairs," I pointed to the ceiling. "Cooper, can I just call you later? I really have a whopping headache."

He looked at me and nodded. "C'mon, I'll walk you to your room."

He held his hand out. I took it and reluctantly allowed him to lead me up the stairs. When I looked over my shoulder, I saw Simon staring ruefully at me and felt as if I were doing the walk of shame. I gave him a subtle smile before turning around.

When we reached the top, Cooper put his hands on my shoulders and looked me square in the eyes. "Are you mad at me?"

"No." I crossed my arms defiantly. "But you could have been a little nicer down there."

"To whom?"

I cocked my head and raised my eyebrows.

"Oh, come on," Cooper responded as he grabbed my hand. "I was kidding. I don't think that guy or anyone out there for that matter would expect you, a classy lady, to fall for a camp kid."

Cooper gave my hand a tight squeeze as he continued. "Speaking of camp, I knew there was something I wanted to tell you. I rented a house in East Hampton for the summer. It's totally like a camp. It's got the whole pool, tennis court, volleyball pit thing going on. I can't believe I forgot to tell you."

"Ugh." I pulled away from his grasp. "I hate the Hamptons scene."

Cooper stared at me with a blank look on his face. "You do?"

I shook my head and rolled my eyes. One of our biggest fights ever was over the fact that I didn't want to get married in East Hampton. I licked my dry lips and wished I had a bottle of water. It felt like a wad of cotton was stuffed in my mouth, and I wasn't sure whether it was from anxiety or all the alcohol we had consumed.

"Wait. I do remember you didn't want to get married out there, *obviously*, but what does that have to do with spending summer weekends there?"

"Um, a lot? The same reasons still apply."

Cooper raised his eyebrows and folded his arms across his chest. "Explain."

"I don't like the pretentious people that hang out there, plain and simple. It's New York City supercharged. Every trust fund Dick and Jane come out for the weekends in their, no offense, convertible whatevers..."

I half expected Cooper's eyes to flash Porsche logos.

"Honestly," I said, with a shrug, "it's a moot point. I'm still here, and when I finally get home, the last thing I want to do anyway is to leave the city."

"The city is dead in the summer," Cooper observed.

I held my finger up in the air. "Precisely my point."

"Okay, okay, point noted." Cooper paused and put his hands on my shoulders. He looked down at me with a deadpan expression. "How about instead we adopt a tribe of children and lock ourselves in the apartment until Labor Day?"

A giggle burst through my tight lips, and I smiled.

"Luce, all I need is you. If I have you, I will do whatever it takes to keep you, my dear." He tilted his head and looked at me. "Do I? Have you, at this point?" He squeezed my hand and frowned. "I know I don't deserve your forgiveness, but I really, truly love you, Lucy Banks."

Cooper massaged the top of my hand with his thumb. As I looked into his eyes, something inside of me softened. I had looked into that same pair of eyes for years. Yes, their owner had seriously let me down, but he'd also been there for quite a bit, too. He definitely was a colossal jackass at times, but those were just deep-rooted insecurities and vulnerabilities that reared their ugly head at times. I gave Cooper's hands a tight squeeze.

"Does that mean you love me too?" he said.

I looked at him thoughtfully. The creases on his forehead deepened as he waited for my response. "Yes, I think it does."

"It does? You do?"

"Of course I do," I answered aloud with conviction. "My feelings never stopped. But you destroyed me, Coop. I've been angry for a long time. I still am."

Cooper nodded solemnly. "I really want to make a go at this when we get back to New York. Please. I'll do it however you want. We can go slow, or we can even move in together," he said excitedly. "I'll give up my place and everything."

I couldn't quite imagine Cooper leaving his posh pad on the Upper West Side to move into my one-bedroom on the Upper East. I felt a tight feeling in my throat that I couldn't quite identify. I pulled my hands away and coughed into a clenched fist.

"I think we're getting ahead of ourselves. Let's talk about the logistics another time. How about we just start with dating for now? We're a long way off from sharing a toothbrush holder."

Cooper wrinkled his nose. I shook my head as I put the key in the door and turned the doorknob. He had a strange thing about having his toothbrush in the same vicinity as anyone else's.

"Okay," Cooper agreed from behind me.

I turned around and saw him chewing his bottom lip thoughtfully.

"Speaking of logistics, I have a question." He tugged on his lips. "How many babies do you want, anyway?"

At that point, my head started to pound. I tucked my lips into a thin line and inhaled slowly through my nose as I pushed the door open. "How about I call you in a bit? I really need to put that, and myself, to rest for now," I said with a strained smile.

"Good idea." He looked content as he gave me a kiss on the cheek. "I'll be waiting."

I got inside the room and after the door had clicked shut, I leaned against it and slid down to the floor. I hugged my shins to my chest and rested my head on my knees. When did my life become so complicated?

I kicked off a Jimmy Choo and grimaced as I rubbed my aching foot. When I took a closer look, I noticed blisters had formed on my pinky toe. My other foot looked even worse.

"Figures," I grumbled. I had a cluster of blisters on my feet and a boyfriend, or whatever he was, who was acting like a blister on my butt. Suddenly, the whole situation felt like a colossal clusterfuck. I didn't know what was worse—Cooper judging Simon or Simon judging Cooper. Cooper acted like such a jerk to Simon and.... *Oh my God*, why was Simon even here?

I sat up tall and in yogic position, I folded my legs and pressed the heels of my feet together. I closed my eyes and took a deep breath. "Let it go..." I chanted on the exhale. "It doesn't matter that Simon's downstairs," I whispered.

Cooper had finally realized the error of his ways, and now we could have the family I've always wanted. Tess knows the truth. She's happy.

"Let it go," I repeated.

Letting go seemed easier said than done. I pressed my knees to the floor and sighed. Had it only been a few hours ago when I felt like a tipsy Cinderella? Now all I felt was miserably sober, doom, and gloom. I sure as hell didn't recall Cinderella being this stressed out when the prince brought *her* a fancy shoe. Feeling more like one of the bratty step sisters, I folded my arms across my chest and kicked Jimmy Choo across the room.

Chapter Fifteen

Three's a crowd.
Facebook Status June 13 at 5:00pm

After deciding that Cinderella's judgment hadn't been impaired by four hours of champagne and wine at a vineyard, I decided to give myself a break. I allowed myself ten more minutes to sulk and then turned to an old reliable pick-me-up, my version of happy hour. I turned on the tub faucets. It was time to pamper myself.

I dug through my backpack and retrieved a rotting banana from a fruit stand in Munich and a packet of honey from tea in London. I mixed them together with the leftover milk from this morning's coffee and whipped up a facemask. Thank you, *Self* magazine, for that tip! Then I lathered conditioner in my hair and wrapped my head in a warm towel that had been soaking in the running tub.

I had one foot in the bubbling tub when I heard a knock at the door.

"Hang on," I yelled as I stepped back onto the cold bathroom tiles. I figured it was probably Cooper, and I'd just talk to him through the door.

No. If we were going to make a go at this, I had to keep it real. He couldn't always expect me to be done up. It's high time he embraced my casual self. Move over, plain Jane. It's time to make room for her even simpler sister.

I flung open the door, and to my surprise, Simon stood there, staring. My heart leaped and then sank. I was wrapped in a towel and smelled like a sour banana smoothie. He flashed his handsome smile, and I was reminded of the first time I had laid eyes on him in London. I hadn't looked so hot that day either.

"Hey, what's up?" Simon said.

My face flushed under his gaze and at that moment, I was actually relieved I had a mask to hide behind.

"Oh, I'm just keeping it real," I said, punching the air.

He didn't recoil in horror. Nor did he shield his eyes. My facemask reacted more than he did. A chunk of banana slid from my face to the floor.

"What?" Simon laughed and bent down to pick it up.

"Never mind. Just an inside joke with myself." I grabbed a tissue from the dresser. "Do you want to come in?" I said, handing him the tissue.

Simon hesitated as he wrapped the banana chunk. "Were you expecting company?"

"No," I exclaimed. "Look at me."

"Well, you opened the door with such gusto. Who knows, maybe you're hosting one of those crazy spa parties or something."

"Oh, no," I assured him with a chuckle. "I never entertain with a mask on. I figured it was Cooper and to tell you the truth, I kind of wanted him to see me like this."

"Whatever you guys are into is totally your business," Simon said, holding up a hand.

"What? No. It's just that he's never seen me like this," I said, waving my hand over my body. "I thought, isn't it about time he does? He should know all sides of me, right?"

Simon nodded thoughtfully and leaned on the doorframe. "I, personally, don't believe in mystery. Full disclosure." He winked, and eyed the towel I clutched protectively.

Another piece of banana started to slide. "Maybe you should come in so I can wash this off. I feel like I'm going to ruin this lovely carpet."

Simon followed my gaze to the well-worn brown carpet that covered the hallway. I noticed he had changed out of flip-flops into navy blue Chuck Taylors.

"Um, I just wanted to talk to you about something." He ran his hands down his neck and folded his arms across his chest. "It won't take long, I promise."

I heard a door slam and voices approaching from down the hall.

"Sure, but will you please come in?" I jumped behind the door. "You've gotten a dose of the real me. There's no need to scare the rest of the guests."

Simon just stared at me as he stuck his hands in his pockets and played with the coins he had inside.

"Hellooo?" I said, waving my hand in front of his face. "Are you still here?"

The jingling sound of the coins came to an abrupt stop.

"I'm sorry," Simon took his hands out of his pockets and rubbed his eyes.

I stepped aside and waited for him to walk into the room. This time I was reminded of the first visit he'd made to my hotel room in Paris.

"Make yourself comfortable." I smiled. "I'm just going to change."

"Lucy?" Simon took a seat on the bed and clasped his hands together. "Do you think I can just talk to you for a quick sec? I kind of regret coming here in the first place and just want to get it over with."

I nodded and tightened the towel wrapped around my head. There I stood looking like Chiquita banana, and yet for some reason, I didn't even care. I was more concerned with what he wanted to talk to me about and why he looked so nervous.

"First of all, please, take what I am about to say as friendly advice."

"Okaaay." I sat on the bed next to him and folded my arms across my towel-covered breasts. I looked at him expectantly.

Simon drew in a breath and licked his lips. "It's about your ex-fiancée. Or maybe you've dropped the 'ex' part by now?" He raised one eyebrow and waited for me to answer.

"I don't like labels." With my toe, I subtly slid one of the Jimmy Choos under the bed.

"Well, Cooper seems to think you do."

I rolled my eyes and waved a hand. "He likes to spoil me."

Simon held up a hand and shook his head quickly. "I'm not going to go there. That's irrelevant. Listen." He paused to grab my arm. My skin tingled from his touch.

"I know we don't know each other well, but I know enough to say that you're a dream woman," he said matter-of-factly. "*My* dream woman, anyway."

I gasped and pointed my finger at my chest in surprise.

"Yes, you, Lucy. You're smart, funny, sexy... And in all fairness to Cooper, I'm sure," he said, holding a hand in the air, "that he has some redeeming qualities. But look at you," he said, waving his hand over my body. "You're gorgeous. More importantly, you're beautiful within." He tapped my breastbone, and a shiver ran up my body.

I swallowed hard and pressed my palms together. "Thank you," I mumbled and looked down.

I may have been speechless on the outside, but my heart sang on the inside. That may have been the nicest compliment I had ever received.

"You've told me some things he's said, and quite frankly, I don't quite see how you guys are together. I don't think he appreciates you and..."

"Luce?" a voice called out in the hallway. My head snapped up so fast that I felt a burning sensation in my neck.

"It's Cooper," I hissed.

My eyes bulged as I stared at Simon. I heard a simultaneous knock at the door. I think the knocking heart in my chest may have been louder.

"Oh, my God," I gasped. "What am I going to say?"

"Relax," Simon whispered and jumped to his feet. "I'll hide. Just please, please promise not to have sex with him." He wore a pained expression on his face. "I really can't imagine hearing..."

I interrupted by punching him in the arm.

"Ow." Simon grimaced and rubbed his arm. "I was being serious."

I shooed Simon away and pointed to the bathroom. While he headed off to take cover, I stood and adjusted my towel.

"I'm coming." I called. I ran to the door and opened it a few cracks.

"Yikes," Cooper said. He took a step backwards into the hallway.

"Gee, thanks," I said dryly. "I wasn't ... err ... expecting any company."

Cooper held up a hand. "I should've called. I just wanted to drop off a cup of coffee and some Tylenol. You seemed to be really hurting when I left you." He held out the offerings, and I opened the door a little wider to take it from his hands.

Oh, you have no idea just how much, I thought to myself. "Thank you so much, Coop. Do you want to..." I couldn't bring myself to finish the question because the last thing I needed was to hold Simon hostage.

"No, no," he answered quickly. "I'll leave you to do your ... girl thing," he said with a face.

"Hey. Am I that scary?"

"No, no," he reassured. "I just think some things are better left to my imagination."

I smiled weakly, knowing full well Simon was within earshot.

"Take the aspirin and drink the coffee. Relax, and when you're all done with *this* ... whatever it is," he said, pointing to my face, "call me."

"You know what, Cooper. I feel somewhat beyond repair today. Let's just meet up in the morning. I'll probably look and feel better in the light of day."

Cooper's face immediately fell. "Are you sure?" He looked so disappointed I almost changed my mind, but Simon's words had rattled me so much that I really needed to do some thinking.

I bit my lip and nodded.

"Okay," Cooper sighed. "Well, I guess last night's dinner was supposed to be just that. A dinner. Today was a bonus, and there's always tomorrow, right?"

"Right." I leaned my head against the doorframe and nodded again.

"Feel better, sweetheart. The car will come pick you up in the morning. I'll be sure to call first."

I blew him a kiss and started to shut the door.

"Oh, and Lucy?" Cooper called.

"Yes?" I popped my head back into the hallway.

"Thank you for giving me another chance. I promise,"—Cooper interlaced his fingers and squeezed his hands together —"you won't be sorry."

I smiled grimly and closed the door.

Within a second, Simon appeared in front of me. We listened to the sound of Cooper's footsteps disappear down the hall.

"Please, please,"—Simon closed his eyes for a brief moment before he reopened them—"don't tell me you have officially taken him back?"

I clenched my jaw and looked at Simon.

"Unbelievable," he muttered.

I squinted and leaned closer. "What did you say?" I said in disbelief.

I folded my arms across my chest and tapped my fingers. "What does that mean? You don't even know him."

Simon gazed into my eyes, and my heart began to race. I inched back so he wouldn't hear the heavy beating.

"I don't have to. Just hearing what he said about your appearance confirmed my entire opinion of him. Lucy, it doesn't matter what you wear, a designer dress or a hotel towel." He tugged on my terry cloth get up.

Wowzers! I felt something I hadn't felt once the entire day with Cooper. All sorts of nerves had come alive, and I clutched my towel protectively.

"You're perfect just the way you are. I'm sorry, but I don't think Cooper loves you for you. He loves the idea of you, but not the reality. Not the Lucy who wants to dress casually. Or the Lucy who can't have babies," he said, gently.

My stomach dropped, and I chewed my lip, while fixing my gaze on the floor.

"He's just too hung up on appearances," Simon continued to rant, "not to mention making millions." He scowled. "Does he really make you happy?"

I paused for a moment. Is anyone really ever truly happy? Oh, whatever. Feeling anger rise within me, I bit my lip and drew in a breath.

"Simon, no offense, but you barely know me. And you definitely don't know Cooper. What gives you the right?" I clasped my fingers together to keep them from shaking.

"I'm sorry," Simon said. "I just think you're much deeper than he is. And that you can do better."

Like who? A camp counselor who doesn't want to grow up?

"I think you should leave," I said quietly, reining in my temper.

"Lucy…"

I walked towards the door and flung it open. I couldn't bring myself to look him in the eyes, so I stared down at the floor instead.

"Jesus Christ, Lucy. Are you mad at me or are you mad at yourself?

You're acting like a total fool."

My head snapped up, and I stood there with my mouth agape. While my inner voice was loud and clear, I couldn't seem to find my outer one.

"Yes, a fool," Simon repeated. "How can you even be with that douche after what he did?"

"Simon, you don't know...." I rubbed my temples.

"No, Lucy, *you* don't know. He broke off your engagement. He broke your heart. Show a little self-respect."

Whether or not I had shown any self-respect, I knew I certainly wasn't at that moment, as I stood there, overexposed in my towel.

"Please, just leave. I can't do this right now."

He walked forward and stopped in front of me. "I was just trying to help," he mumbled to the floor.

"Help me feel like a fool? Help me doubt my own life? Mission accomplished." I stepped aside, and I too, looked down, hoping to signal our conversation was over.

When I saw his feet pass, I slammed the door behind him. And then there was one.

* * * *

I woke up in the middle of the night, dying of unquenchable thirst. Little elves were hammering away inside my head. The dry mouth, I could chalk up to too much alcohol and not enough water, but the pain in my head, well that was just a side effect from Simon, that pain in my ass.

Damn him, the know-it-all who knows nothing. I had such a lovely day with Cooper at the vineyards and probably would've been perfectly happy if I hadn't run into Simon. As I'd tossed and turned all night, thoughts of his insecure ramblings rattled around in my head.

I yawned and squeezed my eyes shut, willing myself to sleep.

Several hours later, the sound of pedestrian traffic beneath my window roused me from my broken sleep. I pressed my forehead as the events from the night before worked their way back into my consciousness.

Don't even go there, I warned myself. I turned on the clock radio and allowed the sounds of Pavarotti to drown out the cacophony in my head. Tess and I only had a few more days until we moved on to Venice, and I refused to allow Simon's nonsense to ruin another moment of my fleeting time in Florence.

I flung my feet to the floor and dragged my lethargic body out of bed. Sounding raspy and off-key, I hummed along with the Italian opera singer as I stumbled over to the window to open the shutters. Bright sunlight flooded the room, and I shielded my eyes to look out into the distance.

The Cyprus trees, copper domes, and terracotta roofs looked like part of a painting, their colors standing out against the clear blue sky. The sun warmed my skin and radiated through my entire body, brightening my mood and uplifting my spirits. It was going to be another glorious day in Florence, and I was determined to make damned sure it was a good one.

I folded my arms on the windowsill and watched the Florentines as they set out on their daily grind. They looked suspiciously happy, which made me realize that a workday with a two-hour siesta probably doesn't qualify as a grind. The more I thought about it, it seemed to qualify more as *grand*. Once again, what a difference a letter can make. The sound of my cell phone interrupted my musing.

I glanced at the caller ID. It was Cooper.

"Good morning," I answered with a smile. "I have the windows open and feel a lovely day on tap. Is it possible the air actually smells like a cross between espresso and Parmesan cheese? I know that may sound like a gross combo, but it's making my mouth water for..." I paused from my babbling to swallow. "A cappuccino and a cheese Danish? Or maybe a fig one? Oh my goodness. My mouth is actually watering. I didn't eat any dinner last night."

"Don't hate me," he pleaded.

"Oh," I cried. "Duh. How could I have forgotten how much you loathe cheese Danish? I must've blocked it out because honestly, I can never, ever imagine—"

"That wasn't what I meant, Lucy," Cooper interrupted. "I have some bad news."

"Whatever it is, don't worry. I'm sure it's not so bad. Is the Mercedes in the shop? I'll have you know I've become a real whiz on mass transit."

Cooper remained silent and I, on the other hand, couldn't shut up. I was feeling rather punchy, or maybe I was just delirious from a bad night's sleep.

"Are your best pants at the cleaners? No time to shave?" My jokes were met with more silence and I felt a familiar twisting in my stomach.

I heard Cooper draw in a breath. "Luce," he began.

"You have to work, don't you?"

"Well, yes and no." Cooper sounded distracted, and I heard the sound of a male voice in the background. It had a very thick Italian accent. "Luce, can you hang on a sec?"

"Yes." I plopped down on the bed, looked straight ahead, and stared at myself in the mirror. The me looking back was clearly annoyed and disappointed.

"I think I like the navy one better. Does it come in charcoal, or maybe olive?" I heard him ask.

As I half-listened to Cooper rattle off names from the darker spectrum of the color wheel, I couldn't help but think of all the times this had happened in the past. The day of my cousin's wedding, when he canceled, forcing me to go dateless at the eleventh hour. The night of my birthday dinner, when he showed up one hour late, after they'd given our table away. The day I left him the message I'd been laid off, when it took him three hours to call me back. Why hadn't I remembered those moments when I was crying my eyes out over Cooper earlier?

"I'm back. Sorry," Cooper sighed as he returned to the line. "The concierge told me about an old man who makes killer suits. I figured while I was here, I'd go see him. The old school Italian tailors are a dying breed in New York, and from the looks of things,"—he lowered his voice—"this guy's also on his way out."

I shook my head in disgust. "Please don't tell me this is why you can't come meet me."

"No. No!" he exclaimed in horror. "I came here early, but it's taking a bit longer than I'd expected. I guess it doesn't really matter though, since I have some issues to take care of anyway. I came here thinking I may as well kill two birds with one stone."

"Am I one of the birds by chance? Reconcile with Lucy and get a custom made wardrobe in the process?"

Cooper laughed. "Cute. No, I'm going to shoot out some emails while getting fitted. I know how much you hate that."

"What? The way you palm your BlackBerry like a teenager holding his penis?"

Cooper chuckled on the other end.

"It's not funny," I scolded.

"Hey, that's not fair. I flew all the way to Florence. That should count for something. I just have to wait for a fax to come," he said. "It needs to be signed asap, and that's the reason I have to hang local. Then after that, I'm all yours. Right now, I'm just multi-tasking. Don't be mad."

"Cooper," I sighed. "I'm not mad, per se. I just can't help but feel like a part of your to-do list. Buy new clothes, return emails, have dinner with Lucy—"

"Hey, let's not forget that you got a new wardrobe too, and I took you on a special date yesterday. I barely took any calls at the vineyard!"

"That's because you didn't get service. Cooper, I don't need things. I need *you*."

"Aw, Luce. I need you, too, honey, and I know you're disappointed, but I promise to make it up to you later. We'll have a nice dinner. And I'm still sending the car, of course."

Without saying a word, I looked up at the ceiling and took a deep breath. He just didn't get it.

"I even packed you a nice picnic," he added in a pleading voice.

I gazed into the mirror with narrowed eyes, exchanging a suspicious look with myself. Unless Cooper had a personality makeover overnight, I hardly thought he could take credit for packing a picnic.

"Luce? Are you there?" Cooper said.

"Yep," I sighed. "I'm here."

We hung up the phone, and I got dressed while trying to figure out what to do. I decided to love the one I was with: Good old reliable, dependable, me. And I deserved the best.

However, contrary to the pleasures of yesterday, today, the best didn't mean a chauffeured car. It meant being me, the real me whom I had started to truly enjoy. I put on a tank top and a skirt I'd bought at a street fair in Munich, and left the room as a semi-single girl who felt confident enough to walk around a new city by herself.

When I stepped outside, the car was waiting out front. The same driver from yesterday must've seen me coming because when I approached the car, he quickly jumped out of the car.

"*Buon pomeriggio!*" he exclaimed, opening the passenger door.

"*Ciao,*" I smiled. "I'm so sorry, but I'm going to walk today." I twisted my hands and looked at him apologetically.

The driver looked at me in confusion, so I held my hands flat and moved them as if they were walking.

"*Ah. Si,*" he nodded. "*Es una bella giornata.*" He pointed a finger up to the sky.

"*Molto.*" I stood up a little straighter and felt proud of my ability to have a two-line conversation.

He reached into the car and extracted the picnic basket. "*Buon appetito,*" he said, handing it to me.

"Oh," I said with surprise as I reluctantly took it from his hand. There were starving backpackers all over the city; I probably shouldn't let a gourmet picnic go to waste. "*Grazie.*"

The driver took off his jacket and while he neatly folded it up and placed it in the backseat, I took a peek inside the basket. There was wine, foie gras, caviar, and all sorts of unrecognizable delicacies. While it looked delicious, something about sightseeing with a premade lunch made me feel as if I were cheating. It was like moving out of your parents' house, but returning home for dinner on your first night alone. I didn't want to be half-independent today. It was going to be all or nothing. I needed to cut the cord.

The driver closed the passenger door and reopened his own. That's when I handed the basket back to him.

"For you. *Per favore.*"

"No? You no like?" His forehead crinkled as he frowned.

"It looks great, but I want..." A man walked by with a long sandwich that he nibbled out of a bag. "That," I said with a firm point of my finger.

The driver took a step back and looked at me as if I were crazy. "*Che?*"

"*Si,*" I smiled. "Enjoy."

He gratefully accepted the basket, got back into the car, and pulled away from the curb. After it had disappeared into traffic, I planted my feet firmly on the crowded sidewalk and looked around the narrow road. It had been a while since I'd been part of the rush hour crowd and it was interesting to see real life in a different city.

Just like in New York, pure chaos was happening around me. Loud conversation, frantic honking, and vibrations from vehicles on the cobblestone street mixed as motorists sped along on their way to work. It was a little before ten, and rush hour still appeared to be in full swing. While all sorts of mini-cars whizzed past, I was surprised to see the majority of the vehicles on the thin cobblestone street were scooters.

A silver one pulled up alongside me, and I could tell immediately its driver was a beautiful woman. Long, auburn hair spilled from beneath her helmet and cascaded down a very tanned back. She wore a cream-colored pencil skirt and halter-top, and the red soles of her black Christian Louboutin pumps peeked out as they rested on the footboard.

When the light turned green, she expertly balanced a cup in one hand, cigarette in the other and left behind a trail of perfume, gasoline, and coffee. She reminded me of an ad for liquor. Or sex.

My cell phone rang, and I saw that it was Tess.

"Hello?" I shouted. I ducked out of the way as an older group of women on a Segway tour came barreling down the sidewalk. I strained to hear Tess over their peals of laughter.

"Hi, Aunt Lu."

"Tess! I feel so out of touch with you. What's happening?"

"You tell me. *Please* tell me you did not have a threesome last night," she said in a hushed tone.

"What?"

Apparently I wasn't the only one who had been thinking about sex.

"Well, first I saw Simon go up to your room, and then moments later, Cooper followed. But Mark dragged me away before I had the chance to see either one of them come down."

"Oh they went down all right. Simon even dragged me down with him."

Tess gasped.

"Not like that," I groaned. I filled Tess in on what had happened.

"Yikes," Tess whispered after I finished the account.

"Yikes is right. I mean, who does Simon think he is? Can you believe he even said those things?" I demanded.

"Well..." Tess didn't have to finish her answer.

The silence on the other end of the phone was an affirmative. Since I was feeling footloose and fancy free, I decided not to even go there. I wasn't in the mood for another lecture.

"So tell me," I quickly interrupted. "How was your night? No twosomes, I hope?"

"Aunt Lu. Give me a little credit, please. Although ... I did get locked and loaded," she said with a giggle. "Mark wrote our names on a lock, fastened it to the bridge and then tossed the keys into the Arno."

"Wow, Tess. That's like the Italian version of writing your names on a tree."

"I know!" she squealed with delight. "The Ponte Vecchio is glorious at night. We drank some wine, I got sloshed, and he was a perfect gentleman," she said matter-of-factly.

I ran my hand through my hair and frowned into the phone. "From what you can remember, anyway," I said doubtfully.

"Oh, I remember everything. He's incredible." Her voice oozed with enthusiasm. "I don't think I ever met a kinder man in my life."

Tess continued to gush, and I was so engrossed in conversation that I was caught off guard when someone bumped into me. I took a step back and whirled around.

"Bella, mi scusi!" A handsome man held the hand of a little girl and looked at me with apologetic eyes. From the looks of their attire, a suit for him and a plaid uniform for her, I guessed he was taking his daughter to school on his way to work.

I smiled and waved my free hand to let him know I wasn't bothered in the slightest. He winked and walked off.

The little girl was so involved in stepping over the cracks in the sidewalk, she didn't notice when her father tossed me another glance over his shoulder. I politely smiled again as I listened to Tess, and he in turn, narrowed an eye and slowly ran his tongue over his upper lip.

I opened my mouth in horror, did an about face, and started to walk briskly down the street in the other direction.

"Ew, ew, ew. I just had my first encounter with a horny Italian man," I hissed into the phone. I felt violated.

"Where are you?" Tess sounded amused. "I've been chewing your ear off and have no clue where you even are."

"I just stepped outside the pensione. I was supposed to go out with

Cooper, but something came up."

"I'm sorry." Tess paused for a moment. "Does that mean that you're free for a little shoppy shop?" she said hopefully. "Yesterday's fashion show really inspired me."

I felt a stab of guilt. "Tess, I'm so sorry. I never even asked you about that. How was it?"

"Oh, it was fun. I've never been to a real runway show, and it was cool to see all the far out fall fashions," she said with a chuckle. "Some of the dresses were amazing. I sat next to a buyer for an Italian department store, who also happens to own a little boutique in the Piazza Santa Trinita. She invited me to a trunk show at her store today. Do you want to come?"

I looked around and wrinkled my nose. "You know what, Tess? It's so nice out, and to tell you the truth, I'm a little more in the mood to bop, rather than shop. You go check it out, but please let me know if you see something for your old auntie."

We said our goodbyes and promised to see each other later in the day. After I hung up the phone, a touch of the blahs came over me.

Tess sounded so elated. And here I was, having just rekindled things with the love of my life, yet I didn't feel one iota of the way she did. Was it because, despite the break we'd just had, we were still nothing more than an old couple who had grown comfortable with each other? I wondered if I ever even had that same excitement for Cooper that Tess had for Mark.

As I moseyed down the street, I decided it was probably a good thing Cooper had cancelled on me. I needed the alone time, and there was no better time than the present to do a little soul searching.

About a block later, I stumbled upon a quaint little garden that seemed to beckon to me from behind a tall wrought iron fence. I ran my finger along the posts and walked by the spring flowers that blossomed between the openings. Red roses, purple irises, and blue hydrangeas burst through the fence and jutted onto the sidewalk, creating a richly colored wall of flowers that brushed against my hip.

By the time I reached the entrance, the sweet, floral smells called for me to enter. I walked under a rose trellis and descended three marble steps. Once inside the garden, I paused to survey the beauty that surrounded me.

Flowerbeds on one side and a labyrinth of neatly trimmed hedges on the other flanked a lush green patch of grass. A pebble path ran directly though the grass, and after I followed the short trail, I came upon a long, narrow alleyway bordered by Cypress trees and classical statues.

On the cobblestone path, a lone daisy grew from one of the cracks. I plucked it from the surrounding weeds and slowly strolled, absentmindedly tearing petals off, murmuring, "loves me, loves me not, loves me, loves me not, loves me, loves me not." When I had one petal left, I held it to my nose and looked around.

Someone sat in the far corner. My jaw dropped a split second later when I recognized Simon. I shut my eyes and quickly opened them. He was still there. I wasn't imagining things. He sat on a short stone wall, sketching on an oversized pad.

Frozen, a strange sensation came over me. It wasn't the fact that I was about to have a heart attack. It was that he looked so intense, lost in his own world, and it dawned on me I'd never thought of him as someone with a talent or a passion. Since the man was unemployed ten months a year, I had judged him to be somewhat of a rebel without a cause. It hadn't crossed my mind he might actually be skilled in other areas of life.

I stared at him for a few moments before I took out my camera and snapped a picture. After violating his privacy, I felt guilty, but quickly recovered and took another. A smile crossed my face and a myriad of unanswered questions filled my mind.

I walked a few steps before stopping again. My stomach sank. His presence affected me so deeply that in my excitement, I'd forgotten about last night's exchange. Should I even say hello? He might not even want to see me. Not knowing if I would ever have another chance to be alone with him again, I took a deep breath and cleared my throat.

"I didn't realize you were such a Renaissance man," I called quickly before I changed my mind.

He looked up in surprise. "Lucy."

Simon jumped off the wall and began striding in my direction. "When in Rome, right?" He fumbled with the pad and closed it.

"I believe this in Florence," I said caustically. Immediately, I regretted my condescending tone. "But I hear you." I smiled sweetly, patting the bag that contained my journal. "I was hoping for a little inspiration myself."

Silence hung in the air, and then we both began to talk at the same time.

Simon's face grew solemn, and he cracked his knuckles. "Please, me first." His eyes pleaded with me. "Lucy, I really owe you an apology. I had no right to say those things to you and should've just minded my own business. You're probably going to marry the guy. I shouldn't have said that." He closed his eyes for a brief moment and shook his head.

"Oh," I said, waving my hand dismissively. I suddenly felt foolish and wondered if perhaps I'd overreacted. "Let's just forget it. You meant well."

"I did," Simon said with relief. "I would like to declare a do-over. Friends?" he said hopefully, extending his hand.

"Friends," I replied.

I opened my hand and the 'loves me' daisy petal fell from my palm. After we shook hands, I placed my things on the ground, picked the petal off the grass and put it in my pocket. I was too superstitious to cast it away. I was hardly in a position to abandon any promises of true love.

"Where's Cooper? Working?" Simon said neutrally.

"That depends who you're asking," I replied.

Simon stared at me for a moment, but whatever he was thinking wasn't showing on his face.

"Well, I'm psyched to see you, and it's rather nice to see the return of the old Lucy," he said sheepishly and tugged on my tank top strap.

"What do you mean?"

Simon gave me a sideways look. "I think you know what I mean." All neutrality had been abandoned.

I blushed. "Technically, this is the new Lucy," I insisted.

"Well then I prefer the old one. Lucy, undone." Simon looked me up and down and smiled. "Although, something tells me your stylist may not agree."

Oh, I was coming undone, all right.

"Okay, okay, enough about Cooper please," I begged, suddenly very tired of the whole thing.

"You're absolutely right." Simon placed a hand on his chest. "My bad. We're starting over, right?"

"Right," I said firmly. "Have you come here by yourself?"

"Yep. Would you like to join me? You know those Italian men. A beautiful girl like you shouldn't be alone. Don't you already have enough men vying for your affection?"

I smiled and drew in a breath. "Do you want to walk a bit?" I motioned towards the entrance of the tree-lined pathway.

I don't know," Simon said, eyes widening. "Are you going to throw me behind a bush and attack me? You know, since you're such a badass and all now."

He clearly didn't have any trouble joking. I hit his arm and walked ahead so he wouldn't see the big smile on my face. "Not funny," I said, wagging my finger behind me.

"I'm just teasing," he replied, catching up to me.

"I know. You actually are funny ... and I'm sorry about last night, too. I shouldn't have gotten so mad." I sighed, "It's just that I don't know who I am, anymore." I looked up at Simon for help.

"What do you mean?" He cocked his head to the side and waited for me to elaborate.

I ran my hands through my hair and sighed. I wondered how much to say. Simon was easy to talk to, which was one of the things I loved about him, but I didn't want to put him in a bad spot. I kept thinking about our conversation from the night before, and about how young he was, and how wrong for me in so many other ways. At least that's what I told myself. It was as if Cooper had rubbed off on me. I had started to build a wall of protection around myself just like he did post childhood. I couldn't open up to Simon and risk hurting myself, or even him, for that matter.

I settled on staying superficial. "A few weeks ago, I was a high-maintenance New Yorker, and now, I eat street meat for goodness sake." I threw up my hands.

"Change is good, Lucy," Simon replied gently. "And so is new meat."

A chuckle escaped me. "How can someone so young be so wise?"

The reflection of myself in Simon's eyes disappeared as he suddenly pulled me in close. I leaned my head on his chest and breathed in the clean scent of his body. I hardly knew him, yet I felt as if I had known him forever. He was just so comfortable. It was a different kind of comfortable than what I had with Cooper. This kind was laced with an intense chemistry that I was suddenly not so comfortable with.

I stepped back and fumbled though my bag. I was looking for nothing in particular and hoped that something useful would find its way into my hands.

"I'm not that young, Lucy," Simon said, suddenly serious. "We're only ten years apart. When I'm seventy, you will be—"

"Almost dead." I was afraid of the way this conversation was going and sipped from the water bottle my hand had miraculously closed upon. I knew I wasn't ready to have another conversation with Simon about our non-relationship. I still had enough talking to do with Cooper and with myself. Besides, there was no point. Simon wasn't boyfriend material, right?

"I'll just be your older, senile friend."

"We'll all be dead one day. Look at all these statues." Simon motioned around him. "Does it really matter in the end?"

He walked ahead to a statue of a man. "This is Jupiter," he said, putting his arm around the figure. "He was in charge of laws and social order. I think he would approve of our friendship and if he didn't, who cares. Life's way too short to give a damn about what other people have to say. I know I don't. That's not how I want to live my life."

"And how do you want to live your life?" I was suddenly dying to know.

"I just want to be honest with myself. Follow my dreams and have no regrets."

"Well said," I agreed. "Do you have any regrets?"

"None yet." Simon started at me thoughtfully.

"Let me take a picture of you and your buddy," I said, holding up my camera in hopes of quelling my inner turmoil. "Say cheese…"

"Cheese." Simon smiled and hugged the statue a little closer as I looked through the lens.

"Let me take one of you." Simon pulled his camera from his pocket.

"No way," I cried. "I don't photograph well."

"That, I find hard to believe," he said with a look. "C'mon." He turned the camera around and held it out in front of us. "I'll take one of us together."

"Sure, why not," I said, forcing my brightest smile at the camera. "I mean, everyone looks gorgeous in a selfie."

Simon pulled me close and bent his knees to adjust himself to my height. He placed his cheek against mine and I felt the smooth touch of his skin as he snapped the picture.

"Nice," he nodded in approval at the picture he just took. "C'mon, check this out. Do we look good together or what?"

I glanced at the photo he had taken and exhaled with relief. I had to agree with him, it actually did come out pretty good. I looked up at him with a closed half-smile. Our eyes locked, and I quickly looked away and tucked my hair behind my ears.

"You don't have to answer me," Simon soothed. "Just please promise that you'll look for me in your next life. All I want is a fair shot to come back as your boyfriend." Simon held his fist out to mine.

I tapped his fist and shook my head. "You're crazy," I said, trying not to fall back into his arms. "Um, do you want to grab something to eat? I'm starving."

Simon didn't answer, and I was becoming warm under his unwavering gaze. My eyes darted away and swept around the park.

"Or we can go to the meditation garden over there? It looks tranquil, serene... I'm sure people from all over the city come here just to pray," I babbled anxiously.

"Hmm," Simon said thoughtfully. "Decisions, decisions. Eat, pray—"

"Love?" I choked, making a feeble attempt at a literary joke.

Simon's eyebrows furrowed, and he inched towards me. My throat constricted as he got closer. I swallowed, closed my eyes, and waited for him to kiss me.

The next thing I knew, Simon was picking something off my cheek. "Make a wish," he said quietly, holding an eyelash in front of me.

I blew it gently and touched my burning hot cheeks. "I wished I could disappear," I muttered, "but that didn't seem to happen."

"Lucy, there's nothing I would like more than to kiss you, but you made your feelings clear last night. I don't want to go there with you. You're not the kind of woman a guy can just forget about."

My heart melted and an inward sigh erupted in the form of a breathless exhale.

"Besides, I don't mess with other guys' girls. Especially now that I've met him and know you're an official couple." Simon stepped back.

"I'm not claimed," I said indignantly. "In case you haven't noticed, there's no ring on my finger. He and I are just testing the waters. Not like I was going to kiss you anyway," I said, defensively. "I just didn't want to make you feel like a fool when I shot you down."

"How kind of you," he said, narrowing his eyes.

"So do you want to eat or what? I passed a great place on my way here. They had all sorts of yummy sandwiches in the window. You know, those long, thin, crusty—"

"Been there," Simon sang as he patted the black messenger bag slung across his body. "I was so torn between the prosciutto and mozzarella, and the tuna with black olives, that lucky for you, I got them both. Don't worry I remember you loathe tuna, so the other one is all yours."

I gazed at him in admiration, touched that he remembered.

"Oh," Simon exclaimed. "We even have dessert. You're probably going to think I'm a total loser carrying around melted chocolate for the past week." He reached into his bag. "I actually meant to give you this last night, but didn't get the chance before you threw me out," he said with a grimace. "It may have gone nicely with your delectable beauty treatment."

I raised an eyebrow as he handed me a little box. I glanced down and read the label—*Maison du Chocolat*.

"How did you know I wanted to go there?" I cried. "This place is rumored to be the best chocolate shop in Paris. I had planned to make a visit while we were there." Of course, I'd been unable to predict we would be making a hasty departure.

"I know that," he replied.

"But how?" I said, incredulous. "Please don't tell me you're a mind reader, too."

"I would love to read what goes on in that pretty head of yours, but no, I'm not a mind reader. Just a good listener. You told me," he said.

"And you remembered," I whispered gratefully. "I don't even recall mentioning it." I clutched the box to my chest and thanked God he wasn't able to read my mind. Chocolate was my favorite aphrodisiac.

We spent the afternoon lounging around the garden and all of the uncomfortable feelings between us completely disappeared. Time seemed to stand as still as the statues around us, and as I wrote in my journal and watched Simon sketch, I knew that even when I was back with Cooper in New York, I would never forget this afternoon as long as I lived.

I learned a lot about Simon and would forever equate the smell of lemons to those carefree hours we spent together among the lemon trees. It was a place where I was truly myself with someone who wouldn't have allowed me to be anything but.

Chapter Sixteen

```
Billy Joel said it best. This is the time
to remember, because it will not last
forever.
Facebook Status June 14 at 4:40pm
```

Neither Simon nor I seemed to be in a hurry to part company, so when he suggested we take the long way back to the pensione, I was more than happy to oblige. We circled the entire neighborhood, twice, before we made it back.

By the time we returned, it had to have been about ninety-five degrees, and I didn't need a mirror to confirm I looked as gross as I felt. I was having too much fun to worry about the fact that my shoulder length hair had frizzed its way up to my chin. I told myself we were just buds, so it really didn't matter what I looked like.

"You are one cool chick," Simon said with a smile. We slowed down as we passed the Loggia dei Lanzi, a building that adjoined the Uffizi Gallery. I peered through its three wide arches into the open-air gallery of Renaissance sculptures.

"Why do you say that?" A flutter of excitement hit as I waited for the explanation behind his compliment.

"Well, most women would be whining non-stop about the long walk in the heat, their feet, the way they look ... something."

"Oh, I get the way I look. I'm just trying not to let *it* get me."

Simon opened his mouth to say something, but something in the gallery caught my eye, and I was too excited to be polite. "Hey." I tugged on Simon's arm. "Is that Michelangelo's David?"

"No, that's a copy and where the original once stood. The real deal is at the Accademia Gallery."

I turned my head to look at Simon and then quickly directed my gaze to the statue. "Oh."

I wasn't sure what I found more surprising. That the copy looked like the real deal or that Simon knew so much about the arts. "It's absolutely beautiful," I murmured.

"Lucy, you are by far the most beautiful thing in the piazza."

Sweat beaded my upper lip, and I used a finger to wipe my mouth as he looked at the statues. Simon turned his attention back to me, and I awkwardly tucked my hair behind my ear.

"Why, thank you. I do have some pretty stiff competition."

I couldn't help but feel flattered by his compliment. I felt like the prettiest woman in the room. I realized I felt that way a lot when I was with Simon, starting from the day we spent together in the vineyard.

He took my arm, and we turned the corner to the pensione. The day had been a slice of heaven, and I really didn't want it to end. The joyful hours in the garden had my head in the clouds, and I wished we could travel back to where we started. Or at least bottle up the wonderful feeling bubbling inside of me.

Then like a cork on a champagne bottle popping, my joy bubbled out as I saw a familiar face outside the pensione. Cooper stood there thumbing his BlackBerry.

That peaceful feeling escaped, and in seeped negative energy. I wasn't sure why I felt the way I did, but whatever the reason, I immediately knew it wasn't normal. The sight of Cooper should not have made my happiness dissipate. It didn't seem like a typical reaction for a woman who had just gotten back together with her boyfriend.

My body tensed as I pulled away from Simon. I placed a hand on my burning stomach and thought about Sal from the vineyard. His words came rushing into my head. "*Il stomaco* never lies."

"Lucy, is everything okay?" Simon asked, with a gentle hand on my arm.

I couldn't bring myself to look him in the eye. Instead, I nodded, marched two paces forward, and forced a smile so big the corners of my mouth twitched.

"Cooper!" I exclaimed, once I stopped in front of him. "What a nice surprise."

Cooper's head snapped up, and he looked us up and down like we had just come out of Oscar the Grouch's trash can. I had grass stains on my pants from sitting in the grass, chocolate on my shirt, and those were just the things I could see. God only knows what sorts of sweat stains I had. Cooper, on the other hand, was dressed to trade at the American Stock Exchange.

I reached up to pull my frizzy poof into a neater ponytail. "You remember Simon, right?" I smiled through gritted teeth. I was hoping he could hear "Mind your manners, please," the telepathic message I was screaming.

Cooper nodded politely. He shoved his hands into his pockets and fixed his gaze on me. "Where you guys coming from? What happened to the car?"

"I decided to go on my own walking tour and hit a local garden. That's when I bumped into Simon. He helped me kill time," I said with a nervous chuckle.

Simon's eyes darted to me, and a trickle of sweat ran down the back of my knee.

"Well, I texted you like five times."

"You did?' I frowned and reached for my phone. I saw he had indeed texted five times as well as called several times too.

"Yikes! Cooper, I'm so sorry. For some reason, I didn't even hear my phone."

"You must've been having so much fun you forgot about me." He frowned.

I looked over at Simon who was carefully checking his own phone, avoiding my gaze. I clicked my tongue and sighed. "Cooper, that was so not the case. We were outside, and I just didn't hear the phone. It was nothing," I said with a cavalier wave of my hand.

I was trying to appease Cooper, but in one second, I'd managed to belittle the hours Simon and I spent together. I felt confused and couldn't seem to think clearly.

"Well, I wanted to tell you that I'm heading home tonight."

"Tonight?" I placed a hand on my chest. I had just kicked Simon to the curb to protect Cooper, and now Cooper was abandoning me again. First he couldn't go to the Gardens, and now he was leaving. "Why?"

Simon cleared his throat. "I'll leave you guys alone."

"Oh, no you won't," Tess called out, suddenly appearing from out of nowhere. Tendrils of hair spilled from out of a messy bun and her flushed cheeks matched the dark pink color of her tank top. Next to her stood Mark, who had a hand wrapped around her waist.

Tess clutched her hands together and squealed. "Aunt Lu, you are not going to believe this." She grabbed my wrist with a sweaty hand and squeezed it. "Someone liked my skirt." Her eyes bulged as she looked at me expectantly.

"The one you're wearing?" I pointed a finger to her skirt. It was the same one I had admired on the train to Amsterdam, as well as the other times she had worn it on the trip. "Why are you so surprised? I love your skirt and must have told you like twenty times."

"I know you do, but you don't count," she said with the wave of her hand.

"Gee, thanks." I rolled my eyes at Mark. He gave me a wink and laughed.

"You know what I mean," she said with her eyebrows raised. "It was that woman. You know, the one I told you about, the buyer. She freaked when I walked into her store."

A head-to-toe chill washed over me. "Really?"

Mark was nodding his head enthusiastically behind her.

"Really. She asked if I'd be interested in making her twenty more to sell at her store."

"To sell? Holy crap!" I threw my arms up and gave Tess a hug. "Wait." I pulled away and looked at Tess searchingly. "You did say yes, right?"

Tess gave me a sideways glance.

"Okay, just making sure." I tucked a piece of loose hair behind Tess's ear and pride oozed out of me when I looked into her eyes. "I told you, you have a real talent."

"I just can't believe someone wants to buy something *I* made." She folded her hands across her chest and cast a dreamy gaze up towards the sky.

"Congratulations, Tess," Cooper said. "I'm excited to say I know a real designer."

"I don't know if I'm worthy of that title, but thanks, Cooper." Tess gave him a polite smile. "It does have a little more cache than 'teacher's assistant at a daycare center'," she said.

Mark cupped her shoulders and planted a kiss on the top of her head. My heart melted from his tender display of affection.

"I'm heading back home tonight, but we'll have a celebratory drink when you get back to New York. You'll be seeing lots of more of me. Right, Luce?" Cooper nudged me with his elbow.

Tess raised an eyebrow, and I nodded in response. As I smiled at her through gritted teeth, I saw a brief look pass between Mark and Simon.

"Listen, I really have to go. Lucy, thanks for helping me kill time today." Simon pressed his lips together and nodded at Cooper. "See you later, man."

"Where are you...?" I heard the desperation in my voice and stopped myself from finishing the question.

Apparently I wasn't the only one who picked up on my tone. I saw the creases in Cooper's forehead deepen as he looked over at me.

"Simon, wait up," Mark called out to his brother.

"Aunt Lu, we'll leave you alone. I want to call my mom anyway. Text me when you get back to your room," Tess said excitedly. She clapped her hands quietly and did a little jump. "Yay!" she exclaimed with glee.

This time, a genuine smile stretched across my face.

Once we were alone, Cooper turned to face me and drew in a slow breath. "So," he exhaled with exaggeration. "What were you guys really doing? Rolling around in the grass? Is that dirt all over your shirt?"

"Are you serious?" The vein protruding from his forehead told me that he was. "Cooper, don't you dare. I wasn't going to sit in a hotel room waiting for you all damn day." My voice sounded impatient and Cooper took a step back.

"I'm sorry," he said. "I know I sound like a dick. I'm just in a bad mood. I was calling you incessantly because I wanted to spend time with you before I left." He stuck his lip out and looked at me with sad puppy dog eyes. While that look had always made me melt, it had less of an effect on me now.

"Well, whose fault was that?" I said pointedly.

I looked away and saw Simon, who had stopped at a coffee stand. A wave of sadness washed over me. Before I could stop myself I wondered what he was doing tonight.

No. I stopped myself right there. Simon and I had finally found friendship, and I wasn't going to ruin that. I would deal with my disappointment over Cooper's defection on my own. It wouldn't be fair to make Simon feel like second fiddle, even though in my heart he felt like more of a first string. Especially, after the fabulous day we had shared.

Was it really such a bad thing to want to see my friend? I seemed to be having a hard time looking away from the sight of Simon's broad shoulders and back flexing as he reached for his coffee. What was wrong with me? I had such a strong attraction towards Simon. It would fade over time, I told myself. There were more important things in a relationship. What those things were and whether or not I had them with Cooper, still remained to be seen.

"Ugh." I closed my eyes and squeezed the bridge of my nose. I opened up an eye and peeked at Cooper.

"I know," he soothed.

I clenched my jaw. No Cooper, you egomaniac, I'm not devastated that you're leaving. I'm devastated that I have become such a whacked out head case. My thoughts were insane. I was insane. I took a breath to collect myself.

I was so lost in thought that I actually jumped when Copper elbowed me to get my attention.

"Look at that." He pointed his chin in the direction of a child who was throwing a tantrum on the sidewalk. From the looks of things, the little boy had dropped his gelato cone on the ground and just couldn't bear the thought of leaving the cherry behind.

"Aw," I said sympathetically, "that's so sad." He had to have been about three-years-old and wore the rest of the gelato on his face and hands. His parents were doing their best to console him and struggling to wipe his hands clean while he kicked and screamed.

"Sad? More like ridiculous. It's the parents' fault for giving the kid his own cone in the first place. Spoon-feed him with a cup. Look at them," he scoffed. "They're practically kissing his ass to make him stop crying."

My mouth flew open, and I looked at Cooper in alarm. It had never occurred to me until that moment that he might expect too much from a child. His own self-expectations were sky high, as were the ones he had set for me. They all seemed to involve appearances and exterior perfection. Would our child have to have the right friends, the right school, the right clothes in addition to the right ice cream manners?

"Don't you worry, my dear," Cooper said, slinging an arm around my shoulders as we walked into the pensione. "That would never happen to us. We'll run a tight ship." He massaged my arm.

That's exactly what worried me. I watched him glance at his phone.

"So, why exactly are you leaving?" I said.

"Something's come up at work." He waved his BlackBerry in the air. "This really can't be helped. If I don't get back, it'll be a real disaster." Cooper paused.

"Luce, I just came to see you for a bit," he went on. "I wanted to make the effort to show you how sorry I was for the way I acted. To be perfectly honest, I didn't think you would want anything more than a dinner. The rest was just an added bonus."

I nodded thoughtfully. All sorts of negativity brewed inside me, but a slow and steady breath managed to calm me down. Yes, his priorities were screwed up, but this was not the time to pick a fight. I wanted to enjoy the rest of my vacation, not feel guilt over a crappy goodbye.

Cooper glanced down at his watch. "Speaking of dinner, my flight leaves in oh, about five hours. Do you want to have a final one? How fast can you pull yourself together?"

I forced a smile. "You're talking to a backpacker. I can be ready in thirty."

Cooper raised one eyebrow. "I'll tell you what, let's make it forty-five."

"Why? Do I look like I could use the extra fifteen minutes?"

Cooper chuckled as he fiddled with one of the cufflinks on his blue and white striped shirt.

"I guess that answers my question. I better go and get a head start. Wait," I commanded, interrupting myself as I entered the lobby. "Just so we're clear, how nice of a dinner are you talking?"

Cooper gave me a sideways look. "You can dress however you want."

I rolled my eyes. "Thanks, Dad. I'll do my best not to embarrass you." I flashed Cooper a smile and blew him a kiss.

"I'll be downstairs waiting," he said, punching buttons on his phone. "I have to call the airlines. Right now, they have me booked for coach."

I gasped and placed a hand on my chest as we entered the lobby. "How horrible."

My irony was lost on Cooper. He nodded solemnly, as he pressed the phone to his ear. "Take your time. Thirty minutes 'til the next available agent." He groaned, pulling the phone away.

"That's the perfect amount of time for an Xbox rematch," Landon yelled, jumping onto the couch. Mark sat down next to him and pulled Tess onto his lap. I smiled to myself and raced up the stairs two at a time.

When I got to my room, I looked at the clock and dialed Morgan. I had tried to leave her out my love life, but now, I was desperate. It was time to call in the big guns.

"C'mon," I pleaded into the phone. It had already rung twice on her end. I walked into the bathroom and turned on the shower. It took about five minutes for the water to heat up, so a head start was a good thing.

"Pick up, pick up...."

"Lucy!" Morgan shrieked into the phone. I held it a foot away and massaged my ear. "I spoke to Tess, and she filled me in on—"

"Isn't it amazing? I think she may have found her true calling."

"Yes, I couldn't be happier for her. But Lu, that wasn't what I was talking about. I've been speaking to her all week. She has filled me in on everything."

I gripped the phone and cringed. "Everything?"

"Everything."

"Okay well, I only have about forty-one minutes until I meet Cooper for dinner, so there's really no time for judgment." I pulled off my leggings.

"Fine. We'll reserve that for a later time. Honestly, I feel like you're starring in an Italian soap opera. Any new developments? By the way, I have Josh Duhamel playing the role of Simon. Am I right?"

I sank down on the edge of the tub with relief. I had feared the wrath of my older sister and was so glad that she wasn't upset with me, but still, I really wasn't in the mood for jokes. I closed my eyes and drew in a slow breath.

"Morgan, I really don't have time for this now. I'm actually kind of upset. Do you have a minute?"

"Yes, of course," Morgan answered quickly. "I just made a cup of tea. Omigod, this really is like a soap."

"Enough with the goddamn soap. Please," I said firmly. There was a silence at the other end of the phone. I bit down on my thumbnail. "I'm sorry. It's just I need some quick advice and know you're so good at that, Morgan."

"You also seem to know I respond well to ass-kissing," she said dryly. "Now start talking."

"Okay. Cooper blew me off today."

"Shocker."

"Anyway," I said impatiently, "I went out by myself and ran into Simon."

Morgan let out a slow whistle.

"Yeah," I said quietly.

"That must've been awkward ... after last night's tiff."

"Wow. Your daughter is quite the details girl." The clock in the bathroom indicated I had about thirty-eight minutes left, so I reminded myself there was no time to be angry with Tess.

"Well, that's the thing. It wasn't awkward at all. Simon apologized, and for once in my life, I didn't hold a grudge. How could I? The guy meant well, and I know you don't know him, but Morgan, he's so charming, it's ridiculous." I walked over to the sink and put toothpaste on my brush.

"Okay, I know you hate this, but I'm a visuals girl, so please humor me. Now I'm picturing Bradley Cooper. Maybe even a young Colin Farrell. You know, the hottie with the sexy accent?"

"Well, Simon's from Chicago and his Midwestern accent isn't as sexy, but he is just as hot. Or haat as he would say." I looked in the mirror and saw my cheeks redden in my reflection.

Morgan laughed into the phone. "Did you hang out for a bit?"

"More than a bit. We spent a few hours at a local garden and then wandered around the city for a while. We were totally sweaty and gross, but completely happy. So, guess who we ran into?"

"Noooo," Morgan groaned.

"Yep. And I could tell immediately he was bothered that I had been out with Simon."

"But he cancelled on you," Morgan said matter-of-factly. "Not only that, but what did he expect, to come here and regain your trust in two days?"

"Well, hang on." I gave my teeth a quick brush and filled her in on the conversations I'd had with Cooper about our future.

Morgan groaned again when I was finished. "Shouldn't you make him work a little harder for you? Do you really think he's changed that much? No offense, but there's no way he's going to move into your little place."

"Who knows?" I anxiously looked at the clock and ran to my closet to select an outfit before I got into the shower.

"Hmph. So were you totally psyched to discover this metamorphosis?"

"Yes and no. I thought I would be. But something seems different. I think *I'm* different." I shook my head and sighed. "There's also the slight issue that I can't stop thinking about Simon. He and I had such a nice day and … I kind of miss his company already." I was surprised by my own words and cringed after I said them.

"Is that weird?" I continued. "I thought he wasn't boyfriend material, but after spending the day with him, well, I don't know. I just love how I feel when I'm with him. I love who I am. He brings out the best in me," I gushed. "Now I feel really nauseous. Or maybe I'm just worried I hurt his feelings and that's what's making my stomach churn."

"Or maybe you just really, truly, enjoy his company. Is that so hard to believe?" Morgan said. "You know, I think it's a good thing Cooper's heading back home. A fan-freakin-tastic thing, actually."

"Morgan," I chided.

"What? You obviously like the guy, Ms. Denial. I think you should talk to him later. Come to terms with it or get whatever it is out of your system before you're fully committed in New York. If that ends up happening," she said reluctantly.

"I should be fully committed all right." I sighed. "In a straight jacket."

"If you're unsure about Cooper..."

"I don't know if unsure is the right word, but spending more time with Simon made me realize just how much work I need to do on Cooper. I mean, we can all use a little improvement, right?"

"Well, that depends," Morgan said skeptically. "What kind of work are you talking about?"

"You know, subtle things. Tweaks."

"Like..."

"Like, I love the way Simon is truly present. I've come to realize that nothing is better than spending a day with someone whose main focus is me. I know that seems selfish, and I don't mean a guy has to be focused on me 24/7, but sometimes I feel I would get more attention from Cooper if I had a delete key."

I heard Morgan laugh on the other end.

"Maybe I should start taking Cooper to Dr. Colter when I get back. I'm sure this is a very common issue in couples therapy. Right?"

"Probably," Morgan agreed.

"And probably much easier to fix than some other things." I sighed. "I just love the way Simon goes with the flow. Would Cooper ever walk around a city for hours? Or anywhere, for that matter? Um, no," I said, answering my own question. "I also like the way Simon does little things for me by himself. Like buying me chocolates in Paris that I mentioned I wanted to try, as opposed to Cooper sending the concierge to shop for me or how about the way he took me on a hot air balloon ride?"

"No!" Morgan cried in disbelief.

"Yep. I guess Tess forgot to tell you that one. It's as if *his* head is in the clouds."

"No," Morgan said firmly. "More like his nose is in the air. The only thing he's good at is throwing money at people. To tell you the truth, I often wonder if he even picked out your engagement ring himself."

"Yes," I said firmly. "He totally did."

"You always wanted an antique ring. He didn't know that?"

"He did," I said reluctantly, "but I guess he thought I would be happier with a big fat diamond. Who isn't? That's water under the bridge anyway. Or at least a three carat diamond on the George Washington Bridge," I added.

"I never thought I would say this, but I actually think you're simpler than I ever thought."

"I think you might be right," I exclaimed with surprise. "You know, growing up poor, Cooper truly believes that money can buy happiness. For him it does. But I don't share that belief and to think I owe this revelation to meeting a younger—not to mention poorer—man. It's nice to be with someone who appreciates the little things in life. I really am going to work on Cooper. I bet I could tweak him a bit."

"Um, Lu, I hate to say this, but your little tweaks are not so little. You act like you're talking about Botox, but what it sounds like to me is a full-on facelift. And honestly, some faces are just too far-gone to be lifted. I wouldn't make that bet."

"What are you saying?" I said, biting my nail.

"You think you're happy being simple with that type of guy, but it seems to me you are just simply happy with *that* guy, in particular. Caviar on an imported cracker from Cooper or crap on a stale rice cake from Simon? From what Tess has told me, I'm thinking you'd take the latter. She told me how sweet he was when you fell off that ladder. Didn't he even bring you a cane? Cooper would have taken the cane and pulled you into hiding like an old sitcom."

"Oh come on. Don't you think you're being a little hard on him?"

"I think you're being a little hard on yourself. Take a page from Simon's easy, breezy book. Instead of changing Cooper to be like Simon, just take Simon as-is. He's ready-made, sweet, and totally fresh."

"Okay, now it sounds like you're talking about a pastry. Newness isn't always goodness you know. Over time, people change, and I'm sure Simon has his own annoyances that will irk me as well. I barely even know the guy."

"Well, ask yourself this," Morgan said carefully, "what was it about Cooper that made you fall for him in the first place? Are there things that don't irk you?"

"Ha." I chortled.

I paused for a moment and scratched my head while I gathered my thoughts. "Well, I guess I felt honored to be with someone who had such sky high standards. Because he chose me, I felt really good about myself. Which is odd because he also makes me feel horribly insecure at the same time. I feel like I always have to apologize for my appearance or don't feel happy with the way I look until he gives me the seal of approval. But when he approves, he really approves. He brings me up in ways I have never known before. It's weird."

"Um, hello? That is called mind-fucking 101. He's a chopper. He builds you up and cuts you down. In the past, you've said you have a weakness for him because of his childhood, his inability to please his mom and make her happy. I get all that and blah blah blah, but I see him having a weakness *because* of that. He needs everything and everyone to be perfect, and he doesn't get the whole unconditional love thing. Your, no offense, crazy brain takes it as a compliment that someone so hard to please chose you, but let me tell you something, Sister, you will always be under the microscope with that one. He's under his own microscope, for goodness sake. Nobody will ever measure up to his standards. Not even himself."

"But Morgan, I've always felt so safe with him," I whined. "He takes care of me. He treats me like a lady. I guess you can say that he's kind of like my Mr. Big."

"You and your romance. There are more important things than being wined and dined, as you very well know. You want to be damn certain that your Mr. Big isn't a big mistake."

I groaned inwardly and chose to ignore her comment. "Speaking of wining and dining, I'd better run. I'm meeting Cooper in thirty-five minutes. Thanks for the pep talk. And I'll *still* take that bet. I'm a firm believer that people can change," I said punching my fist in the air, even though I wasn't truly convinced. Especially, after hearing all my inner thoughts come to life.

"Oh!" Morgan exclaimed. "That reminds me. Can you pick me up a leather wallet, with a zippered compartment for change? Maybe a nice brown one?"

"You got it."

"*Grazie*. Text me later. I hate cliff hangers."

"You need to get a life."

I hung up the phone and jumped in the shower. Moments later, when I stepped out of the bathroom in a towel, I noticed an unmarked envelope sticking under my door. I plopped on the bed and opened it up to find

Simon's sketch of the tree-lined passageway. It was the most beautiful gift I'd ever received. I traced a finger along the edge of the drawing he'd created with his own two hands.

Morgan was right. There were more important things than being wined and dined, and I knew that. You couldn't put a price on a gift from the heart. I put the drawing down and fell back onto the bed in despair, pulling my ratty old nightshirt from behind my head. It had been rolled up in a ball, along with a lacy bra Cooper had included in the gift bags.

"Somebody, help me," I groaned to the ceiling as I held my beloved t-shirt in one hand and the fancy bra in the other. What a difference between the two guys. I had loved playing dress up with Cooper, but after five years, maybe it was time to stop playing and just be me. I was beginning to get to know that person and definitely wanted to see more of her.

I sat up with a start. Quickly, I threw on a dress, twisted my hair into a bun, and applied a coat of lip-gloss. Smacking my lips together, I picked up my purse and headed down the stairs. As I came around the corner, I heard my nephew's voice. I realized he was talking to Cooper.

"Dude, what's your beef with Xbox," Landon asked.

I slowed down on the landing to listen and peered over the banister. "Don't disparage the greatest invention known to man, *ever*. Just play," Landon said, holding up a joystick. "It's tennis. You might surprise yourself and be a natural." He pretended to serve a ball in midair.

"I'm pretty solid on the court," Cooper said dryly. "I really don't think I would surprise myself with some dumb game."

"It's just for fun."

"I didn't make it this far in life playing video games," Cooper snapped.

"Oh, lighten up," Mark said. "My brother plays all the time. It doesn't affect his career."

"Is that what your brother calls it? A career?" Cooper said in a nasty tone.

I stopped dead in my tracks. I opened my mouth to speak, but the words wouldn't come out. Instead of entering the common room, I walked right out the door. I decided to leave Mark to shove the joystick up Cooper's ass for insulting his brother. As I picked up the phone to call my sister again, the last thing I heard was Mark's voice.

"Didn't your mom ever teach you never to judge a book by its cover?" Kudos to him for taking the high road. He'd handled it a lot better than I would have.

I speed-dialed my sister. "Morgan? It's me again," I said quickly as she answered. I stepped onto the sidewalk and quickly ducked into a leather shop beside the pensione.

"Wow. Twice in one—"

"Listen," I said with my voice breaking. "I'm really upset."

"Oh, honey," Morgan cooed. "What happened?"

"Oh, I'm just such a mess," I whispered. "Simon left me a sketch of the garden and oh my God, Morgan, you should see it. The best part is that he made it for *me*, with his own two hands. I feel like I've been so blind and—"

"Okay, take a deep breath," she interrupted. "When exactly is Cooper leaving?" She sounded like a sergeant in the army getting ready to deploy a missile.

"I don't know. Sometime after we have dinner."

I looked around the store and remembered the promise I'd made to Morgan.

"Did you say you wanted a zipper close or a snap?"

"What?" she said.

"The wallet. I'm in a leather store. Just answer the question."

"Why are you worried about this now? Have a nice meal, say your goodbyes, and go find Simon. You have a few days to hang with him before Venice. That's plenty of time to figure things out. You're out of the U.S. You've already crossed the border, so in my opinion, whatever emotional borders you also cross shouldn't count."

"You're right." I had to laugh despite the crappy way I was feeling. I chose a wallet for Morgan and on my way to the register, a brown one caught my eye. It was handsome and rugged, reminding me of Simon and the disheveled way he had carried his cash in Paris. I tossed it onto the counter.

"Cooper will be waiting for you in New York. You need to use the rest of this trip to clear your head and make damn sure," she said firmly, "that he's the man you want to marry."

The word 'marry' caused my temple to pulsate. I closed my eyes and rubbed the center of my forehead. "Do you think he is?" I said weakly. "Everything feels so different all of a sudden."

I held the phone away from my mouth and looked at the store clerk. "Morgan, hang on a sec. Can you gift wrap that?" I said. The woman behind the counter looked at me quizzically and I pointed to a roll of wrapping paper that sat next to the register.

"Ah." she cried. "*Si.*"

"*Grazie,*" I nodded.

"Lu, nothing is different all of a sudden. *You're* different, but in a good way. It doesn't matter what I think. What matters is what you think, right? How do you feel when you're with Cooper, when he's not cutting you down like a woodsman?"

Despite the stress I was feeling, I giggled into the phone. "Sorry, the image of Cooper with an ax makes me laugh."

"Well, the man you should marry is the one who makes you feel complete. Not broken into pieces." I imagined my sister smiling into the phone. "You already told me how good you feel with Simon, but does Cooper give you that same feeling? Who makes you feel truly happy?"

"Hey, there you are," a voice exclaimed behind me.

I turned around and came face to face with Cooper. "It's Cooper," I said into the phone, forcing a smile.

"Well, there you go," Morgan said dryly. "I guess that solves that one."

I heard a trace of bitterness in her voice.

"No," I replied hastily. "Cooper's here. Right in front of me," I explained, rolling my eyes at Cooper. "I'll call you later."

"Oh!" Morgan exclaimed. "Okay," she said firmly. "Just say your goodbyes like a big girl. Don't stir the pot. Act, don't react. You've always had a tendency to—"

"Okay byeeeeee," I sang. "Sorry," I said turning to Cooper. "My sister is a bit slow on the uptake."

"No, I'm sorry," Cooper apologized. "My flight's been cancelled, so I actually have a car coming for me now. I need to get to the airport early. I'm standing by for a different flight. First class, of course."

"Of course."

"I needed to get out of there anyway. That Mark rubs me the wrong way." He shook his head and pulled me in close. "Baby, I'm really going to miss you."

"Well, this isn't good bye," I said, putting my head on his chest. I couldn't bring myself to look him in the eyes.

"Right," he murmured. "What's another couple of weeks when we'll be together forever?" He moved his hands down to my shoulders and stepped back so he could see me. His hands caressed the sides of my neck.

I looked him square in the eyes, trying to formulate a reply.

"The first thing we're going to do," Cooper continued, saving me from a response, "is go to our favorite little spot on Fifth. That is, after we retire that beloved tank top of yours."

I felt like the hands massaging my neck were starting to close in on my throat. I swallowed nervously. He dropped his hands to the small of my back, and my skin began to crawl.

"You know what?" I said slowly pulling back. "The Peninsula Hotel is hardly a little spot and for the record," I said, pausing to swallow again. "I hate that place." I was surprised that I actually felt slightly liberated.

Cooper gave me a sideways look. "You do? Since when?"

I smiled gratefully as the clerk handed me my purchases, and I walked ahead of Cooper, leading him back to the street.

"Oh, probably since the first time you took me there," I said, nodding my head. "I hate everything about it, and come to think of it, that's not all I hate. I hate the way you tend to make me feel."

I watched his eyes widen and felt a thrill. A surge of confidence slowly replaced my anxiety.

"The way *I* make you feel?" Cooper said, incredulous. "I treat you like a princess."

"Yes, you do. Princess Perfect." I frowned. "Cooper, I'm not perfect, and I'm okay with that. I love my tank top. And you know what I wear to bed these days? A college t-shirt from 1992. I love it in its entirety. Stretched out and ripped up."

Cooper's mouth hung open, and the more of a rise I got out of him, the more satisfaction I felt.

"I don't like to wear the matching bra and underwear sets you bought from *La Perla*," I said dramatically, for effect. "Silk from the south of France," I scoffed. "Who gives a rat's ass? Cotton rocks, and the last thing

I need to worry about is making sets."

Cooper continued to stare at me, dumbfounded.

"You know what else I hate?"

He shook his head slowly as if he were afraid to answer.

"Sharing sorbets. I want my own goddamn dessert. A big, fat real one," I cried, holding my hands out. "Each time you make me share a half a cup of raspberry whatever the hell it is, I go home and eat my own pint. Not of sorbet," I said with a finger in the air. "Ben and Jerry's. Full fat," I whispered with malice.

Cooper took a step back as if he feared me. "Why didn't you tell me any of this?"

"The things you were offering were the things I thought I should want. Whenever I did speak up, you acted like I was foolish, so I began to think I was. I hid my own opinions and denied my feelings. That was *my* mistake," I said sadly. "And now, for the first time in a very long while, I finally know who I am and what I want."

"Where's this coming from, all of a sudden?"

"I don't know." I shrugged. "My feelings must've gotten smothered in all the fancy clothes you gave me. This is for the months of heartache you put me through."

"If you weren't ready to forgive me, why didn't you just say so?"

"Good question!" I practically shouted into the air. A couple walked by and gave me a strange look.

"Shhh." Cooper silenced me with his hand.

"Oh, whatever. Who cares what strangers think?"

I swallowed the lump that had risen in my throat. "We're so different, Cooper. I was going to take you back," I cried in disbelief, clasping my hands together in a tight fist. "Now, I've just realized that would be the biggest mistake I could ever make. You dumped me on the West Side Highway. The West Side *fucking* Highway. All because I have rotten eggs," I spat.

"But worse, Cooper, as humiliating as that is, I have realized," I continued, my voice getting softer as my anger shifted to sadness, "that we were never meant to be at all."

"I thought we'd been having fun. Just last night we talked about moving in together." The vein from before was back, and it was bulgier than ever.

"*You* talked about moving in together," I reminded him. "I'm sorry," I said with a hand on my chest. "I was really trying to fall back in love with you again."

Cooper's face registered hurt and then quickly recovered to a more neutral expression. "Well, I'm sorry to hear that," he said matter-of-factly. "It sounds like you've made up your mind, and truthfully, I don't even know who you are anymore."

"Well, this is the real me," I said.

I looked at him with tears in my eyes, realizing that this time, we were finished for good. I felt awful that he had to fly halfway across the world for me to realize this, but it was exhilarating to know I'd been pining away for something I no longer wanted.

"And that's the real you," I said, pointing a finger to his chest. "And you're just not the right man for me. Let's be honest. I'm probably not the right woman for you either. We want different things out of life, and both of us deserve someone who will allow us to remain true to ourselves. We can try to change for one another, but neither of us will be happy in the end. We are who we are." I drew in a shaky breath and slowly exhaled, surprised by how good the truth sounded. For once, the three amigos and I were on the same page. My stomach felt better, and while my heart may have been racing, it felt lifted, and my head felt a thousand pounds lighter.

Cooper paused and released a long sigh. "I guess," he said reluctantly. "I really don't know what to say."

"I'd say you probably don't like this version of me, huh?" I said with a grimace in attempt to lighten the mood.

"Eh," Cooper sniffed ruefully. "Not so much," he said with a tight smile. "Honestly, Luce, I just want for you to be happy. That's what you really deserve."

We stared at each other for a long minute until he finally looked away. "I better go…" He trailed off, glancing down at his phone.

I sniffed and wiped away the tears that had fallen onto my cheek. Without another word, Cooper turned on his heel and walked off.

"Bravo! Bravo!" cried a tinny female voice from far away. I looked around, but all I saw was a defeated Cooper walking onto the street.

"Lucy? Lu?" It sounded as if my sister was stuffed into my purse, and

I realized I hadn't hung up the phone.

"Oh my God!" I cried, snatching it out of my bag.

"Did you hear—"

"Every word!" Morgan shouted. I held the receiver away from my ear. "I couldn't be more proud of you, but how do you feel?"

"Sad, but liberated," I smiled with relief.

"Good. Now, hang up with me, for real this time, and go talk to Simon," she ordered. "Unless you want to keep me on hold? I was about to do laundry but would much rather listen to you."

"Good bye, Morgan," I sang and firmly hit the button to end the call.

Chapter Seventeen

Life's too short for sorbet. There are better scoops in the case, so skip the sorbet and go right to the gelato. And while you're at it, make it a double. Facebook Status June 14 at 9:30pm

To: Tess (mobile)
From: Lucy
10:00pm

Hi Tess—Are you hanging with the guys?

From: Tess (mobile)
To: Lucy
10:01pm

Just Mark. Landon went to bed early. Did Cooper find you?

To: Tess (mobile)
From: Lucy
10:02pm

Oh, he found me alright. I'll fill you in later. Have you seen Simon?

Jeannine Henvey

```
From: Tess (mobile)
To: Lucy
10:05pm


Simon's gone. ☹ He went to Rome to meet up
with Mark's friend Chaz. Remember that
clown from London? Anyway, he's heading
back to Chicago on Sunday. He didn't say
bye?
```

* * * *

Simon was gone? I'd been so busy rehearsing what to say and trying to make myself perfect before I saw Simon, that I'd missed him.

Maybe if I ran to the window I could still catch him? I was halfway to the bathroom door when I realized how ridiculous that was. This wasn't a Julia Roberts movie. I wasn't going to be able to dramatically throw open my window and see my prince standing on the sidewalk. I sunk down on the toilet in despair, hit the redial button on my phone, and waited for Morgan to pick up.

"Hello, Love Doctor, may I help you?"

"No," I replied sadly into the phone. "No one can. I blew it, Morgan. Simon already left."

Morgan gasped. "Left? What do you mean? Where is he?"

"Rome," I whimpered into the phone.

"Oh, Lu...."

"I've come full circle. I came here alone and am leaving alone. Might I add, feeling way worse than when I started this journey."

I looked around the pensione bathroom, at the bare fixtures and plain white towel on the rack. What was I doing here? At that moment, all I wanted was to be back home curled on my familiar couch under my favorite afghan.

My voice dropped as I pleaded with Morgan. "Would you mind if I ceased my chaperone duties and just came home? I know we're only at the halfway point, but Landon was supposed to meet up with us again next week, and Tess is in great hands with Mark. Please? She's a good girl,

250

Morgan. They're going to do whatever they're going to do, whether I'm here or not. I just ... I just want to be home now." I fought back tears and waited for Morgan's response.

"I know," Morgan sighed. "I'd rather not think about what Tess is going to do or not do. Lu, I had such high hopes for you on this trip. I'm sorry. Come home. If that's what you need now, it's fine with me."

"*You* had high hopes?" I laughed bitterly, thinking of all my dreams of finding myself when we started this trip. "I feel like I'm right back to where I started: heartbroken, confused and alone."

"Don't be so hard on yourself," Morgan said in gentle tone. "Remember, I heard what you said to Cooper. It seems to me you learned quite a bit about the person you are when you got out from under his thumb."

"True, and I've regained an interest in writing," I added. "So what if I'm going to die alone? I'm just going to lock myself in my apartment and write."

"Listen Lucy, regarding Cooper, you did the right thing kicking him to the curb. I'm sorry, but Simon was right. The guy's a narcissistic a-hole."

"Tell me how you really feel," I said dryly.

"Okay," Morgan continued. "He had some hell of a nerve showing up expecting you to—"

"I was kidding. I don't need to take any more abuse about Cooper. I was blind and in denial. Plain and simple. Now I've lost Simon in the process. Just when I decided to remove the bubble wrap from my heart and not be afraid to get hurt... Arrggh," I groaned loudly.

"Can you call him?" Morgan offered.

"And say what? Morgan, he's gonzo. I was mean and unappreciative. I totally deserve this."

Morgan let out a loud sigh into the phone. "Go get a good night's sleep. You can book a flight when you wake up. Everything looks better in the morning."

"I hope so." I crossed my fingers in the air. "I'm going to give Tess the head's up that I'm coming home before I hit the hay."

"Go to bed," she said firmly. "I'll take care of telling Tess. Actually, eat a gelato and then go to bed. Sugar therapy."

"Good idea. The perfect way to bid *adieu* to sorbet," I sighed. "Thanks, Morgan. Love you."

"Love you too, Lu."

* * * *

The next morning, as the sun crept into my room and the sounds of Florence entered, I woke up with a smile on my face—until I opened my eyes and saw my empty cup of gelato. Memories rushed back from the night before.

After talking to Morgan, I had thrown myself a gelato-fueled pity party, while reliving all of my moments with Simon and wondering how I was going to move on alone in New York. Finally, exhausted and out of gelato, I had dried my eyes with a napkin, thrown it into the empty cup, and set the cup on top of Simon's sketch before passing out on top of the sheets. Now when I focused on the cup, I nearly burst into tears again.

"Oh no." I reached for the cup. As I lifted it, a chocolate ring was left behind, circling the beautiful patch of roses Simon had drawn. I couldn't hold back the tears that filled my eyes any longer, and I fell back onto the bed, sobbing.

"I thought things were supposed to look better in the morning, *Morgan*. This is all I have left of Simon," I yelled at the ceiling.

Tears slid off my cheeks and dripped onto my neck. I jumped to my feet and rubbed my eyes. I just had to get out of the room, even though my legs had returned to the depression-induced lead-like state they were in before I had embarked on the journey. I forced myself to get dressed and decided to walk over to the piazza to grab a coffee. Maybe caffeine would help.

Because it was a Sunday morning, the piazza was fairly dead. I forced a returned smile at an older couple who sat nestled on a bench with a shared newspaper splayed across their laps. Church bells rang in the distance, and a pair of nuns speed-walked down the cobblestone street, arms linked together. As I watched them turn a corner I suddenly felt like a missing link with no one to hold onto. There were a few other people passing through, and as I looked for a good place to wallow, a familiar face caught my eye.

I did a double take and confirmed I was right. It was Mark's friend,

Chaz. As I looked at him stretched out on a chair, with his backpack as a footrest, an alarm went off in my head. If Chaz was here, then Simon must be, too.

I hurried over in his direction, causing my just-purchased cappuccino to splash on my arm. I probably burned off a patch of arm hair, but I didn't care. I was too happy to feel pain.

"Chaz? Do you remember me?" I said when I was a few feet away. My hand shook as he turned to look up at me. I grasped the cup more firmly with both hands to hold it steady.

Chaz's face broke into a grin. "Remember you?" He jumped to his feet. "How could I forget the hottest cougar I've ever met in my life?"

In London he had offended me, but today, I was too excited to be put off by his backhanded compliment. "I thought you were in Rome? With Simon, no?" I wondered if my tone sounded as light as I had intended.

"We were." Chaz casually pulled up a chair for me to join him. "Where by the way, I spent the entire night listening to Simon go on and on and *on* about you. I told him, 'dude you should've tapped that...'"

My heartbeat quickened and I sat on my hands to keep them steady. "He mentioned me?"

"That would be an understatement. You do realize you were the reason he left Florence, right?"

"Um..."

"He couldn't stand the thought of seeing you and your boyfriend another day."

"But he came back with you, right?" *Please God, please, please, please....*

"No," Chaz frowned. "He's flying home tomorrow."

I closed my eyes in despair and swallowed the lump that had risen in my throat. Unfortunately, my tear ducts didn't get the message. Before I knew it, tears rolled down my cheeks. I looked at Chaz apologetically.

"I'm sorry." I sniffed. "You must think I'm crazy. It's just that... I blew it. Big time."

I buried my face in my hands. "I know I just met the guy, and it sounds silly, but I felt more for him than I felt for my ex. We broke up by the way." I looked back at Chaz and paused to wipe my running nose with my sleeve. "Of course, this all becomes clear to me when it's too late." I sniffled and my nose made an unattractive sound. "Still think I'm hot?" I said weakly through my tears, trying to cover up my embarrassment.

Chaz handed me the napkin that had been wrapped around his coffee cup. Showing more maturity than I would have given him credit for, he seemed to know better than to respond to my question.

I continued to babble. "Thank you." I sniffed, taking the tissue. "I was so afraid to put myself out there that I tried to focus on the negatives, which weren't really so negative after all. I kept telling myself Simon was too young, too unsettled... Like it really matters that he's a camp counselor? It all seems so silly now, and—"

Chaz held one hand in the air and the other to his throat as he struggled to swallow the sip of coffee he had just taken.

"Are you okay?" I leaned toward him.

Chaz nodded and drew in a breath. "Holy shit balls, I totally thought I was gonna spit that all over you. Simon's not a camp counselor!" He laughed so hard his shoulders shook.

I looked at him quizzically. "Yes he is. He told me he works at a camp." I used the tissue to wipe my eyes.

"He owns the damn camp. He started like three of them for underprivileged kids from inner cities. I think he's opening two more in New York, actually."

"What?" I gasped, unable to believe what I heard.

How had I misunderstood something like that? My mind raced as I thought back to all the conversations Simon and I had had about his job. There weren't many now that I thought of it. Suddenly I was angry. I had certainly referred to his job as 'camp counselor' enough times. He could have corrected me. Had he been laughing at me all that time?

"Why didn't he tell me this?"

Chaz shrugged. "Who knows? The man's a mystery."

Suddenly, Simon wasn't who I thought he was, and I felt stupid for not seeing him more clearly. Here I had been beating myself up for not being truthful with him or with myself, thinking he was a model of honesty and openness. But, it turns out, he'd kept the truth from me, too.

"If you ask me, the man's a liar," I accused.

"No," Chaz said with a finger in the air. "I don't think so. Simon isn't like that. Think about it, Lucy. Did he lie? Or did you just assume?"

I thought back again to my conversations with Simon. Oh God. Chaz was right. Simon had never said he was a counselor. I had been so preoccupied with myself, I had jumped to conclusions about his job. About him, really. I looked down at my feet as confusion swept over me again.

"Yeah, I guess, but—"

"But nothing. You know what they say about people who assume," Chaz said in a know-it-all tone.

"They make an ass out of you and me," I mocked, looking up again. "That's exactly what I feel like. A big, fat ass." I crossed my arms and sighed.

"Let's not get carried away now." Chaz winked before peeking around my chair to get a glimpse of my butt. So much for Mr. Mature.

I shot him a look in return and sat up straighter. "I just can't believe he allowed me to think that. You'd think he'd be proud enough to say it."

"I'd say, and I would probably use it as a pickup line myself. But not everyone needs to walk around touting their goodness." He removed a pastry from his bag and held it out to me. "Bite?"

I detected the faint smell of sugar and cinnamon and paused to swallow. "No thanks," I sniffed before heaving another long sigh. "I guess you're right."

I watched him take a bite and had to admit that those were pretty insightful comments coming from a perv named Chaz. Everyone was just full of surprises. I stared absentmindedly across the piazza.

"I can't believe this," I murmured after a few minutes had passed. "Who is this guy? It's like I don't even know him."

"Please, that's nothing." Chaz looked both ways and leaned towards me. "I'm assuming he probably didn't tell you how he made his fortune either, huh?"

My mouth dropped open. I stared at Chaz. I was completely dumbfounded. Simon had a fortune? A fortune he had earned himself?

"Of course he didn't," Chaz said hitting his own head. "Two minutes ago you thought he was a camp counselor."

"So?" I drew in a breath, as I waited for Chaz to elaborate. "Let me guess. He saved a child from a burning building and got a handsome reward?"

"No, but that's a good one," Chaz said with a laugh. "Nothing quite so noble. More along the lines of intelligent." I leaned my elbows on the table, eager to hear more. "He invented some sort of gadget, so business travelers can work wirelessly in flight. That's all I know. The only reason I even know that is because he has major pull with one of the airlines."

I massaged my temples and looked down at the table. "Unbelievable," I muttered. "I can't believe he kept all of that a secret. Why?" I was feeling completely offended. "You think you know someone…" I trailed off and shook my head.

I jumped up and looked down at Chaz, who had been staring at me curiously. "I'm sorry, but inventing something was definitely worth a mention. That's part of who he is, for shit's sake. He told me his summer job takes up so much time that he likes to take the rest of the year off."

"And?" Chaz shrugged his shoulder nonchalantly.

I shook my head at Chaz's ignorance. "Maybe that would've been a good time to tell me about his little invention? How it afforded him the opportunity to live like a laid-back wanderer?"

Chaz scratched his head. "Yeah, you got a point."

"Thank you." I smiled sarcastically. "Listen, I have to go. I don't mean to be rude."

Chaz scratched his head and leaned back in his chair. "Where are you going? Are you okay? I feel bad leaving you like this."

"You're not leaving me. I'm leaving you." I attempted a smile. "I'll be fine. I'm booked on a four o'clock flight this afternoon, so I better go pack and all that fun stuff. Plus, I'm going to spend the morning with Tess. One last fling before I leave."

I realized I was babbling, but my mind was racing with everything I'd just heard. I wanted to get away and think it through, on my own.

"Nice seeing you again, Chaz." I cut off my babbling with a short wave before starting to walk away.

"You too, Lucy." Chaz kicked his feet onto the chair I'd been sitting on and took another bite of his pastry.

I turned around one last time as the scent of his breakfast wafted toward me. My stomach grumbled. "Where did you get that?"

Chaz pointed his finger towards a small pastry shop tucked away in the corner of the piazza. "Get the *Torta di Ricotta*," he said, once he finished chewing.

"Thanks."

"Lucy?" Chaz waved his phone in the air. "I have Simon's email address if you want to get in touch. Or you could find him on Twitter if that's your thing."

"Nah, I have nothing to say." I turned around and went in search of my last indulgent Italian breakfast.

I was too down and out to tweet. I needed to eat. My mind wandered as I kicked a small rock down the cobblestone street.

If only I could kick my thoughts of Simon to the curb. I wished we'd never met. No, that wasn't true. I knew now that I wasn't dead inside and I was capable of enjoying another man's company. Simon showed me those things.

If we hadn't met, maybe I wouldn't have realized the type of man I could have. Hell, maybe I'd still think Cooper was Mr. Right. Boy, had I been wrong. So maybe I was in a better place than where I'd started from.

I'd spent the past three months mourning the loss of Cooper. I'd completely glamorized who he was and how he'd made me feel and embellished the relationship we'd shared. At least my eyes had been opened, and I had a true sense of resolution on that front. I kicked the rock hard and watched it disappear across the courtyard. Closure.

* * * *

After I devoured my *Torta di Ricotta,* along with the one I had bought for Tess, I headed back to the pensione. I was in the midst of a packing debacle when I heard a knock at the door.

"Aunt Lu? It's me."

"It's open," I called out.

Tess walked into the room and eyed my overstuffed backpack on the bed.

"Hi," I said, cringing.

"You didn't change your mind?" Tess wrinkled her nose and plopped down on my bed. The white halter dress she wore brought out her tan, and she looked fresh and clean with wet hair that hung loose down her bare back.

I bit my thumbnail and shook my head. "I'm sorry."

"I totally understand, Aunt Lu. Really." She placed a hand on her chest and looked at me gravely. "I can't thank you enough for coming with me in the first place. Thanks to you, I met Mark." Her eyes shone as she beamed at me.

"I'm so happy for you, Tessie. And let's not forget your new career." I forced a smile, hoping to mask the sadness I felt inside. "Is he going to go with you to Venice?"

She nodded eagerly, and I blinked rapidly to keep the tears from falling.

"Well, promise me you will wear that beautiful dress," I sniffed. "You look gorgeous."

I paused to wipe my eyes with a knuckle. "I only have enough room in my backpack to take home what I came with. I think Burberry, Chanel, and Prada should see more of Europe." I thrust a neatly folded pile of clothes into Tess's arms. The tags were still on most of the gifts Cooper had given me.

Tess clicked her tongue and had a wistful look on her face. "Aunt Lu, thank you, but I don't want you to leave." She pouted as she placed the pile onto a wooden chair. "I'm excited to be with Mark, but if I had a choice, I would still rather you come with us."

A slow grin spread across my face. Tess's genuine sweetness never failed to warm my heart. "You know what, honey? I'm ready to go home. We started this trip by saying how we were sick of doing what we were 'supposed' to do," I said. "The old me would've gotten back together with Cooper because that was the next logical step. But the new me has learned from past mistakes and is paving a brand new road," I said with pride.

"Um, I believe a wise woman once called it 'the parkway to possibilities'," Tess smiled.

I chuckled. "That day in the Amsterdam diner feels like a year ago, doesn't it? Since then I'd found closure with Cooper, and it's now time to close this chapter too and start fresh in New York."

"Aunt Lu, you're going to get off to a great start back home. I just know it." She threw her arms around me and gave me a quick hug. "In the meantime, I'd like to send you off with a flourish. I read about a great spa down the street. Their signature massage is made with Tuscan grapes and herbs."

I raised my shoulders to my ears and drew in a deep breath. "Ahhh...." I said, exhaling. "Now you're talking." I stuffed my pajamas into my backpack and grabbed my purse. "I will deal with this later." I held the door open for Tess and looked back at the pile of clothes that were strewn on my bed. "Ciao for now, baby."

* * * *

Later that afternoon, I boarded the plane at Peretola and squeezed my way into the seat assigned to me. It was a middle seat, and I was sandwiched between an obese man who began snoring as soon as we took off and a teenage boy whose headset did little to muffle the sounds from his iPod. I was counting the hours until we touched down in New York when a flight attendant came over and placed a hand on my arm.

"Excuse me, ma'am?"

"Yes?" I frowned.

"I'm sorry to bother you," she said in a hushed tone. "There are some empty seats up in first. You might be more comfortable—"

"Oh wow. Yes, thank you." Maybe Tess was right. I was getting off to a great start already with a free upgrade. I grabbed my carry-on bag, climbed over the sleeping man, and followed the flight attendant all the way to the first row.

She leaned down and picked up a box of chocolates sitting on one of the seats. "We've been saving these for you," she smiled mysteriously. "They'll go great with our complimentary champagne." She pointed to a glass already poured and sitting on the armrest.

"Gosh... Thank you," I said, narrowing my eyes.

I wondered what I had done to deserve such rock star treatment. I certainly wasn't about to question it. She took my carry-on, and I slid down into the wide seat, closing my eyes in peace. Because I'd slept like crap the past two nights, I must've fallen asleep within seconds. I dreamed I was picking grapes on a farm.

Then I heard a man's voice. "Excuse me, miss?"

In my dream it was one of the other grape pickers, but even though I acknowledged him, the voice wouldn't go away.

"Miss?" I heard again. It took me a few seconds to wake up and make the shift back to reality.

"Would you like to trade seats with me? You'll have a much better view this evening when the plane lands in New York."

My eyes flew open, and I turned to the direction of the voice. Seated next to me was none other than Simon. I dug my nails into my palms, and the pain I'd inflicted upon myself confirmed the fact that I wasn't dreaming. My mouth hung open as I gaped at him.

"Umm, Lucy? You okay?" Simon's voice broke the awkward silence and brought me back to reality.

"Wh...what are you... How did you..." I stammered.

"I have some pull around here." He smiled modestly.

"Ah, so this is the airline." God, what a response. My heart hammered in my chest. I didn't know what to say. I couldn't believe Simon was sitting next to me. I literally had to bite the inside of my cheeks to keep from smiling.

"Uh, Chaz filled me in on all of your accomplishments."

"No doubt, all the boring details." He looked uncomfortable as he shifted in his seat. "Chaz isn't one to hold back."

"Thank God someone isn't," I said with a hint of sarcasm, starting to recover from my shock. "Just so you know, the details were far from boring. You happen to be the first inventor I've ever met who happens to run camps."

I cocked my head to the side and gave him a look. The anger I'd felt earlier when I'd learned Simon hadn't told me the whole truth about himself had started to seep back, mixing with a feeling of having been ignorant to have assumed so much and not asked more questions.

"There's more to the story." Simon grinned, placing his hand on my arm. A current of warmth spread through my body. "First of all, I'm not an inventor. I worked on a thesis back in business school," he said, with a wave of his hand, "and happened to come up with something that took off. It's a snooze, but it made me enough money so I can help out causes I believe in. Hence, the camp."

"Wow, that's amazing, Simon. Truly." I said. "But, why didn't you tell me any of this?" My cheeks reddened as I spoke. "Why did you let me think you were a counselor? I kind of feel like a fool." I looked down at my lap as I confessed this.

"I'm sorry. It's just that I prefer to fly anonymously. No pun intended," he said sheepishly.

"I'm sorry, but I still don't understand," I frowned, looking at him searchingly. "I feel like I don't even know you."

"You do know me, Lucy," Simon said firmly. "I just omitted a few minor—"

"Major." I was starting to shift back to feeling as if I had been betrayed.

"Okay, major tidbits." He sighed and looked out the window briefly before turning back and putting his hand on my arm. "Listen." He paused, as if thinking about whether or not to continue.

Searching my face, he seemed to make a decision and kept talking. "You're right. I didn't tell you absolutely everything. I guess I wasn't sure how you felt about me and wasn't sure how much I should tell you. I didn't think it mattered what I do or how I live. I should have told you more. I've been dating divas, and honestly I'm sick of it. They don't like me because of who I am, but because of my wallet. I wanted a fresh start."

My stomach clenched at that. I could understand Simon's feelings. A fresh start had been my motivation, too. I looked into his eyes as he continued.

"It's just that I wanted you to get to know me for me without any preconceived notions. My parents have a lot of money, and all my life, it's been an issue. We grew up modestly despite the money, and as a result, people have found them to be a bit strange. I mean, why would anyone want to drive a Chevy when you could drive a BMW, right?"

"Right?" I said, unsure what to say.

"Well, those are my parents for you. A strong work ethic, big on charity—"

"Ah," I nodded thoughtfully, beginning to soften again. "Tess mentioned how growing up, you and Mark had to forfeit your gifts to the needy children in the area."

"Yeah," he said with a face. "Kind of sucked at the time, but now I get it. My grandfather was made of money, and I guess they didn't want us to think everyone else was. So between the family bucks and my invention, it's hard for anyone to see me without a dollar sign in front of my name. The women I meet are so fixated on my bank account. I just wanted to meet someone who likes me for me."

As I looked at Simon and realized he was being truthful, I knew he hadn't meant to mislead me, and I hadn't meant to assume the worst about him. Maybe this was the fate Tess and Morgan were talking about when they had come to my apartment that day. Maybe he was the man for me, but in order for me to see that he was the right man, I had to understand my own tendency to jump to conclusions about other people. Like the conclusion I had made about Cooper—assuming that because he had it all, he was the best man for my heart.

"Makes perfect sense," I said with certainty. "And just so you know, I like you for you," I offered shyly. "More than like you." I held my breath as I waited for him to respond.

"Well, what do you know? That's perfect, because it just so happens that the only bank I'm interested in," he said, taking hold of my hands, "is Lucy Banks."

I couldn't help but roll my eyes at the corniness of his line, but as I exhaled, a grin spread across my face at the sentiment. I bit my lip when a thought crossed my mind. "This *is* the real you, right?"

"Full disclosure. Scout's honor," Simon said, raising two fingers side by side.

"Careful," I warned. "In London, that means to F off."

"Look at you! Down with the local lingo. I'd say you've come pretty far from that angry woman in search of a charger," Simon said, giving my hand a squeeze.

My entire body tingled from his touch. I had come pretty far.

"I'm so happy Chaz ran into you this morning. When we said good bye last night in front of the store, I honestly didn't think I'd ever see you again."

I reached for my glass of champagne. "To Chaz."

"To Chaz." Simon smiled and tapped his glass softly against mine.

"Wait," I said, suddenly a little confused. What did my running into Chaz have to do with seeing Simon on the plane? "Why are we toasting Chaz again? Because he told me the truth about you?"

"Because he called me after you left him in the piazza. He happened to mention what flight you taking, that you were single, and, well, kind of into me."

"Just a tad." I held my fingers open an inch and winked. Simon's cheeks turned pink, and he ran his free hand through his hair. I had a burning desire to rumple his hair, kiss his forehead, his cheeks....

I took a big sip of the champagne, suddenly remembering the gift I'd bought him before all the craziness went down. I struggled to swallow before I laughed aloud.

"How ironic is this," I said, reaching into my bag to fish out the wallet. "I bought a little something for you last night, *before* I knew about your cash flow." I chuckled and handed it over.

Simon looked at me quizzically before tearing off the paper. I bit my nail and waited for his reaction. He held the wallet and laughed before a serious look appeared on his face. "You're the best, Lucy. I can't tell you how much this means to me."

"Oh, it was nothing," I said, blushing from his compliment. "I remembered the way you rolled your money in a ball and thought it might come in handy. Maybe I should have bought a bigger one." I winked, and as Simon smiled at me, I could actually feel the warmth coming from his eyes.

I shook my head in wonder and squeezed his hands. "I can't believe you're here," I whispered.

"From day one, the only thing I wanted was to make you feel the way you deserve to feel. Tell me something," Simon murmured, leaning towards me. "Is this the *Pretty Woman* moment you've been waiting for?"

I inched closer to him and gave him a soft kiss. "Now it is," I whispered with a smile.

About the Author

Jeannine Henvey, a Long Island native, graduated magna cum laude from Hofstra University with a Master of Arts in Industrial/Organizational Psychology.

After graduate school she moved to Manhattan where she mastered the art of job hopping. She finally landed in publishing where she had a long stint as a promotional writer for many popular women's magazines.

Jeannine had backpacked around Europe with three of her friends in between undergrad and grad school. Whether in a youth hostel, on the EuroRail, sitting in a pub, or at a sidewalk cafe, she kept a journal throughout the two month trip. Over the years, she had come across the book and put it away, knowing that one day she would do something special with it. It was that journal that inspired her to write *Tales From a Broad*.

When she's not traveling the world with her fictitious characters, Jeannine is happily grounded with her husband and three children on Long Island.

https://www.facebook.com/jhenvey
http://www.jeanninehenvey.com